the wild road home

A NOVEL

MELISSA PAYNE

LAKE UNION
PUBLISHING

Published by Lake Union Publishing, Seattle

www.apub.com

Amazon, the Amazon logo, and Lake Union are trademarks of Amazon.com, Inc., or its affiliates.

ISBN-13: 9781662515743 (paperback)
ISBN-13: 9781662515736 (digital)

Cover design by Caroline Teagle Johnson
Cover images: © Justin Mullet / Stocksy; © Cosma Andrei Romania / Stocksy; © Franconiaphoto / Getty

Printed in the United States of America

PRAISE FOR MELISSA PAYNE

A Light in the Forest

"The authentic characters and their realistic struggles make this introspective tale entirely believable. Vega's resilience is sure to endear her to readers."

—*Publishers Weekly*

"*A Light in the Forest* is a thrilling portrait of women finding their footing when all odds seem stacked against them."

—BookTrib

the
wild
road
home

OTHER TITLES BY MELISSA PAYNE

To Mom, for teaching me true strength, resilience, and courage.

One

Daisy took his breath away. Sun drifted through the curtains catching on the white of her hair and slipping down the grooves in her cheeks, igniting the gold in her green eyes. Like she glowed from the inside out. She smiled, meeting his gaze squarely, and the directness tickled his old bones the way it did when he'd first met her. God how he loved this woman.

"What's this for?" She fiddled with the wrapper of a cupcake. He'd tried making his own, but baking had been her domain, and Mack had forgotten to use the baking soda or powder or whatever was needed to make it taste like cake. On his way here, he'd stopped at the store and bought the first ones he saw. Decorated in red, white, and blue icing for the Fourth of July. They'd been married on the fourth. Daisy had picked the date, said that if a country this divided had stayed together against the odds, it was a good omen. Forty-eight years later, both of them saddled with a loss that had torn them apart before they glued themselves back together, Mack figured Daisy'd been right.

He scooted his chair closer to the bed. "Happy anniversary, Daisy."

She frowned and put the cupcake back in the clear plastic box. "I don't think so." Her gaze flitted to the window.

The bite he'd taken turned to sawdust, and Mack spit it on a napkin, stuffed everything into the box. His upper lip quivered, and Mack had to give himself a minute. He tapped a fist against a burning in his chest, coughed to keep it from escaping into his throat. "Goddang heartburn," he muttered.

Daisy laughed. "That's called emotion, Mack. It's the price of love."

He froze. It was something she'd said often to him during his heartburn episodes. A response he believed proved that she was still in there, sparking a hope that hurt worse each time it burned out. But Mack wasn't a quitter. The doctors said she was progressing fast, that she may live only four to eight years, if that. Like that meant her life had less meaning. Mack had used the computer at the library to look it up. They were wrong. Sometimes people lived twenty years. And Daisy was the exception; they just didn't know it because they'd never met anyone like her. Strong-willed, tenacious, able to angle a fish, gut an elk, and make the sweetest berry pie from fruit she'd foraged herself.

"Well, Daisy, love goddang burns." He held his breath, waited for the laugh that always followed, light and tinkling like wind chimes dancing in the breeze.

She stared out the window and didn't make a sound.

Mack jiggled his leg. He'd made a decision earlier, but now that he was here, he was immobilized and didn't quite know where to start. He scratched the side of his neck. "Daisy, I . . . well, the truth is I can't stay at the motel anymore."

Her eyes met his, a flicker of interest. "Is that so?"

He gave a solemn nod. "It is."

"Is it about the money?"

When she sounded like her old self, Mack could pretend it was just the two of them alone at home. "We never were the best at watching our finances," he said.

Daisy fiddled with the edge of the blanket she had tucked around her waist. "We watched them," she said. A familiar exchange. "Watched them walk right out the door with a liar and a cheat from Jackson."

Mack's smile held back a trembling in his chin. "We sure did." An ache spread down his arm, a longing to hold her, kiss her on the top of the head, and tell her that everything was going to be okay.

Daisy's eyes trailed to his missing limb. "What happened to your arm?"

Mack touched the stump of his left arm. She asked every time he visited. He smiled, making sure that when he spoke, it was as if he were telling it for the very first time. "That's quite a tale. Would you like to hear it?"

"Yes."

"It was the kind of day you love. A deep-blue sky, full sun, but not enough to make you sweat. The kind of warm where you can wear sandals with your jeans. You always say that's the best kind of weather." Mack laughed. "You don't love the snow." Daisy listened, eyes bright but not connecting. Like Mack was reading a story. "I never was sure why you moved here; your expectations were always a little higher than Wyoming could deliver." He put his palm over her hand, patted lightly, and kept it there until she moved hers away. Tried not to feel the hurt. She didn't mean it.

Back when he'd met her, Daisy had been a weather disturbance all on her own. Upending Mack's life with her beauty, her wit, and a strength of character that drilled down to her core. "We were out picking berries. Jesse had filled his bag and his stomach." The image of Jesse's sticky fingers and stained lips made him smile. He cleared his throat, paused. For Daisy, time was an hourglass, granules that disappeared with breathtaking speed. But Mack was a pack mule, weighed down by all the moments, good and bad. "A mama grizzly came charging from a patch of bushes, straight at us."

"That bear tore off your arm." Even though she sounded distant, Daisy raised her eyebrows in an amused way.

Encouraged, Mack smiled. "She sure did. But you came to the rescue when you emptied the entire can of bear spray. Got both me and

3

the bear." His eyes had burned for a solid week. Daisy was worried he'd end up one-armed and blind.

"She was protecting her young."

"Yep."

"Mack lost his arm like that too."

He looked away, fighting with a lump in his throat but encouraged by the conversation regardless. "Is that so?"

"Typical Mack." She yawned, eyes closing, Daisy sinking because her memories were anchors that dragged her down. "Always willing to do anything for the people he loves." She yawned again.

He felt his chance slipping away. "I was thinking something, Daisy."

"Mmmm."

"That you and me could go live in the cabin we built for Jesse." He moved to the edge of his seat. Mack couldn't afford to stay another night. He had to go back to Pike River, his job, the trailer, and visit when he could. But he couldn't bear the thought of leaving her here alone with nurses, shift changes, and old people who had to have someone wipe their mouths. He knew what she needed. Familiar surroundings. Not the trailer where they were forced to live after they lost everything, and not this goddarn nursing home that had stripped her of all her petals. "You need to be home, Daisy."

She rested her head against the bed and seemed to be watching a pair of robins flitting in and out of a tree outside the window.

A frustrated tingling ran down his arm to his fingertips. He checked over his shoulder—the door to her room was closed most of the way. He needed her to understand. "I got it all fixed up. Been canning, the way you taught me, and I got plenty of meat stored. Even got us a generator to power up a space heater for when it's so cold you can see your breath."

She pulled at her fingers and hummed quietly to herself.

Undeterred, Mack continued, his heart beating faster. "It was our plan, remem—" He swallowed the rest of the word. *Remember?* Such a cruel sentiment. One thrown about like it had no meaning. He hovered his fingers over her hands, not wanting to startle her, letting the heat from her skin warm him like a fire in the woods. "Our plan was to live on our own terms once we sold the business." He studied the framed cross-stitch that she'd hung above the kitchen sink, the sign following them from the house to the trailer and here to her nursing home room, where he'd leaned it against the window so she could see it every day. A Ralph Waldo Emerson quote that Daisy loved. BUILD, THEREFORE, YOUR OWN WORLD. Something she'd done when she'd left her family to move out west all on her own, something she and Mack had done together when they got married, and then again, when what they'd loved most in this world had disappeared.

This time he touched her hand, her skin soft against his calloused fingertips. "I swore to take care of you, Daisy." She stared at her lap, and Mack wished he could tip her chin up and look into her green eyes when he spoke. Instead, he leaned his head against the hospital bed rail and said softly, "I can't do that in this place." He rubbed the back of his neck, embarrassed. He hadn't noticed how bad things had gotten for her. One day he was sure she'd beat the odds and the next she was sitting in a doctor's office with a blank sheet of paper in front of her and the doctor's words hanging thick in the silence. *Draw a clock at two o'clock.* In the truck on the way home, Daisy with her arms wrapped tightly across her chest, a moody gray sky reflected in her frown. *Don't tell anyone, please.* He'd kept his promise, but life got harder and Mack found it difficult to do things himself, including finding work as a fishing guide. One small outfit had hired him but only because the owner had gotten a start working for Mack and only when they needed an extra guide. Mack wasn't as good as he'd been—even he knew it. His mind was on Daisy, and the distraction did not help.

But they needed the money, so he scheduled half-day trips only, made sure Daisy was safe at home, kept the TV on, lunch in marked containers in the fridge, and for a short time it had worked. Then the incident happened and everyone got involved and she'd ended up so far away from him he couldn't sleep at night. In his last night in the motel, he'd tossed and turned, imagining himself back in the trailer without her. He just couldn't do it. So he'd come up with an idea better suited to lovesick young people, but around Daisy, Mack had always felt a little like a teenage boy.

"I have a plan," he said. "You and I can live off the grid the way we've always dreamed." His knee jiggled up and down.

Her face softened. "Jesse's cabin."

"That's right." Mack blinked hard. "Listen, Daisy, I promise to take care of you this time. I . . . I know it's been hard, and I'm sorry. I just got a little stuck, that's all. They were wrong about me, and you know it."

She used to say that one of the things she loved most about him was his strength. He'd flex his small biceps and make her laugh. *Not that kind of strength,* she'd say. *I love how people underestimate you.* She'd run her fingers down his arm, squeeze his hand. *My father dominates every room he's in. He suffocates everyone around him.* Her kiss on Mack's lips was light, playful, her breath like strawberries. *When I'm with you, I can breathe.* The amazing thing about Daisy: as much as Mack loved her, she loved him equally back. He never could understand why, but he wasn't one to question a woman's mind.

She was listening to him; he could tell by the squint of her left eye. "The doctors were wrong about you too." He stood and pulled a rucksack from the floor, went to the little closet, and started pulling clothes from hangers. There weren't many. "You told me once that loving someone wasn't enough, and you're right." He stuffed a couple of her shirts on top of her pants, not taking the time to fold them the way she would. He glanced at the door, nervous. "So I'm taking you out of this goddarn place, and we're going to Jesse's cabin, and when it's time, well, we'll go together."

She sat up in bed, eyes wide, alarmed. "What are you doing?"

He closed the bag and returned to her side, pulling back the covers. "I'm busting you out, Daisy girl," he said gently. He took her hand—long, delicate fingers that lay limp in his own. "Let's go home? Okay? You and me." His voice rose, uncertain. "We don't work without the other."

Daisy shook her head, tried to pull her hand out of his grip, fear in her eyes. "Leave me alone."

Mack held on, sure that the pieces of her that still knew him would squeeze his hand and follow him out of there.

She pushed away from him until her back was against the mattress again. Green eyes bright with tears. "I don't know you!" She turned back to the window, the confused wrinkle in her forehead easing. Daisy loved nature, preferring the feel of the wind on her skin, the warmth of the sun on her face, the pine-scented air. He rolled over the wheelchair he'd taken from the hallway, grabbed her quilt from the bed. A desperate hollowness in his stomach. "You don't want to be here, Daisy." He laid the cross-stitch on top of the bag. "Let's go where the air is fresh and we can build our own world." He tried again, taking her hand. She was shaking now, and pulling away. "Please, Daisy. You'll be happy there, I promise. You, me." He swallowed, willing to say anything that might get her to leave. "And Jesse." She went stiff, and then he was holding all her weight in the tug of her delicate wrist. Something popped, and Daisy cried out. Mack let go, horrified. "Are you okay?"

She cradled her wrist to her chest, face wet. "Go away."

He leaned heavily against the bed, his heart in pieces on the floor. "Please, Daisy, please come with me."

Daisy was crying now, guttural sobs that shook her entire body.

"What's happening?" A nurse rushed into the room. "Oh, Daisy, are you okay?" A sharp look at Mack.

He didn't know this nurse; he didn't want to know any of them. Daisy was never supposed to be here in the first place.

The nurse was touching Daisy's wrist, asking her what hurt, and his wife, the woman who'd married him under a bur oak, bore him a son in the middle of an ice storm, and left him when that was the only thing that might save them both, said, "Where's Mack?"

A punch to his gut every time.

"He came to visit you today, Daisy. Looks like he brought cupcakes too. What a treat." The nurse spoke in soothing tones, tucking and folding the blankets around Daisy's waist.

Daisy laid her head against the pillow, gazed out the window again. The sobs had stopped, forgotten with the passing minutes. Mack stood with the packed rucksack by his feet, quilt folded over the back of the wheelchair, stunned. The wave of frustration that had overcome him seconds before had receded, leaving behind an ache in his chest.

The nurse's eyes narrowed. "Were you trying to *take* her somewhere?"

He couldn't answer without lying.

"Listen, Mack, I don't know how much you talk to Peggy." A softness in her voice. She knew his name. He looked at her again; maybe he did recognize her? Her tag said Janiece. With her nose rings, she looked too young to be working here.

They'd taken Daisy away from him, but at least they'd appointed Daisy's lifelong friend, Peggy, as her legal guardian. As much as Mack wanted to be grateful, it stung to think of his wife's well-being in anyone's hands but his. Peggy had reached out, especially lately, taping Post-it notes to his motel door, leaving messages with the nurses for him to call her. He'd avoided her for now; she didn't deserve his anger. "We haven't talked much."

"Oh." Janiece sucked in her bottom lip and handed Daisy a cup with a straw. "Listen, they just found out that Daisy's cancer is back. They don't think—"

Air turned solid in his lungs. "We did those treatments last time, and they worked just fine."

"Yes, but—"

Mack picked up his hat from the end of the bed, placed it on his head, grateful for the shadow it lay over his eyes, wishing it would stop the image of Daisy rifling through a filing cabinet in the corner of their bedroom. Leftover tears had stained her face. She'd learned that she wasn't forgetful; instead she was a truck barreling down memory lane into oblivion.

Mack had leaned against the doorway, hand in his pocket, heart beating fast. *They're wrong about you, Daisy. They don't know you like I do.*

You're not a doctor, Mack. A pile of discarded folders on the carpet beside her. *Where is it, Mack?*

Why do you need your will?

She'd stopped, stared at him. *I'll forget him.*

I won't let you. You beat cancer; you'll beat this too.

She'd crumpled onto the edge of the bed, face in her hands. *This isn't cancer. It can't be stopped.*

He'd knelt on the floor in front of her, placed his hand on her thigh. She pressed her forehead to his, arms around his neck. Her back moved up and down with her breaths like it did when Daisy did her stretches on the rubber mat. Slowly and with meaning. *It's going to get so bad, Mack.* His heart had quickened with a shared panic. There had been no optimism in the doctor's frank tone. *Get your things in order.*

Mack felt a tremble run through her body. *I don't want to live like that. When it's time, you take care of me like you would one of your dying horses and put me down. We're kinder to animals than human beings.*

He'd tried to pull away, but she kept a strong grip around his neck. *Daisy.*

I'm not scared of dying. She lifted her head, tears dried, the look in her eyes so fierce Mack dropped his gaze. *Swear to me, Mack.*

Mack relaxed into her grip and did the one thing he'd promised never to do. He lied. *I swear.*

The memory broke apart with Daisy's soft humming. A song she'd sung to Jesse when he was a baby. Mack rubbed the trembling from his chin and listened. When it ended he forced himself to focus on the problem at hand. Her cancer was back. Cancer was something she could beat. When the doctors told her about the dementia, she'd been so scared. Of the burden she'd be to him when things got bad. Of not remembering the important things. But Mack knew something Daisy never understood. The world was a better place with her in it. He'd be damned if he let cancer win.

"Is it about the money?" he said to the nurse. Last time they'd barely had enough to pay for the treatments.

"I think you need to speak with—"

He waved her away. It was about the money; of course it was. After they'd lost Anders Outfitters to a lying accountant, money for Mack and Daisy had been in short supply for all of the last ten years. And now with her cancer back, it meant Daisy's life had a price on it.

Take care of me like you would one of your dying horses. Mack shook his head until her words fell away. There was little he wouldn't do for those he loved. He pushed his hat up and kissed her on the forehead, gently, inhaling her scent one last time. His eyes burned so goddang bad the room had gone blurry. "I love you, Daisy girl." He backed out of the room. At the doorway he paused, imprinting all the details of her face into memory. The sweep of her hair across her forehead, the arch of her eyebrows, the curve of her cheek that ran smack dab into full lips. She'd be upset with him if she knew his plan. But Mack had known deep down in his old broken heart that he would never do what she wanted.

~

The canoe was hooked securely to the top of his truck. Mack wiped a palm along his jeans, sweaty from the work of getting it up there. It was early, before first light, the birds not yet stirring and the air a mixture of pine and mud from the overnight rain. He gave the double-wide one last look. This hadn't been their home. It had been a fallback when they'd lost the house where Daisy had her garden and Jesse had his treehouse. The only place to lay their heads after the last of the Anders Outfitters inventory had been sold off to pay the overwhelming debt accrued by an embezzling accountant.

In its prime, Anders Outfitters had been the premier company in town, with a history of good service, the best guides, lucrative hunting and fishing trips, and satisfied guests who came back season after season. Mack and Daisy had led the company to its heyday, even beating out the slicker corporate outfitters that had started to spring up. Mack had a local touch that won most folks over. If things had been different, maybe they would have recognized the house of cards they were standing on. But Mack and Daisy's world had already imploded; they didn't think they had anything more to lose.

He tightened the strap across the canoe once more and did a final check. Everything he needed was already at the cabin. The only thing he had to take from the lake was his pack that held water and food for the long hike back. He'd updated his last will and testament to make sure his life insurance payout would be used to help with any of Daisy's medical expenses. It was all he had left to give.

Jesse appeared as his ten-year-old self, soaking wet, his fingertips waterlogged. Not real. Not a ghost. Just Mack's guilt tightly bound to his side. Mack pressed his lips together and breathed in until the image of his boy disappeared. Jesse's presence was a harbinger of what was to come. It was drastic, Mack knew, and seemed fool-headed and rash, but when the cancer was treated, he would sneak her away from that goddang home like he'd planned to before. It wouldn't be easy, but Mack was convinced that out there, Daisy would come alive with memory, remembered or automatic, and they'd live out the rest of their days together, surrounded by happy times and peace.

He climbed into the truck and hesitated, staring up at the trailer that was never supposed to be their home, the distorted end to a life that had held so much love, so much potential for a happily ever after. He squeezed his temple between his thumb and fingers. *Goodbye, Daisy.* Opened his eyes. It was time. He twisted over to pull the driver's door closed with his right hand when Peggy's voice stopped him.

"Early morning, Mack."

He hung his head, exhaled. Bad timing.

In the dark, her hair appeared first, blonde sprouts that shot out from her scalp, around her face, and down past her shoulders. Wild lioness hair that didn't match the business owner she was. She leaned against the open door, hands stuck in the pockets of her work overalls. "Why are you avoiding me?"

"Men don't avoid people, Peggy, you know that. I needed to be alone."

She took something from her pocket, gum, unwrapped a piece, and stuck it in her mouth. Peggy was no fool, but Mack didn't need her to be. He just needed her to believe him.

"Don't pull the man versus woman bullshit on me, Mack. You've been avoiding me. Just like Daisy did when she was first diagnosed."

Peggy's flared nostrils caught the glow of Mack's porch light. He felt bad about that time, only a few years ago but in many ways a lifetime. Back when Daisy was just forgetful, or so they'd hoped.

"Since the state folks came snooping around. Since the court hearing. I've stopped by, I've left notes on your door and your truck and wherever else I thought you might see them." She squinted. "I know you need space, but you also need friends."

She wasn't wrong. He hunched his shoulders and looked straight ahead. The truth was he didn't want Peggy to see Daisy like that. He'd kept hoping it was temporary, something he could fix. They did sudoku together, memory exercises he found on the computer. They'd go for hikes because he'd read that exercise was good for the brain, fish, spend a few nights at the cabin when the snow had melted enough for them to get up there. He kept hoping she'd get better. Instead she got worse and worse, and Mack was the only one left holding on to the dream.

"Mack?" A soft note in Peggy's voice that tightened his grip on the wheel.

"I can't afford the motel anymore."

"I could float you a few more nights . . ." She trailed off, sounding uncomfortable in the offer. Mack wouldn't take it, and they both knew it.

"I got a few trips with Derek this week, good money, big tippers supposedly," he said.

"Good, good."

Silence followed. Peggy had always been more of Daisy's friend, but Mack had known her since they were kids ditching Sunday school to go fishing. He thumped his fingers on the steering wheel. It was getting late, and he needed to be up at the lake before the daily summer rush. He couldn't pull this off with people around. "She doesn't belong there."

"I know," Peggy said, and after a pause, "Listen, Mack, there's something you need to know."

Heat stung his face. "That Daisy's cancer is back?"

"Janiece told you?"

He took a breath. "I'm going to do whatever it takes to get her well." He sounded gruff. Mack always sounded tougher than he meant. "And I'm sorry we haven't been more social." Five years. That's how much time had passed since the diagnosis. Not enough time for Mack to catch a full breath. Daisy had struggled knowing others would see her deteriorate, and Mack had done whatever he could to protect her, even if that had meant allowing decades-old friendships to crumble. Peggy had been persistent, refusing to be put off quite so easily as others. Eventually, though, even Peggy's visits lessened. "I know you love her," he said.

"Of course I do."

"She's too young for this." Mack squeezed the stump of his left arm. Daisy wasn't even in her seventies. "So we do whatever we can to help her get well." Three hundred thousand dollars and change. That's all he had left to give. Money from a life insurance policy he'd bought in full to help a young man in town when he was just starting out. A single premium policy, the man had called it. Back then Mack had a few nickels to rub together. Figured with his young son and wife depending on him, it wouldn't hurt to have a backup. Now it would help pay for chemo and radiation and whatever else would make her well. He'd promised to take care of her, and goddang it that's exactly what he intended to do. "When she's better, well, maybe we can bring her home. That place is killing her."

Peggy made a noise in her throat. "But, Mack, you can't fix Alzheimer's."

He shifted in the seat, agitated but ignoring her. Some things were just too dang big to take in all at once. "She can beat cancer. She's done it before. Her body is strong. I know Daisy. She's a fighter." A thin ribbon of gold along the eastern horizon set Mack's pulse hurrying. "Early bird, Peggy. I need to get on the water."

But she wouldn't move. "I need you to hear me out. Daisy reached out to me a few years ago. Just in case . . ." The woman sounded almost meek, and that started alarm bells clanging for Mack. Peggy was anything but meek. She sniffed. "She doesn't want this, Mack."

He bristled at the intimacy in her words. Like Peggy knew something he didn't. "Want what?"

She shifted her weight and stood a little too close to Mack, making him feel trapped. She was a tall woman, and she carried her height with ease. "You two are the love story of the century. You know that, right? Everyone here knows it. And it's goddamn beautiful."

Mack couldn't speak.

"And I know you want to take care of her and protect her and do everything you promised you'd do. But I know Daisy too, and she doesn't want to live like this."

Shock stiffened his body. "Like what?"

"You know what I mean." The typical lightness in her voice had vanished. "She knew you couldn't do it yourself."

"What are you saying?" It sounded like she was giving up.

A quiet sigh. "Daisy knew you'd fight for her until the end."

"Of course I goddang will."

"But that's not what she wants."

The silence that followed had lost all comfort. Mack's hand tightened into a fist, and he wanted to turn the key, drive away, and pretend this conversation had never happened. "She moved out here with twenty-five dollars, that old car, and—"

"Those damn sandals." A smile in her voice. "She's a hell of a woman."

"She came back." His breath snagged. Daisy had left him once, and Peggy knew how difficult those years had been for Mack. She'd had a front-row seat.

"She always said she didn't work without you." Peggy put a hand on Mack's shoulder, squeezed.

He tried to speak, but everything had turned into a sticky ball in his throat.

Peggy sniffed. "Listen, I can arrange . . . we could bring her home."

"After they treat her cancer?"

"No, Mack, she doesn't—"

"To die?" The idea sucked all the air from his lungs. "You'd give up on her like that?"

"Mack." So much not said in one word.

A wisp in the air, a familiar smell that stung his nose. *Can I go fishing with you, Dad?* A tremble in his chin. Mack took hold of it and squeezed, his resolve hardening. "Daisy fought when I'd given up. I can fight for her now." He started the truck, twisted around to grab the door handle, but Peggy stood still. "Move, please. I have to go." His face was stiff with anger.

In the dark, he couldn't see her eyes. If Peggy wanted, she could grab him by the collar and drag him from the car. But she wasn't like that. For all her innate physical strength, she was pragmatic and intelligent, and combined with her compassion, Mack and Daisy had always considered her to be one of the finest people they knew. But in this case, she was dead wrong.

Finally, she stepped aside. Mack reached for the door handle. "I'll see you later."

"Okay, but this isn't over, Mack. We have to talk."

He gave in. "When I get back." It didn't matter what he said; he wasn't coming back, but he was sure that Peggy would do the right thing with his insurance money. She loved Daisy too much not to.

Two

The smell of the house burned her nose. Brandi pressed her thumb and finger against her nostrils. Cat piss and rotten meat. Had it smelled this bad when she'd lived here? She stepped around empty beer cans, deflated trash bags, a dried-up hot dog hanging off a paper plate. Her toe hit an ashtray, and gray smoke particles shot into the air. She coughed, froze. Her heart beat loudly. Where was her brother?

With the lamps off and the blinds hanging closed, the busted ones let the only light inside. It tracked across the walls and onto the floor in yellow blobs. Unpaid electric bills would account for some of the stink. She shook her head, disgusted. Classic Mom. Pay for drugs but not for essentials.

She tiptoed down the hallway, echoes of the past in the old squishy carpet under her shoes, ingrained into the wood-paneled walls that once held her mom's photographs. Most were gone now. Stolen or sold to pay for more of her habit. But there was one, outside the bedroom that had been Brandi's and later the one she shared with Sy. Hanging crooked, the glass cracked, half-gone. But the photo had been her favorite. One snapped on a dry summer day when her mother had taken her to see the wild horses. They'd sat in the grass on the side of a dirt road and waited for hours. Nancy had packed a cooler with sandwiches and orange slices, her camera hooked to a stand on the ground in front of her. Brandi could taste the sweetness of the orange, and the memory hurt like a scab she'd picked at too early.

She looked inside her old bedroom. "Sy?" she hissed. Dark and musty, the bed shoved into a corner, no sheet on the stained mattress. A nervous shot of energy through her fingertips. Where was he? She opened the closet and was hit with an acidic rush of soiled bedsheets that had been balled up into a corner. It stung her eyes. She gasped, blinking, and felt the filth of her childhood home in a noose tightening around her neck. She'd gotten out. Through bad decisions and juvie, but at least she'd gotten out.

"Sy? Are you here?" she whispered, afraid to wake anything that might be sleeping. "It's me, Brandi." She knelt to look under the bed. No Sy. Got back to her feet, looked around the room, panic threatening the strength in her legs. Sy had gotten the worst of their mom. At least Brandi had had the wild horses and Mrs. T.

She'd come home to check on her brother as soon as she could, fibbed actually about where she was going, but she had to know he was okay. Blood hammered in her temples; she'd been delusional to think Sy would ever be okay with Nancy as his mom.

A hacking cough from across the hall. She jumped, hand to her chest, and peeked out, noticing Nancy sprawled across her bed. Brandi stepped closer, hands in claws and ready to defend herself. Her mother always had a boyfriend, and those boyfriends all had the same name: *Asshole.* Usually violent, always dumb, definitely criminals. But only her mom was on the bed, tangled in the sheets, one arm pinned underneath her. It eased her jitters, and Brandi moved into her mother's room. When Nancy crashed, she was as pathetic and docile as an injured puppy.

Maybe Sy was with her. She kept her breaths shallow and her footsteps light and looked into the closet, under the bed. Her mother slept on, snoring lightly. No Sy.

A shift from the bed and Nancy's gravelly voice. "Kenny?"

Must be the newest asshole.

Her mother sat straight up and locked eyes with Brandi. "Brandi?" Listless, confused, meth leaving her cells dried up and screaming for more. This was always what had given Brandi false hope. The rare times when there was more Nancy than meth. So pitiful when the high was stale. Sometimes remorseful. When Brandi was younger, it had fooled her. Not anymore.

She felt her face harden when she looked at her mom. "Where's Sy, Nancy?"

Her mother stared, something in her face that surprised Brandi, like longing. "You look so much older."

"Where's Sy, Nancy?" Brandi repeated. She'd been out of juvie for a month, and a group home had been her best option.

Nancy moved to the edge of the bed, head in her hands. "I'm your *mom*, Brandi."

"Where the fuck is my brother?" She spoke through clenched teeth.

The front door slammed and Brandi jumped, the walls moving in, trapping her.

"Don't be here," Nancy said, a nervous tremor in her voice. "Not now."

Sweat down her back, panic squirming through her muscles, but she stood her ground. "Where's Sy?"

Nancy leaned forward onto her hands, swaying, shoulders hunched. "I don't know. I don't know." Her mewls like a fork scraping across a plate to Brandi's ears.

Brandi left the room and tiptoed down the hallway, stopping in her tracks. A man in the living room, wolfing down a hamburger straight from the bag. He sat facing the opposite side of the room and didn't see her behind him.

"Get your ass up, Nancy!" Another bite of burger. "Now!" The word muffled by bread and pickles and meat.

Brandi inched toward the door. The big asshole scratched at his neck and behind his ears, his body jerking like one of those puppets with strings. "I'm gonna take a piss, and then you better be the fuck awake." He stood, dropping the food wrapper to the floor, and walked to the kitchen and out the back door.

Pissing outside. *Classy asshole.* Brandi was hurrying to the front door when she noticed the couch pulled away from the wall. Spiky tips of brown hair above the back cushions. *Sy.* She hurled herself onto the couch, but when she peeked over the cushions, her forehead met the tip of a gun barrel and she lurched backward.

Her heart snagged between beats. "Sy?" Carefully she leaned over.

He had smooshed himself into the smallest space possible, with his shoulder pressed into the wall and his knees almost to his chin. He rested the handle of the revolver between his legs, the muzzle pointed up at her. He was only five, but he didn't seem big enough. More like a stretched-out version of the toddler he'd been. Too small, too skinny, fear glazing his eyes.

She moved away from the opening, trying to breathe, to think. She couldn't leave him here. Not like this. Not without Mrs. T next door to give him a safe place to hide.

The kitchen door slammed, and Brandi inhaled and did the only thing she could think to do. She grabbed the gun by its barrel and jerked it out of Sy's hands. Then she took him by his arm, digging lower to get a hold around his waist, and yanked his body upward. He was so light he flew up and out, and they both landed on the couch.

"What the fuck?"

Kenny the asshole loomed over them, twitching. Brandi kept hold of Sy with one hand, gun in the other, and leveled it at the man. Carefully she got to her feet without taking her eyes off Kenny, a firm grip on Sy's hand keeping her own from trembling. "I'm babysitting my little brother, so you and my mom can do whatever the hell it is you're going to do." She swallowed hard; the gun was heavy, the barrel drooping and her body buzzing with fear.

Nancy emerged from the hallway, hair in a frizzy helmet around her pale and puffy face. Brandi wanted to hate her. Had tried once by filling an entire journal with three simple words. *I hate Mom.* It hadn't worked.

Carissa said that kids had a gene that made it biologically impossible for them to hate their parents.

"You let her get your gun, Nancy?" Kenny took a step closer.

Nancy shook her head, pulled at her fingers. "No, I don't know how she got it."

Brandi backed toward the door, keeping the revolver aimed toward Kenny. "You know it's loaded, asshole." It was the kind of thing that always got her in trouble. Not thinking before she spoke.

Kenny stopped moving, but his nostrils flared.

"Brandi, what are you doing?" Her mom was moving closer, hands out in front of her.

Brandi swung the gun between the two of them, clumsy, afraid she looked as clueless as she felt holding this piece of metal. "I'm taking Sy someplace safe."

At the door, Sy suddenly dropped to his knees to grab for something off the floor. Brandi stumbled, and she had to take her eyes off Kenny and her mom to keep her footing. Kenny lurched forward, hands out. In a panic, Brandi's finger pulled the trigger, and she fired a wild shot that left her arm tingling. It missed Kenny.

She gulped. She could have killed him.

Now he was in a full rage. "You fucking bitch!"

"Kenny, no!" Nancy, sounding vaguely like a mother, rushed to the man like her skinny ass could stop him.

Brandi pushed over a table, threw an empty bottle that hit him in the face, and grabbed Sy by the collar of his shirt, pulling him out the front door. Her hands shook, eyes dragging the street. Where the fuck was Carissa? She'd driven Brandi here and was supposed to be waiting, but her car was nowhere to be seen.

A dusty RAV4 was parked in the driveway. They sprinted to it, and Brandi could not believe her luck. Keys in the ignition. Kenny really was a dumb asshole. She pushed Sy into the driver's seat. "Scoot over!" she screamed, then jumped in after him, tossing the gun into the back seat. Turned the keys, engine roared to life. The front door banged open, Kenny, with her mom trailing behind, pounding on his back. Frantic, she shoved the gearshift, and the RAV4 sailed forward instead of backward, tapping Kenny's knees and knocking him over. She slammed on the brakes. "Oh shit, oh shit!" She tried again, this time finding Reverse and stomping on the gas. They went backward over the grass, the curb, narrowly missing her mom's Subaru parked on the street. Kenny was on his feet, unhurt and running straight for them. She shifted to Drive and tore out of there, close enough that she nearly hit him again when he lunged for the car. Again she missed and they sped forward, down the residential street. Brandi's chest hurt from gulping in air. A glance in the rearview mirror. Was that her mom's Subaru coming after them? Her knee jiggled. The road ended on a main drag, and she hardly stopped before she swung the car right and accelerated.

Blood pulsed in her ears; she glanced at Sy. He sat with his feet up on the seat, head dug in between his knees, hiding his face. In his arm, he held a *Minecraft* stuffie squished to his side.

"Hey, Syborg, it's me, Brandi." She was out of breath. "I'm your sister. Do you remember me?"

He didn't answer. She didn't expect him to.

Where the hell was she going? Another look in the rearview mirror. Would they come after her? She'd just kidnapped a kid, stolen a car and a gun. Sweat turned slimy in her armpits.

Whispers of a memory tickled her ear. Aunt Heather. *4425 Delgado Street, Casper.*

"Hey, Sy, you want to go visit Aunt Heather?"

Again no answer. Brandi shrugged. Signs pointed her out of town, and when she got to the highway, she drove as fast as she could, her spine tingling every time she checked the rearview mirror.

Three

Mack picked his way along the edge of a small river, toes submerged, heels balancing on rocks dug into the wet bank. He cast into a deeper pool, his rod modified to fit across his chest where he wore a rod holder, allowing him the full use of his one arm to maneuver the line, his body practiced to feel for the vibration, the tug of a fish. When he lost his arm, Mack thought he'd never angle again. It took time to fashion his own system, similar to this but much cruder and less efficient. But he'd made do. Years later, he'd been guiding a trip when one of his clients, fascinated by Mack's cobbled-together rod, asked if he'd work with him to produce it on a larger scale for disabled veterans. Years later, that man started a nonprofit doing just that. As a thank-you, he gave Mack a complete system of his own, including a knot tyer. Everything Mack needed to fish independently. The man had later sent more modified rods for Mack's disabled guests, and soon Mack was teaching men and women that fishing could be enjoyed by everyone.

I knew God took that arm for some reason, Daisy would say.

A bear took my goddang arm. He and Daisy had different views of the world. *God decided not to stop her.*

Her soft laugh ended in a sigh. *And look at all the good it's done.*

Mack sniffed, wiped the tip of his nose on the shoulder of his jacket. River water misted late-afternoon air, cool and a little bit humid. The scent of mud and weeds picked up by a fluttering breeze surrounded him with earthy memories of teaching Jesse how to cast and dance the fly through the water, tease the fish. Jesse had loved it.

Too much.

Mack blinked, coughed against a sudden rise of acid. "Goddang heartburn," he muttered. A deep weariness washed over him, encasing his heart and settling deep into his limbs. Time to call it a day. He gathered his gear, neatly folding and storing it in his pack. It was getting late anyway, and the hike back was long. He'd planned to forage along the way before the wildlife emerged into the blue of dusk.

He'd turned from the water—there'd been a patch of elderberries he'd spotted on his way to the river—and headed in that direction when he saw the grizzly cubs through the bushes. They wrestled, playful groans puncturing the quiet. Mack stopped in his tracks, cursed himself for being caught up in thoughts of the past. His memories were all he had left, and they swarmed around him like ghosts, distracting and unfulfilling.

But he knew better than to let his guard down. This time of year the looming winter drove the bears to fill their bellies before hibernation. They weren't territorial, but a sow would protect her young if she felt threatened, and if Mack surprised her she'd feel threatened. Many of his clients, after hearing how he lost his arm, marveled at his lack of fear. He'd say the same thing every time. *Out here, animals are part of the land. They have just as much right to be here as I do.*

The cubs stopped their playing to stare in his direction. Mack backed away, alertness turning his skin electric, and carefully walked down the bank, never turning his back to the animals. The grizzly appeared just behind her cubs. She smelled him. Mack sensed it from the way the animal's fur bristled along her shoulder blades, the heavy inhale, followed by a huff and a shake of her fattened body. A stiff wind pushed against his cowboy hat but it stayed put, faded and worn and as used to the Wyoming winds as his old body. He tightened the strap of the canvas sack so that the bulk of it rested firm across his back and tried to keep his feet light and silent. He fingered the gun belted to his thigh, animal stink heavy in his nostrils.

He moved slowly. The bear eyed Mack through the bushes, swaying but not coming any closer. If she was going to attack, she'd a done it by now. As it was, the grizzly must have sensed that Mack was as desperate to fatten up before winter as she was, because she turned her attention back to the elderberries and her cubs. Keeping an eye on the bear, Mack continued backing away. Once he reached the clearing, he turned around and released the air pent up in his lungs.

The hike back to his cabin was a long one. He'd wandered far on this trip to the creek, harvesting dandelion roots for tea, his fingers stained from plucking gooseberries, popping a few into his mouth as he walked. Mack had taught Daisy to fish, and she'd enjoyed it too, but her true love was foraging, finding anything wild that she could harvest for food or use for medicinal purposes. Like elderberry root for Mack's aching knees.

He stopped, tapped his chest until the heartburn settled. He caught himself thinking about Daisy like she was the one who'd died and he wasn't the ghost who roamed the woods alone. Nearly three months ago he'd left her at the nursing home, her face etched into his memory, his hand empty without hers to hold. He felt the loss of her in a diminished appetite, most days forcing himself to eat. Her words from years ago had wrapped themselves around his heart like barbed wire. *Take care of me like you would one of your dying horses.*

Daisy was blunt. It's what he'd first loved about her. The way she didn't sugarcoat or pretend that there was any other way of being than honest. She'd been a late addition to his first solo guided fishing expedition. He found out later she'd traded with his father for the cost of the trip and mucked the horse stalls for a week. Thrifty even then. He'd been seventeen and she'd been twenty. A city girl wearing bell-bottom jeans and sandals that would never cut it in this rugged land. Looking like she'd lived her entire life in hotels and taxicabs. Mack had handed her a pair of hip waders, struck mute by her dark-green eyes and strawberry blonde hair. But also feeling just a tad full of himself. *What's a pretty girl like you doing in the Wild West?* She'd kicked off her sandals and stuck her bare feet right into the boots. *Same as everyone else. Trying to be free.* She'd stood, adjusting the waders, then speared him with a look that caused his spine to compress. *So why don't you teach me how to fish so I don't have to put up with boys like you making me feel pretty and helpless?* Afterward, he'd heard she was living in a tent by the river and working at the feedstore. It had taken him a year to work up the courage to ask her out. Another year to ask her to marry him. And before she said yes, she made him promise to be her best friend first, her husband second, and to eat more vegetables, because contrary to what he might think, meat wasn't the only food God made.

Mack pulled on the canvas bag so that it hung across his hip, ran his finger along the old fabric. Something squeezed his throat. The bag had been Daisy's. One she'd worn as a permanent accessory like some women wear necklaces or earrings. Always there as a just in case. She'd made one for Jesse, and together they'd roam the woods while Daisy poked around for seeds and roots and Jesse shoved rocks into his bag and ate wild raspberries.

Clouds moved swiftly across the sun, and there was a coolness to the early-fall air, reminding Mack of the long and dark nights to come.

After leaving Daisy, he'd gone back home to figure out how she'd get the life insurance payout the fastest. According to the internet, drowning was the quickest way to being declared dead without a body. The fact had sunk like a hook into his heart, and sorrow bobbed to the surface. He'd almost given up on the whole thing. After a few minutes, Mack had decided it was a fitting death for him. Daisy might have agreed.

So he chose a lake that reached over six hundred feet deep in spots, proving recovery difficult to near impossible. There'd been a man just last summer who'd drowned with his boating party right there watching him. They'd never found him, even after several recovery missions. With

Mack's age and his missing arm, he didn't think it would be a leap to come to the conclusion that the lake had swallowed him too.

The water had been flat that morning, the fading moon wavering across its glassy surface. He'd rowed himself using a paddle he'd adapted for his one arm and welcomed the ache in his muscles. When he was far enough out, he'd sat still, listening to the water knock the sides of his canoe, the splash of a fish in the distance. Thought about his son on that long-ago morning. Breathed in air laced with the tang of lake water, the mineral earthiness of its muddy bottom. Closed his eyes and saw pale limbs in dark water. Drowning was quiet and cruel. The panic of a summer morning years before painted the early dawn with images that never faded. Daisy's screams forever imprinted inside his head. Mack had slept late. Minutes that changed everything.

He started to rock the canoe, getting more violent, leaning heavily toward one side until his head dipped far enough below him and stole his balance. When it capsized, cold water stalled his breath and water-logged his body. He didn't have to fight; this could be his end. He'd imagined a tug on his ankle, the dip of his nose below the surface, silty water slipping down his throat. The panicked thudding of his heart. A blackness that came with letting go. Water in his ears, and in the plugged silence Mack saw Jesse's body limp in the water, no struggle, no fight, and Mack couldn't do it. He refused to leave before Daisy.

It had taken him much longer than he'd expected to reach the shore, but he'd made it, and the hours-long hike to the cabin had returned the warmth to his core. That was three months ago. Since then, Mack had settled into his new existence. Counting the minutes and the hours, thoughts of Daisy following him each day, dreams of Jesse waking him in a cold sweat every night since. He ignored the dreams and focused on what he hoped: Peggy finding the will, filing the claim, the payment funding treatments that would decimate her cancer and give Daisy a fighting chance to—

He halted, hand on the thin trunk of an aspen. It nagged at Mack. This incomplete thought. The aloneness of the woods played tricks on him, taunted him with questions he didn't want to answer. Peggy's words swirling around him. *She doesn't want this, Mack.*

He punched the wood. Peggy didn't know what Daisy wanted. But Mack did. Daisy had chosen life. Cleaved in two by their shared loss, she'd saved them both by leaving Mack all those years ago. Someone had to, and it sure as heck wasn't going to be Mack. He didn't think he could breathe without her.

You can't fix Alzheimer's.

"Damn it, Peggy." He shook his head. Things had gotten worse for Daisy, but Alzheimer's was an old person's disease and Daisy was too young. Without treatment, cancer would eat her away, a slow and painful death. Wasn't that worse? How could Peggy want something different for her friend? Especially when Mack could save her? He rubbed his hand down the trunk, dusty white residue on his palm. He knew the disease would take her eventually, but he hoped for a peaceful end, maybe in her sleep here at the cabin with Mack holding her hand.

He moved higher and deeper into the woods, and when he reached a rise, he turned. From here, he could see the very edge of town peeking out from between two hills, glimpse the river beyond the clearing. Thoughts of the cubs reminded him of the stuffed bear Jesse used to carry with him everywhere, even after the head wore off the body. Mack touched the stump of his left arm. In the end, it wasn't a bear that took everything Mack loved. Sometimes he wondered if Daisy's forgetting was a gift. If being the last one remembering was his penance.

Something caught Mack's attention. Miles off, coming from town, a small SUV, dull sunlight glinting against the metal. Driving like it was being chased and down a road that Mack knew went nowhere. An old Forest Service road. The vehicle disappeared behind a rise. He waited for it to turn around and go back toward civilization. And waited.

The SUV didn't reappear, and Mack hesitated, sat on the ground, and plucked a long piece of straw, chewing on the end. An uneasy feeling settled in his gut. He couldn't explain why. It wasn't any of his business where that car was going. Still he stayed. Past the time he should have and when the walk back would be covered in dark. It didn't matter to him. He knew this land like a man knows the curves of his woman's backside. But whoever had driven that old car didn't know that four-wheel drive or a four-legged ride was the only way to get any farther.

There was no point in staying. He couldn't help and he wouldn't besides, but his feet remained firm where he stood. Daisy's voice pestered him. *What if they need help?* That woman would not have hesitated to march straight down there to see if the car got stuck in a ditch or the mud, would have offered to use their old truck to tow them out, would have scolded the driver for coming out into the woods unprepared. Mack grunted a laugh, spit out the straw, and stood. Daisy always forgot how she first came out here. Running from a family legacy of wealth and expectation with a few dollars, a Pinto with bad tires, and those damn sandals. As unprepared as anyone Mack had ever seen.

He headed in the direction of his cabin, hand close to his gun, on the lookout for more wildlife. It was getting on to dusk, and the animals would be active. Whoever was driving that car likely had no good reason to be out in the woods this time of day, and if that was the case, Mack wanted nothing to do with it.

~

Brandi had been driving for an hour, thinking she must be heading in the right direction but also 100 percent sure she was lost. A creeping sensation across her shoulders that her mom and Kenny were following her. The crazed look in Kenny's eyes popped up whenever she thought about what she'd just done. In one of her many glances in the rearview mirror, Brandi thought she saw what looked like her mom's Subaru barreling after them, and she swerved the RAV4 onto the first side road she saw.

Now that road had disappeared into ruts so deep Brandi thought they might swallow the car whole. And worse, they were in the middle of nowhere. It was totally possible that Brandi had overreacted. Chances were that her mom and Kenny had gotten high and forgotten all about her by now.

The SUV hit something so hard it made her teeth slam against each other, and Sy rolled from his tight ball on the passenger seat and into the footwell, jerking him out of his hibernation. She stopped the car. "That did not feel right."

Sy crawled back onto the seat and curled up like nothing had happened, tucking his head under his skinny arm so his whole face was hidden. She glanced at his arm, a pang in her chest. He'd broken it when he was four. Woken up from a nap, looking for her. She hated to think about it because as much as she loved him and took care of him, even dreamed of being his actual mom, he'd broken his arm because she'd left him alone.

His silence bothered her. "Hey, so I'm sorry about the gun going off like that," she said. "It was an accident. True fact: I've never even held a gun before." It had shocked her to feel the powerful jolt of the bullet, the recoil of the gun. Kenny was a terrible person—it didn't take a genius to know that—but Brandi wasn't the kind of girl who killed people. "Hey, Syborg, are you okay?" she said.

No response, no acknowledgment that Brandi even existed.

"I guess you don't remember me, do you. I used to read to you and take you to the park and stuff like that." She'd put him in a stroller and push him to the park down the road. It was bare-bones as parks went. An old metal slide, the kind of monkey bars that burned her fingers, and a couple of swings. She'd hold him on her lap and swing. He'd giggle and make all the cute baby noises. Back then she thought she'd make a pretty kick-ass teenage mom. Back then she'd also thought her mom would get better.

Brandi couldn't even remember when the drug use started for Nancy, but it was like one of those Polaroids where the picture darkens with time. One day her mom was a nature photographer who sold her photos at little stores and in a shoebox by the register at the liquor store where she knew the owner. Her dream was to be the John Fielder of Wyoming. The only reason Brandi remembered that was from all the Colorado books they'd had scattered around the house. Some of Brandi's very early memories were of snuggling next to her mom while Nancy flipped through the pages, pointing out the camera angle here, use of shadows and color there.

There'd been this one boyfriend. Also a photographer. Brandi couldn't remember his face or even the color of his hair, but when he slithered into her thoughts, she felt cold all over. He was the first of the assholes but also the worst because he'd been the one to introduce Nancy to meth, and from there it had been a muddy downhill slide. Brandi had been really young, but she remembered the hunger pangs that made her cry, the fear that kept her awake, tapping on her mom's face to wake her up. Then Aunt Heather took her away, and all Brandi remembered of that time was how safe she felt. So safe her memories jelled together into one big glob of warmth.

Brandi shook her head and breathed in. "I know you're probably saying to yourself, *Who the hell is this girl, and where the hell are we?*" She craned her neck, looked through the windshield at the rangeland that surrounded them, mountains in the distance. "First, don't start cussing. It's a hard habit to break, trust me." She smiled at her joke. "Also, I'm your sister Brandi, and I love you so, so much, Sy." It was true—he'd been her baby right up until the day she was sent to juvie. She'd written him letters and told him she'd do good so she could come home and take care of him again. He never wrote back, but the first time she went to juvie he wasn't even a year old, and the second time he was just four and couldn't even hold a crayon right. But she'd hoped her mom would read her letters to him, because while her mom had made bad decisions, she wasn't a monster. "And did you know the coolest thing ever? You and me have the same birthday, only thirteen years apart. Do you know what that makes us?" She waited for him to speak.

He stayed curled into a half-moon, head hidden under his arms. Brandi swallowed past a lump, pinched herself in the thigh for feeling hurt. It wasn't his fault he didn't remember her. "It means we're birthday twins!" On his first birthday, Brandi had baked them both a strawberry cake with strawberry icing; she'd even added real strawberries to the top. All of it she'd stolen, because how else was she going to make a cake? "Do you remember the strawberry cake I made you?" The icing she'd used turned his fingers red and the bathwater pink. She looked out the car window, sighed at the expanse of land covered in spiky grasses and prickly shrubs. "Listen, Syborg, in case you're worried, I'm not moving us out to this wasteland." She puffed up her chest, reminding herself that she did know what she was doing even if she had decided it on the fly and after stealing a car, a gun, and her brother. "I'm taking you to Aunt Heather. She took me in once when Mom was real bad like now, and Aunt Heather, she's just so cool. You're gonna love her."

Uneasiness tickled her stomach. Aunt Heather hadn't bothered to show up in the last few years. She was pretty sure Heather had never met Sy. Brandi had no idea why, but she figured her aunt must have finally cut things off with Nancy. She couldn't blame her. Brandi would do the same thing if she could, but she'd had Sy to think about. She rolled her shoulders and pushed away the hurt that bubbled up to her throat. A part of her had felt abandoned; she tried to remind herself that it wasn't Heather's job to make sure Nancy was a good mom. She pushed the thoughts away. For all she knew, Heather had spent the last few years trying to find them.

"Anyway, she lives in Casper." Brandi waved a hand at their surroundings. "This is not Casper, obviously, but I'll get us out of here." She put her hand on the door handle, thinking of the loud thunk she'd heard earlier. "Just as soon as I make sure the car is okay."

She stalled. Brandi wasn't an outdoor girl. She loved inside and carpet and faucets with water. She'd never been into hiking or camping or anything to do with being outside. It was remote and scary AF out here. The kind of place where people got probed by aliens. She breathed in and pushed open the door. "I'm getting out now!" Voice raised to sound like a badass. She wasn't, but she was good at pretending. "I'll be right back, Sy." No response. Brandi shrugged and decided that his silence was Sy saying *okay* back. And also *I love you* and *I've missed you so much* and *thanks for saving me from asshole Kenny*. In her head, Sy was as talkative as she was.

A breeze kicked up dust around her feet, gritty in her eyes. She wrapped her arms across her chest. The mountains were eating the sun, and it was cooler already. She walked around the SUV. What had she hit? Immediately she saw the problem. A flat tire. "Oh, shit no." She pressed a palm to her forehead. Prickles across her shoulders at the sound of small feet scurrying through branches and leaves. In the distance the howl of an animal. She tensed. She knew nothing about changing a tire. Hell, she didn't even have her license. They were lucky she'd driven them this far without wrecking. It was too big out here. Too much sky, too much land, too much of everything except people. She was used to noise—in juvie and at the group home the sound of girls, talking, laughing, fighting, taking up space even if they were sleeping. But out here it was empty and unnatural. She shivered.

Brandi sat on the ground, arms around her shins, and rocked. What the fuck was she supposed to do now? She stared at the tire until the sun was gone, then decided to try Carissa. Maybe she knew how to change a flat. Besides, the girl needed to tell her why she'd ditched her. Her cheap Walmart phone had a single bar of service. She raised her eyebrows, impressed. It was a piece of shit that only made phone calls, but it found a signal in the middle of nowhere. "Dope," she said to no one and dialed Carissa's number.

Carissa answered after one ring. "What."

"Why'd you ditch me today?" There was no pretending with Carissa. They were who they were with each other, and that about summed up their friendship.

A sigh from Carissa came through the phone, and Brandi pictured her friend admiring her nails on the other end. Since leaving juvie, Carissa had a bad habit of spending money on things she shouldn't, like a full set.

"Me ditch you?" Carissa said. "You're the one who wasn't there when I came back."

"Came back from where?" Hearing someone else's voice calmed Brandi a bit, helped her ignore the chills that ran up her spine from being so alone.

"There was a Taco Johns just around the corner! You know I can't pass up a Taco Johns. Please." Music in the background. "But you've gotten yourself in some serious trouble, B. What the hell—" Her voice cut out. "—thinking? And where the fu—"

Again, it cut out. "What do you mean I'm in trouble, Carissa?" She spoke loud enough to get through the bad reception.

Silence until, ". . . they came to the group home. Your mom said she was worried about you. Said you had Sy, and she wasn't sure what you were going to do. You're in loads of trouble, B."

A tremor ran down Brandi's thighs. They had tried to follow her. She didn't think her mom even knew where she was living after she'd gotten out of juvie. She pressed an arm into her stomach.

"They said they were worried about you, like, that was bullshit obviously. But seriously, what were you thinking? And that's something coming from me."

It was true. Carissa had a long track record, and unlike Brandi's, hers included armed robbery, but she'd only been eleven at the time. Her choices were seriously flawed.

"And where the hell are you, anyway?"

"In the middle of nowhere." She tapped her foot on the ground in disbelief that her mother had come after her. The dark tiptoed around her, thick in the trees and bushes, settling over the mountains. They were alone out here, and the idea of it made her anxious and sweaty. "Do you know how to change a tire?"

Carissa laughed, obnoxious and loud. "Have you seen my nails, bitch? You think these hands have ever changed a tire?"

"No." Brandi pulled at the ends of her hair, scared to look around now that everything was just a little dimmer. "I think I need help, Carissa." She didn't want to admit it, but they were stuck.

Carissa didn't say anything.

"I'm serious, girl. We're lost and I don't know the first thing about flat tires and Sy is, like, traumatized and I'm probably ruining him forever." She loved him and had even had dreams of trying to adopt him when she turned eighteen. Instead, she'd made everything so much worse. Her head dropped into her hand. "Carissa! Say something."

Dead air. She pulled the phone away from her ear. Cheap phone. Her arm cocked back, and she wanted to throw it at the big rock across the way, watch the worthless thing bust into a million pieces.

A coyote howled, and Brandi sprang to her feet, raced around the car, and jumped inside, breathing hard. Sy had moved to the back seat, where he'd curled into his now familiar ball. With a jolt, she remembered throwing the gun back there. Brandi leaned over, found it on the floor, and picked it up with her fingers, staying far away from the trigger. It took her some time, but she figured out how to push the latch forward to get the cylinder open and drop five bullets into her hand. She studied the cylinder, space for six bullets, and one of those she'd accidentally shot at asshole Kenny. She smiled to herself, wondered if asshole pissed himself. According to Carissa, that was a thing.

She opened the glove compartment, threw the bullets inside, closed the cylinder, and slid the gun under her seat.

She leaned her head against the window, a thousand-pound weight crushing her chest. *Breathe, Brandi, f-ing breathe.* Her heart raced, the car claustrophobic. Better in here than out there in the wild with things that wanted to kill them, but inside, cluttered with Kenny's trash, a stink similar to the house, she wanted to pull her skin off.

It was getting dark, and there was no way they could walk anywhere or have enough light left for Brandi to even begin messing with the tire. Plus it all seemed impossible and more than she could handle. For now, Sy was asleep in the back and away from anything bad that could have happened to him at home. If nothing else, Brandi had done that for him. They could survive one night in the car, and then she'd figure out a plan tomorrow.

She wrapped her arms across her body, suddenly so tired she felt like she might sleep despite the coyotes howling their heads off. She'd try at least.

Four

Mack woke up after a restless night to frost spread across the ground, early for this time of year. The fire had burned down to embers in the stove, and the tip of his nose had gone cold and wet from dripping. He moved his fingers and toes, then stretched his body, warming up bit by bit. A couple of months off the grid had taught him two things: he knew how to survive, and he was old. At sixty-seven, his own father had still been leading hunting expeditions, moving like a man half his age and strong until the end. Within minutes of shooting an antelope through its heart, he'd keeled over from a heart attack that killed him on the spot. In contrast, Mack had grown wiry on his limited diet, muscles poking through his skin, his body doing what he told it to but without the quickness he remembered in his father. Living on limited supplies and whatever he could trap, fish, or hunt was taking its toll quicker than he thought it would. It made sense, Mack supposed. He'd lost his stamina over the past year between trying to find work as a guide and watching over Daisy.

He stoked the fire back to life, adding thin twigs once the coals ignited a small flame, blowing gently and shutting the door. He filled the percolator with water and coffee grounds and set it on top of the stove. This morning he craved the bitterness of coffee. It wasn't a staple he could replace, so he used it sparingly, hoping his stores would last for as long as possible. Mack eased into a canvas chair, a crackle in his right knee. He sighed into the cool quiet, thoughts of Daisy lingering in the frosted air.

Alzheimer's hadn't been a complete surprise. There had been little things at first. Keys in the fridge, milk in the bathroom. They'd laughed. Daisy had called it her "loose change" moments. Much later, after the doctor's appointment, after Daisy had begun pulling away from her friends and on a cold winter afternoon when the snow flew sideways through winter grass, Mack came home early from work to find Daisy and Peggy at the kitchen table. Documents were spread under their coffee cups, a portable file box at Daisy's feet. He hung up his keys, slid out of his jacket, and poured himself a cup. He sipped, letting the bitterness of the liquid fight the sting of betrayal at seeing the two women together with Daisy's last will and testament. *What are you doing?*

Daisy put the papers into a folder, held it to her chest, and for a second Mack had thought she wasn't going to answer. They'd lost everything when the business went belly-up, and with no beneficiaries and no property, the only thing that had mattered to Mack was Daisy getting his life insurance payout if he died first. What could Daisy want with her will?

I added Peggy as an executor.

I'm your executor. His stomach shifted uneasily. Daisy never lied. She'd always said that a lie was the beginning of the end. But this didn't feel like the truth.

Daisy relaxed her grip on the folder. *But I need a backup in case you go first.*

Mack nodded. It made sense. Still, it seemed like a half-truth, and he noticed that Peggy was staring into her coffee cup, and that set the red flags flying. *You're going to be okay, Daisy,* he'd said.

She smiled, but it was thin, without her usual brilliance, and her bottom lip trembled. *You swore to me, Mack.*

He knew what she meant. Did Peggy? But the woman had turned away so that her back was to him, pretending to study the papers in front of her. Mack could not meet his wife's gaze. She'd see the lie in him. So he stared at her hands because he couldn't bear the naked vulnerability on her face. Her hands were always so beautiful. Delicate, long fingers that danced over piano keys—elegant, like birds in the air, when she talked. And when he spoke it was to those goddang beautiful hands. *I swear to take care of you until the end of my days or yours, whichever comes first.* Silence, and when he'd finally looked up he'd wished he hadn't, because she was crying. Big, messy tears dripped off her chin, and he hoped she understood. Mack would never be able to go through with what she'd asked.

The water in the percolator popped, and it was loud in the cabin, snapping Mack away from the past. He pulled out a strip of jerky, tugged on the tough meat, and chewed. He'd left a piece of himself with Daisy, same as he'd left a piece of himself in the ground with Jesse, and being out here alone made him feel emptier for it.

Outside the sky had lightened into a pearly blue; the sun peeked around the trees and slid through the window. A warm glow spread like butter on toast across the small cabin. Mack pulled a pair of socks from a bin under his cot, took hold of one in his hand, and inched it onto his foot. He tugged; the cotton snagged on the dried cracks of his heel, then wrinkled into place. He repeated on the other foot. He'd never had a prosthetic. They were expensive and uncomfortable, and maybe he hadn't given it much of a go, but Mack figured that like a wild animal, he'd adjust to the missing limb. Daisy liked to remind him that he was not an animal. There were a few things they disagreed about—but that was marriage. An ache in his chest. God how he missed her.

At night when sleep danced with the owls, he sometimes wondered if he should have let himself sink to the bottom of the lake instead of this half-life where Daisy lived just out of his reach and Jesse's absence grew like a black hole.

Mack coughed, waited for the heartburn feeling to pass through his chest. Solitude brought out all the ghosts. At night, his son haunted the cabin in that in-between time just before sleep when Mack's mind cut loose from his body. He'd feel something solid yet invisible taking up space, the floorboards creaking, and with it, an unbearable weight pressing down on him.

Mack poured the steaming coffee into his mug and sat back in the camp chair, surveying the interior of the cabin. He and Daisy had built it by hand, each log fitted together with pieces of their broken hearts. On the floor, a square metal plate that Daisy had inscribed with:

JESSE'S CABIN

1987–1997

It was built on a small slice of land that had been in Mack's family for generations, remote and rugged and not worth the trouble of selling. A good spot for hunting or a few nights camping. It had been Jesse's favorite place. *Can we live here?* he'd whispered from his sleeping bag after the lantern had been dimmed. Mack smiled into the dark. *When you're older we'll build a cabin here together. How does that sound?* Jesse had squealed and launched himself between Daisy's and Mack's sleeping bags. *How you going to build a whole cabin with one arm?* Mack had tickled Jesse, who howled giggles. *I can do anything.* Jesse, breathless, snuggled up to Daisy. *You can't cut your fingernails. Mommy has to do that.* Daisy had laughed.

Anything else I can't do?

Jesse had sighed, and Mack heard him click his tongue. *Nope, that's it, I guess.*

He sipped the hot coffee, let it scald his tongue and burn away the memory.

Mack pulled the bedsheets into place, tucking them under the mattress. Daisy never started a day without a made bed, and he'd grown to appreciate it too, especially in this tight space. He slid his arm into a thick flannel, pinned the other sleeve up and around his stump, and yawned to clear the cobwebs. His mental list of to-dos grew longer the closer winter got: fish, check his traps, re-chink the south side of the cabin. But his thoughts kept drifting off topic. Back to the car from the day before and Daisy's voice in his head. *What if they need help?*

Mack muttered to himself, feeling that familiar powerlessness that overcame him when he knew Daisy was right. There were a few traps he could check on his way to where he'd seen the car. The day wouldn't be a total loss. He drained the coffee, leftover grounds and all, and headed out for the long hike back.

~

Brandi woke up with a crick in her neck and her mouth sticky and dry. *Gross.* She rubbed at her eyes, itchy from a long night spent imagining one shape after another crawling from the dark nothingness, wiggling through the air vents and into their mouths while they slept. So she'd tried to keep her eyes from closing and instead fell asleep with her mouth wide open, jerking awake to drool running down her chin and a crick in her neck. Like an idiot.

It felt early. The sun hid behind sheer clouds shimmering pink and yellow. She yawned. No need for a phone to tell her the time. It felt like the butt crack. Frosty air overnight had turned her feet cold, and she had to move her fingers to warm them up. She wiped her runny nose on the sleeve of her sweatshirt.

A quick stretch of her legs, then arms, twisting to crack her spine. Sy in the back with his hands away from his face, mouth hung open, fast asleep. She turned, resting her chin on the back of the seat, and studied him. Different, longer, lankier, but still her baby brother, the same little boy who used to fall asleep beside her, arms and legs clinging to her like a tiny koala bear. She'd been gone only a little more than a year. Had he really forgotten her? She reached out and lightly brushed her fingertips along his knee, jerked her hand back when he twitched.

She turned around, rested a foot on the dashboard, thirsty, so thirsty. Sy must be too. It had been hours since she'd had water, and she had no idea the last time he'd had a drop. Brandi didn't know much about surviving in the outdoors, but she did know that people died without water.

Outside was less scary in the daytime when the sun chased away shadows. Maybe there was a river or a creek or something out there. She could go look. A little water would go a long way. Quietly, she got out of the SUV and went around back, easing the door open and rooting around until she found an old fast-food cup. Checked once more on Sy. Out cold. Thought about the gun under her seat. She couldn't leave Sy alone with ammo and a gun. She'd had a friend in second grade who shot his little sister dead. He'd only been playing around. Brandi opened her door, grabbed the revolver, and slid it into the waistband of her jeans and under her oversize sweatshirt. Nodded to herself. Already a better mom than Nancy.

She started walking, glancing every few minutes behind her at the car and hoping that water would not be that hard to find.

~

This time he was more careful, keeping an eye out for the bear and her cubs, making sure he didn't lose himself in thoughts again. When he spied the small SUV, one side sunk deep in a rut, back tire flat as a pancake, he grimaced. He stayed in a grove of aspens, watching. It could be kids from town, he supposed, who'd come out to make some trouble. Or a couple sweet on each other getting into trouble. The fact that they hadn't changed the tire made Mack think they were too young, or stupid he supposed, to know how. An anxious jitter slid down his leg. He wished he'd never come back.

One of the doors was open, and from this angle, Mack thought the car looked empty. He waited, pulling a piece of deer jerky from his pack, chewing on it. After a while, he moved closer to get a better view. Yep, car looked empty. He'd almost convinced himself it was okay to leave. That even Daisy would agree. He'd done all he could. And surely whoever it was that had gotten themselves stuck had headed back to town by now. It was only about ten or so miles to the nearest gas station.

Then he saw something that stopped him cold. The dirty heel of a small shoe poking out from behind one of the tires. His pulse beat faster. The foot jerked, then disappeared. Was that a little kid? Hiding? Or hurt? Mack felt the air whoosh from his lungs. This wasn't good. Not good at all. Sweat built up along his back, and his biceps tensed. He couldn't leave a little kid out here alone.

Movement under the car. *Ah hell.* It was a kid. And something else. A snake, from the looks of it, curled up under the edge of the tire the kid was hiding behind. Mack heard the faint rattle of its tail, agitated at the body too close to its nesting spot. Prairie rattlers didn't attack unless threatened, and right now the kid was threatening.

He felt powerless. The same feeling that had turned him mute when the state people showed up at his trailer unannounced, claiming that Daisy wasn't in a safe situation. She'd taken to wandering when he wasn't looking. Caused an accident that could have killed people. So she was sent to the nursing home in Lander that smelled like a place where people went to die. They said he wasn't capable of caring for her. They were wrong. He knew it and Daisy knew it.

The snake's rattle turned up a notch from a warning to a threat. Mack felt the time when he could do anything to help slipping away. A small head appeared around the front of the tire. A whimpering. The kid heard the snake. The kid was scared. Mack moved quickly from the grove, staying on the balls of his feet, pulling a knife from a sheath strapped to his waist. The snake's head was raised, tongue flicking. A moment of indecision. Kill it or grab it? His knife was big, and the small space between the bottom of the SUV and the ground upped his chance of missing or only injuring the snake. He sheathed the knife and instead darted his hand under the car, grabbing the snake just below its head and yanking it out, tossing it far into the bush. It slithered away with an angry rattle.

Thoughts of leaving right then. The kid was safe now. But he couldn't do it. Knelt down, hand on the front grille, and dipped his head until it nearly rested on the ground. A small face was already turned up, staring at him.

The kid didn't look a thing like Jesse, except for the stuffed something or other he held squished against his chest. He was young, maybe six, Mack wasn't sure, but it was the look in his eyes that triggered something in Mack. Not fear or sadness or worry. Just, blank, kinda empty. Like the kid couldn't take in anything more. Jesse had been a happy kid, full of light. What had happened to steal it from this boy?

Mack rested on his heels, looked around. The boy hadn't driven here himself, so whoever had was probably close by. Anger knocked on his gut. Unless they'd dumped him the way people did with dogs. Drive 'em out a long road and never look back. His throat tightened. He shouldn't be here; it was too big a risk, and it would ruin everything he'd done to help Daisy.

But he couldn't very well leave this kid alone.

The kid's eyes darted around like the snake might come back. "It's long gone now." Mack opened his canteen. "You want some water?"

The boy crawled out from under the car. He wore pajamas that hung from his frame, all skin and bones and dark circles under his eyes, his hair sticking out in every direction like no one had taken a comb to it in weeks. Mack handed him the water and the boy drank, water slipping down his chin as he gulped.

"Easy there." Mack's voice was hoarse.

The boy stared at Mack's stump. Amused, Mack wiggled it. The bear had come upon them fast, no warning. His arm had merely slowed the sow down enough for Daisy to grab her bear spray. It made everything just a bit harder than it ought to be, but it was a sacrifice worthy of protecting his family and proof that at one point he had done everything he could to keep them safe.

Mack stood. The boy would die out here—he knew that for sure. If it wasn't by dehydration first, it would be by exposure or animal. Daisy would do the right thing. After they lost Jesse, she was always trying to do the right thing. Like she could make up for that one moment over and over again.

He was about to speak when something flew from the trees and hit his shoulder. A rock. Then another, glancing off his forehead, and another, hitting his knee. Mack reached for his gun, but the boy had moved so that he stood in front of him like his small body could do anything to stop the assault.

But it did. The rocks stopped flying, and a voice called out, "Get away from him, Sy!" A girl's voice. "He's a dirty old man, and he's gonna do nasty things to you. Run!"

Sy didn't move, and Mack took his hand away from the gun.

The girl appeared from behind a shrub, hand raised with a rock the size of a baseball. Older than the boy but only a teenager. Young to be out here all alone. She stared at Mack, defiance in the pinch of her lips and the straightness of her shoulders, fear in the shake of her hand that grasped the rock.

"Listen, girl, I don't want any trouble."

The girl's eyes flicked to the boy, and in her expression Mack saw a protectiveness he recognized. The kind that glinted in Daisy's eyes the minute she became a mother. Or in the teeth of the bear when she tore into his arm to protect her cubs. The girl pulled something from her waistband, and Mack's blood ran cold. A gun. She aimed it at him.

Sy crumpled to the ground and scurried back under the car, a bug returning to its rock.

"Put your gun on the ground," she said. "And leave." Anger in the twitch of an eye.

He should walk away, not drop his gun. But damn if Daisy's voice hadn't gotten as loud as the Wyoming winds. He carefully took it from its holster and set it on the ground at his feet.

"Kick it away from you."

He hesitated, irritated he'd gotten himself into this predicament.

"Kick it!" she yelled.

He did.

"Now get out of here."

"I can't," he said simply.

"I'll kill you." There was a slight tremble in her voice, and Mack sensed fear tearing holes in her tough exterior. It softened him but didn't change the situation.

"You need help, and I'm the only one here who can."

"We don't need—"

Sy scrambled from under the car and scooped up Mack's gun. His heart stopped. "No, boy!"

The boy held the gun close to his stomach, the weight of it pulling his hands lower, the tip of the barrel wobbling but pointed in the direction of the girl.

Her eyes were wide and her mouth dropped open. "Sy, buddy, no." Her voice had gone soft, weaker than before.

Tears ran down Sy's face, but he wasn't crying, at least not the way Mack knew crying looked like. The boy was a statue, no emotion betraying him, except for the tears.

"Give me the gun, boy," Mack said. Sy didn't move. Mack turned his attention to the girl. "I can help you change your tire."

She looked from Mack to the boy. The seconds felt like hours until she nodded, tucking her gun back into the waistband of her jeans. "Okay."

"Give me the gun, boy," Mack said again, in the kind of tone he'd use so as not to spook a wild horse.

Sy blinked and handed the gun to Mack, who slid it into its holster, breathed out. Nobody moved. The morning had warmed; the dusty scent of heated soil rose from the ground. The girl rushed over to Sy, pulling him away from Mack until they were on the opposite side of the SUV. She held the boy's body to her own and shot daggers at Mack. "You can fix the tire now."

Mack sighed and waved the stump of his left arm at the girl. "I'll be needing your help."

Five

The nervous energy from seconds ago leaked from Brandi's legs, and she wanted to give in, sit down on the ground, and shake. But she couldn't.

Thank God she'd come back as soon as she had. The farther she got away from the SUV, the more she worried that she'd get lost and abandon Sy to a terrible death. She couldn't stand the thought.

When she saw the old man talking to Sy, she freaked out. She'd grabbed for the rocks first, remembered the gun second. She pressed a hand to her heart; it still thundered from the shock of it.

The man rummaged around in the back of the RAV4 for something called a jack to fix the tire. Sy sat cross-legged on the ground, elbows on his knees, stuffie in his lap, and watched him like it was a reality show. Brandi sighed, sat down by her brother, and watched too. The man grunted when he lifted something from the back of the SUV. It looked like a weapon. She gripped the handle of the gun.

"Easy," he said. "That's the jack." He set it on the ground, then stared at her. "I need your help now."

She frowned, pushed to her feet, and reluctantly walked over, tense and ready for anything. Nothing about the old guy screamed *safe*, but Brandi had never changed a tire, and that literally left her with no choice. Plus he was doing what he said he'd do. This guy might think there was something in it for him afterward, but he could eat dirt if he thought she'd do something to him.

The old guy had set his hat on the ground, and Brandi was surprised to see that the long white hair that grew down over his ears didn't make it to the top of his head. It looked hilarious. She almost laughed, stopped herself. No reason to make him angry. But if he went for his gun or got weird with her, she'd crack his bald skull with a rock.

He handed her a metal armlike thing. "Loosen the lug nuts first." He pointed to the bolts on the wheel. "You do that before you lift the tire off the ground."

She tapped the end of the metal arm on the ground. "Why?"

"So it's easier to get the lug nuts off."

She shrugged and fitted the end of the thing onto the nut and tried to turn it. Nothing. She tried again. "Freaking ass."

The man gave her a look, and she gave him one back. He didn't get to make her feel small. She breathed through her nostrils and tried to calm down, but her heart still raced. Juvie hadn't been the worst thing to happen to her. At least there she'd had a program she was working on. Getting noticed for things she did right. Feeling like she had a purpose even if that purpose was to not be the worst girl there. And she'd learned something too. If she wanted to make it out here, it was up to her; she had to think things through and use her "process" to cool down. That's what Ms. Hanno had taught her. Brandi swallowed hard. Ms. Hanno had been her counselor. Young and mousy, but funny and nice and Brandi's favorite human being she'd ever met. Except for her mom's neighbor Mrs. Tallula. And Aunt Heather. But they'd both up and vanished from Brandi's life, and it got them fired from that particular list. At least with Ms. Hanno, Brandi had been the one to leave.

Brandi grunted with effort, and still the bolts didn't move. Frustration cinched her lips together. She closed her eyes, counted to ten, and tried again. Nothing. She threw the metal arm on the ground. "This isn't working. Do you even know what you're doing?"

He narrowed his eyes, not saying a word. Sy scooted over from where he was sitting, interested—Brandi could tell by the tiny light in his eyes that was focused mostly on the old man. What was it with him?

Brandi picked up the arm, tapped the end on the ground in front of the old man. "Hello? Are you in there?"

The man worked his jaw, looked at the sky, then back at Brandi. "Just because something's hard doesn't make it impossible."

"Don't I know it." She fitted the metal arm to the end of the bolt and started at it again. Brandi was a sucker for inspirational sayings. Must be an old people thing to know so many. Mrs. T had her fair share scattered around her house, on little knitted pillows, in frames on the walls, on her coffee cup.

Brandi'd called her Mrs. T because saying all those *l*'s had been a real tongue twister when she was ten. Mrs. T found Brandi on her front porch one rainy summer day. *As wet as a dog and shaking like one too.* Mrs. T loved telling the story. Brandi didn't remember that part. For her, it started at Mrs. T's round kitchen table, sitting in her shiny metal chairs with red vinyl seats. The ones that released air like a whoopee cushion when Brandi sat down. It was the sweetness of lemonade on her tongue, and the toasted popcorn Mrs. T served in a big metal bowl, butter shiny on her fingertips. It was the potent whiff of whatever Mrs. T put into her coffee in the morning or over ice in the afternoon that made her eyes water when she sniffed it.

Brandi did know that she started going to Mrs. T's after the photographer boyfriend moved in. In Brandi's memory, he'd ruined everything, taking away the mom who made dinner and had dance parties and replacing her with a stranger with googly eyes and a smile that didn't match her face anymore.

She'd wondered why Aunt Heather didn't show up like she had when Brandi was four. Or why she stopped visiting. But Brandi wasn't about to wait for her aunt to save her, so she'd figured out a way to save herself. Some nights she'd sleep on Mrs. T's couch or watch TV after school. On the days when Mrs. T ran out of alcohol, Brandi stayed home. Things changed when her mother was pregnant with Sy. She got sober, made dinner, packed lunches with notes that said *I love you,* took pictures again. Then Sy was born, and it didn't take long before it started back up again and Brandi was bringing Sy with her to Mrs. T.'s.

Brandi's arms ached with effort, frustration building behind her eyes. The dumb bolt still hadn't budged. Sweat beaded across her forehead. Her biceps strained when she pushed on the arm, but still, nothing loosened. She had to fight the urge to throw the metal arm as far as she could or use it to break one of the windows. It didn't help that the old man had brought up all her memories of Mrs. T. As Brandi got older, the woman had started to change. She'd fly off the handle for no reason, breaking dishes in her anger, or she'd call Brandi by a different name, sometimes talking to her like she didn't know her at all. They drifted, and when her son moved in, Brandi stopped going.

The last time she'd seen the woman had been from the back of a cop car. There was no food or milk in the house, and her little brother was screaming his head off. Brandi climbed through Mrs. T.'s window to get inside, and the old woman's good-for-nothing son, who was on the couch drinking beer and eating all of Mrs. T.'s popcorn, called the cops.

"You're turning it the wrong way." Apart from Mrs. T, Brandi didn't know any old people. Was he lost out here like she was?

"What?"

"Turn it counterclockwise." He waited; she stared at him. "The other way."

Brandi shrugged and did what he said. It took some muscle but it worked, and soon she'd loosened the bolt. "Why didn't you tell me about that clockwise shit in the first place?"

He grunted. "I was giving you a chance to figure it out first. The best learning comes from doing."

She curled her lip up and rolled her eyes. "Didn't know I was in school." The rest of the bolts loosened with no problem.

"You ever change a tire before?" the man asked.

"Does it look like it?"

"Your daddy never taught you?"

Brandi made a face. "I don't know what that is."

With his one hand, he set the jack under the car behind the tire, took the metal arm she'd used to loosen the bolts, and fitted it onto the end. Looked at her again.

Message received. She grabbed the arm and started to turn, amazed at how easily the car lifted. Her brother sat on the ground in his dirty pajamas and stared. No smile, no sign in his eyes that he gave a flipping damn. Brandi didn't know what to make of him. Worry clouded her vision, turned the tire into a rubber blob.

The old man talked her through the rest of it, and he didn't use many more words than Sy to do it. Brandi didn't know Sy like she used to. But he was her brother, half of him at least. She'd done the right thing by taking him, she knew it. Their mother would choose herself over and over again, and Sy would always be on the losing side of things. She rolled her shoulders, her nose hairs still holding on to the stink of filth in that house.

"Hey, Syborg, you ever change a tire before?"

He shook his head the tiniest bit. A spike of excitement. It was a response. Better than nothing. She grinned. "Well, rule number one: always loosen the nuts first." She gave the old man a look. "And don't wait for your dad to show you, 'cause those guys don't know shit."

The old man let air out of his nose in what Brandi guessed was exasperation. It was a common response to her. She didn't know why. Personally, Brandi found herself charming AF.

Finally, the new tire was on. Brandi stood back, crossed her arms, and made a face. "That wasn't hard."

When the man stood, his bones popped so loud Brandi could hear it. He replaced his hat and started to move away, shaking his head and mumbling, "Not that hard." He pulled the strap of a bag over his head and set something brown and shriveled on the hood of the car. "That's some jerky. Think the little one's hungry." He nodded like he was having a conversation with someone else. "You two be careful. There was a mama grizzly and her young by the river just last evening."

Brandi's mouth hung open. A fucking grizzly bear? Was he serious? She might have lived in Wyoming her entire life, but she'd carefully avoided anything to do with the outdoors. "Um, what? How do I be careful around that?"

"Just don't surprise her."

"What if I do?"

The man looked like he was steadying himself against something. Maybe her questions. "Back away slowly."

"I'll be running, thank you." Did he think she was an idiot?

"Then you might trigger an attack."

Her skin went cold. "What do I do then?"

The man sighed. "Play dead and wait for the bear to leave. As long as you're not a threat, she'll leave you alone."

And then, like what he'd said hadn't just raised the hair on her arms, he started to walk away.

For a moment, Brandi couldn't move. He was just going to leave. Like that? With killer teddy bears roaming freely around? Her skin prickled. When he'd seemed a threat, it was easy to feel tough. But last night, out here, pitch-black dark, with the howls of coyotes in the distance, she'd been so scared she'd almost pissed herself. A cry came from Sy's direction, animallike and earsplitting. The boy ran past Brandi and to the man, still making that godawful sound. When he got to the old guy, Sy threw his arms around the man's shins.

She ran over to her brother, grabbed him by the armpits, and pulled. He fought her, kicking and still making that horrible sound. They fell backward, Sy resting against her, Brandi's arms firm around him. She was afraid to let go. Scared he might run away from her. "What the hell's wrong with you, Sy!" His little body went limp, but Brandi held on, her heart pounding into his back. The old man stared down at them, and Brandi sensed pity in his frown. "He's been through some stuff," she said.

The man nodded, then knelt in front of Sy. "Good on you, boy. Yelling means you're alive. No shame in that." He pulled another shriveled brown stick from his pack. "Jerky."

Sy moved to take it, and Brandi let him go. He tugged on it with his front teeth.

He handed one to Brandi, and her stomach growled.

She was starving. It was tough and tasted salty. Threads of it stuck in her teeth, but it was food and she had no complaints. "Thanks."

He sat down, opened a canteen, and gave it to Sy, who took several gulps, coughing on the last one. Then the man motioned for Sy to give it to her. She sipped; it tasted clean, slightly metallic, but good, so good that she had to make herself slow down and stop so they didn't drink all the man's water.

The sun had heated the air, and Brandi, who thought her toes had fallen off from the cold overnight, had started to sweat.

"Where're you headed?"

She squinted at the old guy. The last thing she'd do was tell this stranger where she was going. "Nunya."

The man took a sip of water, eyes on her. "Never heard of it. That in Montana?"

She didn't know if he was kidding or not. His skin was creased and leathery, and he was skinny, like all he ate was that jerky. Everything about him looked old, from his wrinkled face to his clothes and all the way down to his boots. Nah, he wasn't kidding.

"You live out here?" she asked. "Or are you lost too?"

The man shifted to his feet, stuck his thumb inside his belt loops, gaze drifting to the SUV. His face softened when he looked at Sy. "Make sure you get back to the main road before you get another flat," he said to Brandi and pointed behind her. "It's that way." He paused, blew air into his cheeks. "Not sure which direction is Nunya."

It tickled her chest and she wanted to laugh, but her stomach was in knots. She didn't have money, and the little orange light had turned on when she was driving. She wasn't sure if they could make it to a gas station without running out and getting stranded again. She pulled at the ends of her hair, panicked.

The weight of the gun tugged at the waistband of her jeans, awkward and alien and making her think about her brother aiming it at her. The year she'd been gone had made her nothing but a stranger to him. Not the girl who'd slept curled beside him when he was two, her hand covering his ears to block out the loud music and raucous voices coming from the living room. Or the one who scrubbed his feet clean, water brown from unwashed floors.

But the man was itching to leave. She knew the signs: not meeting her gaze, feet tapping the earth, body angled just slightly away. And it pissed her off because right now they needed his help, and she hated that they had to depend on a complete stranger. He hadn't done anything weird like look at her the way her mom's assholes did, and he did what he said he'd do and helped fix the tire—even if she had done most of it. With the stump, he seemed less of a threat, and sad, like his arm wasn't the only thing he'd lost.

The sun had risen higher, warming her arms, but the cold from the night before lingered in the tips of her fingers. Last night the landscape turned spooky: dim starlight making eerie patterns on the ground, minuscule bits of light catching on odd shadows. It was the kind of place a skinwalker haunted, she was sure of it. Her friend Carissa had told her stories of her grandfather's ranch and all the scary shit that happened there, like cows with no insides and weird noises and things that looked like people but weren't. Brandi hadn't believed a single word until last night, alone in the car with nothing for miles around but coyotes and bears and things that wanted to eat her from the inside out. The one-armed man was a kitty cat compared to all that.

"Mister, we need gas." She straightened her shoulders, felt her face tighten, hoping it locked the fear behind her eyes and mouth. "Can you help us?"

But he was already shaking his head, and the rejection joined the knives of so many others lodged in her back. She rolled her shoulders.

Fuck him. She'd just have to figure out a way to get them out of here on her own. She could do it. She'd been only thirteen when Sy was born, but she'd done all the things an adult was supposed to do: feed him, change his diaper, put that ointment on his bottom when his own poop gave him blisters, rock him to sleep. She didn't need this falling-apart old man to save them.

The man stabbed the tip of his boot into the ground, and for a second he looked like he was having a conversation with himself, shaking his head, breathing out hard in disagreement. Then he pointed to something in the distance and said to Brandi, "It's thatta way, about ten miles. Gas station's owned by a fella named Zeke. He'll help you."

He started to walk away, and her bravado from seconds before disintegrated. Sy stood, staring at the old man's back, his *Minecraft* stuffie in a grip so tight his knuckles were bone white. A sound came from his throat, and Brandi sensed the screaming was about to start. Her heart raced. The old man moved faster than she expected, cresting a small rise and disappearing on the other side of it. She took her brother's hand and started walking in the direction the man had gone.

Her toe smashed into a rock, and in her thin Converses it hurt, but she kept walking. Sy stumbled beside her in his effort to keep up, but at least he wasn't dragging his feet or screaming. He didn't want the man to leave them either. "Rule number one, Sy: walk fast when chasing after one-armed old men." She laughed at herself. Damn, she was funny sometimes.

"Rule number one." Sy whispered it, a sound so light it could have also been nothing. But it wasn't to Brandi. She squeezed his hand, he didn't squeeze back, and since Brandi didn't believe in miracles, it didn't bother her.

They crested the hill. "Damn," she said. The man was halfway across the clearing and already headed up a ridge that disappeared into trees. They were practically running, Sy panting like a dog. "Hang with me, Sy," she said, and he nodded.

Their aunt Heather lived in Casper, an artsy lady with pink hair and studs up her ears and really soft hands that had held Brandi's when she'd whispered, *Are you safe?* When Brandi was four, Heather took her away from Nancy. Brandi still felt the tears hot in her eyes and heard her own cries, but she never remembered who it was for. With Aunt Heather, she played in paint with her bare hands, read books that had flaps to lift and things to touch. Her belly was always full, and her sheets were always clean. She learned the alphabet, and at night she snuggled with Heather's chocolate-colored cat with green eyes that glowed in the dark.

Nancy came for her two years later. Brandi still felt the confusing push and pull of wanting to be with her mom but not wanting to leave the safe cocoon of her life with Aunt Heather. Things with her mom were good for a while, and then they weren't, and then they moved to another town and Aunt Heather never came around again. Once Sy was born, all Brandi wanted was to keep him safe. He gave her purpose and strength, even if she made some stupid mistakes that got her taken away from him. At least she'd tried to protect him. It was more than her mother had done.

They got to the trees, and Brandi shivered. It was shaded, cooler, with no clear path forward. They stepped over fallen logs; branches snagged her hair, and panic turned her breaths jagged. No sign of the man. She stopped, turned. From here she couldn't see the car. *Shit.* Cold sweat in her armpits. No idea where she was. No one to help. Alone. The woods were quiet, the man was gone, and with him their last chance at getting help. She sank down, knees drawn up, hugging her legs with one arm, the other still holding Sy's hand. His palm had gone sweaty, but his grip was so tight her fingers tingled. He crouched into a ball by her side, breathing hard.

"I just need a minute to think, okay?" No response. Back at the house, she'd been so panicked that she'd just run with no clue where she was going. But when her thoughts went to Aunt Heather and the address she'd made Brandi memorize when she lived there, she knew it was the exact right place to go: 4425 Delgado Street. *So you always know how to get home.* She wiped the back of her hand across her eyes, jiggled her leg, fighting a wave of anger that threatened to come down on her head.

She pushed to her feet. The old man was the only person around. They needed to catch up. "You okay, Sy?" The boy nodded again. "We're going to find that old man, and he's going to help us get gas, and then we'll find Aunt Heather. Okay?" No answer. Brandi shrugged, but with her plan made, she felt a rush of optimistic energy. That was one of her good qualities, Ms. Hanno had said—her optimism even when things were hard. "Let's go, Sy."

They walked through the woods, slower now because of the fallen logs and tight spaces between trees, up a steep hill, and Brandi prayed that they didn't disappear the way that people did out here. Like that girl runner that Carissa told her about one night. Went for a run in the forest and was never seen again. Brandi tightened her grip on Sy's hand and tried to walk faster. They had to find the man before one of those skinwalkers found them.

Six

The kids were following him. *Dang it.* He'd hoofed it up the hill, assuming they'd do what he said and go to the gas station. It wasn't too far, and if they ran out of gas, they could walk the rest of the way. Jesse had been able to hike for miles when he was that little boy's age. They'd be fine. Zeke was a good man, grandfather to fifteen kids, a veteran; he'd get the tire fixed and the kids on their way to wherever the hell Nunya was. Weather was fine too. Mack smelled the air—didn't seem like anything was coming.

He pushed himself up the hill, uneasiness plucking at the hairs of his chest. If the girl didn't have money for gas, what the heck was she doing out here? He shook his head, scrunched his nose, and kept walking, staying light on his feet, calf muscles propelling him forward, his body built by this terrain, accustomed to the burn that spread up his legs from a lifetime exertion of hiking across valleys and over hills. The farther away he got, the more his thoughts fell behind, slinking back to the kids. The boy had near broke his heart. The way he'd grabbed on to Mack's legs, only letting go when his sister pulled him off. That horrible cry. Jesse had done something like that once, when Mack was leaving on a hunting expedition with bigwigs from California. They'd chosen his outfit over the slick corporate one that had moved into the area a few years before. It was a big deal. The corporate one had higher-quality food; he offered more of a homegrown fare. They had something called *glamping* that the rich folk apparently loved because it meant their butts never actually touched the ground. Mack's clients were always fully on the ground, behinds and all. Jesse had cried angry tears. He was desperate to do all the things his father did.

Heartburn spread from the center of his chest outward. Mack came to a stop, saw his boy, ten years old, black hair in curls above his eyes, sparking a flint into a tent of small twigs. *I'm gonna catch a fish for your anniversary.*

Daisy had tilted her head to catch the sun on her face, arms resting on the canvas sides of the camp chair. *You're making dinner for us?*

Jesse blew carefully on a spark, smoke building before a flame caught. *Yeah, I figure so.* He added more small twigs, gently protecting the young flame, growing it the way he'd seen his parents do. *First thing tomorrow morning. I'll catch the early buggers.*

Daisy had laughed. Mack too. Their boy was a perfect mix of each of them: precocious, adventurous, and independent. Fiercely so. Daisy had leaned forward in the camp chair, chin in her palm, hair catching its own fire from the sun. *Don't go out on the boat without one of us. Understand?*

He smiled when he blew on the fire, a sizable flame now, eating quickly through the small twigs. *Yeah, okay.*

From the valley below came a cry that ripped Mack away from the past so quickly he gripped the space over his heart. It sounded like the girl. Mack's hand balled into a fist. He couldn't leave them out here.

"It'll ruin everything," he told himself and Daisy, as if she were listening.

There was no imaginary response, because Mack knew exactly what Daisy would want. It was in her soul to think about others. She was outlandish with her generosity, unapologetic about her beliefs, sure of herself in a way that in the beginning had intimidated Mack.

On one of their dates, she'd wanted to learn how to bow hunt.

Have you ever shot an arrow? he'd asked.

No. I grew up with a cook, remember? Her family came from generational wealth, and Daisy had watched how it twisted her parents' marriage, turned siblings into competitors, money the beating heart of the family. Daisy had wanted something different. When she'd left, her father had threatened to disown her; when she'd married Mack, he'd done just that.

On their date, he'd brought her to an archery range, stood behind her to look for the proper shape of her draw, and watched as her first arrow sailed right into the ground. She'd laughed, loving it even with a bad shot. She never gave up until she hit the target, and then she kept going until she'd hit it fifteen more times. Never a bull's-eye on that first day, but with her light touch and graceful shot, she'd become an excellent hunter in the years to come.

Afterward, they'd sat at the base of a tree, a summer breeze cool against their skin. Her hair was in two silky braids that hung past her shoulders, and it exposed her delicate neck, the freckles sprinkled across her nose, the arch of her eyebrows. He'd wanted to run his finger along her jaw, tip up her chin, and kiss her. But Mack wasn't so bold. He played the long game, and he already knew that Daisy was the woman he intended to grow old with. So he'd kept his hands and his thoughts to himself and enjoyed the light scent of vanilla that tickled the air whenever he sat this close to her. They'd looked at the mountains, snowy tops glittering in the late-afternoon sun.

Her sigh was full of contentment. *I love it here.*

Why? Mack hoped he had something to do with the why.

She smiled and pointed to the mountains. *Because of those.* She twirled the arrow they'd used for archery practice. *Because of this.* It had green fletching that reflected her eyes. He'd picked them for that reason. She ran her hand over a patch of dandelions. *Because of everything that's free and real and mine if I know how to harvest it.* She'd turned her head, caught him square with those knee-buckling eyes. Mack was glad his rump was already seated. *And because of men like you.*

He'd gulped. *Me?*

She'd laughed, a sound like mountain water over rocks. *Well, you're still a boy, but you're going to make a fine man.* She'd plucked a dandelion in its moon phase, brought the white puff ball to her lips, and blown all the seeds into the air. With her lips still puckered she'd given him a side glance, then thrown her head back and laughed.

Years later, Mack heard Daisy tell Jesse that if he blew all the seeds off a dandelion and made a wish, then the person he loved would love him back.

The memory was warm and painful at the same time. Most of his memories were this way now. Happiness and grief, the twisted roots of the same tree.

The girl hollered for help, and Mack pounded a fist into his thigh and forced himself to keep walking. If Daisy were in his position, he didn't doubt that she'd help those kids no matter what. One of her ways to cope had been to help children. Raising money for an organization that gave college scholarships to local students. Starting a program with Anders Outfitters that taught kids how to fish and forage. She'd thrown herself into giving back, and she would have never left that girl and boy to begin with.

The cry again, muffled, more a whimper that echoed up the slope and finally stopped him in his tracks, head hung. Jesse in the crinkle of leaves behind him. In the silence that woke him in the middle of the night, a late morning that cost them everything. *Help them, Dad.* Jesse had his mother's heart. Mack had found it difficult to be around kids afterward. But ignoring the girl's cries for help, that he couldn't do.

"Dang it all to heck." He turned and started running back to the kids.

Going downhill was faster—he used the trees to slow his descent. The girl's cries started up again. Angry cries, barely covering pain. He spied them in a grove of aspens. She sat on the ground, leg out in front of her and holding her ankle. The boy crouched beside her, worrying the arm of his stuffed robot and staring at the girl.

"Ow ow ow!" She rubbed at her ankle.

Mack figured she'd twisted it, maybe a sprain. A heavy ball landed hard in his gut. He'd need to lead them out of here. Branches rustled when he stepped out from behind the tree and the girl yelped, reaching for the gun.

"Hey now, it's just me." Mack held his hand in front of him.

The gun lowered and the girl's mouth twisted. "Why'd you walk so fast? We couldn't keep up."

"I didn't invite you." It was the truth, even if it came out sounding harsher than he meant.

She squinted one eye. "I hurt my ankle." The girl had a toughness to her that Mack recognized, one that had been knitted into sinew from hard times, bad luck, and whatever else had her on the run with a boy who wouldn't speak. He didn't know her, but he knew what happened when people you thought you could trust failed. Anders Outfitters had been Mack's inheritance. A family business that had stood the test of time and generations of Anderses, and he and Daisy had put their souls into the company. It was all they'd had left. Until they were blindsided by the accountant who'd abused their trust to siphon money that wasn't his, rotting the company from the inside out. Daisy had tried to take the blame. *I hired Peter.*

He was recommended. He'd been a nephew of a woman who'd let Daisy camp on her land when she'd first moved out to Wyoming. Daisy was loyal and happy to return the favor. And Mack was forever grateful to anyone who'd helped Daisy stick around long enough for him to ask her out.

Still. He lives in Jackson. Too much greed in a city like that. She'd bitten her nails to the quick, shouldered the blame until it weakened the straightness of her spine.

Finally, he'd said the only thing he knew would let some sense in. *The company is gone like Jesse, and I figure we either decide to live anyways or hang ourselves from the rafters and get it over with.*

It had shocked her, eyes bugging wide before a smile wiped away the tight press of her lips. Then she'd laughed, and so had Mack, because sometimes that was all that was left to do.

The girl sat with her back bowed, shoulders hunched. Like Daisy. Splintering under the weight of her world.

Mack sighed. "Why didn't you go to the gas station like I told you to?" he said.

The girl pressed her lips together. The boy tugged on the arm of his stuffed robot.

He decided to be more direct. "What're you doing out here alone?"

The girl's eyes blazed. "What're *you* doing out here alone?" she repeated.

Mack sighed.

She flung her hands in the air. "We're going to see my aunt in Casper."

It was the truth—Mack could tell by the way her face remained smooth. Liars always had a wrinkle somewhere that gave them away. "She know you're coming?"

The girl's shoulders rounded. "She will when we get there." She breathed out. "Mister, we need your help. I have no money for gas, the tank's almost empty, and I need to get my brother to Casper because my aunt's a safe place and that's what he needs right now. Right, Syborg?"

"Rule number one?" His voice was soft, like the kid was afraid of being heard.

"Hell yeah, that's a rule number one: you deserve to feel safe."

Mack felt the heartburn behind his eyes and kicked the dirt.

"We won't say anything, you know. If you're hiding from something, I mean, we won't say anything, I promise. It's none of our business. We just need gas, you know, and maybe some food. I'll pay you back. One day, I mean. I'm good for it." The girl's brownish-red hair curled around her face, sticking to the side of her neck where the heat of the sun hit her skin. A weariness had crept into her voice. "My name's Brandi, and this is Sy."

That last bit, offering her name, it meant something. Pieces of truth given as a trade.

Mack cleared his throat, decided. "I'll help you get gas."

Brandi smiled, and it transformed her entire self, making her look like the teenage girl she was. Shame heated his face for not having offered before now. "But we have to wait until it's dark."

"Aye, aye, Captain," she said in a high-pitched, singsong voice.

Mack stared at her, confused.

"SpongeBob?" When he didn't respond, she giggled. "It's like the only show on TV in juvie."

The only thing she said that Mack understood was juvie. And it meant the girl had something to lose. He felt the tiniest bit better. Likely she didn't want to bring any more attention to her and Sy than he wanted for himself.

"Can you walk?"

She stood lightly on both feet, putting more weight on the uninjured one. "I can try." Stretched her hand out to Sy. The boy took it, holding it close to his body, probably terrified to be left behind.

Mack picked up a stick, tested its height, and handed it to Brandi. "I'll find you a better one, but this will do for now." He started to walk, and behind him Brandi snorted.

"Guess that means we should follow him, huh, Sy?" The boy didn't respond, and Brandi's laugh tickled Mack's ears. "Doesn't waste much air on talking, does he? Rule number one: only talk when you have something to say. That is one rule I'll never be able to follow, huh, Sy?" Sy was quiet and Brandi laughed again.

Mack kept his pace slow, and the girl and her brother followed him down the mountain.

Seven

The ground was hard and uneven and her ankle didn't really hurt at all, but she had to act like it did. She'd been banking on the idea that the old guy wasn't made of cardboard. That he'd never leave two kids alone in the forest with wild animals and skinwalkers creeping around. Faking an injury seemed like a long shot, so when he'd appeared, Brandi had been so relieved she about cried her eyes out for real. She hadn't, of course. Crying got her nothing. Never changed her mom, or made dinner, or locked the door when one of the *assholes* snuck inside her bedroom.

She smiled to herself, trying to make it look like a grimace. It had worked, but her fake limp made walking hard. *Ironic.* She giggled and pressed the stick into the ground like a cane, her other hand getting squeezed to death by Sy. It was awkward, but Brandi didn't care. She loved that Sy needed her.

Earlier, she'd thought they'd lost the man, and Brandi had gotten so turned around in the trees she was sure they'd never make it out alive. Now the old man walked slow, his stride so short he could be a bride walking down the aisle. Brandi rolled her eyes. He didn't have to make a thing of it. "Are we there yet?"

The man pointed, and when Brandi followed she saw the glint of metal beyond the valley and tucked just under a small rise. "Shit, that's far." Her fake ankle injury burned.

He kept walking, and Brandi gave up trying to get him or Sy to talk. She put one foot in front of the other and kept her eyes on the back of him. His skin was sun dark and rolled loose over his bones, and his pants hung from his skinny waist and over his butt like a deflated balloon. Brandi had more meat on her left wrist than this guy had on his entire body. It looked natural on him, though, like someone had taken a hammer and chipped him from this rugged place.

A breeze pushed into her hair, unglued where sweat smooshed it against her skin. The sun was warm, but something colder swirled in the air—winter laughing, because out here, the cold won, even on a fall day that made her sweat. It reminded her of how cold and sleepless the night before had been. She walked faster.

The group home would have reported her missing by now. A sharp cramp in her side. She'd left juvie as one of the warden's favorites. He'd never said so; she'd just known. Guessed it from the way he and her counselor smiled when she was around.

There'd been a girl there who'd hated Brandi. Something about how Brandi was too happy and it annoyed the fuck out of this girl. She'd pick at Brandi in class, making fun when she got a problem wrong, calling her names, pushing her in line. The thing that girl never understood was that Brandi was happy until she wasn't, and it was from this place that her impulsiveness lived. When Brandi couldn't smile anymore or make jokes because of this girl's constant harassment, Brandi beat the crap out of her. There were no more words after that. There were, however, the consequences that followed: the isolation room, losing her hard-earned privileges, extended time on her sentence, and worst of all, the disappointed wrinkle in Warden Trujillo's forehead. But Ms. Hanno doubled down on her efforts to rehabilitate Brandi, and six months later, Brandi was working hard on her process and making Ms. Hanno proud as hell.

She liked that feeling of accomplishment. Of someone noticing her. Like maybe she could be special in some way and to someone. Mrs. T used to tell her she had a light inside, and Brandi had liked to think that was true. Of course, Mrs. T also claimed that Jesus appeared to her in a pancake, but who was Brandi to disagree?

Sun hot on her back and Sy's hand slippery in her own. She looked at the top of his head and felt her breath catch. She'd done it again. Ruined her forward progress. She'd missed curfew and a meeting with her probation officer. She didn't want to go back to juvie or disappoint the warden. She didn't want to be a screwup, even if that's all she'd ever been. Brandi wanted more.

Sy walked putting one foot in front of the other, eyes on the ground, bony shoulders poking through his top. She swallowed hard. All of it was worth it if she got Sy to Aunt Heather. She ruffled his head and smiled to herself. All of it.

The man stopped so they could rest, take sips of water. She and Sy were drinking all his water, and Brandi felt bad about that, but she was also burning with thirst. Her brother looked a little gray, and it worried her. The closer they got to the car the more Brandi's legs trembled. She couldn't wait to be away from this place.

Sy never let go of her hand, and while he wasn't exactly talkative, Brandi figured this was a massive improvement to him pointing the gun at her. When they finally reached the car, it felt like days had passed instead of a few hours. Brandi leaned heavily against it, patted her pretend-hurt ankle, and looked back the way they'd come. The valley led up into the tree line that spread green icing over the top of the mountain for miles and miles. She swallowed hard. They really could have gotten lost.

The old man stood a few feet away, arms crossed, leaning against a big rock.

Brandi stared at him, annoyed. "Are we gonna go?"

He shook his head. "Wait for dark."

"Why?" She was eighteen and ready to be given answers when she asked a question, not told the way kids were. If she wanted to live like an adult, make her own choices, get her own job, a place to live, then that started with answers. She inhaled and made sure it was loud enough to be heard.

He studied her from under the brim of his hat, and she thought his eyebrows rose in an amused kind of way.

"Why do we need to wait for the dark?" she asked again, fighting an urge to kick the ground.

Another long pause from the old guy, and Brandi thought she might punch a rock.

"So nobody sees us." He knelt, fell back on his butt with his legs stretched out in front of him, and leaned his head against the rock, hat tilted to cover his face.

Sy tugged on her hand, and she looked down. His cheeks were red, and the smell shocked her even if it shouldn't have. Had she asked the poor kid if he needed to use the bathroom? Ashamed, she led him around to the other side of the car. "It's okay, buddy. Accidents happen. I think I saw sweatpants in the back." Sy looked at the ground, and Brandi wanted to hug him, smell and all, but she was afraid it would make it worse for him so she opened the door instead. The old SUV had a stained fabric interior infused with cigarette smoke. Trash was ankle-deep in the back: old fast-food bags, napkins, a few pieces of discarded clothes.

The sweatpants were stuffed under the passenger seat, and when she pulled them out she saw a small duffel bag hidden underneath. A jolt shot through her fingertips. Lucky them. It could be an overnight bag. Maybe with clothes that would fit Sy, get him out of his dirty pajamas.

She pulled the bag into her lap and unzipped it. A thick silence filled her ears, broken by the pulse of blood in her temples. Small bags of crystals filled the bag.

"No, oh fuck no." She yanked the zipper closed, threw the bag onto the floor, and kicked it under the passenger seat. Like it could bite, which it could. Meth was a vampire that sucked all the good out of a person. She pressed her hands into her thighs to stop them from shaking.

You are my sunshine. Her mother's favorite song to sing when Brandi was little. Her cool hand on Brandi's feverish forehead. *Poor baby.* Vicks VapoRub massaged into circles on her chest, humidifier humming, the cocoon of her mother's body, and Brandi's naive belief that it would always be this way. Brandi kicked the seat in front of her. She wanted to scream. Wanted to throw those memories into a fire and watch the heat bubbles rise, the images blacken and peel away. Watch them turn to ash.

A bag full of meth. Her mom must be dealing now too. Or at least asshole was. She scratched the underside of her arm with her fingernail, pressing into her flesh, wishing she could push a magic button and feel anything but this constant pain, this bitter disappointment in a woman whose only real motherly accomplishment had been in giving birth.

Sy whimpered and Brandi turned. He stood outside the SUV, stink rising off him, and trying to cover the soiled areas of his jammie pants with his hands. He was the only thing that kept her from becoming unhinged. He needed her to stay in control. Sy needed her to be an adult.

"Hey, buddy," she whispered. "I'm so sorry I didn't come home right away." Her mother never visited her in juvie. In court, Nancy had acted like Brandi was the problem. When Brandi got out, a group home was her fresh start. Maybe she'd fooled herself into believing that Mrs. T would be there for Sy. The truth was that Brandi was afraid to go home. Because if she was sucked back into the hamster wheel of her mom's addiction, Brandi didn't think she'd survive.

Outside, the old guy shifted, lifting his hat above his eyes and staring at her through the window. She piled trash in front of the duffel to keep it hidden; she'd have to get rid of it as soon as possible. Grabbed the sweatpants and a roll of paper towels she found in the cargo area behind her and scrambled out of the car. If the old guy knew about the meth, he'd never help them.

"Come on, Sy, let's go over there." She led him away from the SUV and the eyes of the old man. Sy was embarrassed enough. "Here,

Syborg, can I take your pants off so we can get you cleaned up?" He nodded, serious and sad.

She knelt in front of him and tugged off his jammie pants. He held on to her shoulders and lifted one leg at a time to help her. It was everywhere. She balled up his pants, trying to keep the mess from getting onto her hands. Pressure on the top of her skull. A feeling that the ground was quicksand and she was sinking fast. The acrid smell watered her eyes. It was too much. Weakening her. She could leave. Let the old guy help Sy. He'd have to. And Brandi could go back to the group home, beg them to let her stay. She couldn't fix her life and Sy's at the same time.

She stopped and sat back on her heels, trying to get a grip, forearm against her nose. Sy met her gaze, and she softened. His eyes were the prettiest brown she'd ever seen. Brown sugar and honey.

"I'm sorry," he whispered.

His words, his tiny voice, cut straight through to her heart. Her body stopped its nervous humming, and she gave him a small smile, touched his little chin. An iron resolve had replaced her nerves. She loved him so much—she would do whatever it took to help him. "You know, my friend Carissa, well, she used to pee her bed every night, and guess what?"

Sy shrugged.

"She slept in the bunk above me, and it was like living under Niagara Falls."

Sy looked at her.

Brandi raised her eyebrows. "See, Niagara Falls is a humongous waterfall. So she peed her bed, and I lived under it, get it?"

For a second Brandi saw his mouth lift the tiniest, teensiest bit.

She smiled. "Yeah, you get it."

The paper towels were running out, and there was still poop sticking to parts of his legs. She'd never get it all off. Her stomach grew queasy, but she kept at it, trying to get him as clean as possible. From behind her came the scuffling sound of boots on earth. The old man appeared beside her, handing her a wetted-down handkerchief. She took it. "Thanks." It wasn't perfect. The poor kid needed a bath, but it was so much better. "Hey, that's not so bad now, is it?"

She helped him step into the sweatpants—they were huge—and used a hair tie from the collection on her wrist to tighten the waistband around his hips like a fabric ponytail. She sat back on her heels, studied her work. *Not bad.* Her mother was a tiny woman, made gaunt by meth. The pants would work well enough until she could find him something better.

She wiped her hands on the only clean part of the handkerchief and then ignored what might be under her fingernails. The light had begun to fade, that late-afternoon kind of bleak that always made her a little sad.

The man stood beside the car. "Let's go," he said.

Brandi breathed out. "Finally."

They got in the car, Brandi in the driver's seat, Sy beside her, and the old man in the back. She drove carefully, and when the car creaked and shifted over the rough road, her knuckles turned white on the steering wheel. She had no idea how much that duffel bag was worth, but probably enough for them to come after her. Enough for asshole to kill her, kill them all. Since yesterday, all she'd thought about was getting out of here and back to civilization. Suddenly it felt dangerous to leave, foolish even. But it wasn't like they could stay.

She glanced in the rearview mirror. The man stared out the window with no clue that a bag full of drugs lay close to his feet. What if he found it? She shivered. There were two types of people in the world: those who did drugs and those who didn't. Which one was he?

She breathed in and drove. There was nothing she could do about it now.

~

The small SUV bounced violently over the ruts. Mack hit his head against the window. "Your struts are bad," he told the girl. From his view in the back, Brandi looked small behind the wheel, young, like she shouldn't even be driving. She caught his eye in the rearview mirror, her face lit from underneath by the dashboard lights. She had brown eyes that were so dark they blended with the pupils. And she liked to narrow them or roll them or open them wide when she was frustrated. Mack had never experienced a teenage girl phase, but he imagined that the way she looked at him about summed it up.

It was fully dark now, too early for the moon, no light catching on the white lines of the road. Dark enough to get Brandi the gas she needed—from here he could see the needle at the empty line. It had taken quite a while to reach the main road, and Mack wondered why the girl had come down that way with so little fuel. "Why'd you turn down this road anyway?"

He could tell the question made her nervous by the way she glanced back at him and shifted in her seat. "I got lost, I told you."

"Someone after you?"

A voice, soft, nothing more than a whisper from the passenger seat. "Bad man."

The car swerved to the right, tires hitting gravel, spinning, losing traction until she righted the wheel and got the car back on the pavement. Headlights bounced like jackrabbits along the horizon. Mack relaxed his grip on the seat in front of him, chilled by the boy's words.

Brandi shifted her head from her brother to the road and back again. "And that's why we left, right, Syborg? Because people can be shit, and you deserve better. Rule number one: never stay somewhere you don't feel safe."

Mack cleared his throat. "What bad man?"

"No one." Brandi talked a little too quickly. "Sy wasn't happy there, you know? And he should be, don't you think? Don't all kids deserve to be happy?"

Mack ran a hand up and down his thigh. Jesse had been a sweet boy with a big heart and love for adventure, his tears releasing as easily as his giggles. When he was Sy's age, Jesse would climb into bed with them on nights when thunder shook the glasses in the cabinet, and Mack would tell him the story of the nocturnal giants who bowled when it rained. His hand shook as it always did when he thought about his boy. A futile wish that he could go back and change the past. Be the one who'd died. His nostrils flared. There'd never been a goddang choice.

Mack realized that Brandi seemed to be waiting for an answer. "Of course kids deserve to be happy." He didn't mean to sound so gruff.

The girl sighed and focused on the road.

Sy had twisted around so that he was on his knees, hands and chin resting on the seat back, staring at Mack. Like the boy heard the chatter in Mack's head. He wondered what had been bad enough for Brandi to take her brother with very little gas, no change of clothes, no food or water. He cleared his throat. "Turn around and put your seat belt on."

Brandi glanced at her brother. "Oh, yeah, Sy, seat belt for sure. Safety first!"

The girl loved her brother. That much was obvious in her tender patience, even when she had to clean up his mess. Sy slipped back into his seat, and Mack heard the seat belt click. He couldn't imagine what they were running from, but Mack figured the sooner he got the kids on their way, the better. He felt Daisy's hand holding his, the way she did whenever they sat on the porch swing on a warm summer evening and watched the stars pop out. A longing to see her dug away at his determination. He squeezed her hand and let go. He'd fill the car with gas and get them on their way. That's all he could do.

~

It took a few miles before dim lights appeared in the distance, shimmering. "There's the gas station," he said.

Only one car in the lot, parked around the side. An older truck that Mack didn't recognize as one of Zeke's. Good, better for him, in case they got caught if it were someone he didn't know. At one point, he'd been friendly with just about everyone in town, but as Daisy got sicker, Mack pulled away and their circle of friends shrank. The last time he'd seen Zeke had been when the two went fishing together, two, maybe three years ago. Mack tapped a fist against his chest; he'd been living like a dead man far longer than he'd realized.

"Pull up beside that car, on the downward slope." Lucky for them, there was a good incline between the cars.

"Why? Doesn't gas come from those?" She pointed at the pumps.

"Stay here."

"Why?" She turned around, eyes wide open. Irritated. The girl asked why a lot. Like she was sick of not knowing. Mack understood. He'd felt that way with every memory Daisy lost.

"Stay. Here." Firm, unyielding. He got out of the car, careful to make no sound when he closed the door, and eased toward the back of the store, where a water spigot was located on the outside of the building. A green hose hung coiled on a hook, not attached. He smiled. Right where it always was. He'd used it often to wash the mud from his tires after filling up. Zeke never minded. Mack pulled a length of hose out from the hook and, with the knife he kept strapped to his hip, cut about eight feet, slicing off the metal end. He used his stump to help him, but it took longer than he wanted. He spit on the ground, frustrated by his progress. When he was done, he slid it over to the other car. He felt bad, for sure, but sometimes things just had to be done.

Through the car window, Sy pressed his face against the glass, robot stuffie beside him, both of them staring at Mack. The words the boy spoke from before painted into the fogged glass left by his breath. *Bad man.* Did it surprise him? The girl had dragged her brother from somewhere with no plan, obviously. He shuddered. Folks came from all kinds of situations. What had happened to these two?

He opened the gas cap of both vehicles, then pushed the end of the hose inside the old truck, snaking it deep into the tank. The small SUV sat lower to the ground and was parked on the downhill side of the slope. Mack hoped it was enough of an angle for the gas to flow. He put his mouth to the hose and carefully sucked the air out. He'd done it often enough in his youth to have a method. He'd been a handful back then. Hanging out with a few of the ranch boys, getting into drink and trouble, spurred by a wildness that came from open spaces and youthful boredom. He wasn't a totally changed man when he'd met Daisy, but it sure was the kick in the pants he needed to start.

As soon as the gasoline touched his tongue, he pinched off the hose and put his thumb on the top to keep it from spurting out. Then he carefully walked over to the RAV4 and shoved the hose inside the hole of the filler. Gasoline squirted onto his hand, but the rest went into the tank. He hoped it would at least be enough to get them to the next gas station.

After a couple of minutes, he heard the flow stutter and then stop, either because he'd drained most of the truck's gas or because the hose lost its suction. Either way, it was enough for now. He shook the hose out and, instead of tossing it away, coiled and nestled it into the back of the RAV4. When he slid into the back seat, it took him a second to notice what was wrong.

The girl wasn't there.

Mack's pulse beat inside his neck. He jumped out of the car, hurried around the corner of the store, and froze. Brandi stood in front of the clerk, gun tucked into the back of her jeans, her hand feeling around her waistband, like she was planning on using it. What in the heck was she thinking? "Goddang it!" Mack hissed to himself, hand on hip, kicking the ground with his cowboy boot. His throat went dry, and something tightened around his body.

He should go right now. Hightail it back to his camp and leave whatever this was far behind. He'd tried to help them, dang it. But again, his feet were glued to the spot by the image of Brandi cleaning Sy after his accident. Her kind touch and soft tone, not wanting to embarrass the boy, he could tell. It was how he'd felt when he'd had to help his wife. Meeting her eyes, a steady hand even at the worst of times because she deserved dignity and respect.

The heartburn moved back up into the top of his throat, and Mack did exactly what he ought to do.

Eight

"Can I have a pack of Camels?" She didn't smoke, but Brandi needed a minute to think. Her hand touched the gun. It wasn't loaded, she reminded herself. She wasn't going to use it anyway. It was there in case she needed to scare the guy into thinking she was tougher than she looked.

"Are you twenty-one?" The guy was like nineteen, maybe, and giving her grief for trying to buy cigarettes. What bullshit.

Brandi snorted. "Yeah, I am. Pack of Camels, *please.*" The metal was cold against her fingers. But the old guy was out there stealing gas and she had no money and Casper was hours away and they were hungry and thirsty and she'd already screwed up hard—what did it matter if she piled more stealing on top?

She added a map of Wyoming to the food, candy, and water, waiting for the guy to put everything into a bag. Then she'd grab it and run. It was only him, and he was probably robbed like, what, twice a week? She bet he'd just shrug and let her go. Her hands shook. She'd stolen before—it wasn't new to her. But after juvie, she'd hoped she could be different. Had wanted to be different. So much of the trouble she'd gotten into had been for her brother. When Nancy stopped being their mom, Brandi didn't have a choice. She gritted her teeth and reached for the bag. She loved her brother, and unlike Nancy, she would sacrifice anything for him.

Her eye caught on flyers stacked on the counter with a list of community announcements. And toward the bottom of the page, a black-and-white picture of a guy with scraggly gray hair underneath a cowboy hat. Brandi made a sound. The same guy outside stealing gas. *Memorial Service for beloved and longtime Pike River resident Mack Anders.* "He's dead?" She didn't mean to say it out loud.

The clerk looked down at the flyer. "Yeah, some local guy, I heard. I bet he offed himself."

For a second she couldn't move, fingertips touching the gun in her waistband. From behind her someone knocked on the glass door, and her heart plummeted. She turned. The old guy stood to the side of the glass doors, most of his face hidden by the frame, the rest in shadow under the brim of his hat. "Cigs are for my grandad," she told the clerk. The guy pinched his lips but turned to get the cigarettes, and when he did she grabbed the bag and a flyer and ran.

"Hey!" he yelled.

Brandi knocked over a display of chips and the one with all the maps by the door, breathless and high on adrenaline. The old guy was in the driver's seat. That surprised her, but she hopped in back anyway.

"Drive," she wheezed, and was surprised when he did—and fast.

She didn't mind the silence this time. It gave her a moment, and she used it to lean into the seat and let the pulsing in her temple ease. Night whooshed past the window, swallowing trees, bushes, rocky outcrops. She looked up, noticed that the needle hadn't moved much beyond empty. Her stomach sank. Would they just end up stranded again?

"You can't wave a gun around like you do and think there aren't gonna be consequences."

"I didn't." Brandi kicked the back of the seat. "Plus, it's not loaded."

"Doesn't matter."

"I didn't use it."

"Doesn't matter. You had your hand on it. That's saying something whether you intend it or not."

"You're not my dad, *Mack*."

Silence.

"How do you know my name?"

She read the flyer to him. "Memorial service for beloved and longtime Pike River resident Mack Anders. Saturday at two p.m. at Jackelope Saloon. First round on Peggy." Brandi laughed. "Did you know you were dead? Or did you plan it? Is Peggy your wife? Is this your way of divorcing her by disappearing into the woods? Oh man, that's harsh. At least it seems like she's celebrating." It sounded funny to her, but when he didn't respond she scooted forward, put her head between the passenger and driver seats. He stared at the road, the hat making it hard for her to see his expression. She felt a pang, glad she hadn't blurted out what the clerk had told her. "Oh, sorry, is it something more than that? My bad, seriously. I didn't mean to be a bitch."

Mack didn't respond, and Brandi bit her lip, annoyed with herself. It was one of the things her counselor said she could work on. Her rashness, she'd called it. Brandi had to look it up because as far as she'd known, rash was like itchy red bumps. But no, according to the dictionary, it meant doing something without thinking about the consequences. She'd had to agree with Ms. Hanno. She was rash AF. Nothing she did was with *careful consideration*; she just did stuff, like robbing the gas station because it seemed like it was her only option to give her brother food. Was there a little thrill to it? Sure, she couldn't lie about that. But she'd probably be just as happy with bungee jumping instead of something that always got her in trouble. Then again, she didn't have many choices when it came to food. She either had it or she didn't.

Mack pulled the car over to the side of the road, and Brandi realized that it was the same service road she'd gotten stuck on. Her heart hammered against her chest. From the looks of it, Mack was dead to everyone who cared about him. It should raise all kinds of warnings, and Brandi couldn't help but feel let down by it, because it meant he had every reason not to help them. She wanted his help. No, they *needed* his help.

Mack put the car in Park, hand on the wheel, and Brandi figured with substantial relief that he was having second thoughts. Then he nodded and turned to Sy. "Be brave." He twisted his head, squinted at Brandi. "Think before you do something." He hefted himself out of the car, closed the door, and started to walk away, the ink-black night scribbling over him like he was never there.

And that's when all hell broke loose.

~

The soil felt good beneath his boots, the crunch of small rocks comforting. It meant that he was back on familiar territory and away from town, where people might recognize him. Hearing Brandi read the flyer had been surreal—cold water accompanied by a shock of disbelief. It had worked. They thought he was dead. Still, so many questions. When would they release the insurance money? How much longer before she got the treatment she needed? He missed her so much it scurried ant-like inside the vessels of his heart. Once she was better he'd go see her, he'd decided. What would the police do with an old, used-up man like him? Send him to prison for fraud? All he wanted was to take care of his wife, *goddang it*. He wrinkled his nose at Peggy's voice. *You can't fix Alzheimer's.* Maybe not. But Daisy had been the strong one after Jesse died. Now it was Mack's turn.

He still felt the shock of hearing Brandi say his name. *First round on Peggy.* Shame pulled his head low. He was an honest man, for the most part, and the idea that his biggest deception had hurt people didn't sit well.

He felt the pull of the cabin in the arches of his feet competing with the needs of the kids in the car behind him. The girl was a hothead, prone to impulsive decisions that got her in trouble. That was clear.

He kept walking, but it was slower than his normal pace. In his mind, Daisy was behind him, standing by the car, hurt and disappointment in the slope of her shoulders. *You don't give up just because something's hard.* It brought him to a halt. He took his hat from his head, cool air rushing over his scalp. She'd left him once. Packed her bags, a note by the coffeemaker. *I forgive myself, Mack, and I've made a promise to live for Jesse. But you're stuck in that morning. I think you've given up and if I don't leave now you'll destroy me.*

She'd been right, of course. He had given up, and after she left things got worse before they got better. But Mack lived. He woke up every morning, made coffee, and put one foot in front of the other, and sometimes, that's all a man could do.

Muffled voices came from inside the car, yelling that intensified when the door opened. He turned. The boy ran toward him, the girl chasing, catching him, and both of them tumbled to the ground. A dust storm tore around them in the headlights of the car.

"What's wrong with you, Sy! He doesn't want to help us—can't you see that? Stop fucking screaming!" Raw anger scraped her voice hoarse, and Mack flinched. *What's wrong with you?* Something he'd said to Daisy when her memory started to evaporate and before he understood that what was lost was never coming back. He'd unraveled the day she asked him to read Jesse his bedtime story because she was too tired. His knee-jerk reaction had been anger. *What's wrong with you, Daisy?* It was only the beginning. The more her memory wavered, the more she brought to life the ghost that tormented Mack's sleep.

Mack pressed his hat into his chest. "Goddang it," he said, and strode over to the struggling kids.

The boy was flailing, punching his sister, scratching her to be let go. "I'm trying to help you, Sy! Stop it!" The boy cried out, scrappy but determined to get away from her.

In the struggle, the oversize sweatpants had fallen from Sy's waist, leaving his bony hip and thigh exposed from where he lay in a tangled embrace with his sister. Mack swallowed. The boy was skin and bones.

He stood above the pair, who were so intent on fighting they didn't seem to notice.

"That's enough," he said.

Brandi went limp, as though Mack's voice had released her from something. Sy scrambled away, trying to pull the sweatpants up, but the knot that had held them to his waist was gone, so he grasped the waistband to keep them from falling down. His chest was rising and falling so fast Mack wondered if he might pass out.

"What's your plan, Brandi?"

It was the first time he'd said her name out loud, and it seemed to surprise her, because she pushed up from the ground, hair a tangled mess and backlit by the yellow glare of the headlights. He couldn't see her face. "I already told you. I'm taking Sy to my aunt Heather in Casper."

"Why?"

"Because he's got no one left to care for him."

"What about your mom?"

"Who?" Brandi stood, wiping dust from her jeans. Sy hadn't moved, a statue with one hand keeping his sweatpants from sliding down. "Well, there is this woman called Nancy who gave birth to me. But she's a tweaker and loves herself more than anything else. Is that a mom?"

Mack replaced his hat. Sometimes she sounded older than he thought she was, and other times the girl could be a child. "How old are you?"

"Eighteen, and what does that have to do with anything?"

"Is your aunt expecting you?"

Brandi's shoulders fell. "No. I tried to call her, but the number I had wasn't hers anymore. And my phone's dead anyway and I don't have a charging cord, but she lives at 4425 Delgado Street and I got a map at that gas station and she promised she would help me if I ever needed it and we do."

While she spoke, Brandi pulled another elastic band from her wrist and knelt in front of Sy, using it to tie a knot into the waistband of his sweatpants. The simple act—kind, thoughtful, even after the boy had tried to scratch her eyes out—hit Mack right in the chest.

"Okay," he said, as much to them as to Daisy. "I'll help you get there."

"What?" Brandi cocked her head. "Why?"

"Because you need it."

"But you're dead, which is weird and probably illegal too, right?"

He rocked on his heels. "Some things can't be avoided."

"Like making sure my brother is safe."

Mack nodded. He didn't know why she was on the run, but it seemed to be for the right reason—helping her brother. In some ways, they weren't that different. "Seems like we both have something to lose," he said.

Silence from the girl. Like she was actually giving it some thought. Maybe she wasn't always so impulsive. "I won't tell on you if you won't tell on me?" she said, a statement and a question all rolled into one.

He wrinkled his nose, wished for time to reverse, to have walked away from the car when he'd first seen it. No matter how he played it in his head, it came out the same: him standing here with Brandi and Sy, making a decision that might ruin everything he was doing to help his wife. *You can't fix Alzheimer's.* He swatted at Peggy's words. He could fix cancer.

"Deal," he said at last.

Sy walked to the car, opened the back door, and hopped inside.

Brandi laughed. "Sy has spoken." She hurried to the driver's side of the car. "I'll drive, but since we're being honest now, I don't have a license."

Mack shrugged, opened the passenger door. "You don't need a license to tell you what you already know. My son was helping me steer my truck when he was seven." They settled into their seats. "And if we're being honest, I'm not supposed to drive at night because I don't see well in the dark."

She smacked the steering wheel. "But you just did anyway. That's dope. Also, I don't know how to get to Casper." Brandi reached for something in the back seat, pulled out a paper map of Wyoming, and started to unfold it across the dashboard. "Also, I don't know how to read a map."

Mack was incredulous. "How were you going to get there if you don't know where it is?"

She shrugged. "I don't know. I figured I'd see a sign or something like that. Carissa said Wyoming's just a huge square and there's not that many cities, you know?"

Mack sighed. "So you were just going to drive until you found it?"

"Yeah," she said, and at least she sounded sheepish. "I guess."

Mack took the map from her and awkwardly folded it with his hand. He didn't need a map. He'd lived here his entire life. "Take a right."

Brandi giggled and in that singsong voice from earlier said, "Aye, aye, Google!" The car rocked when she hit the gas, sliding on dirt and rocks, then righted itself on the paved road. Mack buckled his seat belt, saying a silent word to whatever lived above the stars. *Please let me stay dead.*

Nine

Wyoming roads were barren ribbons that went nowhere fast but never seemed to get there either. At least that's how it felt to Brandi. She'd left Nancy's house with a vague idea of where Casper was. East or north, or a combination of the two. But how to get there was an entirely other matter, and at the time she'd been so panicked by what she'd done that she'd just driven, fast, convinced she was being chased.

It was light out when she'd left yesterday, and driving during the day was totally different. At night, tiny bodies scurried across the road, eyes catching the headlights. She jumped and tapped the brakes almost every time.

"Easy," Mack said, his voice a low, slow rumble. Brandi liked it. Nothing in her life had ever been unhurried. It had all felt like a race where in the end, everyone she loved ran off a cliff.

"How far is Casper?" she asked after what felt like miles and miles of silence.

"About five hours or so."

"Damn, that's long." She glanced at the gas gauge. "Do we have enough gas?"

"No."

She pressed her lips together. At the group home and before, in juvie, Brandi was the talker. Always in the middle, goofing around, making people laugh, trying to stay out of conflicts with other girls. With Sy and Mack, she could be in one of the isolation rooms they sent girls who made trouble, stuck with her thoughts. She'd been there once or twice. She shuddered. *No, thank you.* "So why'd you fake your own death?"

She didn't really think he'd answer, had a bunch of questions loaded when he didn't. When he did, she had to keep her jaw from hitting her lap.

"My wife has Alzheimer's."

"What's that?"

"It takes memories."

"Oh, that's horrible." Silence grew like an ink stain. "What's she like?"

He didn't answer, and Brandi figured she'd asked something too personal and tapped the steering wheel, thinking of anything else to talk about.

Mack took his hat off and rested it on his lap. "She's beautiful inside and out."

Brandi felt a pang. "That's really sweet." The outside world flew by the windows, one mile after another. "You know, I think Mrs. T had that or something like it. She kinda started to forget about me." It had been gradual, things Brandi ignored. But the night Mrs. T's son called the cops on Brandi, she knew something was really wrong. She'd been handcuffed, standing outside the house and demanding they wake up Mrs. T. *She knows me! I swear. She doesn't care. Please! Just ask her.* Mrs. T had come out then, her wig gone, the hair she had left patchy, and wearing a thin nightgown that showed the lumpy curves of her body. It felt too personal and wrong for all these strangers to see her like that. But when Mrs. T had looked at Brandi her heart sank to her toes. Something was missing. *Ma'am, do you know this girl?* Mrs. T shook her head, arms wrapped across her chest. *Where's Abe?* That had been her husband who'd died before Brandi ever met Mrs. T. Pictures of him were scattered all over the house.

Brandi scrunched her nose, hating the memory. She'd forgiven Mrs. T; it wasn't her fault, but it still hurt.

"Mrs. T was our neighbor, right, Sy? You remember her?" She stretched up to look in the rearview mirror, but Sy was nowhere to be seen. "Sy!" Her heart raced and she twisted in her seat to look behind her, taking the steering wheel with her, and felt the car veer sharply to the right, earth beneath the tires.

Mack had to lean way across with his one arm to grab the wheel and get her back on the road. A burning spread in her cheeks.

"Eyes on the road," Mack said. "He's sleeping."

"Sorry, sorry! I just, well, I told you I don't have a license, right?"

"Yep."

Her thumbs tapped the wheel. "Anyway, Mrs. T used to invite me over for dinner and snacks, and sometimes we'd have movie night with popcorn she made on her stove instead of the microwave." Just thinking about it filled the car with buttery memories, and her mouth watered. "I think it's an old people thing to make popcorn on the stove. Do you do that too?"

More silence. And Brandi fidgeted in her seat, convinced she talked too much even though talking was where she was happiest.

"I made it over a fire for my son when we camped."

Brandi smiled, relieved. "That's cool. I bet he loved it. I loved Mrs. T's popcorn, but mostly I loved being at her house instead of mine." Lights from the dashboard turned everything blue, comforting even in its alien light. Better in here driving than out there with ginormous bears and skinwalkers.

"Does your mom know you have Sy?"

The question came out of nowhere even though it really shouldn't have surprised Brandi. She turned carefully to check on Sy and saw his little face from the corner of her eye. Sleeping. "I was thirteen the first time I went to juvie. Got caught stealing batteries."

"Batteries, huh?"

"Our electricity had been shut off, and I couldn't change Sy's diaper in the dark anymore. Kept getting poop on my hands." She shuddered, thinking of Sy's recent accident.

"They arrested you for a few batteries?"

She gave him a side look. "I might have stolen a few other things too. And it might not have been my first time getting caught." A small rodent darted in front of the car, froze, then scurried back the way it had come. Brandi didn't jerk the wheel or slam on the brakes; she gave herself a mental pat on the back for staying calm. She was a kick-ass driver. "The thing I hated was worrying about Sy. He was just a baby." She glanced around again. Still sleeping. "That's when my mom decided to try and get clean. I mean, good for her, you know, but also, like, what a bitch. Like, she couldn't do that when I was around? So when I got out, I thought, cool, we're gonna be a normal family for once." Brandi stopped to breathe, vaguely depressed. She'd been old enough to know it wouldn't last, young enough to dream that anything was possible. She thought she was better now, but Carissa told her she was too optimistic. That she better start seeing the bad shit or she was always going to be let down, and that kind of hurt cut deep. Brandi didn't know how to change like that. She was who she was.

She squinted at the road and breathed in. "When I got home, I think she stayed clean for two weeks." Her mother had shaken her awake in the middle of the night, antsy, pacing the bedroom and pulling at her hair. *Sy's been kidnapped. I can't find him. He's been kidnapped.*

Brandi had shot to her feet, cotton spinning in her head from too little sleep and trying to understand what her mother was saying. She pushed past Nancy and ran to Sy's crib. Empty. Brandi's stomach gave a sickening drop. *Mom, what did you do?* She ran from room to room, her mother following her like a stupid chicken, flapping her arms, completely useless. There was no sign of Sy. In the living room, she saw the pipe, inhaled the chemical-sweet remnants of her mom's last smoke, and if she wasn't sick from worry about Sy, she would have punched Nancy right in the face. A soft cry came from the bedrooms. Brandi followed it to her mom's room. She fell to her knees, lifted up the bed skirt. Baby Sy had been stuffed under the bed, naked except for a blanket tied around him, no diaper, and soaking wet. Brandi pulled him out and held him against her chest, trying to soothe his frantic cries. She glared at her mom. *I wish you were dead,* she told her.

Nancy was staring at her hands, and Brandi pressed Sy closer, prepared for this version of her mom. The one who preferred numbness to honesty. The one who was predictable. This Nancy couldn't hurt Brandi anymore. But when her mom looked at Brandi it was with such tenderness she felt it like a slap, and she stumbled back.

You used to love me. Her mom reached out a trembling hand, touched Brandi's arm, Sy's little head. Tears down her face. *You've always been a better version of me.*

Brandi had a counselor once who said that the definition of insanity was doing the same shit over and over and thinking there'd be a different result. Or something like that. So Brandi stopped waiting for her mom to love her more than drugs. It was never going to happen. Once she let that go, she did feel better, a little harder too maybe, but not so easily hurt and weakened by the whim of her mom's addiction. But this gentle touch, her words, in an instant crumbled everything Brandi had built to protect herself.

Nancy had pulled her hand back and crossed her arms, a soft smile that touched her eyes too. *I'll always love you.*

In those words, a flash of the woman who'd taken Brandi to see the wild horses, the sweet burst of orange on her tongue, and the power shifted easily, tickling Brandi's heart with old pain.

She'd hardened her face and did the only thing she knew that would save her from crumbling: she rebuilt her wall one word at a time. *I hate you, Nancy.* She walked out of the room and from the hallway yelled, *I fucking hate you!*

Nancy didn't follow. Brandi took Sy into their room, staring at the door hoping she would. She laid Sy on the ground. He looked up at her, baby rolls in his neck, fists in the air knocking her in the chin. She smiled and ignored the pain in her chest. *I love you, Sy, always and forever.* She'd cleaned and changed him, rocked him until his eyes fluttered closed, and lay down on the floor beside his crib, watching him sleep.

"Anyway, once she was back on meth it got bad, real bad. And then I got arrested again." Her spine curved forward. Shit was heavy sometimes. "I was only gonna take some food and light bulbs from Mrs. T's house. She was cool with it. Except she was sleeping, so I broke in through a screen window that was open. I didn't do any damage or anything. But Mrs. T's asshole of a son was on her couch, eating all her food, acting like he owned the place, and he called the cops on me." She curled her upper lip, still disgusted by that man. Mrs. T deserved better than him. "Anyway, that one got me sent to juvie. And you know what? I didn't mind it. And you know why? Because in juvie I had clean sheets and food and no creep trying to get into my room when my mom was so high she didn't know or didn't care."

Mack had taken his hat off and laid it in his lap. He didn't respond, but she could tell he was listening. And it felt good to talk. Like it had with Ms. Hanno.

"Brandi?"

She loved the sound of Mack's voice. He could narrate kids' shows or something. It was that kind of voice. Like nothing bothered him and everything would be okay if he was around. Carissa told her she was always looking for a dad. That's why she'd liked the warden so much.

From the seat behind them came a rustling, then Sy's little head popped in between the seats. "Did you get some sleep, Syborg? Are you hungry?" She reached for the bag behind her, straining in her seat so she could stretch her arm long. "Eyes on the road," Mack said, and twisted around to get the bag himself. He looked inside and made a disappointed sound. "This is all junk."

"Yeah, so. Junk is delicious."

"You need real food."

"Well, there wasn't any of that to take or I would have. Maybe."

Mack looked at her, as though just now understanding something. "There's free food everywhere."

"Huh?"

The car dinged. Low gas. Again. Brandi hissed, annoyed. They'd been driving forever, and she hadn't seen a single store since Pike River. "What's the point of gas if it's always running out?"

At that, of all the things she'd said that she thought were more hilarious, Mack laughed. It was a funny laugh too, higher pitched than she'd expected. "There's a gas station not too far up the road," he said. "We'll get more there."

"Do you have money now?"

"No more than I had before."

She laughed. They made a good team. Like Shrek and Donkey. She settled in and drove, letting another round of silence fill the car. But she was okay with it this time because for now, someone else was in charge, and all she had to do was drive.

~

Mack leaned against the headrest. His eyes drooped, and the road ahead blurred all the way. It had been like Brandi was telling someone else's story, not her own. She spoke in an upbeat manner, even making jokes, somehow keeping the whole sordid tale light. But it was heavy and hard to hear and had obviously led to Brandi taking her brother and running. It deepened a growing respect for her. Despite everything she'd gone through, she was scrappy, with a determination that made it seem possible she could beat the odds.

In some ways, Brandi reminded him of Jesse. There wasn't much that would stop his son from getting what he wanted. Daisy had kept bees, and Jesse would dip his fingers into the freshly collected honey when she wasn't looking and lick them clean. He was always a little sticky. But he'd been determined, like Brandi. Mack could see it in the way he practiced with his bow, wanting to be as good as his mom, or working his little fingers to thread a worm onto a hook.

He's a genius, Daisy used to say.

And Mack always agreed.

And stubborn.

Mack would nod with a smile. The boy refused to potty train; often he'd be having too much fun outside to bother. The last time he came in smelling like a cow patty, Daisy took him by the hand and made him strip his own pants off, dump the mess into the toilet, and then scrub his pants clean all by himself. Little Jesse had cried angry tears but after that, he never had another accident. A sound stuck in Mack's throat, and he coughed to cover it up.

"You okay?" Brandi said.

"Just swallowed my spit wrong."

"Oh my God, Carissa used to do that all the time. We were best friends in juvie, and then we went to the same group home. Cool, huh? Anyway, it happened in her sleep and everything. Woke me up every time, and I'd think she was literally dying."

He didn't mind her chatter. In the silence of the past few months, his mistakes had grown mouths. Brandi kept the noise at bay.

"But you know who did die?" Brandi said. "Mrs. T. And nobody thought to tell me. It happened when I was in juvie. I loved that woman like a grandmother. I mean, she wasn't perfect or anything. She couldn't drive because she'd had too many DUIs, and her son was a piece of shit who took advantage of her, and she just let him. But with me, she was always there, you know? Until she forgot me, I guess, but I mean, shit, nobody's perfect."

Brandi shared very personal things in such a casual way it kept surprising Mack, and he found he wanted to offer her something in return. "Daisy clips her toenails on the sofa. Lets them pile up, one nail at a time until she's got a pile of ten. Sometimes she'd brush them off onto the carpet when she thought I wasn't looking. Used to say that's what vacuuming was for."

Brandi laughed. "Ew, gross!"

"She's not perfect either. But I love her, and sometimes that's all it takes."

"Did your wife die?"

The question startled him, and he looked out the window, catching his faint reflection in the glass. Long hooked nose, stubbled cheeks—he never could grow a real beard—old man jowls. He liked to think that Daisy remembered his younger self. A sharp pain in his side.

"She lives in a nursing home."

"Oh, that's . . ." She paused. "Nice?"

"It's not nice at all."

From behind them came the rustle of Sy moving among the trash; then the little boy's hand appeared through the opening between the seats. Mack turned to find the boy staring at him. His small hand found the end of Mack's stump; Sy cupped it and held on. Mack stared at the boy's attempt at comfort, and it found its way deep into his throat and camped out. His own hand lingered over Sy's, patting gently.

After a few minutes, Mack said, "So this aunt of yours—"

"Heather."

"She doesn't know you're coming, that right?"

"Uh-huh." She sounded guarded suddenly. "But she'll be fine with it, I mean, I think she will."

He tried to be gentle, because it seemed like she'd put all her eggs into this one basket. "And how do you know?"

"Because I lived with her when I was real little. My mom was chasing the dragon again, and I guess Heather found out and came and got me." She gave Mack a side look with a dramatic eye twitch. "Before that, my mom had been sober for like nine years. Can you believe that, Mack? Heather told me she got into bad stuff in high school—well, they both did, but Heather hated how it made her feel, you know, that shit kills your motivation. So Aunt Heather turned good, and my mom went full druggie. Dropped out of school, moved in with a loser boyfriend." She lifted her eyebrows. "First of a long line of assholes. She was homeless too, but Aunt Heather did some kind of intervention thing, and Mom went to rehab. And like, she legit got sober. Got her GED, went to a community college, then to the University of Wyoming, where she got a whatever degree you need for photography. Then she had me and a real job taking pictures of dead people for the cops, and wedding pics, plus all her landscapes and animals. She wanted to be a famous photographer. It was a big fucking deal, you know?"

Sy still grasped the end of his stump, resting his head against the side of Mack's seat and listening to his sister like she was telling him a bedtime story.

It was another verbal dump; Brandi told all the bad things at once, Mack realized. He wondered if it hurt less to say it all together. He took hold of his chin and squeezed. "Did you like living with your aunt?" He hoped those were good memories.

"Yeah. I don't remember much, but I think that's because it was good? And when it's good, it doesn't stick in the same way like when it hurts. Hurts are like a tattoo because it never goes away, you know?"

Mack remembered waking up inside an empty tent. Canvas glowing from the late-morning sun. A sound like that of a wounded animal coming from the banks of the lake. Heart beating, the zipper snagging so badly he had to rip the tent flap open with his hand and teeth. He fell to his hand, rocks biting into his palm, arm buckling. Then his feet were under him and he was running. Every goddang second of that morning seared into his brain. "Yeah," he croaked. "I know."

Sy must have understood the pain in his voice, because he squeezed Mack's stump.

Brandi continued. "But then she did it again. Went to rehab, got her life back on track, said adios to the asshole who was my father, and asked for me back. I think I was around your age, Syborg, when I went back with Mom." She pulled in her lower lip. "Heather still visited, though. I know she didn't trust Mom. And then Nancy fucked it all up again, and we lost everything, and I never saw Heather again." She gave Sy a sad smile. "Did you ever meet her, Sy?"

The boy shook his head.

Brandi sighed. "I figured either Mom didn't want Heather butting in and taking her kids again, or Heather just got fed up with fixing

Nancy's disasters." Her chin trembled in the dashboard lights. "You know what I do know, Syborg?"

He shrugged.

"Aunt Heather will be so excited to see you! I just know it. And you're gonna looove it there, I promise."

Sy moved back into his seat, and when Mack turned his head to look, the boy had his arms wrapped around his skinny chest, head against the door panel, eyes closed. He saw Brandi turn her head, glance in the rearview mirror to check on her brother.

"You'll see, Sy," she said. "You'll see."

Mack watched the dark landscape pass. Brandi tapped the steering wheel and jiggled her nondriving leg up and down. Mack didn't have a good feeling about this aunt.

Ahead were the first lights they'd seen in a while, and his breath whistled softly through his teeth. He was grateful for a chance to break the sad tension in the car. And relieved—he hadn't been entirely sure they wouldn't run out of gas.

Brandi made a little noise of excitement. "Hell yeah, we're saved!" She hardly kept anything inside, like her thoughts were pets she kept on a leash, bounding around her. "I thought for sure we'd be sleeping outside again. No, thank you!" She shot a quick glance at her brother. "Hey, Syborg, you have to go to the bathroom again?"

Sy returned to his spot by Mack's side, hand lightly gripping his stump. Like Mack's lost arm was the one thing the kid could rely on. The boy's nearness brought Jesse back, his presence so strong Mack couldn't breathe. This had happened before, a rush of memory taking form. It was the boy, Mack knew. His vulnerability, his need for protection, that was raising Mack's son from the dead.

He cracked the window, lifted up his head to feel the air splash across his face. Little Jesse had loved physical contact: holding hands, sitting on Mack's lap for a story at bedtime, falling asleep tucked into his mother's arms. Even as he grew older, the boy didn't shy away from emotion. Daisy's child through and through. Angry tears, carefree laughter, giving Mack's hand a squeeze when they walked. He wished with all his soul that he could go back in time and never let go.

Lights from the gas station ran across the dashboard when Brandi pulled in. It was an old station with four pumps, but the spotlights were new, flashbulb-bright. A man in a Carhartt jacket filled his pickup truck, his blond hair turned silver by the lighting. Another car was parked in front, with a third in the shadows along the side of the small building.

"Pull around—"

"To the side. It's my second time stealing gas, you know." Brandi snorted a laugh and parked next to a dusty CR-V.

After a few minutes, the guy by the pumps hopped into his truck and pulled away. Mack waited a few more minutes, giving whoever was inside the store time to leave.

"Stay. Here." Mack held her gaze, emphasizing each word just as he'd done at the first gas station. Apart from tying her to the steering wheel, he didn't know how else to get her to listen.

Brandi held up her hands and bugged her eyes. "Relax."

He eased out of the RAV4 and stuck his head back inside. "But keep a lookout."

She grinned. "Should we have a code word, or wait, I can make a bird sound." She cupped the side of her mouth and in a hoarse whisper let out a, "*Caw! Caw!*" Sy, who had moved so that his elbows were on the center armrest, chin in his palms, made a tiny sound that could have been a laugh. Brandi heard it too and jerked her head back. "Sy, did you just laugh?" She clicked her tongue and leaned back, looking pleased. "Syborg's not such a borg after all."

Mack gave the little boy a tight smile, then closed the door and stepped carefully toward the front of the building. He poked his head around the corner. The car was gone. Turning around, he saw something by the dumpster and nearly whooped out loud at his luck. An old gas can, lying on its side. He went over to pick it up and blew air out of his nose—there was a hole where the spout was supposed to be.

95

"Goddang it." He stared at it, a plan circling his head. He climbed up to look inside the dumpster, using the biceps part of his missing arm to hook himself against the metal. Squinted into the dark interior and waited for his eyes to adjust. Just as he had hoped, water bottles, several of them.

He checked behind him—the parking lot was empty—then hefted himself up so that he balanced on his belly. The air compressed in his lungs, and he took shorter breaths. With his good arm, he reached forward and using his fingertips rolled a bottle toward him until he could grab it and toss it to the ground. He grabbed another one for a backup, the metal digging painfully into his ribs before he scooted back and jumped off. His knee buckled when he did, causing him to spin around before landing on his butt. He sat there for a minute. "Goddarn old bones."

To get up he rolled to his knees and pushed with his hand, one foot at a time. Sy's face was pressed to the window again, watching. From the back of the RAV4, Mack pulled the hose, pried open the gas tank lid of the CR-V, removed the cap, and stuffed the hose inside. He'd fill the gas can, then use the water bottle as a funnel to get it into the RAV4. It wouldn't be perfect, but it would do.

While the fuel spilled into the can, Mack used his knife to saw off one end of the water bottle, trying to work as fast as he could. Sweat beaded under his arms, his pulse raced, and, as he'd done many times since the bear attack, he cursed his lost arm for his slowness.

No cars in the parking lot, none on the highway, a quiet night with the sound of fuel splashing inside the metal can. Regardless, Mack was filled with the kind of dread he'd felt the day he woke up to find Jesse gone. Something bad was going to happen.

Ten

He'd told her not to move. And Brandi wasn't a rule breaker. Sure, she stole and did other things that broke the law, but she saw that as surviving. Like on those shows where they put naked people out in the middle of nowhere and then they win a bunch of money if they make it to the place where a helicopter saves their lives. Brandi's life was like that. Except she got to wear clothes. *Score.* The rest of it—food, finding a safe place to sleep, evading meth heads, taking care of her little brother—that was all up to her. And in the end, there was no bunch of money. No helicopter. Just more surviving.

But Mack was a good one, she'd decided. It was in his eyes. Mrs. T had those eyes. Even if sometimes they were glassy from too many Silly Willys as she called them. Some kind of whiskey combination she liked to drink at night. But it didn't make her bad. It just made her sometimes unreliable. Her mother was a different story. Meth had wiped away all the goodness and left nothing in her eyes but a thirst for more, more, more. Brandi guessed that alcohol would have done the same thing, that maybe Nancy had just been born that way. Chills ran up her back. Was Brandi like that? Would she screw over everybody she loved for a high? Brandi had decided long ago that she never wanted to find out.

From beside her, Sy squeaked. He hadn't taken his eyes off Mack since he'd left the car. It hurt Brandi's heart just a little bit. Why couldn't he trust her the way he trusted this stranger? She bit her lip. Maybe it was because she looked so much like their mom. Same thick brownish-red hair that was never curly or straight. Just some in between that made drying it take forever and always looked like a helmet.

Headlights on the highway and Brandi's heart raced. They passed by and she relaxed. She craned her head to check on Mack. He was butt-up inside a dumpster; it made her giggle. How long was this going to take? She should be out there helping him, be his other arm. "Stay here," she said to Sy in the same tone Mack had used with her. Sy just stared at her. "I'll take that as a yes."

She started around the car when she heard a sound from the front of the store. A door closing. She froze. Must be whoever worked there. She glanced behind her. And whoever owned this car. *Oh shit.* She hurried back to the car, flung open her door, and grabbed the map of Wyoming from inside. Walked around the corner and ran straight into some guy's squishy stomach. He yelped and grabbed her by the arms like she was gonna knock him off his feet.

"Whoa! You scared the shit out of me." His black hair hung in frizzy waves around his ears; acne scars thick to his temples. Interest in the glint of his eyes that looked her up and down. A pack of cigarettes and a lighter in one hand. Must have been a smoke break for the creep.

She tried not to look disgusted. "Yeah, sorry."

He looked out over the deserted parking lot to the empty road and the shadowy dots of sagebrush that rolled across acres and acres of empty land. Nobody and nothing for miles. She felt the aloneness in an anxious fluttering. From this angle, at least he couldn't see Mack or the cars. Brandi's nose twitched at the slight smell of gasoline in the air.

"Did you walk here?"

"Huh? No, course not." She walked to the glass doors, gripped the handle. "You working or not?" Trying not to sound rude. How long would it take Mack? Her skin crawled when the guy smiled, licking his lips and following her inside. He was the only one working.

She walked to the back of the store, picking up bags of chips, rock candy, those candy peanuts that only live at gas stations, granola bars to be healthy for Mack, and bottled waters, placed them all on the counter.

Added gum and whatever else was at the front of the store, just wanting to keep him occupied and away from the outside or her.

"Can you show me how to get to Casper?" She handed him the map she'd brought from the car, proud of her quick thinking.

He traced a finger along the highway they were on, then to another, listing off numbers she didn't hear. She gave the door a quick look to see if Mack had pulled the car around, anything to let her know he was done. A jittery feeling in her thighs. She wanted out of there.

"You all alone?" His mustache was sparse, like he'd just had a glass of chocolate milk and wiped some of it off. It looked stupid.

She tried to keep her upper lip from curling. "What? No, of course I'm not alone." She backed away from the counter, his bad vibes pinching the skin on her arms. She searched for something to say, itching to stretch the physical space between them.

"Where's the bathroom?" Bathrooms had locks, and she could wait a minute in there until she was sure Mack was done.

His eyes narrowed. "Aren't you gonna pay first?"

She held her stomach, tried to look embarrassed. "Girl stuff, sorry."

He pointed toward the back of the store, past the energy drinks.

"I'll be right back to pay for all that stuff," she said, hoping he wouldn't go finish his cigarette break. When she walked away, she felt him staring at her ass and made her hand into a fist. Imagined the crunch of his nose under her knuckles. She'd do it too, or kick him in the balls, whichever needed to happen first.

The narrow hallway to the bathroom was dark, lit only by a buzzing bulb. She edged past store crates of beer, soda, and cleaning supplies, the floor dingy, nasty black schmeg in the corners. She closed the door behind her and turned the lock. It spun in the handle. *Fucking useless.* Sweat beaded under her thick hair. She waited for a few minutes, long enough to hopefully give Mack the time he needed to steal the gas. She washed her hands with soap that smelled sharp and astringent, dried them on her jeans because the paper towel dispenser was empty. *Lazy creep.*

When she opened the door her heart plummeted, falling in a squishy heap to the floor.

He filled the hallway, a weird mint-and-man-perfume smell stinging her nostrils. "Hey." His soft voice made her skin itch.

Memories flooded her; images from the past burned inside her eyelids. Waking up to one of the assholes with his hand over her mouth and nose, her body writhing under the force of his arm on her chest. Sy asleep in his crib, her mother not there, and Brandi powerless and without a soul in the world to protect her. Of everything, that had been the truth that ripped her heart in two. That led to her willingness to do whatever it took, like stealing or breaking into her neighbor's house.

She had nobody.

Later it had fueled her in a different way. Made her want to be something, somebody. To say, *Fuck you, world, I deserve better!* And for a while she believed it. But not anymore. Because here she was, on the run, nowhere to turn, with her brother to protect, and this asshole licking his lips like she was his own plaything. Like she was nothing. Like she *had* nobody.

And that was the truth.

"I don't see a car out there. You need help?" He touched her hair, ran his cigarette-stinking finger down her shoulder, along her arm, grazing her boob. She couldn't move, trapped by his body, wilted by a fear that overrode a voice screaming inside her head to *run!* She wanted her body to boil over with a hot rage, she wanted to take his head and bash it on her knee in some kind of ninja move she'd never learned but wished she had. She wanted to be the badass she was inside.

She stood there, unmoving. Maybe this was all she'd ever be. A heaviness pressed down on her skull. She wanted so much more than that.

"Get your goddang hands off her."

Brandi's legs gave out at the sound of Mack's voice, and she grabbed on to the edge of the sink to keep from dropping to the floor. The guy's eyes widened, his mouth gaping like a fish on a hook. Mack stood to the side with the barrel of his gun pressed into the man's head. On the other end of the gun, the old man looked bigger, a cowboy swagger in his steady hold on the trigger. But the thought of Mack hurting or killing someone for her was all wrong. She wrapped her arms tight across her chest, a protest building inside. "Don't, Mack." Her voice as weak as the rest of her.

But Mack's eyes were trained on the man. "Hands in the air and back out slowly."

The guy did as he was told. "Hey, man, I thought the toilet paper was empty. I was only trying to help."

"I said move." Even Brandi straightened up at Mack's cold anger. Asshole did as he was told, hands up, backing slowly out of the hallway.

Mack met her gaze, unflinching kindness, even as Brandi wanted to wrap her arms around her body, shame in the slump of her shoulders. He turned and followed the guy. "Lay stomach down on the goddang floor."

Brandi stayed where she was, sucking in all the air she could. The numbness turned to shaking, and she squeezed her arms to hug herself tighter. *Calm down.* She left the bathroom; Mack stood with his gun pointed at the other guy's back and glanced her way.

Her lips wobbled. She gave him a thumbs-up.

"Put your hands behind your neck."

The guy did as he was told, and Brandi relaxed enough to smirk at his fear. Not so tough against a one-armed old guy with a gun. *Asshole.* She went to the register, found a bag, and filled it with all the stuff she hadn't bought, plus a few more things.

"Hey, man, she's stealing!" He spoke to Mack like the two of them were on the same team. Brandi wanted to kick him in the face, but Mack got there first with one to his side. She would have kicked harder.

"You want me to call the police, tell them what you were about to do to that little girl?"

The guy flinched. "Don't kill me, man, please. I'm not like that. I thought she was into me. She was flirting and shit."

Mack leaned down and pressed the gun to the back of the guy's neck. Brandi froze; the guy whimpered. "Not another lying word." Asshole's shoulders shuddered like he might actually be crying, and Brandi relaxed, smiling because this, this was just too good. And if Mack was the kind of man who killed, he would have done it. She felt confident in her judgment. She knew people.

Mack waited until Brandi was at the door before he backed away, keeping his body between her and the crying asshole. She pushed backward through the door, held it open with her foot for Mack. Outside, the night air slipped cold over her sweaty scalp.

She ran to the car, threw the bag of snacks at Sy, started the engine, and before Mack had closed his door, she was back on the highway and driving as fast as she could without the old man telling her to slow down. She was used to bad decisions, constantly surrounded by them. Her own, her mother's, her friends'. And part of her believed they'd been about a minute from someone doing something that made everything so much worse. She might talk tough, but inside, Brandi cared. About life, about right and wrong, about consequences. She just hadn't been given the chance yet to prove it. When the darkness swallowed the gas station lights behind them, the tension released from her shoulders and Brandi slumped forward, so relieved she'd gone boneless.

"Thank you," she whispered, glad she could look at the road and not Mack, afraid of what she might see. Irritation? Blame? Or worse, nothing. "I was just trying to help. He'd come outside to smoke, and he was going to see what you were doing."

"I know. Sy told me."

She raised her eyebrows. "He did?"

"He said enough for me to know."

Stars overhead, night smearing across the windows. Brandi's hands had started to shake, and there was a burning pressure behind her eyes.

"Sorry, I'm so sorry," she said, unable to stop. "I'm so sorry."

Mack's voice, low, warm, rumbling. Like a TV grandpa. "That wasn't your fault."

Her heart hugged the blame tight. She should have screamed no, pushed him out of the way, not stood there like a dumbass. Like she wanted it.

"It wasn't your fault," Mack said again. "Brandi?" He'd leaned forward, hat off. "It wasn't your fault. Do you hear me?"

Her nose was running. "I didn't want it. Like he . . . like he said I did." She wiped away the snot with the back of her hand. "I was so . . ." She wanted to stop there, hold it in, because telling someone else made it real. "I was scared."

"Course you were." Mack said it like it was the most natural thing. "Sometimes bigger and scarier things take pieces of us whether we want them to or not." He wiggled his stump in such a funny way Brandi almost laughed. "But it still doesn't make it your fault. That's something you keep telling yourself until you believe it."

Brandi pinched her lip between her teeth and nodded. It was true—she'd heard it from Ms. Hanno. Wrote something similar in a journal once. But hearing Mack say it out loud meant something, if only to give her the permission to believe it herself.

~

It didn't show, but inside Mack's heart thumped an angry beat against his chest. He'd never witnessed anything so brazen and wrong in his entire life, and he couldn't stop thinking about how he very nearly didn't go inside. When he'd realized she was gone, Sy had hugged his stuffed robot to his chest, chewing on one corner of its square head. *The girl went there.* He'd pointed toward the front of the store.

Mack had breathed through his teeth. *Why?*

Sy had shrugged.

Mack had hesitated. He could leave—the girl would do her own thing no matter what he said. But she had that goddarn gun, loaded or not, and he didn't believe she had the good sense not to wave it around again. He kicked the tire. Sy stared at him through the car window with that blank look of his. It cut right to Mack's heart. A kid his age should be building forts, not so scared he hardly spoke.

Mack had made a promise to help them get to Casper, and that's exactly what he intended to do. He strode to the front, yanked open the door. It was empty, no clerk at the register, no Brandi stuffing food into her pockets, the faintest sound of whimpering from the back. He'd hurried across the store staying light on his feet, Brandi's terrified mewls of protest growing louder, sticking like burrs into his heart.

He'd turned the corner to find the man touching her like he had a goddang right to, and the look on her face, like someone had told her she deserved it. His gun was in his hand and pressed against the man's temple so quickly Mack had little memory of making the decision to do it. It had been instinct. His finger on the trigger, a momentary thought. He could shoot this guy.

Now in the car, processing everything that had just happened, the idea that the guy might try it again with some other lost girl, dang it if Mack didn't still wish he had.

Brandi drove, her left knee bouncing up and down. The way she kept apologizing like she was to blame for the deplorable behavior of that man cut Mack to the quick. He had said the only thing he knew to be true, and it had seemed to calm her down. *It's not your fault.*

"Damn, it's still low." Brandi's eyes were on the dash. "At least it's not pointing straight at the E. Do we have enough to get to Casper?"

And this girl had planned to drive there by herself. "No," Mack said.

"Oh." She tapped the wheel to a tune only she heard. "You know what I'm hoping? That you took enough so that asshole back there runs out of gas on a lonely country road and then gets kidnapped by some beast who just got out of prison, and then he gets it right up the—"

"Brandi," Mack said. "Sy's listening."

She craned her neck to look in the rearview mirror, smiling at her brother. "And karma does the rest. Right, Sy?"

"Are you hurt?" Sy's voice was delicate and as small as he was.

Brandi opened her mouth, surprised, Mack thought, by the boy speaking directly to her. "Nah, Mack here saved the day. You were right to trust him, Sy. Rule number one: learn to trust good people."

Mack's eyes burned. "Goddang heartburn," he muttered.

"Mrs. T thought she was having a heart attack once. Turns out she just needed Tums." Brandi gave him a serious look. "You sure it's not a heart attack?"

He pushed air through his lips. "It's not a goddarn heart attack."

Brandi made a face. "Okay, okay."

Mack felt a small hand on his stump and turned to find Sy had moved up and was nearly nose to nose with him. "You smell like a grandpa."

"I do?" Mack was amused and also wondered if a grandpa smelled like his cabin with the dirt floor or the grime that had worked its way into his skin from his few months living off grid.

"Uh-huh," Sy said.

"Hey, Syborg, I got you all sorts of yummy treats."

Mack heard the bag rustle, then Sy handed him candy on a stick.

"Would you like me to open it?" Mack asked.

Sy nodded. "Please?"

"Sure can." He tore off the plastic cover with his teeth and gave it back to the boy, the feel of the wooden handle with the knob on the end painfully familiar. "My son loved rock candy too."

Sy crunched the treat, sounding like a real kid for once, and Mack figured a little sugar wouldn't hurt. The boy had the rest of his life to eat healthy.

The car sailed forward, tires smooth on the road, a comfortable warmth in the air. No lights except for the stars spreading across the expanse of the nighttime sky. Daisy had lived in the city; Mack only knew country life. She'd marveled at the differences. *Everything out here is just so big.*

Like what?

They'd sat on his father's porch steps, gazing up at the sky. She'd pointed. *Like that.*

You don't have stars in the city?

She gazed up, the light from inside slipping down the line of her jaw. Mack had to sit on his hands to keep from touching her. *Not like here,* she'd said. *It's more like an afterthought, but out here, it's a part of you. You know?*

Mack had nodded even though he didn't really understand, because this was all he'd ever known.

Brandi yawned. Mack followed, not realizing until that moment how bone-tired he was. The wind had picked up and pushed against the windows. The car swayed a bit, an overcorrection from Brandi.

"Gonna blow me off the road," she said.

"Not this wind. It's too weak."

Brandi glanced at him. "You're telling me wind can actually do that? I was being funny."

"Just keep both hands on the wheel and—"

"Eyes on the road, I get it." She sounded exasperated but also amused. "Is that how a dad sounds?"

He wasn't sure why it stung. Maybe it was hearing that word and all the things that came with it. Mack had never held a baby before his own, and Jesse's tiny body was so frail, so vulnerable. It hadn't helped that his birth had nearly been a funeral. Mack squeezed the back of his neck. Later, Daisy liked to say that maybe he was supposed to have died on the day he was born and all the years in between had been a gift.

There had been a relentless May snowstorm that day with a sweeping wind that iced the roads and everything else in its wake. Quick and brutal, shutting down highways, freezing new buds on branches. Daisy had gone into labor at home, already determined to have the baby there anyway.

Hospitals are for sick people, she'd said.

The midwife was expected that evening but with the weather, she never made it. With each contraction, Mack felt a quickening in his own gut and a feeling he'd hardly experienced: panic. He knew how to survive—how to gut a fish, process an animal, cure skin to use in shoes, fur for hats and gloves. But delivering his own baby wasn't part of that skill set.

I need you, Mack.

Daisy. Forever sure of herself in all situations. She'd become his compass. Even with her belly twisting, her body spreading itself to allow for this new life, Daisy remained the calm in the storm. Ice spit at the windows, wind howled across the plains. Mack had washed his hands, rolled up his sleeves. *I got you, Daisy.*

I know, Mack. That's why I married you. She breathed through her teeth, another fresh round of pain spasming her rounded stomach, and grunted her next words. *Get. This. Baby. Out. Of. Me!*

In the end, Jesse slid out easily enough, at least that's what Daisy said, and started life as quietly as he'd ended it. No tears, no indication that he was in trouble except for his utter stillness. Daisy cried out, and Mack felt the weight of his son's life in his arms, light as a feather and a breath away from over. He rested his tiny body on the bed and instinctively laid his fingers on the frail bones of his chest, right by his heart. Maybe it was the shock of Mack's cold skin, or maybe baby Jesse just needed a minute to acclimate to his new world, but right then his lips vibrated around a cry.

Daisy had laughed. Mack had cried himself at the shock of it all.

"Mack?" Brandi's voice pulled him out of the past.

He sucked in air and had to look out the car window to collect himself. He repositioned in his seat, pulling the seat belt away from his chest. He needed some space to clear his head from all the memories that had come along for the ride.

"Why are you acting dead if your wife is still alive?"

Mack sighed. The girl thought everyone's business was free information. Still, the desolate road stretched long and dark ahead of them. Mack started talking. "She'd taken to wandering." He slapped his hat against his thighs. He hadn't wanted to leave her to go to work, but they needed the money. He should have reached out, asked for help. But after her diagnosis, she pulled away from her friends, easily embarrassed by her confusion. Mack didn't have the heart to push her, so their isolation from others evolved naturally.

It felt like it happened overnight. Daisy's mind unraveled like fishing line, making daily tasks more difficult. Soon Mack was helping her get dressed, making sure she got to the bathroom and other tasks that he knew would have humiliated her. He didn't mind, because he'd promised to love her even in the bad times, and goddang it, he wasn't going to ask someone else to take care of her.

"This one day . . ." Heartburn turned his chest to fire. "She walked out onto the main highway and caused an eighteen-wheeler to jackknife. Shut down the road for hours. The driver was okay, but . . ." He sniffed, touched the brim of his hat. Peggy had come to find him, her face so pale he thought she was about to pass out. "Daisy was sitting in the middle of the road, crying and refusing to get up until I came to get her." His heart had plummeted when he'd seen her. Her once-silky strawberry hair in a white tangle around her face, confusion clouding her eyes and running so deep her hands shook. He'd knelt in front of her. *I got you, Daisy.* She'd looked at him, a flicker inside of the woman who was the calm in every storm, battling with the unknown. He'd taken her hand, held it firm, and pulled her to her feet. *Can you help me find Mack?* It had broken him all the way through, but he'd put his arm around her and hugged her close. *You bet.* "It got a lot of attention, and a couple of days later the state people showed up. They decided I couldn't keep Daisy safe and that she needed to go into a home."

He caught Brandi staring at him, mouth hung open.

"Eyes on the—"

"That's not fair."

The sentiment sounded childish, but it didn't make it wrong. She was right. Nothing about it was fair.

"How could they take your own wife away from you? I thought they only did that to kids."

It took him a moment to wrap his thoughts around what she'd casually implied. An ache in his side for her and for Sy. Both he and Daisy had loved being parents, as hard as it had been at times. Jesse had been their shining light. His hand formed a fist, knuckles kneading his thigh. She was right: some things just weren't fair.

"Like why wasn't Sy taken away from my mom? Sometimes nothing makes sense, you know, Mack?"

A phantom laugh from the back seat, and he felt the apparition of Jesse sitting next to Sy, listening to every word. At Sy's age, Jesse had been prone to giggles. His little hands worked on tying knots and catching fish. In contrast, Sy was a ghost of a kid. Quiet, waifish, slowly disappearing. Mack swallowed. He'd do anything to have Jesse back, but he knew his boy had lived a good life. "Sometimes nothing makes sense at all."

"Yeah."

They were quiet for a while, the sway of the car heavy in Mack's eyelids. The road a relentless line forward, bordered by dark outlines of sagebrush in cracked earth. A monotonous drive. He forced his eyes open, not wanting Brandi to drive alone.

Brandi shifted in her seat. "So are you dead because you want to break her out and then go live in the woods where no one can bother you and you two can be old together?"

For some reason, it made him laugh. It might have been the simplicity of it along with the fact that it had been close to his plan. He and Daisy had often talked about finding some land and living on their own terms. The little cabin wasn't ideal, but he'd figured he could make it work for her.

"You laugh at the weirdest things."

"You say funny things."

She flipped her hair over one shoulder. "I am hilarious. Ask Carissa."

Mack smiled into the night.

"I still don't get why you being dead helps your wife."

He sighed. In for a penny, as Daisy would say. "Daisy has cancer. If I'm dead, she gets a little bit of money that can help pay for her treatments."

"Oh, I'm sorry." She paused a beat. "Like insurance money? I know all about that. There's this girl at my group home who is ob-sessed with true crime. And let me tell you, insurance money is almost always the reason—well, for like a husband to kill his wife, not usually why they pretend to be dead. Or maybe it is. Who knows? But it's stealing, I do know that." She leaned over to elbow him. "We're similar, you and me." The delight in her voice turned serious. "Isn't she lonely without you?"

He rubbed his stump, thought of Daisy's face in the minutes after the bear attack. Stricken with panic, twisting her own shirt into a tour-niquet around Mack's arm. Walking him out of that forest with Jesse on one side, Mack leaning heavily into her on the other.

"She deserves life." He sniffed, Peggy's words crowding around him. *Maybe that's not what she wants.* He shook it off. Daisy was a fighter. "And if I can give that to her, why wouldn't I?"

"Yeah, of course." Brandi's left leg jiggled up and down. "So I guess you did it, huh?"

He looked at her, confused.

"Did what?"

"Tricked them!" With one hand on the wheel, she pulled some-thing from her pocket and handed it to him. It was the flyer for his memorial service. "They don't have those for people who are alive, do they?"

Mack shook his head. "They do not." She was right. It had worked. Regret swelled, surprising him. He should be relieved; instead, he felt like he'd lost something he'd never get back. The cabin felt a bit like a real grave.

"Is her nursing home close to you? Like, can you at least spy on her through a window or something like that sometimes? Just so you won't, you know, be all alone forever?" Pity in her voice. He heard it and maybe felt a bit of it for himself too.

But Mack steeled himself against it. Daisy would be surrounded by friends. Peggy would see to it. She had always been the loyal sort. "Daisy's in Lander." Mack would much rather take on the burden of being alone if it meant he could provide comfort and healing for his wife. He had to remind himself that once she was cured of the cancer he'd find a way to take her to the cabin. She'd be so much happier there. It was in her soul to live free. He winced, still hating to think of her in that place with a small window separating her from the smell of trees, the sound of birds. When he visited her there she'd say the same thing. *I don't like this place.* She'd grip his hand. *Where's Jesse? Let's go to the pond.* The pond had dried up the year after they lost Jesse. In the beginning, Mack used to correct her. Thinking if he told her the facts she'd remember. It would only agitate her. As time moved on, he'd learned that what was important wasn't telling her she was wrong; it was living with her where she was. It brought her peace. So he'd squeezed her hand back. *Jesse will love that.*

"Don't you miss her?" A child's question. Asked with no sense of how deeply it cut.

"Every second."

"I'm so sorry, Mack."

Wind slammed against the car, metal creaking, turning the window cold with its whispers of winter. "In a little bit, you'll want to get on 28 toward Lander." He leaned back in the seat, set his hat on his head, pulling it low to cover his face. There wasn't much of anything but road and sagebrush between here and Lander and a pass to climb, but for the most part, the pavement was dry and straight. Brandi would be fine for a little bit on her own. He just hoped they had enough gas to get over the pass.

Eleven

Mack was resting, Sy was quiet as a mouse as usual, and Brandi's head was spinning with everything that had happened in what, a couple of days? She sang to herself as she drove, a death metal song that she'd be screaming into the night if she were alone. Ms. Hanno said music was perfect for soothing her anger. Ms. Hanno had meant that classical stuff that bored Brandi to tears. Brandi preferred the kind of music that filled all the spaces in her head, the kind that thumped so hard inside her veins it completely consumed her, leaving her no choice but to focus on the beat of the drums, the screech of the electric guitar, and her own voice singing along.

The road climbed and the land stretched up in shadows outside the windows. From the corners of her eyes, figures leaped from bush to bush, following them, laughing as they kept pace with the car. She shivered. There was nothing for miles and miles and miles. No light, no other cars, nothing. Mack breathed deeply, and Brandi glanced at the old man and smiled to herself. At least they weren't alone. She felt safe with Mack. The safest she'd felt in a long time.

The headlights were yellow on the road, small cones that illuminated the pavement only immediately in front of the car. Which was why she didn't see the black-and-white lump hurtle itself across the road or why, she told herself later, she didn't hit the brakes or swerve to avoid hitting it. Instead, she screamed and pushed the gas harder, and the car jerked sickeningly up and down on one side.

Mack sat up, hat falling to his lap. "Whoa—"

She swerved into a pull-off and was out of the car in a flash, throat tightening. It was dark, so dark. She grew up in a small town, but she'd gravitated to gaming and friends who hung around places cocooned by dim streetlights. She always forgot how big and open and *empty* the rest of Wyoming was. Out here, she was small and irrelevant.

The smell hit her first, and she pressed a palm over her nose, letting her watery eyes adjust. There, on the side of the road, its white fur a faint glow in the starlight. Motionless, battered, and dead. She stumbled back, repelled by the sour stink and the life she'd taken. In the dark, she cried. She couldn't help it, and she knew it was stupid.

Footsteps on the gravel behind her.

"I didn't mean to kill it. It came out of nowhere." A deep sorrow burrowed inside her chest.

Mack's voice behind her. "It happens." He touched her shoulder, and she looked up but couldn't see his face in the night. "That spray will get into your hair and clothes quick. Let's move back to the car."

She stood and followed. Now that her eyes had adjusted to the dark, she saw what looked like a small cabin on wheels parked at the other end of the large U-shaped pull-off. It was dark, and if there were people inside they were probably sleeping this late at night. Brandi was tired so deep down she felt it behind her eyes. Mack led her to the RAV4, where the stink was less pungent. Brandi leaned against the SUV, arms crossed, and stared toward the lump. Headlights down the highway, gears shifting on a truck, brighter, closer, louder, and when it passed, the skunk's mangled and bloody body was illuminated entirely. Brandi winced, felt a tug in her chest and new tears in her eyes.

"You know, I used to want to be a veterinarian," she said.

"I can see that."

Brandi snorted. "I was ten! Back then I thought all they did was play with animals. Did you know they have to put them down too?"

Mack sniffed. He didn't need to answer. As she got older, Brandi realized there were a lot of things that people knew that she didn't

113

because her life had been about surviving, finding food, sleeping through the night, and there was no one around to make sure she knew the obvious things, like that vets do more than love and cuddle animals.

"There was this cat who slept under Mrs. T's porch. He was kinda mean, but I think he really liked me." That cat had scratched the hell out of her, leaving bright-red welts up and down her arms. Brandi figured he was scared, so she held him tighter. She loved that cat. "I called him Scratch." Eventually, Scratch got used to Brandi, even sitting in her lap once. But mostly he left a trail of dead mice around the porch. "One day he wasn't there. I looked under the porch, nothing. Around back, nothing." She stopped, pressed a hand over her heart. It still hurt. "I heard a car and then Scratch cried out. He was up by the road, and the car was driving away. They hadn't even stopped to find out if someone loved him enough to miss him." But the worst part had been that he wasn't dead, so she'd scooped him up and begged Mrs. T to take her someplace to see if they could fix him. "Mrs. T took me to the vet even though she wasn't supposed to be driving because of all her DUIs and even though she definitely shouldn't have been driving with the way her breath smelled." Brandi had rushed inside, Scratch motionless in her arms but still breathing. The vet was a young woman who worked mostly on big animals like horses and cows. She laid Scratch on an exam table and gently stroked one ear. Brandi had never been to the doctor. She had no idea how it worked.

Fix him, please.

The vet's blue eyes were kind. *The most loving thing you can do is to put him down.*

Put him down where? Brandi had been an idiot.

The vet looked surprised by Brandi's ignorance. *He's dying, but we can help make it less painful by doing it for him.*

A cool wind blew from the other direction, taking the stink of the skunk with it for the moment. "The vet gave him a shot, and his eyes clouded over and he was gone." She snapped her fingers. "Like that."

After a few minutes, Mack cleared his throat. "I'm sorry, Brandi."

"Yeah, anyway, I'd memorized that car and the license plate and I watched for that asshole, and the next time that car drove down my street, I busted the back windshield with a rock." Brandi laughed to herself. "And nobody was hurt, except for the car, and I didn't even get caught." A fact she couldn't help but be a little bit proud of. "So I guess that's why I have a soft spot for animals."

"There's nothing wrong with loving animals."

She kicked at the dirt, a little embarrassed by her reaction. "Even if it's over a damn skunk?"

"Even then. My son had a habit of finding motherless baby birds."

"Ha, like you."

Mack made a noise in his throat. "I suppose."

"So what'd he do with the birds?" It was possible that in Mack's neck of the woods, baby bird was delicious.

"He fed them from an eye dropper, kept them warm, and when they were big enough, he let them go."

"Cool."

"The dark-eyed juncos he'd raised came back year after year to have their babies."

"Still?"

"We don't live there anymore." Mack's voice had flattened, and Brandi sucked in her bottom lip, afraid she'd said something wrong. Mack walked around to the passenger side. "You okay to drive?"

"Yeah." She felt cooler, wishing the warmth of the moment had lasted just a bit longer. As much as she wanted to get Sy to Casper, she also wanted to slow everything down.

Her seat belt clicked into place and she turned the key, but the engine sputtered and died, the needle at E. "Oh, that again."

Mack sighed.

"What are we going to do?" Sy was in back, where he'd been sleeping this entire time.

Mack slid his hat to cover his face. "Sleep. We'll figure it out in the morning."

She climbed in back and curled up on one end, resting her head against the window, and tried not to think about how they were out of gas and in the middle of nowhere with the skinwalkers and grizzly bears. Again.

At least this time they had Mack.

~

His rumbling stomach woke him up well before dawn. The kids were still sleeping, and he didn't want to wake them. They lay curled around each other in the back seat, exhausted, the kind of tired that came from losing everything. He got out of the car and stretched, taking in their surroundings. They were close to the top of the pass, parked on one end of a large pull-off. A tiny house on wheels, looking abandoned without the truck to pull it, took up the other side of the gravel area.

In the early dawn glow, he had a better idea of where they were. Not far from a creek filled with trout, likely active on this cool fall morning. He had his fishing gear in his bag, flint for a fire, and they could be filling their bellies by lunch. Mack left quietly, dumping water from one of the bottles Brandi had stolen into his canteen, and headed out.

The hike felt good after the time in the car, the events of last night, and the lingering anger Mack still felt at what the man had tried to do to Brandi. The girl was tough, but Mack didn't think anyone could be that tough without something else giving.

He cast the line, letting the fly dance through the water, and breathed in the crisp air, the bubble of cold mountain water slipping over rocks familiar and comforting.

Later, he walked back with two good-size trout clipped to his belt loop and enough time to call it a late lunch. But when he got to the pull-off, the SUV was empty. He dropped his bag on the hood, laid the fish beside it, pulse loud in his ears. He hadn't thought about waking Brandi up to tell her where he was going; he was used to leaving early, to Daisy knowing exactly where he'd be. He hit his thigh with his fist, angry at himself for not thinking. Had she hitchhiked? That would be something she'd do. *Dang it!* He hardly knew her, but the responsibility he felt for the pair tugged at his throat. They probably thought he'd abandoned them.

He stood in the middle of the lot, hand hanging uselessly by his side and with no idea what to do next.

"Macky!"

Sy's voice, louder than Mack had ever heard it and saying his name for the first time too. Mack swallowed back a sudden rush of heartburn to his throat. From the direction of the tiny cabin, Sy ran toward him. Brandi stood in the doorway with her arms folded.

It was a large lot, and in the middle Sy stopped to collect his pants, which had started to drop, and held them firm at his waist, then half skipped, half walked the rest of the way to Mack, where he flung one arm around Mack's waist. "You came back."

Mack let himself be hugged, stunned by the boy's unearned attachment to him.

"You smell fishy."

"Got us some lunch."

"The new girl will like it."

Mack flicked his eyes in the direction of the camper, the muscles across his back tightening with suspicion. A woman had appeared beside Brandi, both looking mad as hell.

"C'mon." Sy took hold of Mack's stump and started walking him in the direction of the cabin.

Mack sighed. What had Brandi gotten herself into now?

The cabin was about the size of Mack's, maybe even a little bigger, but the wheels made it portable. Brandi frowned at him from the doorway, but Mack sensed her relief in the smallest twitch of her nose.

The woman hopped down. She was young, possibly in her twenties, he wasn't sure. The older he got, the harder it was to guess. Her short hair was peroxide blonde with a braided black rat tail that hung over one shoulder. "She thought you'd left 'em." Her eyes were blue and squinted behind thick black glasses that covered half her face. "You can't just leave without telling them you'll be back, you know."

He directed his words to Brandi. "I went fishing." Sy squeezed his stump.

Brandi blinked, her mouth soft. "Okay." She stepped down from the cabin's minuscule front porch and joined the woman. "This is Pepper."

Pepper smiled, and it made the hoop that hung in the space between her nostrils dance. Mack shook his head. *Young people.*

"At least you came back," Pepper said. "You're already a better man than Gus." She hopped back inside the cabin, came out wearing a large gray sweatshirt that hung halfway to her knees and read MOUNTAIN COLLEGE. Opened a cooler and pulled out a Diet Coke. She raised an eyebrow, and Mack noticed it had been shaved right through the middle. "Want one?"

Mack shook his head.

Pepper smiled, sipped from the can, and looked Mack up and down. "You're like the real deal, huh? Gus thought he was the real deal, but that son of a bitch couldn't handle two weeks changing the dirt in the toilet." She gestured to the cabin. "It's a composting toilet. European too. The best in the market because *Gus* wanted nothing but the best."

Brandi sat on the cooler, ankle over one knee. "Gus left," she told Mack.

Sy joined her and gave a solemn nod.

Mack worked out how to respond and only came up with, "I've got trout. You hungry?"

Brandi and Sy nodded, and Pepper clapped her hands. "Fish tacos? I've got tortillas and salsa and some *queso fresco*," she said.

"Sounds yum," Brandi said. "What do you think, Mack?"

Mack didn't know what a fish taco was, but he could guess. "I'll make the fire."

"Nonsense," Pepper said. "Use my kitchen."

~

When she woke to find Mack gone, Brandi couldn't think. A first for her, since her brain never stopped. And unlike before, daytime made everything worse. Nothing but sagebrush surrounded them, divided by a lonely straight cut of road. A small herd of antelope grazed in the distance. She'd paced around the car, pulling at her fingers, panic fluttering inside her chest, and finally woken Sy, tugging at his arm, telling him they needed to go now. They'd hitchhike, she'd decided. But Sy wouldn't budge, and when she'd tried to drag him toward the road he screamed that eardrum-busting shriek, and it had woken Pepper, who'd busted out of her house with a can of bear spray. The antelope bounded quickly away. Pepper was the kind of friendly that Brandi felt like a hug. No suspicion, no doubt, willing to believe whatever Brandi said. So Brandi told her they were traveling with their grandad, and while it was a lie, Brandi decided it was also kinda true. They were traveling with Mack. And he was definitely old enough to be a grandad.

Now they sat in Pepper's teeny tiny kitchen watching Mack cook up the fish while Pepper laid out tortillas, cheese, and lime wedges and filled the house with her chatter. Brandi loved being around someone who talked almost as much as, maybe even more than, her. She wondered what Mack thought.

"Gus and I wanted to live off grid, you know, have no one to answer to but ourselves, not reliant on jobs and the grind and the money gods." Sy watched Pepper but sat close to Brandi on the small bench seat. He was gradually warming up to her, and she loved it. "So we saved up and bought this place and we came to Wyoming, since it's *the* place to live remote."

Mack slid the fish from the skillet onto a cutting board, and Pepper used a fork to shred it for the tacos before making up plates for each of them. They all sat at the table and ate, and inside her little house with all the wild outside, Brandi felt like she could breathe, buoyed by the optimism that came with it.

Mack finished his taco, wiped his mouth, and sat back. He'd taken his hat off and without it, Brandi thought he looked older. She wondered how old he was. "You said your husband left?" It was the first he'd spoken since offering up the fish.

Pepper laughed. "Oh, we're not married, thank God. I don't believe in institutions, and that one tops the list. But yeah, he left. Took the truck and his precious ATV and was gone before I woke up." She sucked at her teeth. "At least I'm young enough to learn from my mistakes, huh?"

"So what are you gonna do?" Brandi asked. They were alike, it seemed to her. Alone with no one but themselves to depend on.

"Well, I called my dad. He's driving from Sturgis with his truck. Actually, he's supposed to be here this afternoon." She sighed. "He never liked Gus."

Brandi couldn't help but feel disappointed. They were nothing alike. Pepper had a support system, she had a family, a way out. Brandi crossed her arms and sat back in her seat, her appetite from before gone.

Sy ate the rest of her taco.

"So you're on a little adventure trip with your grandkids. That's pretty sweet. Where're you all headed?"

"We're going to visit our grandmother," Brandi said quickly, wanting to make it seem like she had someone too. She was grateful when Mack didn't correct her.

"She's a nurse," Sy said, surprising Brandi, and Mack too from the way his eyebrows raised.

"No, Syborg, she *lives* in a nursing home."

Mack stood, replaced his hat, seeming much larger in the small room than he actually was. "Thank you for lunch." He stopped at the door, turned. "You're wrong about marriage being an institution. If you do it right, it makes you free."

He left, Sy fast on his heels and Brandi getting up to follow. Pepper's mouth hung slightly open. "The old codger hardly speaks, and then he drops some real knowledge."

Brandi watched the old man lope across the parking area, Sy by his side. "He's weird like that."

"A good weird though, huh?"

Brandi smiled. "Yeah, the good kind." She hesitated at the door. Pepper's small cabin smelled like fish, but it was also homey, with a hint of cinnamon from a candle she burned on the counter. They weren't the same. Pepper had a safety net. She had people who cared enough to haul her back home. But Brandi did see something of herself in the woman's optimism. Brandi had that too. She looked around the space: towels hung to dry on the stairs leading to a loft, knickknacks on display in cubbyholes, pictures of her travels in frames on the walls. Brandi would be happy in a place like this. Maybe someday she'd have something just like it.

Mack headed toward the RAV4 and slid into the driver's seat. Sy stood in the open doorway, watching. "Let's hope this works." He turned the key. Nothing.

He'd been hoping it would start, that last night they'd just been tired and needed the rest. But the pass was steep enough to drain what little he'd been able to siphon. He hit the steering wheel with his hand. "Goddang it."

"It's like totally out of gas, huh?" Brandi joined them, leaning against the SUV and staring out at the sagebrush. "What in the hell are we gonna do now?"

Mack had no easy answer apart from walking. But from here it would be a very long walk, longer than either of the kids could do.

"Too bad we don't have a dad like Pepper's to save the day." The girl said it to be funny, Mack knew, but he also felt the bitterness that came with it, and he couldn't blame her. "So, Mack, what do we do now?"

Mack pushed out of the car, stood beside Brandi. "I think you need to ask Pepper and her dad to give you and Sy a ride to Casper."

"What?" The one word was bruised with hurt. He felt a little like he was abandoning them too. A breeze kicked up the smell of grass and sage twisted through with sour remnants of dead skunk. Brandi lifted her face to the air and breathed it all in in one long and loud pull. "Fine." Her face had gone stiff, lips pressed together. "C'mon, Sy." She held out her hand to her brother. Sy's thin body swayed toward Mack like a magnet that Mack felt in the tug on his heart. "Please." Her voice a pitiful plea. The boy looked up at Brandi and touched the ponytail of his sweatpants, remembering, Mack hoped, her tenderness. Then he took Brandi's hand, and Mack saw her surprise betrayed by a lift of an eyebrow. "Oh, okay, Syborg." Brandi didn't look Mack in the eye when she said, "See you around, Mack." They walked across the lot, Sy with a glance back toward Mack, Brandi with a lift in her chin, shoulders straight.

Pepper stood outside her cabin, beating a small rug against the side of it. Mack watched Brandi approach, one arm hugging her stomach, the other holding Sy's and looking less confident than he'd grown used to expecting from her. Pepper was nodding, then gave a look at Mack across the lot, then was nodding again. She gave Brandi a hug, and the kids headed back over.

Mack straightened—looked like the kids had a ride. But the ground felt less stable, shifting from a sudden sense of loss that surprised him.

Brandi returned with her chin raised, her face determined. "Yeah, so we're all good. He should be here by dark. Thanks for, you know, getting us this far, I guess." She chewed on her bottom lip, looking at everything but Mack. "Guess you can go fish and walk your way back."

"I'll stay until you get on your way."

She sniffed. "That's your choice, I guess."

~

She walked away from the old man. He didn't owe them anything. In fact, he'd gotten them this far and kept them both safe, so why this

122

mushy spot in her chest that made it hard to breathe? There was a plaque of some kind in the center of the pull-off. She walked Sy over to it and with her back to Mack, she let her bottom lip tremble. *C'mon, Brandi!* She'd started this trip without him, and she didn't need him to finish it. She stared out over cracked earth, the land undulating gently in all directions toward distant mountains. Cotton-ball clouds white against a deep-blue sky. And she felt as small as she was. A speck of nothing compared to all this. The idea was weirdly comforting.

Sy let go of her hand. "Macky," he said in his soft voice. She sensed the old man beside them, and for once she let silence speak for her. She brushed a frizzy wad of hair out of her face, biting her tongue, her insides twisted through with gratefulness that the old man helped them get this far and anger that he could so easily leave them. Carissa was right. She did have a daddy complex. Like this old man would stick with them. He couldn't even save his wife. She gave up—silence made everything more confusing—and started to read the plaque. It was about the Oregon Trail. She brightened, remembering it from school. "Hey, Sy, you learned anything about the Oregon Trail yet?"

He sat on the ground at Mack's feet, skinny shoulders bowed under his dirty pajama top, and shrugged.

"Basically, it was used by a bunch of people in the old days, that's old with an *e*." She smiled at her own joke. "And it took years—"

"Five or six months," Mack interrupted, and Brandi shot him an annoyed look.

"Lots of *months* to go ten thousand miles."

"Two thousand," Mack said. Sy squinted up at them, and Brandi was pretty sure he was smiling the eensiest bit.

"Okay, two thousand miles, that's still a lot by the way, and it was super dangerous and hard as hell, and they rode in wagons with wooden wheels or they walked, and a lot of times they never made it. People died all over the place."

"Did they run out of gas too?" Sy asked, and Brandi laughed and sat down beside him, drawing her knees up.

Little by little, Sy was coming out of his shell, and the fact that he'd chosen her earlier over Mack meant she was doing something right. Her heart expanded so much it inched up her throat. "Nah, they didn't run out of gas, because they didn't have any to run out of in the first place." Sy had perked up, his eyes a shade brighter than before, interested. Brandi loved it. "And sometimes they got stuck. In fact, there was this one group, the Dahmer party, that got stuck in all this snow and ended up eating people to survive. And it happened right here." She stuck a finger into the crusty dirt.

Sy made a face. "Gross."

"Yeah, gross."

From above them, Mack cleared his throat. "It was the Donner party, and it happened in California."

It was coming back to Brandi. "Yeah, they left their wagon train to take some shortcut."

"They took the Hastings Cutoff."

"Right, that one." Brandi didn't mind Mack's corrections; it felt like she was in school. She'd really liked school and learning about history and people doing stuff that seemed impossible. Made her feel like even she could do something important one day. "Well, it was too late in the year, so they got stuck because of the snow." Pronghorns loped gracefully across the plains, the whites of their bellies dancing with the effort. "Rule number one, Sy."

Sy raised his eyebrows.

"Stick with the wagon train."

Sy turned serious. "Okay."

She stole a glance at Mack. The old man stared across the brown and green vista. She did the same, imagining the wooden clap of wagons jerking over the sagebrush. She hugged herself, wishing they didn't have to leave the old man. He was safe. He was known. She sighed, resigned. "So how do you know so much about the Oregon Trail, Mack?"

"Daisy and I liked to read about it. We ran an expedition company, and it was a little piece of history that our guests enjoyed learning about." He lifted his hat, then settled it back down, blew air through his lips, kicked at the ground with his boot. "Brandi." His voice was gruff, her name a call to attention, and Brandi sat up straighter. "Pepper seems honest. She can get you to Casper faster than I can. You and Sy need to be with your aunt Heather." He moved his mouth like he chewed tobacco. "And I need—"

"You need to be dead. I get it, Mack." And she did, for real this time. The thing about the world that Brandi already knew: everybody had their own shit to shovel. And Mack's was a mountain. She nodded, the truth a balm, smoothing away the hurt she'd felt at him leaving. She'd started this whole thing. It was her mountain and hers alone. The wind kicked up, sending her hair flying around her face in big chunks of frizz. "Do you know why all those people did the Oregon Trail?" she asked Sy.

He shrugged.

"So they could have a better life." She tapped him with her elbow. "Like you and me, Syborg. That's what we're doing. Finding you a better life."

"You too?"

Her throat tightened at his question. It was a good one, because she didn't know. She didn't think Aunt Heather would want anything to do with a damaged eighteen-year-old. She didn't really know if her aunt would want anything to do with Sy. Brandi's hands were fists. There was a whole lot she didn't know. But the one thing being older was teaching her—the truth usually sucked, and Sy didn't need to know it. "Yeah, me too."

They sat like that for a while, watching the sun sink lower to the horizon, Sy leaning lightly against her, Mack standing beside them, and nobody saying a thing.

~

Pepper seemed safe, and Mack knew that going with her was the fastest way for the kids to get to Casper. So why did it feel like he was bailing on them?

It was well past dusk when a large blue pickup truck pulled into the lot and backed up to the cabin. Pepper's dad got out of the truck, and Mack saw the woman launch herself into her father's arms. The man patted his daughter's back and held her until her shoulders stopped shuddering. He blinked, touched by the scene. Felt the ghostly weight of his son in the crook of his arm, pulled into his chest for a hug. He'd give anything for one more hug.

It took some time and the rest of the evening light, but eventually the pair hitched the cabin to the truck. Sy held on to Mack's stump, robot stuffie tight under his other arm. Brandi rhythmically shifted her weight from one side to the other. The brake light glowed red in the dark, then dimmed when the truck drove across the lot toward Mack and the kids, the cabin bouncing and creaking on its wheels. Something crept up to his throat. In a few minutes Brandi and Sy would be on their way to Casper, and Mack could go back to his cabin. But he wasn't ready to say goodbye. He shoved his hand into a pocket, forced himself to stay quiet. This was best for the kids and for him. Sy stood so close that his entire side felt glued to Mack's leg, the boy's head against his hip.

Pepper hopped out of the passenger side, opened the doors behind her, and one by one hefted out two five-gallon plastic containers, setting them heavily onto the ground at their feet. Mack's old heart let out an extra beat. Pepper straightened and pushed her glasses up the bridge of her nose. She smiled. "For you."

Brandi's nose wrinkled at the smell. Her face was blue in the evening light. "Gas?"

"You said you'd run out." Pepper laughed. "So I asked my dad to pick some up. You're going to visit your grandmother, right?" She looked at Mack. "Take it, please. Go see your wife."

Mack swallowed. He should say no, insist the kids go with them. It would be faster, safer. But Mack had a feeling, an instinct. How he knew where the fish would be biting, or the exact moment to take a shot when he was hunting. Or the way he'd felt the first time he'd met Daisy. A feeling he'd ignored for a few more minutes of sleep the morning Jesse drowned.

Brandi was looking at him, her hair wild around her face, mouth in an O. He wanted to see the kids all the way to Casper. He needed to know they were safe. "Thank you," he said.

Pepper swiped a hand in the air. "Family should stick together, right?" She pushed air through her lips. "Unless of course your name is Gus."

Brandi, who had been quiet the whole time, suddenly launched herself forward and threw her arms around the woman. Pepper laughed and hugged her back, rustled Sy's hair, and hurried to the truck. "Safe travels!" she called to them.

"Same to you," Mack and Brandi said at the same time.

Brandi picked up a container, grunting, and duck-walked over to the car. Mack joined her with the other one. Sy followed. Even in the dim light, he saw the girl's broad smile. "Guess you're stuck with us now, Mack. You believe that, Sy?" She leaned against the RAV4, tossed her head back. "I guess we're just too charming."

Sy nodded and mirrored his sister's head toss. "Yeah, guess we are."

Mack shook his head, smiling at their antics, the tension from before gone. He'd done the right thing. Daisy would agree. He emptied the first container into the SUV, the glug-glug of the liquid splashing into the tank a satisfying sound. After the second one, Brandi slid into the driver's seat and turned the key. "Over half a tank! Think we can make it all the way to Casper on this?"

"I think we might."

Mack and Sy joined Brandi in the car, and she drove to the edge of the lot, stopping and looking both ways down the empty road.

Mack figured she'd gotten turned around. "Turn right."

"Yeah, I know." She had both hands on the wheel, bending forward. "Thanks for sticking with us."

Mack coughed away the creeping heartburn. "Yep." He turned. "Put your seat belt on," he told Sy.

The car jerked onto the road, and Mack settled back for the few hours they had left to Casper.

Twelve

When Pepper gave them the containers filled with gas, Brandi couldn't believe her eyes. They had gas, finally, but it also meant that they didn't have to leave Mack yet.

She thought of how much Mack loved his wife. Enough to live alone in the woods. Sacrificing for someone who probably didn't remember him anymore. Brandi had never had anyone love her that much. She'd had a boyfriend once. And only once. He'd been really sweet and maybe not real smart, but he was nice to her and bought her a box of candy hearts on Valentine's Day. Then Brandi had to go and screw it all up by breaking into Mrs. T's house and getting arrested. Last she'd heard, he was some other girl's baby daddy.

Brandi felt so sad for Mack. And for Daisy. And for herself and for Sy and for all the sad things in the world that happened to everyone. But she was annoyed by something. Mack had only talked about his son from when he was a kid. She wondered if he'd grown up into a good-for-nothing like Mrs. T's son. Brandi hated that for Mack.

The old man had leaned back, hat over his face, and seemed to be asleep. Sy had curled up in the back with his arms covering his head. He'd slept a lot since she'd taken him. As though he hadn't slept through a single one of all the nights she'd been away. The thought gave her a pang. Getting away from her mom had been at the expense of her own brother's happiness. Brandi pinched her inner thigh hard, and a shock of pain traveled her leg. She deserved the pain and so much more.

Inside juvie, she'd had dreams of adopting Sy and together becoming a tiny, happy family. She'd hoped that if she explained how she'd loved him his whole life and had always made sure he'd had food and clean clothes and a safe bedroom, they'd see that she was perfect. That she was basically already his mom.

Ms. Hanno had made the truth crystal clear. It wasn't going to happen. With Brandi's record so far, it wasn't an option, especially not with Sy still in full custody of his mother. *Why don't you focus on yourself?* She'd been gentle when she'd said it, because Ms. Hanno understood Brandi. There were some people who were born to do their jobs. Ms. Hanno was one of them.

The wind shook the car and Brandi braced her arms, ready for the gust that would sweep them off the road. Out here it seemed the wind had nowhere to hide. It died as quickly as it appeared and she relaxed, allowing her thoughts to wander back to a time that glowed faintly with good memories and a visit from Aunt Heather.

Brandi and her mom were living at a house in a different town, maybe Jackson. She remembered that home only in bits and pieces. A little apartment behind a garage with a concrete patio and a kiddy pool where they sat with their feet in cold hose water on hot summer days. It was the good years. People were buying her mom's photos—Brandi had known that even if she'd only been a little kid because they'd celebrate with root beer floats each time one sold. They'd been out on the patio, Heather and Nancy sitting in folding chairs, toes dipping into and out of the water. Brandi was on the concrete making shapes on a piece of paper with a Spirograph set Aunt Heather had brought as a gift. A late-spring sun greedy for summer warmth prickled Brandi's arms with a light heat.

You seem happy, Nancy.

Her mother had laughed, but it wasn't the funny kind. *Do I?* There was a bitterness in her voice. Brandi peeked up from her red, blue, and yellow ellipses. Nancy held a soda can between her fingers, head tilted back to the sun, neck exposed. *Happy doesn't keep me clean. You know that, right, Heather?* Brandi turned back to the sand. She was old enough to know when a conversation wasn't about her. *I haven't used since Brandi came home. I'm in recovery, where I'll be for the rest of my life.*

I know. Aunt Heather whispered like she was sharing a secret.

But I'm not that person anymore. Here her mother's voice had trembled. *You can't take her away again.*

I won't. As long as you keep providing for her and stay clean.

Brandi held a bigger plastic circle with one hand and with the tip of the marker inside a smaller circle made loops on the page, adding more pressure each time, her hand, the paper, absorbing the tense exchange.

My photos are good, maybe even really good. I might even be great someday.

Aunt Heather had leaned forward in her seat, touching the arm of her mom's chair. Nancy stared at the can in her hand.

How would I know that? You don't reach out, Nancy. I want to be a part of your life. I want to know my niece. I miss you both so much.

Brandi couldn't remember what happened after that. Except that her aunt visited a few more times, bringing books and toys and cooking elaborate meals with vegetables Brandi hid in a napkin and flushed down the toilet. Aunt Heather would tell stories that made Nancy laugh, and the three of them piled on the couch to watch Disney Channel shows together. Those good days obscured the storm clouds brewing on the horizon. Brandi didn't notice until the sun disappeared behind them, taking all the good with it. A few years later, Nancy moved them to a new town, with a new boyfriend, and Brandi never saw Heather again.

Did Aunt Heather know about Sy? Was she the same person, or had she become like Brandi's mother? Brandi tried not to think about it, because if Aunt Heather had moved or didn't want anything to do with her and Sy, she had nowhere else to turn.

The car sailed forward, and the driving kept all her fears from bugging her with the what-ifs. As far as Brandi was concerned, she'd made her choice, and there was no point worrying. It would either work out or it wouldn't. She sucked on her lip. It would work out. It had to.

A sign for the road Mack had mentioned loomed out of the darkness, its reflective numbers shiny. CASPER. She pursed her lips, struck by a thought. Another sign said LANDER. Goose bumps across her skin from where the jerk had touched her. The way he stood in the doorway, blocking her way, expectant and ready to take whatever he wanted from her. A queasiness at how easily he could have. Except for Mack. Who for no reason had stopped it even though he could have easily left her and Sy behind and saved himself. He had Daisy to be dead for.

Brandi smiled to herself and kept her foot on the gas, headlights slipping off the sign for Casper and shooting forward. *To Lander.* Mack would be mad, she was sure, but Brandi figured it might be nice for him to be close to his wife, even if it was just from the parking lot. It wasn't much, but it was the only way she knew how to truly thank him.

~

The car hit a pothole, and Mack's eyes flew open. He shot up, hat falling from his head, to find the car surrounded by streetlights and a few buildings. It couldn't be Casper. He hadn't slept that long. He gripped the edge of his seat. Dang it, Brandi must have missed the turn.

The girl was grinning at him, and Mack's stomach sank. She was up to something.

"I hope you know where it is."

Sy had scooched up between the seats, staring at Mack with what looked like a tiny smile on his face. It struck Mack with a deep sadness. Whenever he thought of Jesse, it was of his smile first because it was nearly always present. Sy's smile was a rare sight.

"Where what is?" But he knew what she was asking. This was Lander, and from the satisfied look on Brandi's face, she knew it.

"The place where Daisy's staying. How do I get there?"

His leg muscles tightened. He was angry—no, he was shocked. Mack told himself to breathe. "I can't visit her, Brandi."

"I know that. I'm not stupid. But we could sit in the parking lot so you could be close to her. I know it's not the same as seeing her, but I thought . . ." She frowned. "I'm sorry. Was this a bad idea?" She sucked on her lip, looked at Sy. "Sometimes I don't think. Rule number one: be a better thinker than I am, okay, Sy? Ms. Hanno says part of my problem, I mean part of my"—she put air quotes around the next word—"*challenges* is that I don't think before I do. Personally, I think that makes me interesting, but not to everyone, I guess." Her smile had faded, replaced with a worried wrinkle in her forehead. "I wanted to do something for you because, you know, well, the asshole and the fact that you didn't leave us last night like I thought you had."

He ran his palm over the bald spot on his head. This was her way of saying thanks. It was dark, late enough that a town like Lander had been quiet for some time. He didn't know anybody here except for Daisy, and Brandi was right: even sitting in the parking lot might ease the pain of missing her. "Take a left here, then your first right."

She did as he said, and when they pulled into an empty parking lot beside the home, Mack's heart turned inside out. It was a squat building with just one floor, sliding glass doors that opened to a foyer with fake wood floors and walls papered in pinkish-red flowers as big as his head. When Mack visited, half the residents would be in the foyer, in wheelchairs, staring out the glass doors as though waiting for somebody to save them. It had made him sick to leave her here.

After she was diagnosed, Daisy had disappeared into their bedroom and gone quiet. Mack had let her be. She didn't speak for a week; then one morning she got out of bed, showered, and was in the kitchen making breakfast. Mack sat at the table and watched as Daisy piled his plate with pancakes, slabs of melted butter slipping over the sides and into a pile of crispy bacon. She added a mug of dark coffee brewed strong. Then she'd sat across from him, sipping her own coffee and pinning him with those green eyes of hers that gutted him like they had the very first time.

You will not take care of me.

She was always a perfect balance, a feminine strength that ran so deep he didn't think there was an end. Nothing stopped her. Not a husband with one arm, a son whose absence was a black hole, a failed business. She never wavered, never weakened, even when that meant leaving Mack to save herself.

He'd met her gaze. *I will take care of you until the end.* He'd taken a bite of pancakes, never breaking eye contact.

The slightest tremble in her bottom lip, but her voice was steel. *I don't want the end. I want—* She'd choked on her coffee, swallowed, and composed herself.

He'd held her hand, humbled. Mack floundered after Jesse died, lost his way, too weighed down by grief to open his goddang eyes to the fact that he wasn't alone. He'd tried the coward's way out without a thought to what it would do to his wife. She'd found ways to move forward, to find joy even in her grief. Mack couldn't see past his own. He'd figured she'd be better without him. He thought it was the only answer. But Daisy had found him, stopped him, her face twisted with betrayal and a sorrow that ran so deep it boiled.

So she left him because she knew she couldn't save herself and him. And for three years he was forced to figure out why living meant something when he'd lost everyone he'd loved.

I'll remember for the both of us.

A light had slipped out of her eyes, turning them flat, and she'd taken her hand away, set it on her lap. *That's what I'm afraid of.*

"What's she like?" Brandi's voice was soft, like they were in church and she was speaking during the sermon.

Mack sighed. "Beautiful, smart, steady when she's not wild, resourceful, kind. She's also stubborn and set in her ways." He coughed, waited for the heartburn to fade. "She never deserved this."

"Mack?"

He looked at her.

"Can I visit her for you? I could tell them I'm her granddaughter or her niece or something like that."

It was in odd moments like this when he felt the loss of his arm, the empty space where once there had been a part of him. He wanted to hug Brandi with both arms. But he couldn't, and Mack wasn't much into physical displays anyway. Still, a moment like this made him wish he was a lot of things he wasn't. A hint of Jesse in the car. His natural exuberance for the smallest of things. Brandi kept reminding Mack of his son. He stroked his beard and breathed in.

"You know, I could just sit with her a bit. Be a visitor. I won't say anything about you being alive, but I could, you know—"

"Yes, please do that."

Brandi's eyes opened wide. "Oh, cool. Okay." She unbuckled, looked back at Sy. "You stay here with Mack, okay? I won't be long."

Sy reached out and held the end of Mack's stump. Seemed to be a thing for him now, and Mack liked the way it felt. From his neck, Mack pulled a necklace over his head. His wedding ring dangled from the chain. "Give this to her."

She put it around her own neck. "You sure?"

"I am." He cleared his throat. "Brandi?"

"Yes?"

"Thank you."

Her smile lit up every crease of her youthful face. "You're welcome, Mack."

"Go to the door on the south side of the building." When she gave him that look of hers, he pointed. "That side. There's an after-hours entrance there." If there was one nice thing he could say about this place, they encouraged family visits, even at night. Daisy had always been a night owl, so Mack had grudgingly appreciated it.

Brandi slipped out of the car and kept her head ducked, walking fast across the lot and to the building. He tapped at his chest with a fist and watched her disappear through the sliding glass doors, overwhelmed by a deep longing to see his wife, to hold her hand, to kiss her on the lips.

Thirteen

"I have to pee."

Brandi had just disappeared around the corner of the building when Sy spoke. He had wiggled up between the seats, resting on his side and staring at Mack. His face was heart-shaped, and his lips, Mack noticed, were dry.

"Real bad."

"Well, then, let's get you to a tree." They were parked at the edge of an empty lot beside the nursing home and behind a row of trees.

Mack got out of the car and led Sy to the edge of the mostly empty parking lot and a stand of thin aspens.

"Aim at one of those." Mack gestured to the white bark. It brought back memories of camping, when Jesse would wake him up in the middle of the night. *Dad, I have to go.* Mack standing beside him with a canopy of stars above them, the outlines of pine-needled branches reaching toward the sky, the hiss of Jesse's pee, all of it wrapped in the cool early-morning quiet. It had been perfect. Mack felt it even then. What he didn't understand was how fragile it was.

Sy stepped forward and pushed the sweatpants to his ankles. The knot Brandi had tied earlier popped off. Again Mack noticed how painfully thin he was, his legs no more than sticks. He looked away. "Goddang it." Anger stoked a fire in his gut; the boy had been abandoned in whatever life Brandi had taken him from. He was lucky to have her.

Sy pulled up his pants and gave him a solemn look. "Goddamn it," he said.

"Excuse me?" Shocked to hear the word on the little boy's tongue.

"That's how you 'opposed to say it." He was very serious, his eyebrows raised like he was helping Mack.

Mack took a knee, picked up the elastic band, and stared at the sweatpants, trying to figure out how he could possibly fit it back on.

"The girl can do it," Sy said.

"Your sister."

The boy said nothing.

"She's trying to help you. Do you understand that, Sy?"

He shrugged.

"What was . . ." Mack pulled at his beard, wished his thoughts translated as easily to words as Daisy's always had. "Were you safe at your home?" Safe. Was Daisy safe in there? Were they treating her cancer? Helping her get better the way she deserved? His mind wandered to the other side of the sliding glass doors, muscles tensed in an effort to ignore a yearning to run inside and hold her. They said he couldn't keep her safe. The truth of it lived in small glimpses of the past. Unmade and dirty bedsheets. Mice droppings in the corners of a kitchen with crusted pans, used plates, and overflowing trash. A home Daisy would never have abided. He hadn't meant for it to get that bad. *Where's Jesse?* She'd taken to looking for him in closets, under beds, behind doors, a never-ending game of hide-and-go-seek. *3-2-1, I'm gonna find you, turkey.* Frantic tears, panic, knees and hands raw from scrambling across the floor, flinging open cabinet doors. Mack on repeat. *Jesse's not here, Daisy. He's not here.* Burrowing into her world and not saying the words that gut-punched him and wore him down until he didn't see the filth.

Mack closed his eyes, forced the past to fade away, and opened them to find that Sy's solemn expression hadn't changed. His brown eyes absorbed everything but didn't let much out. Reminded him of a hunted animal when it's expertly shot, a peaceful surrender on the outside belying the ravage of the bullet. Mack wondered at the damage to Sy's insides.

The boy leaned in close until his nose was inches from Mack's face. "I was scared of the zombies," he whispered.

"Zombies, huh?"

"If I go asleep, they eat my brains."

"That must of made it hard to sleep, then," Mack said.

Sy nodded and in the orange glow of the streetlight, Mack noticed the dirt on his face, the state of his clothes, and, this close up, the smell of unwashed hair, fuzzy teeth. "I bet you'd like to take a bath, huh, Sy? Maybe get some clean clothes?"

"I got poop on me. The girl wasn't mad, though."

"Brandi. Your sister's name is Brandi."

Sy didn't blink.

Mack stood and together they walked to the SUV. Mack leaned against its side and breathed in the fresh night air. Sy did the same. "Getting a bit musty in the car, isn't it, Sy?" The SUV had an unpleasant smell to it, a chemical kind of stink that he couldn't place. "And, Sy? It's goddang it or just dang it."

"Why?"

Mack blew air through his nose, amused. Questioning everything, just like his sister. "It's a bit nicer to say."

Sy touched Mack's missing arm. "Did a zombie eat your arm?"

Mack wiggled the stump, which made Sy giggle. "Oh, no, it wasn't so scary as that. It was just a regular old grizzly bear."

Sy's eyes went round. "Was he humongous?"

"She was a bigun, that's for sure."

"But why?"

"Because she thought I was going to hurt her cubs."

"Were you?"

"Oh, no." Sy craned his neck to look up at Mack, so Mack sat on his heels, hips balanced against the car. "See, we were just out for a morning walk, picking berries and minding our own business." Sy moved so that he leaned a bit into Mack; the kid seemed to crave the contact. Like Jesse had. Mack sniffed. "All of a sudden, this sow charged out of the trees and straight at us."

"Were you scared?"

"That's a funny thing. I was scared. But I also wanted to protect my wife and boy."

Sy squatted down like Mack, listening.

"Sometimes we do things even when we're scared or maybe because of it." Mack held up his stump. "So I slowed her down with my arm."

A smile broke across Sy's face, showing missing teeth and dimples on both cheeks. "And she ate it instead of your boy! Goddang it!" Sy giggled, holding his stomach even though the giggles were only in his chest. The moment passed, and something closed behind his eyes. "I hate being scared."

Mack nodded, feeling a pang at the boy's words. "I know, bud."

~

The glass doors slid open to a confined area with another set of doors that didn't open. To her left was a small table with a sign-in sheet for after-hours visitors. It was just nine thirty. Brandi bit at her nail. Didn't old people go to bed super early? She wrote a name, Brandi Anders, and filled in *Daisy Anders* under the slot for who she was visiting. She hesitated, wrote *granddaughter* under *relation to resident*. Then she rang the little doorbell and waited.

It took another ring and more waiting before a disheveled woman in fluorescent-pink scrubs opened the doors. She glanced at the sign-in sheet, gave Brandi a quick look before tearing off a sticker that read Visitor and handing it to her. "Have you visited before?"

Brandi pushed the sticker against her sweatshirt. "No."

"Room 107. Down that hallway. Daisy's a night owl, so I'm sure she'll be happy to see you." The woman in scrubs hurried away, her black Crocs quiet on the floor.

"That was easy," Brandi murmured to the empty lobby. The hallway lights were dimmed, and Brandi tiptoed. It felt like the middle of the night. Most of the doors were closed, some cracked, television lights flashing blue and white inside. Each door had a homemade paper sign with the person's name. Brandi smiled: Don on the back of a Colorado Rockies jersey, Judy on a teapot. With its musty wallpaper and dark hallways, the place was dreary, there was no denying it. The detention center had been like that. Old-ass showers with mold in the corners and hair in the drain. Bland colors everywhere except for the purple shirts her unit wore. But, like here, there'd be small bright spots. Construction-paper gardens with electric-yellow suns, motivational sayings about failure and success on the bathroom stalls. All from someone who cared enough about the girls to try and warm the place up with a few cheesy slogans and fake flowers. Most of the girls thought it was stupid. But it wasn't a small thing to Brandi. She loved the idea that even in a place where the staff was paid nothing and the girls drowned in their own trauma, there was someone who loved their job. Someone who decided that their mission in life was to make depressing places better.

Brandi thought that was pretty cool.

She got to room 107 and touched the picture taped to the closed door. Daisy was written in the black center of a flower with yellow petals. *Pretty.* She breathed in and knocked.

Nothing. Her fingers drew nervous circles into her hip. Knocked again. Mack's wedding ring felt heavy against the bones of her chest. Coming here was another one of her "rash" decisions. Daisy was a total stranger. Mack was a total stranger. What was she thinking?

The door opened to a room flooded with light, and standing in the doorway was the prettiest old lady Brandi had ever seen. She wore a white robe over pink pajama pants and fuzzy slippers, and her hair was pulled into a girlish ponytail. Brandi decided right then that she would have a ponytail when she was old too. But it was her eyes that blew Brandi away. This dark-green color that flashed golden when it caught the dim hallway light, and despite her white hair, she had strawberry blonde eyebrows and dark lashes that any girl would kill for. "Wow, Mack wasn't crazy. You're fucking beautiful!"

Daisy's lips pursed and Brandi rounded her eyes, getting the same feeling she got when she'd cussed in front of Warden Trujillo.

"Sorry! I mean, Mack talked about you like you're drop-dead gorgeous, and I thought he was probably saying it from love, you know? But, like, you really are!"

Daisy touched her hair with one hand, looked past Brandi. "Mack's here?" Her soft voice shook, and her back slumped when she leaned heavily over a walker.

"Oh, sorry, no, not right here, but I told him I'd visit you." Brandi swallowed. "Can I come in?"

With a lot of effort, Daisy pushed the walker across the small room and carefully eased into one of those big comfy rockers. Brandi found a folded plastic chair in the corner and set it opposite Daisy, who stared out the darkened window, maybe looking at her own reflection or the framed pictures that crowded the windowsill. Brandi couldn't tell.

"So, um, well, how are you?"

Daisy didn't answer.

Brandi noticed a picture of Mack and Daisy, probably on their wedding day. She giggled and picked it up to take a closer look. Mack had long hair even then, with a hilarious-looking thin mustache that wiggled around the corners of his mouth. He wore a bell-bottom powder-blue suit and cowboy boots, and next to Daisy, he could have been a stand-in for the actual groom. Not that he wasn't kinda cute in his own way, but Daisy, she was just on a whole other level.

"The monkeys came with the rain again today."

Brandi looked up from the photo of Daisy as a young woman to the one huddled and shrunken in her chair. She seemed so lost. Brandi blinked many times. "Did you say monkeys?"

Daisy's reflection nodded. "They come with the rain."

It had been a clear blue sky all day. "Oh, did it rain here today?"

Daisy pulled at her fingertips.

"Carissa, that's my friend, well, she had a cocaine problem. Anyway, she said once she got so high she saw Bigfoot." Brandi pulled at the frayed edges of a hole in her jeans, ripping it so that it exposed her entire knee.

Daisy turned at the sound, eyes narrowed at Brandi's jeans. "Did you fall? I can mend those for you."

"It's the style actually—" At the confusion in Daisy's eyes, Brandi stopped. "Sure, thanks, that's nice of you."

Daisy nodded, turned back to the window. "Jesse fell off his bike and got a hole in his brand-new jeans."

"Is Jesse your son? Mack likes to talk about him too. He must be a good dad, because Sy really likes him." Brandi rested an ankle on her thigh, leaned back in the chair. "Sy's my little brother." Brandi rocked the tips of her toes back and forth on the floor, searching for things to talk about. "He's always hungry."

"Little brother?" Daisy rocked the chair, then pulled a leather bag from a pocket on the side and handed it to Brandi. Her hand shook so badly the bag flopped in the air. "You'll be needing this."

"Mack has one just like it!"

"Just make sure you put the leaves on the bottom to make a nest for the raspberries. No sense smooshing the berries." Daisy smiled then, shaking her head. "Jesse eats the berries as soon as he picks them."

"I bet Sy would do the same. That kid's eaten all the snacks I got for him." She was getting the hang of the awkwardness, even enjoying the conversation. Monkeys and all.

"Sy?"

"My little brother. The one who's hungry all the time."

Daisy's upper lip started to tremble. "Have you seen Jesse? He went fishing and I can't find him." She leaned forward and gripped the arms of the chair, and the sudden shift alarmed Brandi. The old woman was getting so upset, and she had no idea why.

"Um, I don't know where Jesse is." She half rose from her chair, looked around just in case Jesse was behind her.

Daisy gripped Brandi's arm with her fingers. "Can you tell him to come home? It's getting dark. Please?" The old woman's voice cracked, weak and pitiful, and Brandi did the only thing that felt right. She lied.

"Yeah, sure, of course, I'll tell him to come home right this minute. But don't worry, I'm sure he's okay."

Another shift in the old woman; someone else slipping inside her skin and turning the light on. She relaxed, leaning back into her chair, and reached for one of the pictures. It trembled in her hands. "He wants Mack to build him a cabin so he can live in the mountains one day. It's in his blood."

"Is that Jesse?" She peeked at the picture in Daisy's hands. A little boy with black hair that hung into his eyes in Mack's arm, holding up a tiny fish like his catch would feed a village. "Oh, he's so cute," Brandi said. "And Mack looks so young!"

"You know Mack?"

Brandi looked up at the ceiling. She was talking too much, but she couldn't just stop now. That would be rude. Besides, she liked Daisy. "We're kinda on the run from my tweaker mom, and Mack's helping us."

"That sounds like Mack."

"It does? Because I don't think he wanted to help us at first."

Daisy laughed, and it was light and feminine. Brandi snort-laughed, and there was nothing girlish about it.

"He's a good man." Daisy's face clouded. "Except he won't do what I want. That's why I called Peggy."

"Who's Peggy?"

"Peggy loves horses."

"Oh, cool." Brandi slid her hands under her thighs and rocked back in her seat. "I've only ever ridden a horse once, and it's when I went shed hunting. Don't even ask me why I went, because I'm not an outdoors kind of girl. But it was about a boy. Pathetic, right?"

Daisy's eyebrows raised with her smile. "Was he the right kind of boy?"

"No, ma'am, he was not."

Daisy laughed softly. "One day you'll find the right kind of boy."

Brandi was warmed by the old woman's romantic optimism. Her only experience had been with the one boy, and that had been mildly disappointing. It had never gone well for her mom. Besides, Brandi had *a lot* of work to do on herself, and she planned to start there. "Carissa thinks every boy she flirts with is the right boy." Daisy laughed like she knew Carissa, and for a second, Brandi felt like she did. She touched the ring under her shirt and pulled it out. "I almost forgot. Mack wanted you to have this."

Daisy stared at the ring but didn't take it, and Brandi worried she'd done the wrong thing. Until the old woman held out her hand, and Brandi let it fall into her wrinkled pink palm. Daisy made a fist around it and held it to her heart, tears on her face. "Thank you."

"He loves you so much, you know." Brandi's throat was almost too tight to speak, but she did anyway. "He'd die for you, that's how much he loves you." Carissa had a boyfriend she talked about all the time, like about all the sex things she did to him and all the babies they were going to have. The girl was ob-sessed. Brandi had thought that was love. Until now.

From the door came a friendly voice. "A late-night party in here, huh, Daisy?"

And just like that, Mack's Daisy slipped away, deflating the woman in the chair, and it was so shocking, Brandi stood abruptly. "Well, Grandma, I've got to go." Backed toward the door, past the cheerful nurse with black hair and a cool-ass nose ring. "And, well, I love you." It felt odd to say, but Brandi wanted this woman to know she was loved, and if Mack couldn't tell her, then she would. "Everybody, you know, loves you."

"I love you too," Daisy said back, and the nurse smiled at Brandi.

When she was in the hall, Brandi felt a sob wanting to come out, and she punched her chest to keep it stuffed inside.

"You okay, honey?"

She swung around to find the nurse standing outside Daisy's door, kindness bleeding from her eyes. Her tag said JANIECE.

"Yeah, no, I mean, it's hard to see her like that, you know?"

"I do."

"Is she doing okay?"

"As well as can be expected. Most days she can't get out of bed. And the cancer has made her so much weaker. Hospice will give her some comfort."

"Why?" She had no idea what hospice meant.

Janiece tilted her head. "To give her peace before she passes."

"From Alzheimer's?" Brandi knew her questions might get her in trouble. Shouldn't the granddaughter know what's what? But she could sense the nurse was saying something important, and she wanted to understand. For Mack.

"From the cancer, sweetheart."

"Oh." Her heart crumpled into a ball. Poor Mack. His Daisy was dying. She crossed her arms—something was wrong. Pieces of conversation floated loose in her memory. Hadn't Mack wanted his money to go toward treating Daisy's cancer? And if they were having a memorial service for him, then they thought he was dead. Anger burned. How could they just let her die? "But Mack . . . I mean Grandpa's dead and all. Didn't he—" The nurse looked at her in a way that Brandi was used to, with suspicion. Brandi swallowed. "I'm pretty sure Grandpa left her money to take care of the cancer and stuff."

The nurse tilted her head, then looked down the hallway and smiled. She looked relieved. "Peggy's here. How lovely for our night owl. She's the one you need to speak with."

"Who?" It was out before she could stop herself.

Janiece pointed down the hall. "Her guardian."

Brandi turned to see a very tall woman with wild blonde hair striding down the hallway. A soundtrack of tense music played in her head. She had to get out of there. "Yeah, right, I know." She forced a smile and a wave. "See you later."

Brandi was a sweaty mess. She didn't want to ruin everything for Mack. The other end of the hallway looked like it ended in a nurses' station. Her only exit was back the way she'd come and past the woman who looked like she could pick Brandi up with two fingers. Brandi's pulse raced, and her lungs couldn't keep up. She moved her feet as fast as she could without running. The woman's work boots squeaked across the tiles, coming closer.

"Hey, Peggy," called Janiece from behind her. "You know Daisy's granddaughter?"

Brandi was almost even with the woman now, and she couldn't help but shift her gaze up. Peggy stared down at her, blonde and gray hair shaggy around her face, a question in her eyes. "What? Hold up," she said and stepped in front of Brandi, a wall of woman. "Who did you say you are?" She spoke in a hushed voice, like she didn't want the nurse to hear.

"Nobody, I'm nobody and I'm leaving." Brandi tried to go, but Peggy blocked her way.

"Thanks, Janiece! Tell Daisy I'll be there in a minute." The nurse disappeared inside the room. Peggy turned her full attention on Brandi.

She squared her shoulders and tried to act confident, like it was her first day of juvie and she was the new girl about to get her ass kicked. "Hey, listen, no harm, okay? I . . . well, I like to visit old people, like community service, you know? Because my grandmother was in a place like this, and I never got to visit her." She searched her brain for any excuse that might make sense. "So sometimes I just like to visit little old ladies, and maybe I lie about who I am." It was lame.

The woman's expression remained the same, neutral, giving nothing away. Brandi dug her nails into her palms.

"Where is he?"

"What? Who?" She shifted her weight, a rabbit caught in the crosshairs.

Peggy leaned down until they were at eye level, making Brandi feel like a child. "Is he here?"

Brandi forced a laugh. "Lady, I have no idea what you're talking about. I told you. I like to visit old people."

Brandi moved around the woman, hands in fists, ready to run but trying to keep her cool. Nothing guiltier than a runner. To her surprise, Peggy didn't try to stop her.

"Tell him we're not treating the cancer."

That stopped Brandi in her tracks. "Why?" she whispered.

"He knows why." Peggy's voice grew soft. "I don't know why you're mixed up with him, but I know that whatever Mack does has purpose, so I'll let it be. But can you tell him something for me?"

Brandi stayed put, head hung.

"She knew what she asked of him was unfair. She just didn't want him to bear it alone. Understand?"

Brandi nodded, her back to the woman, chin trembling. This felt too big for her, too much weight to carry with all the other stuff on her shoulders, and she wanted to crumple to the floor and give up.

"Tell him—"

She exploded into a sprint and darted out the front doors. The woman may have followed, but Brandi never looked back.

~

"Drive, Mack! Drive!" A breathless Brandi, crying out as she ran toward the car, set Mack's heartbeat galloping. He opened the back door, helped Sy scramble inside, then took the driver's seat and started the car, foot to the gas. Brandi jumped inside, squeaked, "Go." And Mack took off. In the rearview mirror, he saw the door to the nursing home open and a familiar figure step outside, but then he jerked the car onto the road and left it all behind.

Brandi's labored breathing settled into silence; the girl pulled into herself. It was a change that Mack didn't like. "What happened in there?"

She slumped low in her seat and stared out the window, chewing on a piece of her hair. "Daisy's so sweet and she's pretty, just like you said."

A hollow ache in his chest and doubt settled in a headache between his eyes.

"Don't you miss her?"

"Every second."

"Don't you think she needs you?"

He didn't have an answer, couldn't fully inflate his lungs. Halos around the streetlights made it hard to see well, and a wetness spreading in his eyes only added to his troubles.

"She loves you. There're pictures of you everywhere and of Jesse. Where is he anyway? Does he visit her?" A hardness in her voice, like she'd already passed judgment.

Mack's hand went numb from his grip on the wheel, and he steeled himself, reminded that Brandi didn't know anything. "What happened in there?" he repeated.

"There was some woman, a guardian or some Avengers shit like that, and she knew I wasn't Daisy's granddaughter. Peggy. Who is she?"

"Peggy's a court-appointed person. And she's a good friend." Mack spied a Goodwill sign ahead and made a decision, pulling into the empty lot. He drove around to the back of the store and turned off the car.

"She can make decisions for Daisy?"

"As her guardian, yes." He shifted in his seat, fighting a desire to drive straight back to the nursing home to see his wife. "Was Daisy okay?" It was all he needed to know.

A pause. "She talked about Jesse and you. I can tell she loves you. There's a really pretty blanket on her bed with all these colorful squares."

The quilt she'd worked on for most of her life, and one she'd folded carefully over the arm of her favorite chair at home.

"And there are pictures everywhere and plants too. Oh, and she gave me this, told me to put leaves in the berries or something like that."

She held up the small foraging bag, the one Daisy had made for Jesse all those lifetimes ago. He sniffed—Daisy always had an eye for need, and it didn't surprise him one bit that she'd sussed that out in Brandi.

"The nurse seemed nice. And her room is homey. It looks like someone loves her."

Mack finally met Brandi's eyes. It was what he needed to hear to know he'd done the right thing. But being this close to Daisy was physically painful. "Let's get your brother some clothes that fit."

"We don't have money." Brandi scrunched up her nose at the dark store. "Anyway, it's closed."

"Has that ever stopped you before?"

She smiled. "Nope. But I am trying to be a new leaf, you know."

He nodded. "The way I see it, there's stealing and there's taking that's for a purpose. Seems to me this one's for a good reason. Sy needs to look his best before he meets this aunt of yours." He pointed. "There's bins overflowing in back. We'll just take from there, and it won't hurt anybody." Daisy had loved Goodwill, both to donate old clothes and for shopping. The woman knew how to find a bargain and was an expert on stretching pennies. He pointed at the cardboard bins lined up along the back of the store. "But I'll need your help."

Brandi turned in her seat, smiling at her brother. "Hear that, Syborg? You're getting out of those poopy old sweatpants." She opened her door. "Time to slay the dragon, Shrek," she said to Mack.

He wrinkled his forehead. "What?"

But the girl just laughed. "C'mon, Sy, let's do some *not* stealing."

Fourteen

The bins smelled like ass. And they overflowed with everything from clothes to shoes, blankets with holes, and art pictures in broken frames. The kind of stuff that couldn't even make it into the store. Like poor people would be grateful for trash. Brandi stood in one of the bins, pinching her nose while she sifted through the junk. Mack was in another bin, a big old raccoon rooting around with his one hand.

Sy stood by the SUV watching, holding his *Minecraft* stuffie with one hand, sucking the thumb of his other hand. Had he sucked his thumb before? It was a pitiful sight. Something she expected from a little baby.

Toward the back of the bin was a bag that didn't look like it belonged. A cloth one from the kind of store where kids without meth moms shopped. With fabric handles that had been knotted twice. She untied it. "Yes!" Inside were carefully folded and *clean* kids' clothes. Brandi punched the air. Here was someone who got it. She hopped out of the bin and hurried over to Sy, calling to Mack. "Found something!"

It wasn't perfect—the clothes were still too big for someone as skinny as her brother—but it was better than what they had now. Better than her mom's sweatpants. Bitterness thinned her lips. The sooner they got rid of anything that reminded them of her, the better. She started to pull the sweatpants off of Sy.

"Not just yet," Mack said, joining them. "One more stop first."

"Why? He smells so bad."

"I know." Mack picked up the bag. "One more stop." Sy trotted after him like a little puppy.

~

Brandi drove this time. She might not have her license and, before this, very little to no actual experience behind the wheel, but she'd decided that of the two of them, she was the safer option. With the way Mack squinted at the road, hugging the white line, crossing the yellow, slowing down to a crawl when he wasn't sure, well, that was enough for Brandi to take over. Plus it was good to do something instead of focusing on what the woman from the nursing home had told her. How could she tell Mack that he'd failed? A spike of anger at being responsible for breaking the old man's heart. Why her?

Mack had told her to head back toward the road that went to Casper, but right before they left the edge of town and the glow of lights, he had her turn into a motel parking lot. The kind of place that had ice machines outside, a broken vacancy sign that glowed ANCY.

Sirens sounded in her head, and Brandi tensed. She'd gotten too comfortable with Mack, too trusting. What did she really know about him? He was pretending to be dead, had a son who seemed like a dick for not visiting his mom, a wife alone and dying.

"Pull—"

"Around back, yeah, I know." Instead, she pulled into a spot in front.

Mack breathed through his teeth, looking over his shoulder, out the window. "Not here."

Brandi put the car in Park, crossed her arms, and glared at Mack. "Why not?" She didn't really think he had anything bad planned, but suspicion was a feeling she was used to. Better than this deep sadness that had settled in her stomach since leaving Daisy. It was like she'd pulled back Mack's skin and glimpsed his most tender places. It made him suddenly vulnerable, and up to this point Brandi hadn't thought of him like that. He was strong and sure and unstoppable.

His hat was on his lap, and without its wide brim, Mack diminished a bit. The sharp angles in his shoulders pressed against his shirt. The truth played on the tip of her tongue. *Daisy wants to die. She doesn't want your money.* But Brandi couldn't bring herself to hurt him like that. Maybe that woman was wrong.

Mack's jaw twitched. "Most of these rooms are empty, and this kind of motel has small windows in the bathroom. I'm going to see if I can work one open, then crawl through and open the front door."

Brandi tried to revive her tough-girl face from before she knew Mack. "And why do we need a motel room?"

Mack seemed unfazed. "So you can give the boy a bath before he meets his aunt." He turned to Sy. "Be nice to feel clean, wouldn't it?"

Brandi was ready for anything else. That he was going to leave them there, that he'd called the cops on her, that he was going to tie them up and gut them with his hunting knife. As much as she'd allowed herself to trust this man, doubts wiggled through the cracks. She'd been failed over and over by people who said they cared about her: her mom, Mrs. T, Aunt Heather. In some sick way, imagining Mack would do the same was comforting in its predictability. So this, offering to put himself at risk to give her brother a chance to wash the filth from his body, was a level of kindness that Brandi felt unprepared for. She blinked and blinked again, words failing.

Sy spoke instead. "We're gonna steal water?"

Mack shook his head. "Nah, we're just going to borrow it for a bit."

"But what if they catch us?" Brandi whispered, suddenly very nervous.

Mack's answer was serious. "Let's not get caught."

Brandi reversed and pulled the car around to the side where the lot became gravel and the area was big enough for semitrucks and trailers to park overnight.

"Stay here," he said to both of them.

Brandi shook her head. "No way. We're coming with you."

Mack looked like he wanted to argue but didn't. "Be quiet, then."

Brandi laughed. "Being quiet isn't a problem for Sy, is it, Syborg?"

"I was talking to you," Mack said with what Brandi thought was a little bit of a smile in his voice.

She gave the back of him a thumbs-up and whispered, "Oooh, burn."

Fifteen

In the end, it wasn't Mack who climbed through the small window.

"You have to turn the bolt, okay?" Mack had already explained it twice before, but he couldn't be sure if Sy understood. "And there's a button on the little handle that you might have to push."

Sy nodded, and Mack and Brandi hoisted him up to the window. The boy wiggled through, and Mack's throat constricted, a train of nerves barreling through his body. What if he got scared or couldn't figure out how to work the lock? What if he started back up with that screaming he'd done before? What if they did get caught?

Brandi had already scurried to the front of the building, ready to dart inside the moment Sy opened the door. Mack stayed put in case the boy came back out the window.

Silence from inside. Mack's heart beating right out of his chest. He lost a sense of where he was, his mind jumping back to another motel room and a squeeze around his throat, his vision purple and black. He hadn't wanted Daisy to be the one to find him, so he'd gone to an old motel off the highway with wooden beams across the ceiling. It would be quick, he'd assured himself. Daisy was strong enough to move forward; Mack was not. With him gone, she could live free. But Daisy had found his note, found him because the one thing he'd forgotten was how goddang stubborn and resourceful she was. The door had been flung open, breaking the lock, Peggy with a crowbar, Daisy rushing inside, tears and rage competing for space in her eyes. *You stupid man,* she'd cried. *You stupid, stupid man.*

"Mack!" Brandi's face was level with the window. "We're in."

He pressed his hand against the building, steadied himself. "I'll stay outside and keep an eye out."

"Okay."

She disappeared, and the sound of running water filtered out through the window. Mack walked carefully around the building, checked the front. No cars other than the ones that were there before. The desk clerk was probably watching TV.

~

Brandi closed the door and with only the one bulb working in the vanity, the light was dim. The water ran hot. She adjusted it to warm, felt it with her fingertips, and when she was satisfied it wouldn't burn him, let it fill the tub. She turned to Sy. He stood with his hand holding the waistband of his sweatpants, the hair tie having popped off again, the other hand squeezing the arm of his stuffie.

She knelt on the floor tiles. "Is it okay if we take off these grody pants?"

He released his grip, and the pants fell to the floor. Brandi ignored the dried brown smudges on his legs and tried to keep her nose from twitching at the smell. She met his eyes and smiled. "Well, that was easy. Now for your shirt." He lifted his arms, and she pulled it up and over his head. The neck hole caught on his head. "Oh no, you're an elephant, Sy." She made an animal sound and worked quickly, worried he might get claustrophobic and freak out at the restraint. Her heart pounded—she would have. But he didn't, staying calm and waiting for her to do the work. "Go away, elephant, I want my Syborg back." She put her fingers between his ears and the collar and gently pried it off, leaving his hair in spikes. There was a difference in the way he stood, letting her help. Like maybe he trusted her a little bit. "Do you remember me at all?" She still felt his baby weight in her arms, the quiet sucking sounds he made on a bottle. She remembered everything.

He shrugged, and Brandi was okay with that. A shrug was better than silence, better than fear or rejection.

"When you were real little, you used to sleep curled up beside me, and guess what?"

His eyebrows rose, interested.

"You farted! Teeny tiny baby Syborg dutch-ovened me!"

He smiled, an honest-to-goodness real smile that looked like he'd just told a hilarious joke and was proud of it. Brandi's heart swelled.

She turned the water off and held out her hand; he took it. "Step on in, Mr. Borg." He settled into the tub. "Too hot?" Shook his head. "Too cold?" Another shake. He slid his entire body into the water and wiggled around like a fish. Brandi laughed. "Then it's just right."

She unwrapped a bar of soap, grabbed a washcloth from under the sink, and held it out. "Mind if I help you get started?"

He sat up, water sluicing over his skin. She scrubbed his back, swallowing hard when she easily counted his ribs. "Slide down and get your hair wet." She found a tiny bottle of shampoo. Sy closed his eyes and leaned his head back while she scrubbed, the corners of his mouth lifted the tiniest bit. He had a little point in his chin that she found very cute. *He must look like his dad,* Brandi thought. She took the washcloth and wiped it around his face, careful to avoid his eyes. "Okay, let's rinse." After she'd gotten all the important parts, she sat back on her knees, elbows on the side of the bathtub, and watched him float the shampoo bottle like a boat.

"Hey, Sy?"

He looked up from driving his boat.

"I . . . well . . . I love you, you know?" She kept going, afraid his silence might sting. "And I didn't want to leave you all alone with Mom. I . . . I was trying to help, I promise."

He'd gone still, listening, and it encouraged her.

"Do you remember me reading to you?" Brandi gave a nervous laugh. "You'd snuggle in my lap, and I'd read you that book about the monster with prickles all over his back. Oh, what was it called?"

"It?"

Brandi shuddered. "Are you talking about that clown? Eww! You've seen that? No way. First, that clown is psycho, and second, you shouldn't watch movies like that."

Something she said seemed to click with him, because his shoulders relaxed and he rolled onto his belly in the water, making soft engine sounds when he pushed the bottle through small waves. "It was really scary."

"Yeah, I know." Encouraged by his response, Brandi tried to play it cool. "Carissa scared me so bad with all her stories about skinwalkers I couldn't sleep at night."

"What's that?"

She made a face. "I don't really know except it looks like a real person or takes over a real person's body or something like that." Sy paled, and Brandi kicked herself for being so stupid. "But it's probably fake." She slouched, irritated with herself, and tried to switch gears. The poor kid had enough to be scared of without adding to it. "But this book I used to read to you was about a monster who was only scary to the mouse who thought he'd made him up. Something like a gorilla? A gru—Gruffalo! That's it! Do you remember that, Sy?"

Water lapped against the sides of the tub. Sy shook his head.

"You loved it, I'm telling you. You used to say, *Bendi, Gufo!*" Brandi laughed at the memory, Sy ran his boat up and down the sides of the tub. It was so kid-like that Brandi felt her eyes get wet. She pressed her palms against them until it passed and opened them to find Sy staring at her. She was suddenly desperate for him to know the truth. "The day they took me away, well, you were napping when I went to Mrs. T's house. We had nothing, I'm telling you, not even a piece of bread. Then all this shit happened with Mrs. T's a-hole son, and I guess you woke up from your nap when I was gone, fell down the stairs, and broke your little arm. I got blamed for that too. Does it hurt anymore?" Her voice caught. "Mom's a liar. You know that, right?"

No response.

"Well, she is." A whisper weaving among the quiet splashes. "I'm sorry I stole you from Mom. I guess I didn't really ask you if you wanted to go with me, but I couldn't just leave you there, Sy. Not with how much I love you and how scared you were." She paused to gather her thoughts because her words were coming out like gunfire, desperate attempts to make him understand. "Aunt Heather has pink hair, and she loves to paint. I bet you'll love that too. She lets you get your hands all messy with paint, and then you use them as brushes." It was one of Brandi's favorite memories. Painting flowers with her fingertips with Aunt Heather. "And she'll take care of you, I swear to you. At least better than Mom." Brandi dunked the washcloth and wrung it out. "There's something wrong with Mom or something that needs fixing, but you can't sit around and wait, because it might never happen."

Sy's soft voice. "Sometimes I think she's a zombie."

Brandi knew the feeling. When the drugs had crawled through all her veins, their mom was gone. "Yeah, I know, Sy. I'm sorry I couldn't make her better for you." She pulled the drain plug, grabbed a thin towel, and held it out. "Ready?" He stepped out of the tub and into the towel. She wrapped it around his body, lingering, the heat from the water steaming through the towel. His body familiar and strange, but her Sy. Still her baby brother. She wanted to flip him over, cradle him like she had when he was a baby. Instead, she dried him off, left the towel around his shoulders, and turned to the bag of clothes. "Let's see how good I am at dumpster diving."

~

He returned to the window and the sounds of the tub draining, wet drops on the floor, and the soft scrubbing of a towel. Brandi's voice.

"Whatever Mom did, or whatever she didn't do, you know it's not your fault, right? None of it's your fault."

Mack's words repeated. His chest tightened.

"Look what I found! A Thomas the Train T-shirt."

"Cool," Sy said.

"And camo sweatpants too. Oh, wow, they actually fit you, Syborg. No more ponytails in your pants."

Mack heard Sy giggle; he smiled to himself. "Hey, kids," he whispered through the window. "We should get going."

"Yes, sir, Mack, sir!" Brandi whispered back.

"Yes, sir, Mack, sir!" Sy repeated, and the two kids quietly laughed together.

Then Brandi was at the window. "Hey, do you think maybe we could just hang here for a few hours? Maybe let Sy get some sleep on a bed instead of cramped in the car?"

It was a bad idea, Mack knew it, but he couldn't tell her no. If a few hours in the motel room could give them rest or peace or a brief sense of security, he wanted them to have it all. "I'll stay in the car, keep an eye out."

"Um, wait, Mack. I think we'll feel safer with you in here with us."

Mack cleared his throat; she sounded so young just then and scared. He curled his hand into a fist, angry at a world without Jesse, a world that would let Daisy forget everything she loved and abandon kids like Brandi and Sy.

"I'll knock twice." He headed around to the front of the motel, checked the lot. Still just the one car, a light burning in the office. He'd stayed here when he visited Daisy, and the only time it was booked solid was when the rodeo was in town. He knocked twice, and when Brandi opened the door he slipped inside. The curtains were closed, and the only light from the bathroom fell across the carpet in a lonely rectangle. Sy was already under the covers, hair damp and drying in curls across his forehead, sucking on a thumb. Mack thought he might be a bit old for it, but he wasn't sure and frankly, he didn't care. The boy deserved whatever comfort he could find. Brandi jumped onto the other side of the bed, and the headboard knocked into the wall.

She looked sheepish. "Yikes, sorry." Carefully positioned herself on top of the covers, knees drawn up. "Sy wants to hear a bedtime story. All I got are ones from juvie." Her eyes widened. "And let me tell you, those are not appropriate. You got any you used to tell your son?"

Mack placed his hat on the end of the bed and sat in a chair by the window.

Sy took his thumb out of his mouth. "Tell me about the bear that ate your arm, Macky."

Brandi raised her eyebrows; Mack smiled at the nickname and the peaceful flutter of the boy's eyelids. "Might be a tad less exciting. That story hasn't changed since I told it to you last."

"Brandi doesn't know it."

He'd said her name, and Brandi reacted as though the boy had shot an arrow straight at her heart, holding both hands over her chest, a shocked grin on her face, and looking at Mack like he shared in her joy. He scratched at his beard and smiled into his hand.

"Yeah, Macky," Brandi said after she'd recovered. "Tell me about the man-eating bear." She scooted down in the bed so that only her head was propped up, arms across her chest.

Mack retold his story, adding a bit more flare this time, the way he used to when Jesse asked to hear it. Giving Daisy full credit, even adding that she may or may not have wrestled the bear off him. By the time he was finished, Sy was asleep and Brandi looked like she might be too. It was likely around midnight. Mack turned off the bathroom light, peeked out the curtain one more time, then returned to his chair. He'd let the kids sleep for a couple of hours, get them moving before dawn.

Mack dozed to Brandi's soft snores, a peaceful surrender to the comfort of the room. The company of these two a weighty responsibility Mack felt between his shoulder blades. But one he didn't mind, its heaviness lightened by a sense of purpose. In the dark, he heard Daisy's chuckle, absolutely delighted.

~

He woke to a frantic voice, Brandi shaking his shoulders. The lights blazed, momentarily blinding him and setting his pulse racing. He jumped to his feet and lurched for a light switch, but all the lamps were on too.

"Goddang it, turn them off!"

"He's gone!"

"What?"

"Sy! He's not here!"

The girl's hair in tangles, her face still wrinkled from the pillow and heavy sleep. Mack strode to the bathroom, empty, pushed the curtain back from the tub, empty. Panic churned in his gut. Why would the kid leave?

Brandi flung open the door, screamed into the night. "Sy!" She left the room, walking out into the parking lot. "Sy!"

Mack tried to keep his cool. Someone would hear her screams. They'd find them, probably call the police. But Sy out there alone was a terrible thought that made the consequences pale in comparison. He turned to grab his hat from the end of the bed where Sy had been sleeping and saw a little robot arm poking out from underneath. He fell to his knees and scrambled across the hard carpet, throat tight. Lifted up the bed skirt, and there he was.

"Sy!" Brandi screamed from the parking lot.

He pushed to his feet, stumbled to the door. "He's here! Brandi, Sy's here." He whispered the last bit, but she heard and sprinted back to the room.

"Where?" She leaned forward, hands on her legs, breathing hard.

Mack pointed, and Brandi knelt on the floor and made a sound that was half laugh, half cry. "Oh, Sy." She reached in and gently pulled him out. He opened his eyes, groggy, closed his eyes again and lay down on the bed. "What were you doing under the bed, you little menace?"

He opened one eye. "I thought I heard a skinwalker."

Brandi snorted. "Nah, that was just Mack. He snores like a freight train." She touched the tip of his nose. "Plus they're not real."

"But you said—"

"They're not real, are they, Mack?" She looked over her shoulder at Mack, eyebrows raised.

Mack had no idea what she was talking about but agreed anyway. "Not one bit."

She nodded at Sy, satisfied.

"But Brandi," Mack said. "You're the one who snores like a train."

Brandi looked at Mack, surprise in the wrinkle creasing her forehead, then back to Sy. "Macky says I snore? It's not true, is it, Sy? Tell me it's not true!" She started to tickle him, and Sy laughed hard and real, wiggling away and across the bed.

Mack didn't want it to end. He turned all the lights back off, and for a few more seconds he let them both be kids. "We have to go," he said at last. "I'm going to go first, make sure no one heard us. You two give me a few minutes, then come to the car. Okay?"

"Sir, yes, sir." Sy's voice in the dark, a companion to Brandi's.

Mack stuck his head out of the door, checked all around. Still quiet and empty. He hurried to the car and waited.

Sixteen

She collected the bag of clothes and stuffed the sweatpants into the bathroom trash. Then she took Sy's hand and they moved to the door. A voice from the other side.

"There were lights on, Don! I know what I saw."

Adrenaline flooded her body. She jumped back into the room, keeping hold of Sy's hand, and quietly shut the bathroom door with its towels strewn across the wet floor. She hurled them both inside a tiny closet, sliding it shut just as the front door opened.

A woman's voice, louder now. It was cramped inside the closet with barely enough room for Brandi to stand up straight. She squeezed Sy's shoulder; he looked up, and she brought a finger to her lips. He pressed his face against her hip.

"I thought I saw lights on in room 129, and nobody is checked into room 129. I want you on the phone in case there's a serial killer here. No, I don't watch too many true crime shows, *Don*." Emphasis on the *d* because Don was likely a dumbass. Brandi got it.

Footsteps coming closer. "The bathroom door is closed. There's probably a body in there. Should I call the cops?" She stood right outside the closet. Sy's shoulders had stiffened, and Brandi pulled him closer, hoping he didn't go into one of his screaming fits. "Get fired?" Irritation in the woman's voice battling with a tremble. "I do not have a habit of calling the cops." A pause. "That time it *was* a fucking ghost, I'm telling you. A lot of people have died here. This place is haunted."

The woman stood facing the bathroom door, and Brandi saw her through the crack, blonde hair in a teased-out ponytail, bedazzled bull rider on her T-shirt, long pink nails that tapped her phone in a nervous dance. "Oh my God, the bed has been slept in. What? Yeah, we've had trouble with the cleaning crew showing up, but this is weird, Don. I'm telling you." Brandi heard her breathe in. "Okay, I'm going to check the bathroom. I don't care about your stupid *recorded* football game—stay on the phone with me!" She made a sound and stared at the phone in disbelief. "He hung up on me. What a prick. If I die it's on you, asshole," the woman told the phone. "Hey, you!" she shouted at the bathroom door. "Cops are on their way!"

Brandi tensed, ready to drag Sy out of there the moment the woman went inside the bathroom. Her leg muscles fired. She didn't want to get caught. Wasn't ready for this time with Sy and Mack to be over. As long as the three of them were together, Brandi could forget what was waiting for her back home. A probation violation, kidnapping, stealing, and whatever else her mom would try to pin on her. It started a whirling inside her chest that spun down her limbs and settled in her feet.

~

He stood by the car and waited. Seconds ticked by, then minutes, and Mack shifted his weight. Something must have happened. He hurried to the front of the motel, and the end of his stump tingled. The door of the room stood open.

As a young man and hunter, Mack had had a reputation. *Slow Joe*, they'd called him. He never rushed a kill, never ran into any situation without thought and planning. Sometimes his prolonged deliberation might cost him a good shot, or clients who wanted their rewards fast and spectacular. Daisy had said it's why he sometimes lost out to the other outfitting companies. Not everyone appreciated his approach.

But none of that crossed his mind as he sprinted toward the motel room.

He pulled up short. A woman stood with her hand on the bathroom door. He froze. Where were the kids? Glanced around the room to see if they were hiding somewhere. His eyes fixed on the accordion-style closet, noticed how it breathed, as though someone stood just behind it, leaning into it but trying not to.

The woman spun around, hand to her chest, and held her phone out like it was a gun. "Don't move!" she screamed, shrill, wavering. "The cops are coming!" He'd scared her, of course. A one-armed man hovering behind her, breathing too quickly, gun holstered on his thigh.

He took his hat from his head, held it in his hand. "Sorry, ma'am. Do you . . ." He hesitated, wondering how he could get the kids out without her noticing. "Have you got any rooms available?"

The woman's chest heaved up and down, her eyes flickering with distrust. He couldn't blame her; he did his best to appear as small and unthreatening as possible. Never breaking eye contact, she pressed a button on her phone. "Don, I'm here with a man who wants a room."

"You do work at a motel, Amy," a tired annoyance loud and clear through the speaker. "Where people rent rooms."

Amy's face hardened around her flattened lips. She sidled past Mack, keeping so far away from him she had to support herself along the edge of the bed with one hand and a knee on the mattress. "The office," she hissed. "You go to the office for that. You don't follow a woman into a room and scare the crap out of her."

Mack set his hat back on his head, tipped the brim at her. "Yes, ma'am. Sorry about that."

Outside, she gestured for him to move ahead of her, then closed and locked the door. "We are walking through the very dark parking lot back to the office, Don."

From the phone, Don cheered. "First down, hell yeah!"

The woman breathed hard through her nose, scurrying ahead until she was inside the office and behind her desk. Mack followed, hoping to God the kids had the smarts to get out of there as quickly as possible and back to the car.

Amy jiggled the mouse to wake up the old computer. "One night?" she said, eyebrows raised.

"Yes, ma'am." He glanced outside, saw Brandi and Sy running, hunched over as though it made them less obvious, and disappearing around the side of the motel. Air inflated his lungs.

She took in his missing arm. "Wait, you've stayed here before, right?"

"Once or twice." He patted his pocket. "I left my wallet in the car," he said. "Be right back."

"The man is getting his *wallet* out of his car, *Don*." The woman's eyes were slits.

"Probably to pay for a *room*, Amy."

Mack left the bickering pair behind and tried to walk casually across the parking lot, only speeding up when the car pulled around to the front, passenger door open.

Brandi behind the wheel. "Come on!"

He hopped inside, his old blood pumping and a smile pushing up the corners of his mouth.

~

After the excitement of the motel had died down, the energy drained from Mack's body. He leaned his head back, his body craving a good night of sleep. A few minutes passed and the car drifted to the right, crossing the white line, then jerked back to the left when Brandi overcorrected.

"Oh shit, sorry!" She yawned, slapped her face.

Mack looked over at her. The girl looked as tired as he felt. The little bit of sleep they'd gotten at the motel and the restless night in the car had only been a tease. He studied the road: flat and open with the occasional dirt or gravel turnoff. "Pull off here." He chose a dirt road with a cattle grate that looked lightly used, figured it'd be as good a place as any to rest for a bit.

"Why?"

"We're tired, Brandi."

"But it's only a couple more hours, right?"

"No sense falling asleep and dying first," he said. He pointed farther down the side road. "Keep going."

"Why?"

Mack sighed. "So we're not sticking out like a sore thumb." Had Jesse questioned everything like this? The years piled on top of small details like that, and he couldn't be sure.

"This is how I got a flat tire, you know."

"Drive slow and not like a bat out of hell and you won't get another one."

"Okay, okay."

"Pull behind those bushes." From here they were partially hidden from the road.

He leaned back and pulled his hat low over his eyes.

"You're going to go to sleep? Just like that?"

He nodded and closed his eyes before she had time to ask another question.

~

Brandi climbed into the back seat. It earned her a glare from Mack, which she deserved since she'd accidentally knocked his hat off.

But there was more room back here, plus it was close to Sy. They'd had a nice moment at the motel, and she didn't want to lose the fragile connection it had left behind. She leaned her head against the door, knees up, feet resting on the seat. After a few minutes, Sy scooted over and laid his head on her thigh. She smiled to herself, gently patted his head, and let sleep wrap itself tightly around her.

Seventeen

Brandi woke to Sy screaming, and when her eyes jerked open she was blinded by the sun. It left blue spots in her vision, and with the screaming, the crick in her neck, and the drool thick on her chin, she was disoriented as hell. How she felt after her first night in juvie. Along with a pit in her stomach that came with the truth of having no real home.

"Hey, Sy, hey, bud, it's okay, you're okay." Mack's movie-star voice eased through the sunspots in her vision, relaxed her the tiniest bit.

She pushed upright and rubbed at her eyes. Her brother was huddled on the other side of the seat, curled into a small ball with his hands covering his ears. Mack leaned over from the front, reaching out with his one good hand to pat Sy's shoulder.

"Wake up, Sy," Mack said. "It was just a dream."

Brandi scooted over and massaged circles into Sy's back. "Yeah, little borg, it's just me and Mack here. No zombies, I promise."

The crying stopped and Sy shifted, peeking up at them in the small space between his elbow and the seat. He looked terrified, and Brandi wanted to throw something, kick something, break something with her bare hands. He didn't deserve to be this scared all the time. She felt the anger in the hardness of her face and the tingling in her spine. Before she upset her brother with it, she scrambled out of the car and gulped in cool morning air.

After a few moments, Mack got out of the car too. He leaned against the driver's side and studied her.

Breaths kept sticking in her throat; she felt like she was drowning. "Is he okay?"

"He's fallen back to sleep. The boy's exhausted."

Brandi started pacing, full of unexplained energy and a growing anger that crawled under her skin. "I have good memories of my mom, you know. Did I ever tell you that?" She spoke fast, like her mom did when she was high and stupid-confident.

Mack shook his head.

"I remember her reading to me, singing to me, snuggling me until I fell asleep. She made pancakes with chocolate sauce and those cherries that come out of a jar. You know those?"

"Daisy put them in Shirley Temples for Jesse."

Brandi scrunched her eyebrows together. "I don't know who Shirley is." She kept pacing, kicking at the scrub brush, hands in and out of fists. "And I had Aunt Heather. I remember what that felt like, you know, being loved." Dark thoughts flowed through her, and Brandi didn't know what to do with them. "Sy doesn't. He didn't get any of that, and he should have, you know?"

Mack nodded.

Heat built behind her eyes; Brandi shut them, waited for it to pass. "I don't know what happened or why she changed. I don't know if it's my fault or nobody's fault. All I know is that she chose meth, and Sy got nothing. At least I remember. I tried to do that for him, you know, love him, but then I was sent away, and he was all alone with . . ." She had to swallow a sob. "A zombie." A scream fingered its way between her ribs, fighting to come out. She bit her arm, and pieces of it escaped in a moan.

Mack didn't move or say anything, and maybe it was because Brandi had her "daddy" complex thing like Carissa said, but she felt comforted anyway. Like his silence was a big warm hug, and in it she was safe to say anything.

But she needed to change the subject. "You and Daisy are good parents. Her eyes got all sweet when she talked about your son. And you, well, look at what you're doing for me and Sy even when you're supposed to be dead and all." She wiped at her nose. "I don't know why your son isn't helping you or Daisy right now. Is it . . ." She should probably stop. It couldn't be a good reason. "Is he a prick like my mom?"

Mack worked his jaw.

Brandi kept pacing, sure she'd said something wrong.

"My son is dead."

She stopped moving, her body suddenly drained of everything. "Oh no. That's . . ." A wave of tears built behind her eyes. She didn't blink, afraid they'd all spill out.

Mack looked off into the distance. "He was just a boy."

"What happened?" She hated that she'd asked, and she tugged at the ends of her hair, irritated with herself. "I'm sorry. I didn't mean—"

"He drowned." Mack squeezed his chin and spoke to the horizon. His voice was unemotional.

Brandi felt his loss anyway. She lowered into a sitting position on the ground, ready to listen. She knew that sometimes the worst emotions hid so far down they were hard to feel anymore. And sometimes it was better that way. She wanted to reach out and hold his hand, but she also knew that a caring touch could make everything crumble, and that wasn't always a good thing. So she sat on her hands.

Mack took a seat, back to the SUV. "We'd gone camping by the lake." His voice wasn't the same low rumble Brandi was used to. It had turned creaky and weak. "A place we went every year to celebrate our wedding anniversary. Jesse, he . . ." Mack dipped his head, and Brandi thought he was going to stop talking altogether. She promised herself she wouldn't pester him to keep going. He could tell her or not—it was his choice.

"He wanted to catch a fish for our dinner. I'm an early riser, but he beat me to it that morning and got out on the water without me." Mack craned his neck and looked at the sky. Brandi didn't see any tears, but she felt like he was crying anyway. She wondered how often he told this story. Probably not much. "We told him to wait for us."

A scuffle of something small in the bushes, birds calling in the distance, and Mack's breathing heavy with pain. Brandi watched an ant scurry across the dirt.

"His life jacket wasn't clipped. We'd never let him out on the water without one, but sometimes he'd get too excited and forget to belt it. Daisy was always after him about it." Mack made a noise in his throat. "A storm overnight had left behind wind and choppy waters. He was ten and had been around water his whole life, but—" Mack's voice broke, and Brandi felt it in her own throat. "They think he hit his head when it capsized. It's why we never heard him scream."

She didn't know what to say. Couldn't think of anything that would make him feel better. So she said the only thing that came to mind. "I'm so sorry, Mack."

He met Brandi's eyes, and he looked different, like he was really seeing her. "I wasn't strong like you are. I fell apart, and it didn't do me any good. It didn't bring him back or take away my guilt. I was a coward." Brandi saw a tremble in his lips, and his eyes blazed. "Your mom might never be who you want her to be, so you'll have to let that go. Forgive her if it helps you. It won't change the past, but it can give you a future. That's something I wished I'd learned before . . ." He trailed off.

"Before what?"

"Before Daisy left me."

"Wha—" This time Brandi stopped herself. She'd never seen a good marriage, but she thought she knew love, and Mack loved Daisy. She didn't need to know anything more than that.

Mack sighed, swatted dirt from his pants, and stood. "Grab that bag that Daisy gave you," he said. "I'm going to teach you how to forage."

It was what she needed, the idea that there was something else to focus on, a rope to climb that kept her from falling down the hole where all the pain lived. "Sir, yes, sir!" she said, only half smiling, the other half stuck in the hole.

～

They set out from the car, Brandi with Jesse's old leather pouch slung across her shoulder, Mack with Daisy's old bag, and Sy in between them, holding on to Brandi's hand, Mack's stump. He hadn't spoken about the accident in decades. It had been a promise that he and Daisy had made after she'd come home. She'd shown up in an old pickup truck, her hair in a ponytail, looking skinnier than usual, hollows catching shadows in her cheeks. He'd been on their front porch shucking a few ears of corn. Peggy was coming for dinner. Tires on the gravel drive and the sight of her stilled the blood pumping through his body. Mack patted down the thinning hair on the top of his head, wishing he'd worn his good work pants, not the ones with the grease stains and the ragged hem around the ankle. If he'd known she was coming home, he'd of washed up, pressed his shirt, pulled a comb through his hair. He stood, holding the half-shucked corn like a bouquet, and waited.

She put one foot on the bottom step, leaned against the railing, and looked up. The evening glow picked out the gold flecks in her eyes. Mack swallowed.

It's been a while. Battle-weary voice but a relaxed slouch to her shoulders, exuding peace. She looked out over the meadow to the ring of trees, the mountains in the distance.

It has, he'd agreed. Her last words before she'd left played in the grass, flitted among the wildflowers. *I can't save you.*

She gestured at the corn. *Need help?*

For a moment, Mack couldn't speak. He'd changed in the years she'd been away, but one thing that hadn't was his love. That had remained steadfast and waiting for one more chance to tell her. Mack held out the corn, and when she took it their fingers touched. *You were right to leave.*

Something about her looked broken, like she'd shattered and been put back together with some pieces in the wrong places. He supposed he looked similar to her. But they were still living, breathing, watching sunsets and sunrises. The choice had been to live or die from the tragedy of losing their son. Both of them had chosen to live, and that might just be enough to save what was between them.

Her fingers moved over his. *I'll say this one last time. I forgive myself.*
Unshed tears turned her green eyes electric. *But if you haven't forgiven
yourself I'll get back in my truck and you'll never see me again.*

Mack released the cob to her and sat down, his legs suddenly too
weak to hold him up. He rested his shaking hand in his lap, and when
he thought his voice had steadied, he met her square in the eyes. *We'll
talk about him every day.*

Daisy nodded. *But we don't ever speak of the accident again.*

Mack squeezed her hand. *Just our memories of Jesse.*

She sat down in the chair beside him, handed him the unshucked
cob. Together they finished pulling off the silky threads and revealed the
tender yellow corn inside. It wasn't perfect. But it was their life, their
love, and they'd chosen to make it as good as it could be.

Brandi was telling Sy a story, something about a monster with
prickles all over his back. It pulled him gently from the past. The pain
in Brandi's muffled cry from earlier hurt his heart, and telling her about
Jesse had near done him in. Mack was a bathtub filled to the brim.

The kids followed him across the open land, dead grass crunching
underfoot. He'd noticed a grouping of sunflowers not far from the road
and led them there. He'd wanted to give them something of their own,
an experience that didn't include meth and trauma and lost childhood.
And it would get his own thoughts firmly into the present where they
belonged.

"I don't see a Walmart anywhere," Brandi said, her step lighter
because the girl knew how to stuff everything down. She elbowed Sy.
"So how're we gonna find any food, Mack?"

Sy giggled, his dream forgotten. "Yeah, Macky, how we gonna find
food with no Walmart?" His voice rising at the end in a pantomime of
Brandi's question.

Mack stopped by the sunflowers.

Brandi lifted one side of her lip. "Dead flowers? That's what you
want us to eat? No wonder you're so skinny."

Sy studied her, put his hands on his hips, and nodded his agreement. "Yeah, Macky."

Mack slid his knife from its sheath. "Brandi, pinch the stem here and hold your other hand out." She did as he asked, looking genuinely interested. He sliced off the head of the sunflower and it fell into her palm, seed head up. "As long as the birds haven't gotten to it first, this is the best time to harvest the seeds, when the flower is wilting or dried and the back has turned black." He used the tip of his knife to scrape across the seed head and expose the seeds inside.

Brandi made a noise. "Those are sunflower seeds! Like real live sunflower seeds! My favorite is dill pickle, but Carissa always got the black pepper. Which one is this?"

Mack gave her a look that made Brandi giggle.

"JK, Mack. But really, that's cool!" She plucked out a few seeds, held them in her palms. "Is it okay to eat it like this?"

Mack nodded.

Brandi put a seed in her mouth, bit down, spit out the shell, and chewed the seed. "It's the real deal. Here, Syborg, do you know how to eat a sunflower seed?" She knelt down, showed him how, then put one into his mouth. He chewed and swallowed immediately and clamped a hand to his mouth, eyes wide, panicked. "It's okay, buddy, it won't kill you to eat the shell. It just doesn't taste so good. Here, try again."

Mack looked away, overcome by the way Brandi loved her brother. The taste of the sunflower seeds painted memories of Daisy and Jesse into the landscape. Daisy roasting the seeds, flavoring them with pepper and a little bit of salt. Filling a small bowl for Jesse and setting it on the table in front of him.

Something tugged on his shirttail. "Can we do more?" Sy said.

They helped Mack cut off more heads, laid them on the ground, and rubbed out the seeds, dropping them into Brandi's pouch and eating as they went, glimpses of Sy's dimple seeming almost normal.

"Where can we find more free food?" Brandi asked.

"Let's go looking," Mack said, happy to keep moving because his heartburn was constant now, a fiery ball in his throat.

They walked, Brandi talking about her friends in juvie and the group home. Although she hadn't been there long enough yet to make real friends, she thought one girl had potential and besides, she pointed out, she always had Carissa. Mack was growing used to her chatter, a comforting buzz that surrounded the three of them. An unexpected sight ahead lifted his mouth. Short trees with cone-shaped clusters of red berries. Something he was used to seeing around town, not so much out here.

"Do you like lemonade?" he said.

Brandi looked at her brother, eyebrows raised in an exaggerated way. "I do. Do you, Sy?"

He nodded, looking serious.

Mack pulled down one of the clusters of berries. "This is a sumac tree. Here, pull off a couple of berries for you and Sy." She did. "Now rub them between your fingers and lick your fingers."

Sy's eyes went wide. "It's like lemons!"

Mack smiled. "Daisy and Jesse used to make lemonade with these berries."

"Cool!" Sy said and out of nowhere flung his skinny arms around Mack's waist and squeezed, hard. "I love free food!"

Unable to speak, Mack simply patted the back of Sy's head. Brandi watched, smiling and maybe a little sad.

The kids set about collecting more berries, and after that Mack found some wild licorice, which turned out to be a dud for Brandi, who said Walmart's was better and way more like real candy. Later, they sat by the car, backs against the metal, a warmth spreading between them, Sy chewing seeds and spitting out shells. A real pro now.

The sun had risen higher. Anxious twitches ran through his muscles; they'd been there too long. Only a couple more hours to Casper and Mack wasn't looking forward to saying goodbye. In such a short time, he'd grown quite used to their company, and it turned the idea of his cabin in the woods bleak with loneliness.

"What was your son like?" Brandi asked.

The question surprised him, but it wasn't unwelcome either. He didn't mind talking about Jesse, as long as he braced himself for the sorrow that came at him like a tidal wave. Sy wandered around the car, collecting rocks.

"Jesse was kind like his mother. And smart like her too. He had my father's dark hair but his mother's green eyes."

"What did he get from you?"

"From me?" Mack had never thought of that before. "I don't know. Maybe his love of the outdoors."

The car was hard against his back. Brandi sat with her legs straight out in front of her. There were huge holes in the baggy knees of her jeans, and she played with the frayed edges, twisting them around her fingers.

"Looks like you need some patches."

"For what?"

He pointed to one of the holes.

She slapped her leg and knocked her heel into the ground, laughing. "Oh man, old people are hilarious. Daisy wanted to fix them for me too." She'd pulled her hair back from her face using one of the many bands around her wrist, and he noticed light-brown freckles under her eyes. She looked so young.

Mack shook his head, mystified. More holes than jeans. He leaned his head against the car, looked up at the clear blue sky. "Careful how much you make fun of your elders. You'll be one too someday. Probably with a whole bunch of little grand-Brandis running around with holes in their jeans."

"You think?" It was said with so much innocence, so much barely concealed hope, that Mack turned from the sky and back to her.

"You don't?"

She shrugged. "I don't have the best role model, you know, seeing as how she's a meth head and can't take care of her own children."

Mack was quiet for a moment, taking it in, then lifted his eyes back to the sky. "Sometimes you only have yourself." He shifted on the hard ground. "Even with all the support in the world, it still comes down to you."

"You could be a Ms. Hanno," Brandi said.

Mack wrinkled his forehead. "A what?"

"A counselor. You give good advice." She sighed, lifted her face to the sun. "Jesse was lucky to have you."

Mack coughed to clear the tightness in his chest. It was said with no guile, just simple truth from a girl who had so little but still had space in her heart to be generous to others. Mack crossed his arm, holding on to his stump, in no hurry to break the moment. They soaked up the sun while Sy quietly balanced stacks of rocks at their outstretched feet.

Eighteen

Brandi enjoyed the break, even sitting on the hard earth with her butt going numb and her legs covered in dust, warmed all over but not hot. The perfect kind of temperature. Mack seemed to be dozing beside her.

Sy had stacked his rocks into two skinny towers by their feet, impressively fitting them together to form a stable shape. Brandi blinked, echoes of her aunt Heather's voice. They'd been walking along a trail while her mother took pictures when they found a stack of rocks alongside the path. Heather had bent down, Brandi beside her. *These are called cairns. They were used to mark routes to food and safe places.* Brandi had lightly touched one of the rocks. Aunt Heather had bent close, her voice a whisper. *Do you feel safe?* Brandi had nodded yes even though sometimes her mom didn't get out of bed and Brandi missed school or breakfast. She'd learned how to make eggs in a pan; once she'd left the stove on, and it blackened the pan and made her hair smell like burning for days. Most of the time things were good, and she loved her mom too much to tell the truth. Heather had patted her back. *But if for some reason you don't, do you remember what I told you?* Brandi remembered and recited back Aunt Heather's address and phone number. She had a good memory.

Brandi leaned forward onto her knees. "Do you know what these are called, Sy?"

He added another rock, shrugged.

"They're called cairns, and they lead the way to food and safe places."

Sy balanced another rock. "Like Macky?"

She glanced over her shoulder. Mack watched them from under the brim of his hat. She smiled. "Yeah, like Macky."

She worked with Sy to add more rocks until it wobbled so high the entire stack tumbled to the ground. They both laughed and did it again. After a while, Brandi sat back on her heels. Clouds flitted low under the sun, scraping away at the warmth, and with it came an urgency that settled in her legs. They were almost to Casper, and everything she'd buried on this pretend road trip was worming its way back to the surface. Her mom, the drugs stuffed under the seat. Sweat beading across her forehead. She'd had no time alone to find somewhere to throw them out. She stood, accidentally knocking over one of the cairns. The rocks scattered and Sy cried out, "Brandi!"

"Sorry, sorry!" She tried to restack them, but they kept falling, and she couldn't help but wonder if it was a bad omen. Finally, she gave up. "We should get going, I guess," she said to no one in particular, half hoping they'd both refuse and that Mack would magically produce a house for all of them to live in eating sunflower seeds and drinking lemonade in some fucked-up happily ever after.

Sy was the first to stand. "Okay."

Brandi and Mack followed, both of them quiet, Brandi wishing it didn't have to end.

~

Brandi was a careful driver, eyes on the road, two hands on the wheel, a nervous habit of checking the rearview mirror a little too often. Mack wondered if it was for a reason.

"You keep checking your mirrors like you think someone's following us," he said.

She gave him a look. "Us? Ha. Me? Maybe."

"Your mom?"

Brandi shrugged. "It's possible. I did steal her boyfriend's car and her kid and—" She stopped abruptly, looking a little sick, glancing into the back seat at Sy.

"And what?"

"Her gun."

Mack looked out his window. The full extent of what she'd done, the chance of it all working the way she'd hoped, seemed slim.

"She came looking for me at the group home." Brandi's lips were flat. "I didn't think she knew where I lived. I . . . I don't know what she'll do to get him back."

"What's your plan after you take Sy to your aunt?"

"Beg them to go easy on me. Hope they don't send me back to juvie."

"What about the police?" He tried to ask it carefully, not wanting to hurt her feelings by pointing out something obvious. "Could you have called them?"

She gave him a side look. "And send Sy to foster care with total strangers? Aunt Heather is family. I know she'll take care of him." Brandi's jaw twitched, and Mack wondered if she realized how little thought she'd given her plan. "He was so scared, Mack, hiding between the sofa and the wall, holding that gun." Her voice was so soft Mack could hardly hear. "He might have killed himself. Or someone else. I couldn't leave him there. I couldn't do that to him, you know?"

The car hit a bump. "I understand why you took him, Brandi. You love him."

"Yeah, exactly."

"But sometimes love isn't enough." It was cold, but it was the truth. "Maybe you need help." He meant the police.

"*Der,*" she said. "That's why we're with you."

"Yeah, Macky," Sy piped up from the back seat.

"But that thing you said about love not being enough, that's bullshit."

Before she left, Daisy had tried to love Mack through the pain of losing their son. But he wore the guilt, shouldered its heavy burden, and couldn't set it down, no matter what she said about forgiveness. There were days she couldn't look at him, dark thoughts flitting behind her eyes. On those days he waited for her words to flay him with her rage and bury the blame where it belonged. In Mack.

But she didn't. Daisy saw a therapist. She joined a grief group. Drove long distances to do both. She committed herself to giving to others, surrounded herself with friends and community. There were days she cried or screamed or chopped firewood until her hands were raw and bleeding. But still, Daisy moved forward while Mack stayed put.

There were some things that love couldn't fix. After finding him in that motel room and pulling the rope from around his neck, Daisy realized that she couldn't love Mack out of his grief. So she left. And forced to be alone with his pain, Mack finally went to a therapist himself, joined a grief group, worked to forgive himself. All the while hoping she'd come home. And then she had, and while some things were never the same between them, it had been a new start.

Mack sniffed, watched the flat landscape blur past the car. "It's just my experience. I loved my son, but I couldn't keep him safe. Daisy loved me, but she couldn't fix what had happened."

Brandi was quiet, sneaking peeks at him from the corner of her eye. "I know girls in juvie who would kill to be loved the way you love Jesse, or love someone else the way you and Daisy love each other. You think the girls are in there because they were loved *too much*?" She blew air out through her nose. "It doesn't make any sense what happened to him, Mack. And I don't have a clue what to say to you to make you feel better. It's not fair. But I can tell you what I know. You know the kind of love that does it for no return, the kind that gives your heart to someone else and doesn't try to get it back, the kind that says no to drugs and yes to food in the house and heat in the winter. The kind that would die for someone." She stopped, glanced at Sy over her shoulder. "That kind of love is abso-fucking enough. Right, Syborg?"

"Rule number one, Brandi?"

She pounded the steering wheel with the palm of her hand. "Hell yeah, that's a rule number one!"

Mack patted the spot above his heart. "Brandi." It came out too loud, harsh, and guttural.

"Yeah?" She sounded surprised at the shift.

He had to swallow to keep his voice from shaking, but what he had to say was important. Something he had to tell himself when the nights were so dark he couldn't see the stars. "There's always someone who cares about you, you hear me? There's always someone whose life is better because of you." He'd had a rope burn around his neck for weeks afterward, his necklace of shame that faded painfully slowly. Daisy would run her fingers along it, her face a mask he couldn't see past. *Did you think about me? That maybe my life is better with you in it?* He'd never been able to answer her without lying. But now all he could see was Brandi's pain and how much hope she'd placed on an aunt she hadn't seen in years to fix the mess she was in. It worried Mack. What would happen to the girl if it all fell apart? "You understand me, Brandi?"

"Yeah, sure, I guess."

"Listen, I know what it's like to give up all hope." He worked his jaw, kept his eyes on the road. "I made a mess of things after Jesse died. I couldn't handle losing him, and I tried—" He stopped, thinking of Sy listening from the back seat, realizing he'd never told a soul outside of Daisy and Peggy. Not even the therapist he saw later. Mack believed that some things were best left to rot in the past. "I don't want that for you."

Brandi audibly gulped. "Are you saying what I think you're saying?"

"I didn't think I had a purpose anymore."

"Oh." She glanced at him quickly before turning back to the road. "But I'm not like that, you know. I mean, I understand why you'd want to give up back then, and who can blame you, but that's not me."

"I just want you to remember in case—"

"In case things don't work out. Is that what you're saying?" There was a hardness to her voice now.

"Yes."

"Well, thanks for your advice, but I'm very optimistic. Ask Ms. Hanno."

He felt deflated. He'd given her the best advice he'd had, and she swatted it away like an annoying fly.

The next few minutes were filled with silence until a deer darted from the bushes, ready to bound across the highway. Brandi tapped the brakes a little too hard; the seat belt tightened across his chest. The deer ran onto the road and froze.

Mack gripped his thigh. "Careful," he said.

Brandi swerved into the oncoming lane, sailing past the deer. It turned and bounded back the way it had come. "That deer have a suicide wish or what?" She clapped a hand over her mouth. "Sorry! I didn't mean to make light of suic—oh!" Her words were interrupted by a sharp inhale, like she'd just remembered something. "Mack!"

"What?"

"That makes sense now."

"What does?"

"When I grabbed that flyer for your memorial service."

Sometimes, Mack was learning, young people spoke in a series of short statements that unspooled at a maddeningly slow speed. "What about it?"

"What the clerk said."

He squeezed the bridge of his nose with his thumb and finger.

"You want everyone to think you're dead so Daisy can get cancer treatment."

"That's right." His scalp tingled; her comments were going in a direction he didn't like.

"But they have to think you died by accident."

He turned to her. She chewed on her bottom lip, seeming unsure of herself suddenly, and for a girl who never lacked in confidence, it set alarm bells tolling. "What are you getting at, Brandi?"

"I don't think your plan worked."

~

She waited until the shoulder opened up enough for her to pull over and put the car in Park before daring to look at Mack. She'd assumed that the clerk was just being an asshole. She hadn't known that Mack had actually tried to kill himself once, so she'd put it out of her mind. What was the point of repeating it? She looked at Mack; he waited for her to speak, his face giving nothing away, his fingers pinching his pant leg. He was worried, and she hated that for him.

Sy scooted forward. For most of their conversation he'd been looking out the window, chin in his palm. She knew because she'd kept checking on him. When the car stopped, he took off his seat belt and scooted up so that his elbows rested between their seats, all ears.

Mack turned in his seat. "Tell me."

She shifted in her seat. "The clerk made a comment about how he bet you offed yourself. But he was a jerk, and, I don't know, you don't really seem the type since, you know, you live out in the middle of nowhere and a bear took your arm once. But when you told me about"—she glanced at Sy—"the thing you tried once, and it seemed like something serious."

Mack's expression didn't change.

She took a breath, wishing now she hadn't brought it up at all. "And what Peggy said."

"What did Peggy say?" He stared out the windshield when he spoke, low and firm.

Her throat tightened. He sat with his one hand open in his lap, and it looked so lonely there without his other hand to hold it. She wished she could say something to make him feel better, but her mind was blank. A truck rumbled past, and the small SUV wobbled.

Sy looked at Brandi, worry creased into the lines of his forehead. Back at Mack. He touched Mack's stump, took the end where Mack's shirtsleeve was folded over it. "Macky?"

Without shifting his gaze, Mack placed his hand over Sy's and patted. Brandi breathed a little easier. For a second she'd wondered if the old man had actually died of a broken heart, right in front of her eyes. She didn't doubt that could happen. It was catching, though, she knew that, because she felt it in a growing pain in her own chest. The next bit would ruin him, she was sure of it, and Brandi didn't know if she could handle that. Her back slumped. "I'm so sorry," she said.

Sy turned, shook his head, face serious. He could sense this was bad, Brandi knew. That it might hurt Mack so much it changed him forever. How was it possible that they'd only just met the old man? A part of Brandi wished they'd never left the woods. That they could have abandoned all the bad things out here, in the real world. Carissa would say life sucked. Better to accept it than to keep hoping it would get better. Brandi almost believed her.

Brandi sat up straight. "Peggy said they're not treating the cancer."

Mack sucked air in so loud she heard it. "They're not?"

Her eyes burned and her lips trembled, making it hard to speak. "Um, I . . . I guess since they can't get the insurance money since, you know."

Mack met her gaze, and it wasn't like his face changed at all—it hadn't—but there was something different too, and it settled in hard lines around his mouth. She pressed her palms to her eyes. *Don't cry. Don't cry.* Crying would make this about her. And if Mack wasn't going to shed water, neither was she.

Silence stifled the car. Sy hadn't moved from his post by Mack's side. There was no way for Brandi to make this better. And with that knowledge a stomach-dropping panic: Carissa was right. Life was shit. For everyone. They were ants, smaller than ants, specks of nothingness.

What did anything matter? She grabbed the door handle. She could run, someplace where she only had to deal with her own depressing shit. Not anyone else's. Hers she could shoulder, but Sy's? Mack's? She'd rather claw her eyes out.

Mack picked up his hat from where he'd leaned it between his leg and the door, put it on, and brought it low over his face. "It's getting on," he said. "Let's get you to Casper."

At his voice, low, calm, her panic from seconds before fluttered away. It was what she needed right then. A sense that someone else was in control. Even if that someone had one arm, survived on dried meat, and had just learned he was about to lose the love of his life.

But if he could keep his shit together, so could she. Brandi put the car in Drive and did just that.

Nineteen

Time was elastic, a rubber band that could stretch and make three days seem like months, or shrink hours into seconds. The rest of the drive to Casper was over. Old buildings lined the main street, an outfitter store with a huge sign that lit up at night, artsy boutiques, and restaurants. A big city compared to what Brandi and Sy were used to.

"How am I going to find where she lives without my phone?" Brandi was a tiny fish, insignificant and lost.

"Ask."

"Oh, right." She pulled into a parking spot outside a restaurant in an old brick building. She snorted. "Sy, it's called Eggington's. Get it? 'Cause they serve eggs."

Sy giggled.

"Wish me luck."

She got out of the car and walked up the ramp to the front door, feeling very exposed in a town with so many buildings and people. She almost missed the skinwalkers. She pulled open the door, and her mouth watered at the smell of maple syrup and bacon. A girl at the front looked up when Brandi walked in. She had blonde hair that waterfalled over her shoulder in a silky ponytail, and her nametag read CHEYENNE. "Sorry, we stop serving at three."

Brandi was used to a certain type of girl. The kind who eyed others with suspicion first, hands ready to claw eyes, pull hair if need be. This girl, with her carefree smile and gentle blue eyes, was nothing like that.

Cheyenne tilted her head, studying Brandi. "But I could get you a soda. Looks like you might need the caffeine."

Brandi resisted the urge to flatten her always-frizzy hair or try to catch her reflection in the window. There was no use. She probably looked exactly how she felt. "Maybe just some water?" Out here, away from reform systems and parole officers, Brandi's voice was quieter than she was used to hearing. Like she didn't want to draw attention to herself. She rolled her shoulders and stood awkwardly by the hostess stand until Cheyenne returned with a cup for Brandi and one for herself. Just two friends hanging out. Brandi sipped. Clean and cold.

"I'm guessing you're not a big-city girl, huh?"

Brandi shook her head, and Cheyenne smiled.

"Me either. I lived on a ranch outside a town of two hundred people. When I moved here, I'd never seen so many people in one place unless it was a funeral."

Words that usually flowed freely stuck inside. Finally, "Why'd you move here?"

"To go to Casper College. I want to be a physical therapist."

"Oh." Brandi had no idea what that was, but she did recognize the college. "My mom went there."

Cheyenne's eyebrows rose. "Oh yeah? What'd she go for?"

"Photography."

"Cool." She brightened. "Are you here to go to Casper too?"

It was a nice idea. Brandi in college. So far out of her reach, especially now. "No, I'm visiting my aunt." The cup shook in her hand. She was so close to getting Sy to Heather. So close to doing what she'd set out to do, and then what? Go back to the group home? Or prison? She shivered. Would her mom and asshole be waiting for her? She thought of the drugs in the bag under the seat. All the problems she'd ignored rose in floodwaters up to her chest. She was going to drown.

"Hey, are you okay?" Cheyenne's eyes flicked to the door and through the window to the street outside. "Do you need help?" she whispered.

"Oh, no, it's nothing like that." The girl must think Brandi's odd behavior meant she'd been abducted or sex trafficked. "It's just been a long trip, that's all. And my phone's dead, so I don't have maps."

Cheyenne looked relieved.

"My aunt lives on 4425 Delgado Street. Do you, like, know where that is?"

She scrunched her eyebrows together. "I don't think so, but here." She pulled out her phone, fingers flying across the keyboard. "It's just south of here, not far at all." She showed the screen to Brandi, tracing her finger along a blue highlighted route. "Wait, I'll write it down." From behind the stand she grabbed a piece of paper and wrote out the directions.

Brandi took them. "Thanks."

"No problem."

She hesitated, wishing this could be her life. Leaving a shift at the diner, studying to be something important, chatting with a friend. But it wasn't, not even close. She turned to leave.

"Wait!" Cheyenne said, and Brandi watched her hurry past the dining area and into the kitchen. She returned a few moments later carrying a paper bag. "Homemade muffins. They throw them out after a few days anyway."

Brandi took the bag. "Thanks," she said.

"No problem," Cheyenne said again with a smile. "Good luck finding your aunt."

Brandi waved and left. The girl's friendliness hit a chord of deep longing that made Brandi feel both lighter and weighed down by all the things just out of her reach. She hurried back to the SUV, nerves tangled inside her chest. Aunt Heather was only minutes away. After the last three days, it all seemed too easy, and she wasn't ready for it to be over.

She slid into the driver's seat, pulled the belt across her shoulder, and buckled it carefully. Then sat with one hand on the wheel, one on the key ready to turn. Maybe there was a part of Brandi that had hoped it would be harder, even impossible. That Mack would suddenly offer to adopt both of them himself and take them home to his cabin in the woods. Except it wasn't a cabin—it was a huge log home, the kind Brandi had seen on those home-improvement shows with soaking tubs and soft beds with thick white comforters. Brandi almost laughed out loud. Carissa was right. She really did have a daddy complex.

"You okay?" For an old man, he was weirdly intuitive.

"Not really."

"Brandi?" Sy's voice reminded her of why they were there in the first place. It was never to build some fantasy world where she had a normal life. *Snap out of it.*

She smiled over her shoulder. "Buckle up, Syborg! We're going to see Aunt Heather."

~

She parked on the street outside 4425 Delgado Street. A one-story home with a small front porch, navy-blue shutters on the windows, nice paint job. Orange and red flowers in colorful containers on either side of a front door decorated with a harvest-themed wreath.

Faint memories, ghostly laughter drifting from the backyard. Did she remember this place? Overcome by a deep sense of contentment, peace. She blinked against a sudden wetness in her eyes. Some part of her had never left Aunt Heather's.

"Wow, this is really nice!" She tried to sound enthusiastic, but it came out strained. "Right, Syborg? Look at that tree in the backyard. Bet you could climb that tree. I bet Aunt Heather already has one of those tire swings, you know, like from the old days? Or you could ask her to hang one. I bet she'd love that."

All Brandi had to go on were memories made fuzzy by time and youth. Goose bumps spread across her arms. She'd been so sure of herself. But now? She caught her lip between her front teeth. Now she wasn't so sure.

Sy sat with his arms hugging his shins, bony shoulders poking through his Thomas the Train shirt, head down and face buried in his legs. Brandi sighed.

Mack had been silent the entire way, and Brandi hadn't tried to get him to talk. But now it was time for her and Sy to leave. Time for Mack to go back home. "I guess we'd better go."

"Yep." Back to his old one-word self.

Sy made a sound and launched himself from the back seat, scrambling through the gap and onto Mack's lap, where he curled into a ball, head against the old man's shoulder. Mack's arm and stump shot away from his body, as surprised as Brandi had been. She reached out, touched Sy's knee. "I know, Syborg, it's hard to say goodbye. Especially to someone like Macky, huh?" The back of Sy's head moved up and down.

Mack held Sy, patting his back. "You'll be just fine, young man. Just fine." He spoke in his deep, soothing tones. "Would you like for me to go with you?"

Mack met Brandi's gaze, and there Brandi saw exactly what she needed. Days ago, the old man had been nothing but a stranger. Now she saw that he truly and genuinely cared about them. And it meant something. She breathed in and steeled herself to do what she'd planned. There was no turning back now. "Nah, we got this, don't we, Sy?"

"I'm scared," Sy whispered against Mack's chest.

"Nothing to be scared of, Sy. No zombies or skinwalkers here," she said.

He shifted so that he was peering up at her now. "What about ginormous grizzly bears?"

"No way. They don't like the city." Her next breath steeled her resolve. "Well, Mack. We've gotta do the thing."

"Sure you don't want me to go with you?"

Here in Casper, surrounded by ranch homes with flowerpots and nice yards, Mack couldn't have looked more out of place, smaller even, if that was possible. And it made his offer the truest of gestures because Brandi knew that inside, his whole heart wanted to be with Daisy.

"There are some things I need to do on my own, I think."

Mack nodded, his eyes bright like he was a grandfather at a fourth-grade band concert. Proud of her. He didn't have to say it. She felt it anyway. Brandi turned her head to the house, waited for the urge to cry to pass. In three days the old man had done more for her than her mother had done in a lifetime. "I don't know how to really thank you, but, well, thank you. We wouldn't have gotten here without you."

He shook his head. "I'd bet on you."

"Yeah, well, it wouldn't have been so much fun, and we definitely would have run out of gas."

"That's a sure bet." Mack gave a half smile and dipped his chin.

"Wait, how are you gonna get back?" It hadn't occurred to her until right then, but they'd brought him all this way without thinking of his return. She reached for the keys, thought of the drugs stuffed under the seat, and moved her hand away, heart beating fast. Mack couldn't take the car. Brandi would never risk him getting into trouble like that. But she couldn't risk Heather finding it either. Panic in the squeeze of her fists. Why hadn't she thought of this before now? "I'm sorry, Mack, I guess I didn't think that far ahead. Impulsive, you know?" After she got Sy settled with Aunt Heather, she'd make up an excuse about needing something from the store and then find a dumpster for the drugs. Her pulse slowed. It was a good plan.

"I'll make my way back." Something was gone from his voice. The warmth and stability that appealed to her, the thing that smelled like old leather and felt like home. Gone cold, a candle blown out. He'd said his goodbyes, and now he had to get back to Daisy. "But I'll wait here for a while, make sure you're both okay."

She swallowed hard, blinked fast. "Where will you go?" she whispered.

Mack looked down at the top of Sy's head. "I'm going to see Daisy."

Brandi's tongue was heavy with all the things she wanted to say but couldn't figure out how. "I'm sorry about Jesse and Daisy and all of that." The words kept catching; she breathed in. "But I hope you know that you're important to me and Sy. Okay?"

"Thank you, Brandi." Sounding weak for the first time since she'd met him. "Now get on. Finish what you started."

She wanted to hug him, but something about it seemed too final. Like it'd mean she'd never see him again. "Sir, yes, sir," she said. She climbed out of the car, went to the passenger side, and opened the door, picking up Sy from where he still lay curled on Mack's lap. She tensed, ready for the screaming, but his little arms threaded around her neck and held on tight. She carried him up the walkway, still holding him when she rang the doorbell and crossed her fingers.

~

He watched them go, jaw clenched so hard his teeth had begun to hurt. It was all he could do to keep from breaking down. Everything he'd done had been for nothing. Worse than nothing because it had cheated him of the last few months with Daisy. The gun on his leg felt hot, heavy with possibility. He was angry too: At Peggy for thinking she knew Daisy better than he did. For what a fool he'd been thinking his plan was going to work in the first place.

Brandi stood by the door to the house, Sy in her arms with his legs clamped around her waist, face buried in her shoulder. As soon as they went inside he'd leave. Hitch a ride to Lander and see his wife. He'd stay in her room, and they'd have to call the police to drag him out, because he would never leave her side again. Maybe he'd even convince her to leave with him this time. Finally get her to the cabin where they could end their days together. The way they'd always planned.

The door opened to a woman with dirty blonde hair in two braids and glasses that looked so ugly Mack figured they were supposed to be stylish. He sat up, leaned forward in his seat wishing he could hear the exchange. Brandi stood tall, chin cocked in that tough way he remembered when he'd first met her—he scratched his beard—three days ago? Shook his head. Impossible.

A pang of unease. The woman was frowning and closing the door, inch by inch. Thinking she could shut the kids out? His body in a vise of indecision. This was supposed to be Brandi's safe haven, and the one person the girl trusted was closing the door on her. Denying her safety. Denying them both love. It boiled under his skin, this unfairness dumped on kids like Brandi and Sy.

Brandi had put Sy down, and the boy clung to her leg. She was getting heated; he could tell by the way she moved her feet. Like a boxer evading blows. Mack couldn't sit there and do nothing. Not after everything they'd been through together. He had to do something. Anything was better than sitting in this goddang car and watching the girl's heart break in two.

~

She didn't know this woman with her stupid glasses and dumb hair that belonged on a girl, not a grown-ass woman with wrinkles around her mouth. But this woman thought she knew Brandi.

"I'm sorry, Brandi, I really am."

No, she wasn't. Fucking liar.

"But Nancy is toxic, and you probably have no idea what she's put Heather through." She blocked the door, standing there like she was some fucking hero protecting her partner from Slender Man.

Brandi let whatever air remained in her lungs out, tried to feel calm, tried to use Ms. Hanno's process to cool down. She knew that yelling always made things worse. She knew that giving in to this simmering rage would only get her in trouble. She knew all of this.

"I know Nancy is toxic. That's why we're here." She tried to look inside the house, but the woman blocked her view. "Where's Aunt Heather? Please, can you just let her know I'm here? And Sy too." She touched his head. "Please? He can't live with my mom anymore. Aunt Heather told me to come to her if we ever needed help. We need her help." Her voice was cracking, and she hated it. She stuck her head toward the crack. "Aunt Heather! It's me, Brandi! Aunt Heather, please come out!"

"I'm sorry, Brandi. I really am. But Heather doesn't want anything to do with you. She just can't bear to say it herself." The woman's voice was firmer now, her fake sympathy disappearing, and she was closing the door on them.

It hit Brandi. The woman had never, not once, looked at Sy. Had carried on the entire conversation with Brandi only. "You're such a fucking coward."

The door kept closing, a pressure that spread to her fingertips, the roots of her hair. A ringing in her ears and Brandi couldn't breathe, she couldn't scream, felt the ground fall away from under her feet. She'd done the right thing. She knew inside her soul it was the right thing. But this world where adults ruled was hopeless. The truth of it whirled around her, and she had nowhere to put it, no *process* that could stop this rage.

It all came rushing out in a scream that burned her throat. Sy fell backward from where he'd clung to her, landing on his butt, scrambling away and staring at her like she was the monster. She screamed again, and it wound around her, squeezing out everything inside. It felt so good to stop trying so hard and to be exactly what she felt. The woman looked scared, no, terrified. Brandi lunged. She had no plan. She wouldn't hurt the woman, she didn't think, but there was nowhere else for everything to go except her fists.

Her foot stopped the door from closing. The woman yelped. Brandi saw a phone in her other hand, trying to dial 911, and it didn't register, only made her angrier. She stuck her fist through the opening and connected with the woman's chin. She cried out, and Brandi grabbed her arm. The phone fell to the floor. From behind her Sy, screaming along with her, crying, and the panic in it made her hesitate. Then there was a tug on her shirt and she was pulled back, away from the woman. The door slammed shut, the woman screaming about the cops on the other side.

"Brandi!" Mack, firm and commanding. "No!" Like she was a street dog. A cold rush of despair dampened the heat from before, and she went limp.

When the tears came they rushed down her face, her neck, soaking the collar of her shirt, blinding her. There was no end to them. Mack led her back to the car, opened the door, and she blindly got inside, curled up into a ball, and didn't try to stop it.

Twenty

He helped Brandi into the back seat of the car. Sy climbed in beside her, tripping over himself to stay close to his sister. Mack drove away as fast as he could. That woman had surely called the cops, especially after Brandi attacked her like that. *Goddang it*, he should have gone with them, given her support, not watched from the car and done nothing to help.

It brought back with terrible clarity the morning Jesse drowned. He'd felt like an observer then, unable to help, watching their world fall apart.

Mack had woken slowly to the sound of leftover rain dripping from the trees, a weak morning sun filtering into the tent, and Daisy's inhuman scream. He'd stumbled outside, heart pushing up through his throat, a panic so deep he couldn't see or speak or call out. Like his body already knew the terrible truth. The canoe floating upside down, Daisy in the cold water, her strokes big and clumsy. Mack behind her, slower with his one arm. They tried to lift the canoe, hoping to find Jesse underneath breathing in a pocket of air. But he was nowhere. Mack dove deep, swimming just below the surface, searching, searching. Nothing but the murky brown depths of the lake. No place for a child. No sign of his boy. He swam back to shore, coughing water up from his lungs, his stomach bloating with desperation. Together they ran up and down the banks, screaming, searching. When they found his life jacket snagged on a branch, Daisy fell to her knees, soundless screams that still pierced his eardrums. Other campers had come. Someone called for help. They'd searched the water, dragged the lake, later finding him not far from their campsite. He might have hit his head on the boat, they'd said. Been unconscious. Might explain why Daisy and Mack never heard him crying out for help, they'd said.

Mack shook himself free of the memory. It was strong and relentless and left him trembling with loss. He looked over his shoulder and saw that Sy had curled up beside Brandi, his hand patting her knee. If Mack had gone with her, maybe she wouldn't have exploded like that. Brandi curled into a tight ball. The crying had stopped, but the silence was worse.

"It's okay, Brandiborg," Sy said. "You're okay."

Mack felt his face tighten. When Mack had gotten out of the car, Sy had been tugging on Brandi's pants, crying. But he'd stopped as soon as Mack got there, and since then he'd been trying to soothe his sister, repeating many of the same things Mack had heard Brandi say.

He cleared his throat. "I'm going to stop in Lander."

"To see Daisy?" Sy asked. The boy obviously listened more than he seemed.

"We'll need gas, and yes, I'd like to see Daisy." His voice caught on her name.

"Is Brandi okay?"

Mack swallowed. "She'll be okay."

"You'll be okay," he repeated to his sister, rubbing Brandi's shoulder. "Aunt Heather is mean. I don't want to live with her."

Mack blinked, pulled the visor down to diminish the glare of the sun.

"What do we do now, Macky?"

"The name's Mack," he said, even though he didn't really mind the nickname.

"I love macky cheese. So you're Macky too." Sy held a hand to his mouth, giggled in that way of his where he moved his chest up and down. A pantomime of something he'd seen but had rarely experienced himself in the chaos of his life.

Mack smiled at him in the rearview mirror. "I can't fight about that, now, can I?"

A full grin from Sy, showing his missing front teeth, shallow dimples. "You could try, but you might lose your other arm."

Laughter pushed out of Mack's diaphragm, surprising him and Sy, who giggled again, and this time it sounded like he was getting the hang of it.

"Brandi?" Mack tried to see her through the rearview mirror, but she'd slunk down so low he only caught her shoulder. "You okay?"

No answer. He frowned, worried. The girl had shown only stamina for the long road, a stubborn optimism in her decisions, no matter how ill-thought-out they might be. This turning inward after her sudden anger and violence toward that woman had melted the girl away, revealing the troubled teen inside.

"If you—" He stopped, chewed on this thought a moment longer. What he was about to offer wasn't smart. Would likely get him into serious trouble. But Daisy was dying, and Mack had nothing much to live for after she was gone. What did he care about getting into a little bit of trouble? "You can hunker down at my cabin for a bit. There's food and water, enough for you to decide what you're going to do next."

"Yay, yay, yay! We can live with Macky!" Sy seemed not to be affected by the woman turning them away. As a matter of fact, it had freed something in the boy. Maybe it was seeing his sister lose it in the way he had so many times himself. Maybe it was knowing that he wasn't alone. A burning in Mack's ears turned into a cough.

"Don't be stupid, Sy." Brandi's voice was harsh. "Mack's not going to live there anymore."

"Oh." Crestfallen. "How come?"

"Because he's probably going to stay with Daisy until she dies, and then he's going to off himself."

Sy made a terrible sound, and Mack had to pull the car over, anger slamming the brake harder than he meant to. He turned around. Brandi hadn't moved, curled into herself, face hidden under her arms.

"Brandi," he barked.

"Don't be so dramatic, Mack," she said from under her arms. "You know it's true, so don't be a liar. Especially to us. We know life's shit. Ask Sy."

A light went out from behind the boy's eyes. His face grew stiff, the haunted emptiness from before creeping back, having never really left in the first place. Speechless, Mack turned from the kids and back to the road, defeated. Such cruel words, her utter indifference to the boy Mack knew she loved.

"You can stay at the cabin as long as you need." He pulled back onto the road, going a little faster this time, Daisy on his mind. He needed to see her, to be with her. After that—the girl's words clung to his skull—after that, he had no plan.

～

The nursing home looked different during the day. Still depressing, still old, but trying to be festive with pumpkins and stacks of hay flanking the front doors. Mack unbuckled, not moving. He didn't want to leave the kids alone. Brandi lay curled into a ball like before, maybe sleeping. Sy had scooted away from his sister and leaned against the door, staring out the window.

"You don't have to wait for me if you don't want to." It wasn't his car, it wasn't theirs either, but still. "But if you want, I can show you where the cabin is, just, later, if that's okay."

No response, no acknowledgment that he'd spoken. Mack sighed. "If you decide to leave, it's been . . ." He stretched his neck, at a loss. "I'm sorry things didn't work out with your aunt. Be brave, both of you." His words sounded thin to his own ears. Sy closed his eyes and laid his head against the hard plastic door.

Mack blinked and got out of the car. He straightened his shirt, smoothed the hair on the sides of his head, then settled his hat on top and walked inside.

"Hello!" A woman dressed up in a gauzy blouse and dangly earrings, sitting at the desk, smiling. "Can I help you?" Eyes catching on his missing appendage.

Mack approached, tucking in his already tucked-in shirt. Could he get into trouble for people believing he'd died? Nothing illegal had come of it, after all. He cleared his throat. "I'm here for my wife."

She smiled, unfazed, not seeming to recognize him. Must be new. "Sign in here, and don't forget your visitor's badge." The phone rang, and she turned from Mack to answer.

He filled in his name, writing carefully because Mack never had any penmanship to speak of. In the spot where it said *relation to resident*, Mack hesitated, then wrote *husband* because goddang it, he wasn't dead anymore so that's what he was. The woman was busy on the phone and didn't check the log; she unpeeled the visitor badge and handed it to Mack with a nod. He stuck it to his shirt and walked down the hall to room 107, wondering what he looked like. Checked his jeans, yep, smudges of dust in the creases, dirt on the toes of his boots. He rubbed his cheek—patchy, unkempt beard. Daisy would be disappointed; she always said she liked a man who took care of himself. A jolt of excitement—he was about to see her.

Her door was open. He stopped, deflated by a sudden paralyzing fear of what he would find after all this time away. He took a moment, then lifted up his spine and walked inside.

Twenty-One

Brandi's eyes were dry, the skin underneath tight and puffy. She dozed, waiting for Mack, unsure what her next steps should be and feeling utterly lost. There'd been no room for doubt, because she didn't have another plan. She'd been so sure that Aunt Heather would help them. But when that other woman stood in her way, protecting Aunt Heather like Brandi and Sy were the skinwalkers, Brandi's optimism crumbled. Carissa had been right: Brandi was too trusting, too desperate for a fairy tale. And she and Sy were on their own. She covered her head with her hands and curled into a tighter ball.

She heard Sy rooting around through the trash on the floor, probably looking for any leftover snacks. A sob glued inside her throat. What would happen to him now? She clenched her teeth, fighting another scream. She'd failed him.

"Brandi?"

Finally, she sat up, cupping her face, lingering in the dark cave of her palms. She couldn't meet his eyes. Didn't want to admit that everything she'd promised him had been a lie.

"Brandi?"

His hand pressed against hers, and she opened her eyes. He sat beside her, tangled hair sticking up in back, smiling despite the fact that Brandi had blown his world to pieces. "Oh, Sy, I'm sorry. I fucked up so bad." She'd cry, if she had any tears left. She touched the rounded baby-soft sides of Sy's face. Her heart hurt. "I don't know what to do."

She thought she was different, more dependable than Nancy because she didn't do drugs. More like a mother because she loved Sy.

"We can live with Macky."

Brandi kissed his forehead, her insides crumpling. "Oh, Syborg." She was so much worse. At least Nancy never promised a fairy tale.

"Here." He opened his palm; inside lay a crystal shard.

She wrinkled her forehead. "Is that the rock candy? I thought you ate it all."

"I found more," he said, and showed her what was in his other hand.

The car started to spin, and a sour panic inched into her mouth.

Sy held one of the small baggies of meth, opened now, and he was pouring more into his other palm. "I'll share with you, Brandiborg."

With a strangled cry, she knocked the baggie out of his hand and grabbed his arm, trapping it between her own and spinning around so her back was shielding him from the poison in his hand. Frantic, she brushed it off his palm, using her shirtsleeve to make sure it was gone.

Sy tried to jerk his arm back but she held on tight, her thoughts in shambles.

"You're hurting me! Owie! Let go!"

She flipped around and pulled him to her, pinning his arms to his sides the way she held the feral cat she'd found under Mrs. T's porch. Tight so he couldn't scratch her. Tears came with her screams. "Did you put that in your mouth? Oh my God, Sy, did you? Did you eat that stuff?"

Sy's body stiffened, his eyes wide and blank with fear.

"Answer me!"

He didn't say a word.

With one arm she opened the door and started screaming. "Help! Mack! Help me!" With Sy still trapped in her arms, she scooted one leg at a time until she was outside the car and standing with him in her arms. She stumbled toward the doors of the nursing home.

~

Daisy's room was empty. The bed had been stripped, all her pictures gone, the colorful quilt missing, and a sterile smell clung to his nostrils. He ran to the bathroom. Empty. Spun around, heavy with dread. A nurse appeared in the doorway. Nose ring glinting, black hair, young. He knew this one. Jenna, Janna. Her tag read JANIECE.

"Mr. Anders?" Confusion in her frown. "I thought you were—"

"Where's my wife?" he croaked. His legs shook, and he braced himself with one hand on the wall. "Is she . . ." He couldn't say it out loud.

The nurse rushed over, unfolded a chair, and set it by Mack. "Sit down."

He did.

"Peggy came to get her." Her voice was measured, kind. "She took her home."

He pushed to his feet. "She doesn't want to die." Hurried to the door. He could fix this. He had to.

"Wait! Mr. Anders!"

The nurse was by his side, hand stretched out to stop him from leaving. "This is what Daisy wanted."

Anger stopped him in his tracks. "You don't know that."

Her hand fell away. "Peggy does. Did you know that Daisy gave her medical power of attorney?"

A rushing in his ears; he couldn't listen to anything this woman said. What did she know? He waved her away and sprinted through the sliding glass doors and straight into Brandi.

"Mack, help, oh please, help!" Sy was in her arms, clinging to her. "He found the meth under the seat. He thought it was candy. We have to get him to a hospital."

His blood froze solid. Meth? In the car this whole time? His legs wobbled, threatened to give out, but he tensed his muscles and ran after her. Meth. The drug that turned Sy's mom into a zombie, racing through Sy's body? Mack thought of Daisy being taken home to die.

Every piece of him wanted to run to her. His heart thumped. But he wouldn't leave this girl, this boy. Couldn't abandon them when they needed him most. *I'm sorry, Daisy.*

~

Brandi sat in the front with Sy, trying to hold him, but he fought her, his screams so shrill she thought her ears might bleed. The more she tried to push his hands away from his face, the harder he fought. "Please, Sy, stop. I just want to make sure you're okay."

The hospital wasn't far, and in minutes Mack had pulled up to the emergency department. Brandi hurled herself out of the car, fighting Sy but not letting him go. She stumbled inside.

"Please! Someone!" Her voice had grown hoarse. "Help me, please!"

A nurse rushed over, bringing a wheelchair with her. "What's wrong?" she asked, calm but concerned, helping Brandi settle Sy into the chair.

"He might have swallowed meth." Brandi wanted time to explain, to say more, blame her dumbass mother. But all that mattered was getting Sy help. "By accident."

The nurse's expression flattened, and the quick look she gave Brandi said it all. Brandi couldn't blame her. Sy was a bag of bones with dark circles under his eyes, looking like he'd just escaped from a haunted house. She thought of the motel and the bath, his giggles, the warmth of his body beside her in the car, offering what little comfort he had to give. Pictured the drug in his system now. Turning him into the zombies that terrified him.

"Stay here." There was no kindness in the nurse's tone, no hint that there could be another story, a different bad guy than Brandi.

They disappeared behind the doors and Brandi fell into a chair, a weight on her shoulders, pushing, pushing until she thought she might break in half. Her lungs stopped expanding, and Brandi couldn't breathe. Panic squirmed through her muscles, coiled in her gut. She needed air. She ran; the doors whooshed open, and Brandi found the trash can just in time to empty what little was in her stomach.

She wiped her mouth with a shaky hand. Someone stood beside her, and she jerked her head away from the sour stink of the trash can. Mack held the duffel bag full of meth in his hand. With a cry, she tore it from his grasp and pushed it down into the trash as far as she could, face hot, rage mixing with the stench of her own sick. Her hands shook. She couldn't look him in the eye. "I'm sorry, Mack. I found it after I stole the car. It's not mine, I swear to God."

"I know that." Mack's deep voice calmed her the smallest bit.

"Hey, you!" From the doors, a security guard. "Come back in here. You're not supposed to leave."

Mack stepped forward like he was going to go with her. It made her want to cry all over again, but she wiped her forearm across her eyes. No more crying. This was her brother. Her responsibility. And if she was ever going to be different from her mother, it started by letting Mack go. He needed to be with Daisy, and Brandi knew he'd never leave them if she didn't tell him to.

She didn't look at him, but she spoke low, through lips that barely moved. "Please leave, Mack. Now. Please. Go back to Daisy. Social services will take care of me and Sy." The security guard waited, eyes narrowed, probably looking for a fight. Hoping for some reason to use his stupid gun.

She sensed Mack behind her. "Go," she hissed. "You'll never see Daisy if they think you had anything to do with this." She swatted at him. "We don't need you anymore. *She* does. Get the fuck out of here."

She walked fast, heart hitting her ribs with each beat, hoping Mack had already left, wishing he would never leave her side.

Twenty-Two

She was right. He should get out of there, go find Daisy, and let everything that had happened in the past three days flit away like her memory. Mack watched Brandi trudge inside; his blood simmered when the security guard took her by the elbow. Like she was a criminal.

He couldn't leave them.

Not with thoughts of Sy getting sick or worse, or of Brandi taking the blame. He didn't know what he could do to help, but it wasn't leaving them to fight all on their own. His hand squeezed in and out of a fist, missing its companion, wishing it could do more than hang limply by his side.

He took a seat on a bench outside the emergency room. He imagined Jesse sitting beside him, could almost smell the shampoo Daisy used on his hair, like fresh air and pine trees. Together they stared out toward the plains, the farthest reaches already in shadow from the setting sun. Jesse had taken after his mother in looks, with her dark-green eyes and straight nose. So handsome, kind and pigheaded like her too, maybe a little like Mack in other ways. He leaned forward. He'd been a fool; it was so clear to him suddenly. A scared fool at that. Afraid to lose Daisy because he didn't know if he could survive another loss. So he'd run away. His head hung, shame heavy across the back of his neck.

An unpleasant watering in his mouth and for a second, Mack thought he might visit the same trash can Brandi just had. He tightened his gut and waited for the moment to pass. He yearned to go back to

Daisy, to hold her hand and kiss her cheeks, and the desire to see her nearly pushed him to his feet.

But Sy was in there, swallowed up by a hospital bed. Maybe dying. And Brandi, blaming herself, so tangled inside the web of her mother's decisions she couldn't see her way out. Mack knew without a doubt where he belonged. Right here. A gust of wind cut through the parking lot. Mack braced against it, hand on his hat. He'd wait for as long as it took.

~

A police car parked; an officer walked inside. Mack sat up straight. Was he here for Brandi? Mack followed. The emergency room was fuller than he'd expected. An elderly woman slumped over in a wheelchair, her husband sitting beside her, thumbing through a car magazine. A young man holding his arm close to his chest. A few more scattered about. But no Brandi. Mack took a seat by the door, hat in his lap.

He waited and waited some more. Switched positions, drank water from the water fountain, used the bathroom. Back to the chair. The doors swished open, a rush of dry, dusty wind diminishing the waiting room's antiseptic smell for a moment. A woman walked in with the wind, adding a smell to the waiting room that tickled his nose hairs in an unpleasant way. She walked up to the desk, her back to Mack, something about her. Skinny, shirt clinging to the bones of her shoulders, pants hanging from her waist. She moved back and forth on her feet. He couldn't hear what she was saying.

The woman backed away from the desk, eyes shifted to a seat close to Mack. She was younger than he'd thought, skin on her face mottled an unhealthy color. She sat down, scratched at her hands. He was staring but he couldn't stop. She looked like—

"Nancy Harris?"

She stood and followed a nurse behind the doors. Mack's entire body had gone still.

She'd looked like Brandi.

~

They put her in a room with a cop, and Brandi sat opposite him, jiggling her knee up and down, tearing her fingernails to pieces. "What the fuck is going on with my brother?" It wasn't the first time she'd asked. "Don't be a dick—tell me something." Her leg muscles cramped with adrenaline. The cop ignored her.

The door opened and a nurse came in, followed by a doctor and a wo—

Brandi's heart dropped to the floor, and a wild rage pushed against the bones of her chest. She leaped to her feet, backs of her knees pressed into the chair, off balance.

"You fucking called her? I told you not to call her! What the hell is wrong with you people?"

The cop moved toward her, hands out in front of him. "Easy," he said.

Brandi knew she was seconds from handcuffs or some kind of restraint. She struggled to remember any of Ms. Hanno's helpful advice. She breathed in and out, hand on her stomach.

"Brandi." The doctor spoke, her voice measured. Like Brandi was the fucking drug addict. "Sy is fine. There's no trace of meth in his system."

She wanted to collapse right there on the floor. Her eyes burned with relief, but the hate she felt for her mother boiled over.

The doctor again. "Your mother said you stole a car and took your brother."

Nancy stood cradling her arms like they didn't work, looking meek, mild, a fucking pussycat. Nothing like Mack. He'd risked everything he had to help them. Brandi stretched her neck, slowly shook her head, hurt and anger a thick braid around her heart. *Don't lose it.* "I was trying to help—" Carissa in her head. *Ask for a lawyer, dumbass. Don't just tell them all your shit.*

"She said the meth is yours."

Ms. Hanno, Carissa, they faded into red. Brandi flew at her mother. "You lying piece of shit!" Grabbed some of her hair, yanked it by the roots, a satisfying crunch as it left her scalp. Strong arms around her, pulling her away, handcuffs on her wrists, and she was pushed into a chair, her shoulder twisting painfully behind her.

"She's been so difficult." Her mother spoke as though she wasn't there. She straightened her mussed hair into a ponytail, which only emphasized the gauntness of her face. How could they believe her? Of the two of them, her mother looked like the drug addict. "We had some hard times when she was younger. I . . . I wasn't perfect." She blew into a tissue.

"How did you get here so fast?" Brandi said.

For the first time, Nancy's eyes drifted over to her. "I figured you'd be on your way to Casper."

Brandi kicked at the floor. Of course her mother had been out looking for them. "You wanted your crank."

Nancy ignored her. "Can I take him home?" she asked the doctor. "I'm sure he'd like to get home."

Thinking of Sy in that house with the zombies, alone, terrified, Brandi thought she was going to be sick again.

The cop cleared his throat. "Ma'am, I need to check the car for drugs."

Brandi couldn't have been the only one to see the minuscule tightening of Nancy's lips. "Of course."

The doctor led the way out the door. "There's some paperwork before he can be released."

Brandi strained against the handcuffs and screamed in frustration when the door closed behind them.

∾

Her fingers were going numb; she wiggled the pins and needles away trying to keep the blood flowing. Her pulse pounded against her temples, and fear gripped her whole body. Sy would go back to that disgusting house. Brandi would be blamed for the meth, and she'd never see him again. Brandi struggled to breathe thinking of her brother, his future. He'd be forced to make decisions like she had, worse maybe, and he'd end up in prison or dead. The unfairness unexploded into a scream. A heavy sadness fizzled it into a cry.

The door opened and closed, but Brandi didn't look up. She wouldn't say anything more to the cop. She'd ask for a lawyer. Do what she should have done from the beginning. If only she'd ditched the drugs before this. Threw them away, flushed them down the toilet at the motel. What had she been thinking?

"Brandi."

His voice. Such a great voice. The kind that would narrate one of those nature shows. He hadn't left. She sighed and raised her head. Mack stood by the door, hat in his hand, and maybe for the first time she really saw him. Lean, rangy, old, with nothing much left to live for. And risking the last bit of time with his wife to help *her*. It gutted her completely, and all she felt was an aching loss.

"Your mom just left with Sy. She took the car."

"Yeah, so?" The only reason Mack had come back was to help. And helping Brandi would only lead to more loss. She thought of Daisy all alone with her disappearing memories of a life with Mack, of the son she loved with all her heart. Mack needed to be with his wife, not trying to help a lost cause. She hardened the skin on her face. "That's how it works for kids like Sy and me. I'm sorry I ever asked for your help, Mack. It didn't make any difference. Just go."

Mack frowned but didn't seem put off by her words the way she'd hoped. A small voice inside her cheered. "I'm not leaving you here, Brandi. Daisy wouldn't want me to. Jesse either. And without you and Sy breaking down out there, I'd never have known about Daisy. You made a big difference." He knelt on the ground in front of her. "Let's get out of here."

She blinked hard and shifted in her seat, pulled at her arms to show him the handcuffs.

He frowned, touched the metal. "We'll have to take care of that later. No time now."

She pulled away and leaned into the chair, the impossibility of it all a weight she couldn't carry anymore. "Just go. Please?" She was running out of fight, optimism; everything seemed so pointless. *She* was pointless. "It's over, Mack."

Something flared in Mack's face then, caught fire and spread to his mouth and eyes. "It's not over, Brandi."

She felt all the fight drain from her body, and she slumped forward.

Hand gentle on her arm, lifting her up. "You have to walk normal, like you don't have handcuffs on."

He moved her toward the door, and she stiffened. "This place isn't that big. They'll see us."

He'd taken his hat off and rested it awkwardly over her hands. In the hallway outside, hurried footsteps, raised voices. "Heard them talking. Big accident on the highway. Multiple injuries," Mack whispered in her ear. "They'll be too distracted."

He opened the door. Doctors and nurses scurried about. Mack gently pushed her forward, lagging behind her to keep his hat on her hands, and together they walked through the frantic waiting room. Brandi tried to act normal, but fear that they'd get caught dragged at her feet. She stared straight ahead at the glare of sunlight through the glass doors. A nurse stepped in front of them, and the tiny flame of hope that Mack's reappearance had given her sputtered.

"Have you been seen?" The woman carried an iPad and didn't look up as she flicked at the screen.

"Yes, ma'am." Mack's voice and a gentle nudge on her back. Brandi walked forward. Her hands had gone numb, shoulders uncomfortably stretched. This would never work.

But then they were pushing open the doors and stepping outside. Brandi breathed in air tinged with cow manure. Nothing had ever tasted so good. "Now what?" she said.

Mack made a noise in his throat that sounded like a groan. "Looks like we'll need to borrow a car."

"Borrow? How?"

Mack gave her a look.

"Oh, you mean steal a car. You know how to do that?"

"Well," he said as if deciding how much to share. "When I was younger than you, I guess I was a bit of a troublemaker. Hung out with the ranch hands and pretended I owned the world for a bit."

"Told you."

Mack's eyebrows raised. "Told me what?"

"That you and I aren't that different."

He lifted his hat, scratched at his bald head, replaced the hat. "Well, now, Brandi, the difference is that back then I rebelled for fun, but you do everything out of love."

She would have smiled if her heart wasn't so heavy.

Twenty-Three

Mack drove as fast as he could without bringing attention to the truck that didn't belong to him. He wasn't a thief. Before he'd met Brandi, he'd only siphoned gas legally, between his own vehicles or equipment. Had never stolen a car before, just hot-wired the occasional ranch truck for fun in his youth. But with Brandi and Sy, Mack had figured it was worth it to do whatever it took to help, despite the occasional twinge of his conscience. But one thing he'd had no reason to have done in his past was to unlock a pair of handcuffs. Once they were out of town, he pulled over. "Lean forward," he told Brandi.

She did and he studied the handcuffs, at a loss. Brandi looked at him over her shoulder. "Do you have a bobby pin or pocketknife or something?" When he looked at her, she shrugged. "Girls get kidnapped all the time, you know. Sex trafficked and stuff. Especially girls like me. Gotta know how to get away."

It shouldn't surprise him, but it tugged at his heart anyway. He pulled out his Swiss Army Knife and followed her directions, using the corkscrew to push down the ratchet and release the handcuffs. She rubbed her wrists and went back to looking out the window.

She was quiet for the rest of the drive, staring out the window. When he parked the car on the side of the road, she said. "Where are we?"

"Pike River." The town was quiet this time of year, empty of tourists who preferred the summer months. The wind keeping others inside.

He started walking along the side of the highway, his back muscles twitching with uncertainty. What happened when the hospital staff and the police realized Brandi was missing? Would they come after her? Throw her in jail? What happened when people learned that Mack wasn't dead? He teetered above all his mistakes; Mack was in the center of a storm of impossibilities, and he wasn't so sure he'd made anything better. Daisy was dying. Sy was scared. Brandi had given up hope. Daisy had always been the calm in the storm, and Mack needed some of that peace to figure out what he was going to do next.

Brandi followed behind him, her feet scuffing the pavement, and pulled so far inside herself she was like a ghost. In the quiet, Mack pictured the fear in the boy's eyes when he spoke of the zombies. The thought of him with one now pulled the ground from under Mack's feet. The wind had picked up, twisting around them, thick with dust. They walked with their heads bowed, the gusts a force that slowed their pace.

"Where are we going?" Her voice was dull, and Mack didn't like it. Not one bit. He missed the fire in the girl and her ungrounded optimism. This shell of her was disturbing.

"Peggy took Daisy home."

"Oh." She looked crestfallen. "That sucks."

"Yep." The air around Pike River smelled like home, dust mixed with the coolness of sage, the metallic bite of river water. The scents a tangle of his childhood, his wedding day, the birth of their son, the essence that rose from a newly turned grave. An extra beat in his heart that unfurled a deep longing to hold his wife. He quickened his pace.

The nurse's words swirled with the dust. *Medical power of attorney.* If that were true, it meant Daisy had gone behind his back. They'd filled out their wills together and had made each other their medical power of attorney. Peggy had been the second choice for both of them. Back then Mack knew she'd want the same as him: for Daisy to be cared for, for her to be well. But now his thoughts zeroed in on the day Peggy had come over. The documents spread across the table. Had Daisy given

Peggy the power to make those decisions instead of him? Mack didn't need to ask why. Haunted by Daisy's directive from so long ago. *When it's time, put me down.* He squeezed his earlobe, panicked by what he didn't know. Had Daisy asked Peggy to do it instead? Electric shocks down his legs turned his walk into a jog.

Peggy lived in a two-story log home on the edge of town. He led Brandi away from the dirt driveway and through a patch of trees, stopping just short of the clearing. Her truck was parked by the workshop. Mack hesitated. He wasn't ready to face Peggy. Afraid, he realized, of what she'd have to say. And he had no idea how he would explain Brandi. A porch spanned the front of the cabin with three dormer windows spaced above. He pointed to the window on the right.

"That's the guest bedroom. Daisy would be in there."

"Okay."

Mack pictured Daisy as she had been: an easy smile, her sharp wit. He hesitated, heart squeezing. He missed her.

"Is your plan to climb through the window or something?"

He looked at the window, imagined himself climbing onto the deck railing and swinging himself up onto the roof with his one good arm. "Don't think I can make that work."

Brandi snorted. "Yeah, no shit. What about knocking?"

Mack forced himself out of the bushes. "Stay here," he said, heart beating in his ears. Daisy wasn't far now. He climbed the steps and stood in front of the door.

It banged open and Peggy appeared, her mouth hanging open, wild blonde hair as startling as her height. Creases spanned her blue eyes. "Oh, for God's sake, Mack. It took you long enough."

He straightened, met Peggy's gaze square. "I'm here to see Daisy."

"I know. But first . . ." She pulled him into a hug that was so tight Mack's hat fell off. "Damn you, Mack. For a minute I actually thought you'd done it. Left her like that, again." Peggy released him, anger in the gruffness of her voice. She wiped her forearm across her eyes, sniffed.

Mack couldn't find the words to respond. Seeing Peggy again, all his anger flopped on the ground like dying fish. She was right. Why had he left Daisy like that? The question weakened him; it all seemed like such a waste now.

Peggy was studying him with a frown, then her eyes trailed over his shoulder. "Hello again."

Mack turned. Brandi stood just outside the bushes, arms crossed. "Why'd you steal Daisy?"

In that moment, Mack loved the girl for her solidarity, her unfiltered honesty.

Peggy sighed and turned. "Come in, both of you."

Brandi looked at Mack.

"Let's go." He put his hat back on his head and walked up the stairs and into the house, Brandi close behind.

~

Peggy's kitchen smelled like flowers and bacon. She sat at the table and kicked out another chair for Mack. "Have a seat."

"No, thanks." He stood with his back to the wall.

"Brandi?" Peggy said.

"How do you know my name?"

"The sign-in sheet."

"Oh." Brandi looked around, likely searching for the source of the smell. Mack heard her stomach growl.

"There's bacon under that paper towel right behind you." Peggy tapped her fingers on the table. "What in the hell were you thinking, Mack?" She spit the words out like rocks.

Mack flinched. He'd focused solely on what Daisy needed and hadn't thought about how all of it had affected Peggy. "I did it for Daisy. You know that, Peggy."

"Leaving her? Now? When she needs you the most? How did that help anything? You ran away. That's how I see it."

Back when Daisy had left him, Peggy visited Mack, coming around for cards or inviting him to pancake breakfasts in town. She wasn't there to pick up the pieces; instead she'd been a true friend, allowing Mack the space he needed to figure things out on his own, sticking close, checking in, reminding him that he wasn't alone. For that, Mack would forever have a soft spot for Peggy. Even when her words were harsh. "I want to see her."

She pressed her lips together.

In the familiar space of her kitchen, desperation nipped at him. "She can beat cancer, you know that, Peggy. The only money I had for her treatments was in that life insurance policy. But I'll find the money somewhere else. Somehow." The words like rocks in his mouth, awkward, heavy. His reasons, once so solid and sure, felt watered down and weak.

Peggy hit the table with her fist. Brandi squeaked, dropping a piece of bacon on the floor. "It's not about the money, Mack! Why are you being so blind?" She rested her hands on her knees. "This is why she came to me."

"Came to you for what?" Mack felt the wind knocked out of him, even though part of him already knew.

"To help her at the end. Because when it comes to Daisy, you won't listen to reason." Peggy's next breath was ragged. "She knew you'd never give up on her. She knew it was too hard for you."

His heart beat a slow and painful beat. Her words were bullets sinking deep into his flesh, and Mack couldn't take any more. "I want to see my wife." He turned from his friend and took the stairs two at a time.

~

Daisy lay in the kind of bed that tilted up, sleeping. Hair brushed into a gleaming crown of white, same beautiful skin, long lashes framing her eyes. Gut-wrenchingly beautiful. Mack swallowed hard, took off his hat, and held it to his chest, where his heart pounded back. Her hands lay on top of the blankets, long slim fingers clasped together. There was a chair opposite the bed. Mack pulled it across the floor and to her side, took a seat. Brandi stayed at the doorway.

Daisy looked peaceful, untroubled. Mack set his hat in his lap, leaned forward so his elbow rested on the mattress, put his hand over hers, and watched his wife sleep.

It might have been minutes or hours later, he wasn't keeping track, when her lids fluttered open to reveal her goddang gorgeous eyes. Mack's chin trembled with his smile. "Hello there, beautiful."

She stared at him for some time, taking him in, neither smiling nor frowning, not much of a reaction at all. Mack tensed, waited.

He'd taken good care of her, he truly had, until he hadn't. It was when she started talking about Jesse like he was still alive, like none of it had happened, that Mack felt the pieces of their life start to come apart and the horror of those early days without Jesse surround him like a pack of wolves.

Daisy blinked, turned her head to stare up at the ceiling.

Mack took her hand in his own; it lay there limp. He started to sing "Take Me Back to Old Wyoming." And when it came to the part she always loved, the part where he'd take her by the waist and pull her close, cheek to cheek, dancing in the warm kitchen with a Wyoming wind crashing against the window, she sang with him.

"To the Daisy with the emerald eyes."

In the silence that followed, Mack felt everything at once, and his head touched the mattress, chest burning.

"Mack loved that song," Daisy said.

Mack's head shot up, and he locked eyes with his wife. The one who had showed up in flimsy sandals and a steely determination to make it on her own. The mother who taught her son how to find wild raspberries and built a cabin to remember him by. The woman who'd forgiven Mack when he couldn't forgive himself. Mack's Daisy.

Tears on his face. "I love you, Daisy girl."

She reached out and slid her fingers along his jaw. Already she had faded, the opaqueness that shut everything out returning to her eyes. "Jesse wants to go looking for strawberries today."

Mack wiped his eyes and smiled. "Is that so?" Rubbed circles in the space between her thumb and finger.

She nodded, frowned. "You look sad."

"I am."

She looked past Mack. "Is that Jesse over there?"

Mack turned. Brandi leaned against the doorway, and she looked behind her too.

"That's Brandi." Right then he made a decision. One he knew Daisy would have wanted. One she would have made herself. "I'm going to help her get her brother back." A gasp from Brandi.

Daisy laid her head back, closed her eyes, weary, Mack could see, and thin, too thin. Her forearms no more than skin draped like gauze over the bones. "I'm going to see Jesse soon."

Mack swallowed hard, squeezed her hand, and let the truth he'd been avoiding come at him. Daisy didn't want to live like this. Mack cradled his face in her palm, breathed in. Cancer wasn't the enemy. Cancer was Daisy's way out. "I know you are, Daisy. Tell him I love him."

Daisy yawned. "He already knows that, silly."

He stood and leaned over to kiss her forehead.

"My husband wouldn't like that," she murmured.

"I'll come back this time, Daisy girl."

"Of course you will." Her eyes fluttered closed and Mack stood, his knees popping when he did. She was asleep, snoring softly. He kissed her again, lingering, and then he pulled away and headed toward the door. Brandi stared at him, mouth slightly open, eyes bright. "Let's go," he said to her, and she followed him down the stairs.

Peggy waited in the kitchen. "She's dying, Mack, but it's what she wants."

He pulled his hat lower and headed for the door, unable to respond, his throat too tight.

Peggy misunderstood his silence. "If you can't honor her wishes, maybe it's best for her if you stayed dead too."

A shot in his back. He stumbled, regained his footing. Brandi reached for his hand, squeezed, and the contact settled in his spine. "I understand, Peggy." He walked out the front door with Brandi by his side.

Twenty-Four

Mack drove the last few miles to a spot closer to his cabin, gave the interior of the truck a quick once-over to make sure he left it in good condition, then slammed the door and walked into the open grassland. He tried to shake off the encounter with Peggy, but the holes it left were filling with doubt.

"Mack, slow down, stop!" Brandi called from behind him. "Where are you going?"

"To my cabin."

"What?" She sounded crushed. "What about Sy? You told Daisy we were going to get him."

"It's getting dark. We need a real meal, maybe a change of clothes, and a good night's rest." He had no idea how they were going to get Sy, but the pair might need a place to stay for a bit, and he'd promised the cabin. He meant to keep that promise, especially if it was the only place for them to go. If something happened, he figured it'd be good if the girl knew the way.

"Oh, okay." Brandi frowned at her dusty pants and splotched shirt. "I don't have anything else to wear."

"I got a few things of Daisy's up at the cabin that should fit you." The early evening grew shadows where coolness whirled about, tickling his ankles. An uneasiness wrapped itself around Mack's middle thinking about Daisy's waning days, Sy somewhere alone and scared. Helping him seemed an impossible task. Getting back to Daisy in time a fantasy.

He didn't have any water left, and neither of them had had any since the hospital, but it wasn't too far. "It'll take a few hours, though," he said. She'd be fine, he told himself. He looked at Brandi's shoes, the canvas kind that looked too frail for the hike. Thought about how she'd injured her ankle on the day he met her and realized she hadn't complained about it once. "Your ankle okay?"

She looked down, shrugged. "I was faking it so you'd come back."

It struck him then, how close he'd come to walking away. And for some goddang reason, Mack laughed. The kind that came from his stomach and up through his chest.

Brandi narrowed her eyes, raised one side of her lip in a disgusted way. Mack laughed a little more, happy to see any hint of her teenage girl fire. She rolled her eyes and started walking; he followed suit.

~

She was sure her feet were bleeding by the time they reached Mack's cabin. And her mouth was dry, throat on fire from a burning thirst. Maybe she was being dramatic. Maybe it was because she knew they didn't have any water that made her feel the loss of it every single step of the way. But then she'd think about Sy, alone with Nancy, scared out of his mind, and she'd suck it up.

Mack kept an even pace, not too slow and not too fast, and they walked most of the way with the rustle of their feet moving over the earth and the chirps of the birds in the trees above them as the only sound.

Brandi didn't think she'd ever known anyone to sacrifice so much for her in her entire life. Still, she was too unsure of her future to feel anything but numb.

They were deep in the woods by now, surrounded by nothing but trees and a darkness that mirrored her own thoughts. They'd turned a corner, and *bam!* There was his cabin. Straight out of a horror movie— small and kind of depressing, especially when she thought of Mack living here alone while his wife withered away in a nursing home. She winced at her own thoughts, dark, hopeless, her usual optimism smoking like a wet fire.

He opened the door and brought out his canteen, brimming to the top. She drank until her stomach hurt. "How did you get it so cold?"

"I pump it in from the source."

She had no idea what that meant, but it tasted so good she didn't care. But the water turned to iron in her mouth. What was Sy doing? Had he eaten? Had water himself? She thought of his skinny arms, his bony legs, imagined him back behind the sofa hiding from the zombies. It was late, and she was tired from the hike and a depression that filled her legs with sand. Mack seemed to pick up on it. He lit a lantern, and it splattered the inside with gold light. A welcome change that made it slightly less like where an ax murderer might live.

"Come on in," he said.

She hesitated, not because she was unsure. She'd trust Mack with anything. In the hours since the hospital, a desolation had taken root. She'd fucked up everything to help Sy, and then she'd fucked that up too, and it had left her with no one and nowhere to go that didn't end in juvie or worse. And who would help Sy now? There was no Aunt Heather, no caring neighbor, no sister. She'd done a terrible thing by giving Sy even a shred of hope that he'd be safe. A crash from the woods, branches snapping—she jumped and hurried inside. "What was that?"

Mack leaned his head out the door. "Could be bear or cat, moose, or wolf or—"

"A skinwalker or a zombie or Bigfoot?" She stood awkwardly on the other side of the cabin, arms crossed and trying not to touch anything. There was hardly any room, and her shoulder bumped into a hanging pot that hit the wall and made a loud clunk.

Mack's eyebrows raised, and he looked at her like she was the crazy one. "Why are all you young people so worried about zombies?"

She shrugged. "Maybe because the fake stuff is more fun." She shivered. "The real stuff is just, too much, you know?"

He seemed to take that in. "Well, that makes sense, then. Zombies it is."

With his one arm, he loaded wood and twigs into the stove, expertly using his fingers like separate tiny hands to hold the small box and light a match. *Cool.*

She thought of his story about fighting the bear. Listening to his rumbly voice, snuggled up next to Sy. Brandi crossed her arms, hugged herself, wishing it were him. "Aren't you scared of bears now?"

The fire crackled, and Mack shut and latched the little door. "That bear was just trying to protect her cubs, and so was I. Out here, you learn to respect the animals and the weather and know your place among them. After that, this is freedom."

She looked around. A narrow cot took up one whole wall, a small square window framed a pitch-black night, the stove gave the heat. A table against the other wall that looked like his kitchen and dining table, and, ew, was that blood? A place to gut stuff. The cabin was an elevator and the space, while neat, was claustrophobic. "Freedom is really small," she said, and yawned. Cozy too. The size of it didn't really matter, she supposed, if she had something that belonged to her and Sy. The thought gave her a pang.

Mack fried up some meat he pulled from wherever the hell meat came from out here—Brandi didn't want to know—and boiled water for rice. Her stomach rumbled even with the mystery meat, and she ate the entire plate of food in minutes, fighting the whole time to keep her eyes from closing. She yawned.

"Get some sleep." He motioned to the bed.

"What about you?"

He pulled the pillow off the bed, took a blanket from a pile on the end, and lay down on his back, fitting almost perfectly into the minimal floor space. Crossed one arm, stump also coming into the middle of his chest, and closed his eyes. Brandi gave him a look that he didn't see. "That's right, you just fall asleep anywhere." She lay back on the bed, using her sweatshirt as a pillow, with her eyes wide open and staring out the little window. Stars had popped out across the black sky, twinkling just like the song said. "Mack?" she whispered.

From the floor, "Hmmm."

"I can't sleep because I know Sy's not sleeping." Was he hiding under his bed? His only comfort in the grip of his stuffie, the suck of his thumb? "We have to get him out of there." She knew it was impossible and could make it even worse for her, but she'd rather go down fighting in a big way than just give up because it might get her in more trouble. That had never stopped her before.

"We will."

It wasn't that she needed Mack's approval. Brandi was going to do what she knew was right. But it helped anyway. Like it wasn't just her against the world. "Did you really mean what you said about us staying here?"

"I did."

A rush of optimism returned, and she punched the bed with her fist, decided. "He'll love it here, and he can meet Daisy."

Mack cleared his throat. "Let's get some sleep."

Brandi smiled to herself in the dark. "Sir, yes, sir," she said softly.

~

Sunlight on her face, poking through her eyelids, and she woke up with a start. Mack stood by the stove, pouring water into a mug.

"Coffee?" he said.

"Gross, no. I mean yuk, no thank you."

"Not a coffee drinker, huh?"

Brandi sat up in bed, pushed her hair out of her face. The cabin smelled like wood and smoke, not a bad smell, cozy this morning, a little less depressing than when she'd first seen it last night. She'd actually slept too, the kind with no dreams. Sadness caught the end of every breath, but no amount of sleep would ever change that until she knew her brother was away from their mom. "I don't drink anything with anything in it. Only water," she said.

Mack's gray eyebrows raised. He had old man eyebrows, pieces of hair poking out like wings. It made Brandi want to brush them down.

"Water, huh?" He sipped the coffee. "Don't kids your age only drink sugar?"

She leaned back against the wall, not ready to leave the comfort of the bed or the reality that faced her as soon as her feet touched the floor. She pulled a blanket around her shoulders, a chill mixing with the heat from the stove.

"I guess."

Mack unfolded the smallest chair Brandi had ever seen, and when he sat down on it, he was so low to the ground it made her laugh. Mack glanced down as if just now realizing how he must look. "This was Jesse's, but it fit so well in here, I kept it."

"Oh, sorry." Mack's son had been just a boy when he'd died. Her entire body hollowed at the thought of Sy dying, but a plan was already forming. She'd wait for asshole to leave and for her mom to be passed out. Then she'd climb in through Sy's window; the lock was broken, had been for ages. He'd go with her this time.

Brandi pulled her fingers through her tangles, smoothed out her hair, and started braiding it. She needed to do something with her hands to stem her nerves.

Afterward, they'd come here and Brandi would learn to love the outdoors the way Mack did. Maybe she'd even learn how to fish like him. She scrunched her nose thinking of slimy fish scales and worms on hooks. Or she could become a vegetarian and eat sunflower seeds. It didn't matter, because Sy would be happy. His hair would turn golden on the ends from being out in the sun, his sallow skin would brown, and he'd laugh so much he'd get dimples. It was a dream, but one she thought could be real because this cabin was remote AF. They'd never find them here. The dream settled her for the moment.

"I heard once that sugar is addicting, like that's why people get fat. And my mom, she's addicted, not just drugs, you know? But also to alcohol and shitty men and cigarettes and probably sugar too." She looped an elastic band around the one braid and then started on the other side. "So it runs in the family, because they say it can, right?" She finished the other braid, loved the feel of her dirty hair off her shoulders. Suddenly chilled, she pulled the blanket around her and leaned against the bumpy cabin wall. "I don't remember when, but at some point I decided I'd better stay away from all that shit." She shrugged under the blanket. "So no sodas or energy drinks or coffee because it's got caffeine, which is addicting too you know, and definitely no alcohol or cigarettes or drugs."

Mack sipped his coffee, letting her talk and really listening, or so it seemed to Brandi. "Very smart of you. But what about candy?"

"What do you mean?"

"All that candy and junk you got for Sy."

She laughed. "Candy doesn't count. And junk is easy to steal and cheap too." She dropped the blanket and stretched her arms, then her legs from a sitting position. "You're hilarious, Mack." She looked around, heard her stomach growl. If she was going to hike all that way back to the truck and then rescue her brother, she needed food. "What's for breakfast?"

~

He made her oatmeal and added some dried fruit to the top for a little bit of sweetness, since Brandi didn't drink sugar but had no problem with it already in her food. He smiled at her reasoning. Both wise and naive at the same time. Like Daisy when she'd moved out west. Knowing in her soul that leaving behind her wealth and privilege was the freedom she needed even if she'd had to learn it all as she went. He knocked a fist against his chest. Daisy was going to die. The truth hacked away at him now, leaving ragged wounds all over his heart. *Put me down.* Her words from long ago his only comfort. She was ready, he reminded himself. He was not.

Brandi made a face after her first bite, but it didn't stop her, and soon her bowl was empty. Mack filled it again, adding a little bit more of the fruit. "Maybe when Sy and I move in, we can get some real sugar for special occasions." The darkness from before had thinned, and Brandi seemed more like her old self. "He'll have to go to school, but I guess I'll need to homeschool him since he can't."

Mack was quiet. He'd only offered for them to stay there, but the girl sounded like she'd planned to make it their home. He didn't have the heart to correct her. Still, he'd tossed and turned all night thinking about the police looking for her. About the trouble she was in. The girl deserved to have someone stand up for her, not squirrel her away like she'd done something wrong.

Brandi was deep in thought. "Well, he can't go to school because then the state people will know where he is, and since I don't have actual custody of him I guess they'll say we kidnapped him or something." She held up a hand as though to stop Mack's protest, but he was quietly taking it all in. "That won't happen, because nobody will think to look here."

Mack. Daisy's soft, pleading tone sifted between his ears, and with it reality tore into Mack's world. He'd tried to take care of Daisy, and he'd failed because he couldn't do it on his own. What would have happened if he'd asked for help instead? And here was Brandi, a mirror image of his own mistakes. A twinge of regret. Mack should have thought this through, given her better advice. The best thing for Sy, and for Brandi, was to get help, and if that meant going to the police, then so be it.

Mack breathed in, doubt in the heaviness of his exhale. Would Brandi agree to his plan? She'd finished her breakfast and had pumped water into the sink to wash out her bowl. He handed her a washcloth. "To wash up if you want." He toed a bag of clothes on the floor by the bed. "Sift through there and see if anything works. Probably not your style, but it's clean." He shrugged into his jacket. "I'll give you some privacy." He needed to tell her soon, let her get accustomed to the idea.

"Wait, where are you going?" Her face had paled. "What about bears? Maybe you shouldn't leave me alone in here with all the food. Don't they smell blood from a thousand miles away?"

He held up his hand. "Brandi, I need to take care of business."

"Huh?"

He gave her a look, and the wrinkle disappeared.

"Oh, right, the 'bathroom' kind of business?" She put quotations around *bathroom*. "Hurry up, then, so we can get going. My mom will probably be passed out at some point this afternoon, and that's the best time to get Sy out."

He hesitated in the doorway and said what needed to be said. "Brandi, I was thinking that we should go to the police," he said. "Maybe if you tell them what you know, about the abuse and the drugs. It might be safer."

Her eyes narrowed. "Are you serious? Did you see what happened at the hospital?"

"He needs stability, consistency, not to be hidden away out here."

Her bottom lip wobbled the tiniest bit. "But Jesse loved it here."

Heartburn spread to his ears. "He did, but Jesse had a family to protect him. He had a home."

She lifted her chin. "I'll protect Sy."

"I know you will, but you . . ." He coughed. "The both of you deserve so much more than this."

Something shifted behind her eyes. "Go ahead and do your business, Mack." She turned her attention back to the pile of clothes.

Mack wanted to say more but decided that for now it was all she could take in. He hurried outside and up the little hill to the outhouse, little more than a hole in the ground inside a man-size wooden hut, but it did the job.

When he returned, he found Brandi in one of Daisy's Yellowstone T-shirts, sitting on an old tree stump outside, Jesse's foraging bag slung across her shoulder. "I'm ready."

"Let me get my things."

She crossed her arms. "I think I should go by myself. I can get him out without them noticing this time, but I can't do that with you. No offense, but you kinda stick out. Plus I don't want you to get in trouble too in case, you know, things don't go right. Daisy needs you."

The distant toll of alarm bells. A little wrinkle had formed near her left eye.

"Brandi, I really think we should go to the police. I'll go with you and back up everything you say. They'll believe us."

She tilted her head, looking at him like she'd never seen him before. "Do you know what happens when the cops get involved? They'll send him to a foster home, Mack, and I'll never see him again." Her voice broke. She started to walk, the bag bouncing heavily off her hip, stopped and looked around. "Can you show me which way to go?"

"Brandi." She wouldn't meet his eyes, but he knew from the way her hands clenched in and out of fists that anger was building inside her.

"I'll need to know the way if Sy and I are going to live here, you know."

Mack wanted to tell her everything would be okay. Wished for it, even prayed quietly inside his head. Hated that he'd been a part of making her believe she could escape all her troubles and live here indefinitely. "Are you sure your aunt . . ." He didn't know where he was going with the thought, but they were at the end of the road, and he was getting desperate. When he thought more about it, there'd been something about the woman blocking the doorway, speaking for Brandi's aunt. Maybe she'd been lying. "What about reaching out to your aunt again?"

Anger flared in her nostrils. "That bitch? No way. Why would you even say that? You don't want us living here or something? Why? Is there not enough room for me, Sy, you, and Daisy?" Her hand rested on the bag, and Mack saw it. The slight outline of his gun inside. The one he'd taken off to go to sleep last night and hadn't yet returned to its holster like he normally would have. An electric shock ran from his toes and through his body, even down into the fingers of his missing arm. The girl would do whatever it took to keep her brother safe.

It hit him between the ribs and straight into his heart. How similar they were. He'd been as impulsive as Brandi. As blinded by his love for Daisy as she was for Sy. A trembling moved up his legs, and Mack fell to sitting on the cabin's front stoop with Daisy's pleas echoing around him. *Let me go. Let me go. Let me go.*

"Hand me the bag."

"Daisy gave it to me."

"Give me the gun, Brandi."

A light went out in Brandi's face, and she returned to the stranger who'd held a gun to him. Eyes blazing, shoulders straight. "I have to save him."

"I know, but not like that. We go to the police. We tell them every-thing. People like you and me . . ." He swallowed. "We have to trust people at some point." He held out his hand, thought of the last few months, the time he'd wasted believing he was doing the right thing. He understood Brandi more at that moment than he ever thought possible.

A light pink brushed the tops of her cheeks and for a second, Mack thought she might run. "Brandi," he said.

Her back rounded forward, and she pulled off the bag and handed it to Mack. He took out the gun and returned it to its holster on his thigh, then handed the bag back to her. "Daisy gave this to you. It's yours."

Brandi turned from Mack, refusing the bag. "Let's go," she said, and started to walk away from the cabin. Mack followed, staying behind a few steps and giving the girl all the space she needed to cool down.

Twenty-Five

Another car. Another road trip, this one much shorter to a town only an hour from Pike River. It was an old town, built by coal mining and bootlegging, but all Wyoming towns had their stories. Brandi couldn't sit still, and the closer they got to her mom's house, the more she moved, jiggling her knee up and down, crossing and uncrossing her arms.

"Can you drive faster?" she asked as they passed through a school zone.

"No."

She unbraided her hair, then braided it again. "I think we should go straight there. Not to the police first. He's not safe, Mack."

He wasn't budging. "This time you're doing it the right way."

"I know it seems stupid, taking your gun, but what if it's the only way? Turn left here." She was giving him directions to the police station, saying she'd been there so many times she could find it with her eyes closed. "My mom is too weak to change, and Kenny is dangerous." She gave Mack a look.

"That's why we need the police, Brandi."

She crossed her arms, kicked the glove compartment. "Fine. Turn right. There it is."

He pulled into a spot. "Ready?" He was a little nervous for her, but he wasn't going to leave her side until the police listened to what she had to say.

"Sure." She got out and so did he.

When he walked around to the front of the truck she was gone, sprinting down the street, her braids flying behind her. "Brandi!" he barked, but the girl ran hard, hurtling through a yard and disappearing between two houses. "Goddang it," he growled, and hopped back into the truck, the engine roaring to life.

He drove slowly down residential streets, peeking between houses, into yards, hoping for a glimpse of the girl, frustrated by his own stupidity. She'd gone along too easily. He should know better by now—Brandi did what she thought was best.

The minutes ticked by and so did Mack's hope of finding her before she got in trouble or hurt. Maybe he should go back to the police, file the report himself. They probably knew exactly where she'd lived. He turned the truck around to do just that when he spotted her. Down the street he was on, staring at a house. He drove toward her, parking opposite the house she stood in front of, and rolled down the window, afraid she'd bolt if he got out.

"Brandi."

She backed away from the house and came over to the truck. "I'm sorry, but it's the only way. It won't take long. Just let me get him, and then we go to the cops. Sy will tell them what it's like." Brandi spoke between breaths shortened by her sprint. "Please, Mack. No one's home, I already checked, but I bet he's in there all alone."

The neighborhood had seen better days, rotted wood porches and yards littered with junk. The house had once been yellow, but neglect had peeled it away, smudged it brown with windblown dirt. And it looked different from the others. Blinds pulled on the windows, emanating an emptiness, no hint of a home. The others had cluttered porches but more of a life lived with less. The driveway was empty. His hand gripped the wheel. He thought of the gun Brandi had had in the car. Who had it now? His own was strapped to his thigh; he couldn't leave it in the car, but he didn't want to escalate anything either.

"I'm coming with you," Mack said.

"What? No, it's better if it's just me." She looked at Mack, and there was such tenderness in her eyes he had to clear his throat. "But thank you. And thanks for, you know, everything. Can you wait here? I'll bring Sy out, and then we go to the police station?"

He should say no, but when it came to Sy, Brandi listened only to her gut. "I'll be right here."

Brandi gave him a small smile, then reached through the window and put her arms awkwardly around him. "Thank you," she whispered. Mack squeezed his eyes shut and patted the back of her head. A part of him wanted to pull her back into the truck and charge into the house himself. But Brandi knew right where to go and would probably be out in minutes. She pulled away, sniffed, and turned to the house, walking with her shoulders broad, her stride long and determined.

～

She felt a confidence she hadn't felt before. Maybe not confidence—something more like righteous anger fueled her. Sy needed her. And unlike the last time she'd taken her brother from this house, they had a relationship now. He trusted her. And he was all she had. That was clear after Mack decided the police were their best buddies. She didn't blame Mack for wanting to try, but Brandi knew better. Still, she believed that Mack wouldn't want to turn Sy over to child services any more than she did after they were all reunited. Carissa would say her optimism was her kryptonite and maybe so, but Brandi felt the most like herself when she believed things would get better.

She stepped onto the porch, careful to skip the sagging stair, nervous energy sprinting laps through her muscles. Her nose wrinkled. Even from outside the house smelled, moldy cheese and stale alcohol. She pushed on the handle and the door opened. Inside, the air floated thick in splashes of light slipping through the blinds. Old leather couch with sections worn through to the fabric underneath, cigarette burn marks, an overwhelming smell of cat pee everywhere. Fast-food bags, empty beer cans, upturned ash bins, the floor one giant trash can. Exactly how it had looked a few days ago but worse somehow. The last few days had changed her—having seen what love could look like, even when it wasn't perfect, made this reality a nightmare. She straightened her shoulders, ignoring the filth and the bad feelings brought on by the house, and instead envisioned the life she and Sy would have with Mack at the cabin. An odd little trio, sure, but still a family. Mack would change his mind about the police. Brandi could be very convincing.

Raised voices from the backyard. Brandi crept through the kitchen, froze. Her mother and her asshole boyfriend in the fenced-in backyard where they'd driven the RAV4 through the gate. Throwing things out of the car and onto the weed-filled grass. They were yelling, screaming; the boyfriend had a knife and was using it to rip open the seats. Pieces of sentences coming through the screen door.

". . . go back to hooking to repay them."

Her boyfriend flew out of the car, eyes glassy and bugged, hulking over to her mom. He brought the knife to her throat. ". . . not with your skinny ass . . . we're dead."

Heart pounding in her ears, Brandi couldn't feel her face. They were looking for the meth.

Her mother pushed the knife away. ". . . that out of my face." Nancy stood, hitting the car door with the palm of her hand. She stared at the house and Brandi gasped, jumped back. Could she see her?

"Brandi?" Sy's soft voice.

Brandi muffled a cry with her fist and whirled around. Her little brother stood in the same Goodwill clothes they'd pulled out of the bin. Already grubbier. One of his eyes was swelling with a bruise; it turned her hands into claws. She fell to her knees in front of him. "Who did this?"

Sy didn't answer.

"Mom?" Brandi wanted to grab a kitchen knife and stab it into something soft. "Asshole?"

The slightest move of his chin. She wanted to scream; instead she pulled him to her and held him tight. "I'm getting you out of here for good."

"He'll kill you," he whispered in her ear.

Cold prickles up her spine. It was a truth her brother should never have lived. She hugged him tighter. "Then let's run," she whispered back, but it was too late. The kitchen door slammed shut behind her, and Sy went rigid in her arms.

Two hands grabbed under her armpits and she flew backward, hitting her head on the edge of something hard. Stars blended into her vision. Asshole stood above her panting, eyes wide with the kind of rage that couldn't be reasoned with. "Where is it, bitch?" He yanked her braids until she was standing, tipped her head back, neck exposed. The cold press of the blade against her throat, and Brandi saw everything she'd imagined for her and Sy shatter like glass.

Her mother was crying, hysterical screams that vibrated Brandi's eardrums. "Tell him, Brandi. Tell him! Please, honey."

Where was Sy? Fear crawled under her skin, and she jerked her body to try to see where he could be. White-hot pain in her neck from where asshole pushed the blade into her skin. "Don't move, bitch." A sourness spread into her mouth.

"Let her go."

Brandi's eyes squeezed shut. *Mack.* A battling tide of relief and remorse. She didn't want him hurt. Kenny whipped her head up, using her body as a shield, knife pressing so deep into her throat she felt it when she swallowed.

Mack stood with his gun drawn, skinny legs bowed in a firm stance, Sy cowering behind him. Brandi thought she might be sick. The two people she cared most about in the whole world together in this nightmare. She struggled against asshole, desperate, searching for a solution, any solution that would get Sy and Mack far away from here.

"Who the hell are you?" Nancy said. "Sy, baby, come here."

Sy didn't move.

"Let her go," Mack repeated. His eyes met Brandi's. He could have been out hunting, a coolness in his voice, his posture, no hurry or concern. It agitated Kenny, who squeezed her neck with the crook of his elbow and used the spine of the knife to scratch at the meth ants crawling under his flesh. She choked, coughed, eyes watered. When he put the blade back to her throat she sucked in air that smelled of his BO. Onions and rotten, mushy apple.

"She's not going anywhere." Kenny spoke fast, his breath hot on her face. The room started to spin, and Brandi's legs buckled. Kenny yanked her up, kneed her in the back. She felt separate from her body, resigned to Kenny's abuse, a hopelessness spreading from her heart outward. All that mattered was for Sy and Mack to be safe.

Nancy stood slightly in front of Brandi, between them and Sy and Mack. Her face had turned a pasty white. "Just tell us where you put the drugs, okay, baby girl? I'm not mad. I know you thought you were helping Sy. But I'm his momma." Nancy smiled, showing teeth stained by cigarettes and drugs. "I'm your momma too, Brandi."

Brandi pressed her lips tight, felt her nostrils flare, and no matter how much she wanted to hate this woman, she couldn't. A sliver of hope remained lodged stubbornly in her heart for the moment her mom would choose Brandi. Nancy pleaded with her now, eyes only on Brandi, really seeing her, and the thought weakened Brandi. She blinked hard, felt her nose run from the effort. Always the child. Forever wanting to believe her mom loved her more than drugs. Brandi bit the inside of her cheek until she tasted blood, felt the pain harden around her heart.

"Baby. They'll kill me."

Knife to her throat, blade cutting just enough to bring her back. Asshole in her ear. "They'll slice your momma to pieces."

Her next breath caught below the blade, her mind spitting out horrific images of her mother tortured, crying, bleeding. Brandi's eyes met Mack's. Still cool as ever, a little slouched but the gun steady, and he stood in front of Sy, keeping him safe. Brandi took in a shallow breath, not wanting to tempt the blade. She knew what she had to do. "I hid it."

Only then did Mack's face give something away, a slight part of his lips. But Nancy had rushed to Brandi, took her by the arms. "Of course you did. Good thinking. Show us, okay? Show us and then everything will be good. Okay?" A desperate shake in her voice. A gleam in her eye that plucked the sliver from Brandi's heart. It was all about the drugs. It was always all about the drugs.

Something hardened to steel inside of Brandi. "Let Sy go."

Her mother pulled back. "What?"

"Let him go with my friend."

"No." The gleam was gone.

A wild desperation threaded through Brandi's muscles, and she pressed her neck into the blade. "Let them go." Nancy's eyes went wide, and Brandi made sure she looked directly at her mom. "Or you can die, because I don't care."

"Get the fuck out of here," Kenny barked at Mack.

Nancy's face dulled.

But Mack didn't move, and Brandi stiffened. She needed him to go now, didn't want to second-guess herself or think about what would happen when they realized she was lying. "Please, Mack, take him, please," she said. "He needs you. Please?"

With the hat, she couldn't see his eyes, had no idea what he could be thinking. "Go with Mack, okay, Sy?" She tried to make her voice calm. It quavered against the blade.

Tears streamed down Sy's face, but his eyes had dulled. She wanted to scream, to tear herself away from Kenny and take her brother someplace where all his nightmares died. She tried to sound confident, reassuring. "After I help Mom I'll find you, okay?"

Nancy opened her mouth, but there was nothing to say, because the truth was that Brandi wasn't coming back. Not with someone like Kenny in charge. Brandi knew it, and her mother knew it too. It fluttered down into the hole where all the bad lived.

Kenny started to move her backward toward the kitchen door, knife digging into her throat. "Get the keys!" he barked at Nancy.

"Brandi!" A hoarse cry from her brother and she turned her head enough to see him fighting against Mack's grip, hands reaching for her. It was all happening too fast. Throat closing, fingers curled into fists, trembling with a need to punch something, tear something apart, anything to release this rage building inside her.

She kept it all inside. Sy didn't need to see anything more. She tried to smile. "Go with Mack, Syborg. I'll see you soon. First I have to help them fix a tire." Her eyes found Mack's, and he stared intently back, shaking his head no. "Please, Mack" was all she managed before she was out the door, dragged on the backs of her heels by Kenny, who'd locked her neck with the crook of his elbow. He shoved her into the car and followed, squeezing in beside her. The confined space with this wastoid made Brandi want to puke. Nancy got into the driver's seat, glanced at Brandi in the rearview mirror. For a second Brandi thought her mom looked scared.

"Where to?" Kenny said.

Brandi looked away from her mom and out the window, picturing the house empty, imagining Sy already safe in the car with Mack. "Pike River." If Mack understood her, maybe, just maybe, he'd do what he said and go to the police. If there was ever a time for cops, Brandi figured it was now.

Twenty-Six

She was gone and Mack couldn't move, stunned. Sy tugged at his stump.

"Macky?" The boy's voice was high-pitched, pleading. Mack rubbed at his face, tried to collect his thoughts. What did the girl think she was doing? The thought left him ice-cold.

"What do we do? Macky?"

Mack didn't have a plan. Brandi had thrown the drugs into the trash at the hospital, and that would be long gone by now. The only answer Mack could come up with pricked his heart with fear. She was rash, unorganized, impulsive, but since he'd met her on the other side of a gun, everything she'd ever done had been for Sy.

"Macky?"

He looked down and flinched. Swelling around Sy's eye, a dark shadow spreading under the skin. He holstered his gun and knelt in front of the boy. He looked nothing like Jesse. Yet there was a likeness in his dependence on the people who loved him to keep him safe. Like Jesse, Sy had been drowning, but this time Mack could help save him and hopefully Brandi too. He looked around the house, repulsed. Filthy, dark, with a cloying dampness that spoke of decay and abandonment. He used his shirtsleeve to gently dry Sy's tears. Had to swallow against a burning rise of heartburn. Anger pulsed from deep inside. He thought back to the first time he saw Sy hiding under the car beside a rattler curled and ready to bite. And Brandi holding the gun, the muzzle wobbling but the girl's gaze steady, unflinching. Both of them raised here inside this house that smelled of loneliness and pain. He was overwhelmed by the sheer heights Brandi had climbed to be the person she was, by the long road ahead for Sy.

"Macky?" Sy's voice, soft and muted.

It was quiet without Brandi, void of the brightness that was as natural to her as breathing. Mack moved his hand in and out of a fist, thinking of that man with the knife and Brandi leading them to drugs that didn't exist. What was her plan?

"Are we going to your cabin now?"

It reminded Mack of what Brandi had said about the tire. He'd thought she meant for it to calm Sy. He stood, flooded by a rush of sureness. It was meant for him. She was taking them out to the spot where Mack had first met her.

Mack touched the boy's cheek. "We're going to get help." He grabbed Sy's hand, and outside the air splashed warm against his face. He helped the boy into the truck and hurried to the other side. If he was right, Brandi would be all alone. Mack pushed the gas pedal down. She'd have to fight like hell to make it out alive.

$\sim$

The sheriff's station was small and quiet. A woman sat at a desk near the front, hair pulled into a tight ponytail, her uniform a dark-brown shirt, collar cinched tight around her neck.

Mack had left his gun in the car, stashed under the seat, nervous to have it out of his possession and in an unlocked vehicle too. He'd parked down the street a bit; no sense in bringing the wrong kind of attention to the stolen truck. He hurried to the desk, difficult with the boy glued to his side.

"Can I help you?"

Mack pulled his hat from his head. "I need to report a missing girl."

"How long has she been missing?"

"Just now. A man, Kenny, I think, and her mom took her. We have to hurry."

The woman raised her eyebrows. "Her mother—"

Mack saw where this was going. "She was kidnapped. Her mother's a drug addict, and they think she's got their drugs but she doesn't." His voice grew hoarse, and frustration inched all the way down to his toes.

"Kidnapped?" she said with a frown. She wore a gold tag that read DEPUTY BRENNEN.

"Yes." He looked at the top of Sy's head and said quietly, "And I need to report child abuse too. But can you please get help for Brandi." Already it was moving too slowly, and Mack felt himself inching backward. He'd go himself. He stopped. Not with Sy.

The woman's eyes trailed to Sy, down his legs and to his bare feet. Mack hadn't been able to find the boy any shoes before they left.

"Okay." But she wasn't moving or making any phone calls or doing anything that looked like reporting.

Mack thought of Brandi's eyes, round circles of fear, but she'd spoken calmly for Sy. Always thinking of her brother first. Mack's biceps tightened. Time somebody thought of Brandi first too. "She's in trouble. There's a drug deal she messed up. Meth."

Deputy Brennen sat back in her chair, folded her arms. "Are you self-reporting?"

"Excuse me?" He was hollering now.

Another deputy walked up. Mack didn't pay any attention until he heard his name.

"Mack Anders?"

Pricks up and down his spine. He'd worked so long at hiding that he forgot he had no reason to hide anymore. He broadened his shoulders, tried to look bigger. If they knew him, then maybe they'd help him. "That's me." He didn't recognize the man. Wondered how the man knew him. He was young, fit, probably in his thirties, with thinning blond hair and looking shocked to see Mack. A buzzing in his head; Brandi needed him. "There's a girl who's been kid—"

"Oh my God, Mack!" The man hugged him, nearly knocking Mack off his feet from the shock of it. "You're alive!"

Mack stepped out of the man's embrace, the panicked beat of his heart vibrating his muscles. He needed to move fast. "I need your he—"

"It's me. Tom, Tom Dell? I worked for you and Daisy? I knew—" The man stopped, his face reddened. "My dad was part of the rescue team that found Jesse. I was just twelve but, well, I . . ."

Mack stopped listening. His knees buckled, and if Tom hadn't still been holding his arm, he might have dropped to the floor. It only took a mention for that day to rush over in a soul-crushing torrent of loss. Jesse's body pulled from the waters. Daisy's guttural cry that shattered the unearthly quiet among the recovery crew. Their solemn faces, most with tears. Mack gasped for air, felt Sy's hand reach up and squeeze his stump. Like a talisman, Sy's touch dissolved the memories. But the urgency to find Brandi had intensified. And Tom's familiar face was exactly what he needed. Daisy would say it wasn't a coincidence.

"Tom, of course." He didn't have time for pleasantries, but he needed Tom's help. "How are you?" The other deputy had turned back to her desk, uninterested in their conversation.

"Well, Mack." He'd taken a step back now, studying Mack, confusion when he noticed Sy. "To be honest, I thought you were dead. Everyone thought you were."

Mack cleared his throat. "I'm not." Felt Sy grip his thigh, hiding, probably scared out of his mind. He patted the back of the boy's head. "Just needed some quiet time," he mumbled. "I didn't think anybody would miss me." Heartburn swirled around his chest, creeping up his throat.

"They dragged that lake more than once. From what my dad saw, there's a whole town missing—"

"Tom!" His raised voice caught the other deputy's attention.

"He came in wanting to report a kidnapping," she said.

If Sy wasn't cowering by his side with a black eye and if Brandi wasn't out there scared out of her mind, hoping Mack would come and save her, he might have lost it just then. Instead, he breathed in and tried not to yell. "I need your help, Tom. Right now."

Tom didn't hesitate. "Okay."

Relief streamed through Mack's body. For a moment he even felt his missing limb all the way down to his fingers, and he curled that hand into a fist. "This is Sy," he said. "His mother uses meth, and her boyfriend punched him in the face. His sister is in danger, and she needs help. I think I know where she might have gone."

Sy moved his face out from behind Mack's thigh. "You do?" Mack saw Tom wince when he noticed the swelling.

To Sy: "I do." And to Tom: "Can you help us?"

Tom searched Mack's face, another glance at Sy, who squeezed Mack's leg between his skinny arms. "I'll do what I can."

Twenty-Seven

Her head ached from where she'd hit it, and the cut on her throat burned, drops of blood dried to her skin, sticky. The asshole had switched his knife for a gun; the gun that Brandi had once leveled at Mack was now pointed at her. Except this time it was loaded.

Her body shook and she couldn't stop it, hated how weak it made her look to the man. But she kept seeing Sy's face, the bruised skin, the tears but no cries. Mack had been right: Brandi couldn't protect her brother alone. She wrapped her arms across her body, her chest tight. She hoped Mack understood what she'd meant when she mentioned the flat tire. If the cops could see how low her mom would go for drugs, how dangerous the assholes were, then maybe they could make Sy safe.

She leaned her head against the window, the glass cool on her forehead. She just had to stall long enough for Mack and the cops to get there in time. And if not—she felt sick—then they'd find her dead body, and Sy would never, ever have to go home to Nancy again.

Brandi breathed in, tried to slow the shaking by focusing on something good. Ms. Hanno had said she'd had an inner strength. Brandi thought that was dope. She'd remembered hearing some story about a girl who had addicts for parents, was homeless as a teen, and then ended up going to Harvard. Brandi didn't know if she cared about college, but she cared about being someone.

Kenny barked something at her mom, shattering the cotton ball of silence she'd tried to build around her and setting loose a fear that ate away at her confidence. What if this was the end? What if there was no Brandi who would rise above her shit life to do something amazing? She pressed the heels of her hands against her eyes, her thoughts poisonous and destructive. Found an open window in her mind, shooed what could have been out the window, and shut it quickly. If she'd never gone back home, Sy would still be there, huddled between a couch and the wall, terrified of zombies. She was probably going to die. The finality of it crawled across her skin. She didn't want to die. She pressed her forearms against her stomach, a fluttery half breath making her feel like she was suffocating. *Calm down, Brandi.* At least she would die knowing she'd been a damn good sister. They could put that on her gravestone.

BRANDI HARRIS

DIED A MOTHERFUCKING HERO TO HER BROTHER

She felt her eyes droop, bone-tired, sapped of everything. She wanted to believe that Mack would get there in time. She didn't really want to be a dead hero.

"You think you're so smart?" Kenny the asshole's voice close to her ear. Then a sharp pain and white light when his fist connected to her cheekbone. Tears sprang to her eyes and she held her face, but she didn't cry.

"Stop it, Kenny!"

Nancy to the rescue. If her face wasn't throbbing, Brandi would have laughed at how way past due it was.

"Where do we turn, Brandi?" Over the last few miles, Nancy had grown quieter, her hands shaking so badly the wheel moved slightly back and forth.

Brandi held the side of her face and looked up. Her heart sank. They were close, about to pass the truck she and Mack had ditched yesterday. "A little further." Another mile or so and she recognized the turnoff. "Here, turn left here."

Kenny put the gun to her ribs; Brandi flinched. "Why'd you take it out here?" He sounded suspicious. Maybe he wasn't such a dumbass after all.

"It seemed like a good place to hide something."

"Yeah, baby girl, yeah, I get that." Softness in Nancy's voice that actually sounded like a mother.

Brandi looked at the back of Nancy's ponytail and was hit hard by a memory of braiding her mom's hair. When she was little, Brandi would find the brush with soft bristles, the one she liked to run across her palm because it gave her goose bumps. Her mom would sit on the floor, Brandi on the couch behind her, and she'd pull the brush through the tangles in her mom's thick hair, mesmerized at the transformation. When it was smooth and shiny, Brandi parted her hair and twisted it into two thick braids. She mostly just knotted the strands and tangled it all up again, but she didn't know. And Nancy would ooh and ahh and tell her how beautiful it was. Then she'd pull her into her lap and kiss and tickle her until Brandi couldn't breathe from laughing so hard. It hurt all over to remember. Brandi covered her ears with her hands, like it could block those kinds of memories from getting in.

The car bounced violently and Brandi's head hit the window, fireworks of pain shooting through her skull. They'd gone as far as she had last time. Her lower belly clenched, a nervous rush making her have to pee. "Stop. It's here, right here." Cold all over and shaking. Kenny with that damn gun pointed at her, his eyes googly and crazed. It wasn't hard to predict her future. Especially once he realized she'd been lying to them. She eyed the road behind them, empty, no truck, no Mack. Brandi thought she was going to be sick. *C'mon, Mack.*

Kenny stuck the barrel into her back and pushed. "Get out." He scooted over and got out behind her, gun digging into her ribs the entire time. Brandi stared at the ground, trying to think of something to say, some way to stall. Mack was coming, she just knew it. Still, doubt tugged at her bowels, whispered in her ear. A man she'd known for three days was on his way to save her? Carissa's voice in her head. *Talk about a daddy complex.*

She walked, Kenny's stinking breath on her neck. Her spine tingled, feeling the imagined bite of a bullet. She'd never been shot before. But Carissa saw it happen to her friend. Said blood was everywhere and he'd pissed himself. Brandi's stomach heaved, black edged into her vision; she was going to pass out. She shut her eyes and inhaled. *Remember Sy. You did this for Sy.* It calmed her, but not enough. She bit at a nail, tried to look behind them to the road. If Mack brought the cops, they'd never send Sy back home. A crack on her skull, white-hot pain across her ear. Kenny with the handle of the gun.

"Stop looking at the road. You think that someone's coming for a bitch like you?" Kenny's laugh was cruel.

Nancy was by her side, close enough that Brandi smelled the oily residue of her unwashed hair. Brandi wrinkled her nose. "Just tell us where you hid it, Brandi. Okay? And then we'll go home and we'll get Sy, and you and me, we can be a family again, right? I . . . I just need the money, you know, and then I want to get clean." She put her arm around Brandi, and it didn't feel forced; it felt natural. Brandi's eyes misted. Once, she would have craved this kind of attention from her mom. Would have wanted to lean into her, bury all the pain and trauma in the circle of her mother's arms. Brandi could have forgiven her mom. Especially if she'd gotten sober. Especially if they became a family again. It was all Brandi had ever wanted.

But Brandi wasn't a child anymore.

She jerked away, and Nancy's arm fell limp to her side, her other hand held it, like she'd been wounded. That made it worse. How easily she gave up.

Twin flares of anger and sorrow battled inside Brandi's chest. She focused on the only reason she'd pulled this stupid stunt—to save Sy—and breathed in. Her eyes scanned the ground, looking for soil that looked disturbed. Asshole was dumb, but he wasn't a total idiot. Then she caught sight of Sy's soiled pajama pants that she'd carelessly thrown across a bush. The shame soft in his eyes when she cleaned him. *I'm sorry.* Echoing in the space around her. A few nights ago she'd been sure they'd die out here. Sweat beaded under her thick hair. She still might.

A push against her back. "You better find it, bitch."

There. Near a bush. What looked like a small opening in the ground, like an old rodent hole or a place where someone desperate had buried drugs.

She pointed to the ground. "Here, right here."

He stared at where she pointed. "It's in the ground?"

Brandi had to struggle to steady her voice. "Yeah, I buried it."

Kenny scratched at his arms, his neck, one side of his mouth lifting and falling. His head swiveled behind him as though he expected someone to be standing there. "Start digging."

She got to her knees, heart in her throat. Quick peek back the way they'd come, hoping for a glimpse of an old man with one arm leading an army of police their way. She'd laugh if she could. How quickly she'd flipped to wanting help from anyone. Even the cops. But fuck, that was exactly what she hoped. She grabbed a sharp rock—how long could she draw this out? Her desire to live a spark desperate for a flame. Maybe she could leap up and throw the rock at him. She'd never played sports and had no idea what kind of aim she had. If she missed, he'd shoot and *bam*, game over.

She scraped the rock across the dirt, not trying too hard. Kenny was tweaking so bad he was dangerous. She'd been around enough addicts to know that in his state, it was all about the next high. One of her fingernails bent back from the force of her digging; the sun on her back; she was overheating.

Nancy knelt beside her, finding a rock of her own, and dug faster. "How far down?" Disbelief in her voice. She knew Brandi was lying. When Brandi was ten she found her mom's drugs and flushed them down the toilet. Nancy wasn't using every day back then, but enough, and it scared Brandi. That day, her mom went ballistic, turning the house upside down, tearing apart beds, furniture, leaving the house in shambles. Brandi hid. And when Nancy found crystals around the toilet seat, she asked what Brandi had done with Mommy's medicine. Brandi lied, and Nancy told her liars went to jail. Being a stupid kid, Brandi confessed right away, and she'd cried that whole night in her room with the covers pulled up over her head.

"How far?" Nancy hissed.

"Pretty far down." Brandi tried to sound confident, tough. She wasn't ten anymore. "I didn't want animals to get it."

They kept digging. The sun was hot on her back and sweat dripped off her nose, dark rings under her armpits. No Mack to save the day. Brandi digging her own grave. What would happen to Sy if they got away with it? She stole a glance at Nancy. Her fingers were dusty brown from her frantic digging. Sy's only chance might be if there was a shred of her mother left that drugs hadn't eaten.

Kenny muttered to himself, then dropped to a knee and pressed his mouth to her ear. "What's taking so fucking long?" The smell of fish when he spoke.

"Your breath stinks." Damn her mouth.

He kicked her and she tumbled to her side, her bladder aching from the impact, drops of pee on her underwear. Just like Carissa's friend. She cradled her stomach. Something had happened to Mack. Maybe the cops didn't believe him or, worse, thought he'd kidnapped Sy. Nobody was coming. Her plan had been stupid, like her. Tears hot behind her eyes.

"Kenny, stop!" Nancy, arms around Brandi, protective. A tightness in Brandi's throat, and a pressure in her chest. *Run!* Thoughts of a bullet in her back made her want to throw up. What if it was like those dreams where someone chased her but her feet were stuck in mud?

Asshole leaned against the car. She and her mother started moving dirt again, their foreheads inches from each other. Her mother kept her head down, but her eyes floated up. "It's not here, is it," she whispered.

"Mom," she said so quietly she hardly heard it above the pounding in her ears.

Nancy slowed her digging, moved her head closer to Brandi's mouth.

"If you really love Sy, give him a better home," Brandi whispered. She felt time slipping away with each scrape across the dirt. There was nothing here, and Kenny would kill her for it. She knew it, Nancy knew it. She wanted to scream, to run, to *fight*. But this, she realized, was her only move.

"I do lo—"

"No." She spit the word out. "If you really love him, get him somewhere safe."

"Like Heather?" Nancy sounded resigned, and in it echoed the hooves of wild horses pounding on cracked earth, the sweet tang of oranges on Brandi's tongue. And the smallest spark of hope.

"No, Heather doesn't want anything to do with us," Brandi said, assaulted by thoughts of her aunt, hiding, letting someone else shoo them away like they were nothing.

"I'm gonna take a piss," Kenny grumbled from above. His feet kicked up dust when he left. Nancy coughed.

"That's not true." Nancy stopped digging, and when Brandi shifted her eyes up, she found her mother staring at her, tears on her cheeks. "She wanted full custody of you. I . . . I didn't want you to go away. You were the only thing I had. So I cut her out."

Brandi turned cold all over, despite the heat. Was it true? Pressure built around her heart. She was desperate for it to be true, but her mother had lied more than a zillion times in her life. Why would she start telling the truth now? She scrunched her eyes closed, and to steady her hands she dug faster. If it were true, then it meant there was still hope for Sy, no matter what happened to Brandi. Her chest loosened the tiniest bit.

She dug, flinging small rocks to the side, pulling out dirt like there was actually something to find, beads of sweat down her nose. Maybe, just maybe, Nancy was telling the truth. "You could still protect Sy, Mom."

"What?"

"You never protected me, but you still have a chance to protect Sy. Call Heather." Brandi closed her eyes, prayed to whatever. *Please, please, please protect my brother. Please, please, please make her do something right. Please?* Her *please* in her head stretched and thinned. She'd prayed when she was little and stopped when nothing changed. Her head hung. Why did she think it would do anything now?

Nancy sat back on her butt, exhausted probably because she was flesh over bones—meth had eaten all her substance. Brandi kept digging, frantic now, terrified to stop because when she did, it was the end.

From behind her the scuff of Kenny's shoes on the dirt, the hard press of the gun against the back of her head. Her stomach turned sour.

"Kenny." Something about the firm quiet of her mother's tone stopped Brandi's frantic digging. "Babe, why don't me and you just let Brandi go? She won't tell no one. Girl's got as much to lose as anyone."

Brandi's body caved inward, her mother's plea digging at the hardened dirt around her own heart.

"Nah, that's not gonna happen. This fucking bitch shot at me, stole my fucking car and drugs. She's got it coming and you know it. Besides, she could be lying."

Her stomach cramped.

Nancy stood, a hand on Brandi's shoulder, and when she did, the lightest of squeezes. "I know when she's lying; it's here for sure." Brandi felt something dangerous slithering through the air. "We're letting her go." A tremble in her voice, her mother swayed just slightly. For once, a prayer answered, and it would do nothing.

Kenny sniffed, then brought back his hand holding the gun and whipped Nancy across her temple. She crumpled to the ground. "No!" Brandi screamed, a reflex for the woman who used to sing her to sleep. She scrambled over, touching her mom's face, blood smearing with dirt across her skin.

He yanked Nancy by her arm until she hung half off the ground, pressing the barrel deep into the bony part of her temple. Nancy winced. "Dig." He let go, and she fell to the ground. She locked eyes with Brandi, and the fear she saw in her mother was real.

Brandi's head spun, and bright white stars twinkled at the edges of her vision. *No way out, no way out.* She dug anyway, if only to delay, still hoping for the soothing tones of Mack's voice.

She saw Kenny's dirty Nike Pros from the corner of her eye, the tip of the gun swinging low. He was talking to himself again. She had to do something, anything. Sy needed her. Better to die fighting than to just let it happen.

A rush of adrenaline lit up her muscles, and she visualized exactly what she was going to do. She lifted up a fraction, twisted to face him. He was looking over his shoulder, his head twitching, focus drifting. Her hand shot out and she saw it grabbing the gun, swinging it around gunslinger-style, finger sliding over the trigger, aiming, shooting, catching him square between the eyes. Like a badass.

But that wasn't what happened.

Her hand shot out, fingers grazed the barrel, missed. Kenny jerked back. "What the fuck!"

And he shot.

Ears ringing, dust in the air. It hit the ground. Her heart pulsed between her ribs. He was a raging asshole now.

"It's not here, is it!" He lifted the gun, took aim.

In the end, Brandi didn't piss herself like Carissa's friend. Not even a little bit. A supernatural calm sprouted from her scalp all the way down to the ground. It was over. She still didn't want to die, but it wasn't her choice anymore. She squeezed her eyes shut. *I love you, Sy.*

A feral shriek, gunfire, and she was pushed backward, her shoulder cracking painfully when it hit the edge of the hole she'd dug. Her mother on the ground, flecks of dirt spinning in a pool of blood. She had only a fraction of a second to process. Kenny stared at Nancy, his eyes bugged. Brandi couldn't move, a scream stuck in her throat.

Her mother's voice in her head. *Run, Brandi!*

Her limbs jerked into action before her mind, and she picked up two rocks, turned, and sprinted up the rise, sliding down the hill to keep low, pausing where the earth sheltered her, breathing hard.

More shots fired, the click of an empty gun. Did he have more bullets? She leaped to her feet, threw the rocks like grenades, and ran through the open meadow. Ahead was the big hill where she'd faked her ankle injury to get Mack to turn around, where she could disappear if she was fast enough. Her legs burned; her mother's dead eyes loomed in the sky above her.

Keep running.

Twenty-Eight

Tom drove the police truck, Mack in the passenger seat jiggling his knee up and down. He'd left a piece of himself back at the station with Sy. The boy, already so traumatized, had just watched his sister dragged away at knifepoint, and now Mack, the only other person he trusted, was leaving him to the care of the woman deputy until someone from social services could show up.

No, Macky, no! He'd let loose with that scream of his, holding on to Mack with all the might his ragtag arms could muster. It turned Mack's eyes so goddang blurry he nearly scooped the boy up and left. *We have to help Brandi, right, Sy?* That had stopped his screaming, but his arms stayed tight around Mack's neck. Hair clinging to the smell of the soap from the motel. Mack swallowed hard and hugged Sy tight. *I'll bring her back, I promise.* That had been the only thing to unlock Sy's arms.

Now he stared out the window, chewing on his tongue. Worry kept him silent, afraid that if he spoke he'd say what he feared the most: that they were too late. He'd told Tom everything, and true to his word, Tom was doing what he could to help. They were driving out to the spot where he'd first met Brandi and Sy. Mack shifted in his seat, touched the holster where his gun should be but, *goddang it*, in his hurry to get help for Brandi he hadn't retrieved it from the truck. His chest was on fire and Mack thought he might burn from the inside out.

They flew past a shuttered gas station that used to keep orange Creamsicles in a freezer cabinet near the front door. Jesse's favorite.

From here, forty minutes still to go. Mack took his hat off, put it back on, the time passing at an excruciating rate. A vision of the knife dragging across Brandi's throat, blood in rivulets down her skin. He shook his head to rid himself of the image and turned his thoughts to Daisy and the last time he'd ridden in a police car.

He was twenty-three, a newly married man on top of the world with his beautiful wife and their big, beautiful future ahead of them. He'd had beers with his friends at the end of a long excursion. Ended up going to the bar and getting in a fight. Broke the other guy's nose and a few ribs. It hadn't been the first time. Mack wasn't a big man, but he was tough, and there'd been a time in his life when he felt the need to prove it.

Daisy came for him the next morning, after a night of sleep on the concrete floor of the jail cell on a busted face. The deputy did a double take when she walked in, as most men did. Strawberry blonde hair hanging in waves down her back, full lips, those green eyes that stopped every man's heart at least once. When they opened his cell door, the deputy looked at Mack, then at Daisy, back at Mack. *You rich or something?*

The truck hit a pothole, and it jarred Mack to the present and to a sign for Pike River. Thirty minutes to go. He squeezed his hand into a fist and let the memory float around him.

Daisy had taken Mack's arm; he was still soggy from the night before, and his eye had swollen shut. They walked out, leaving the deputy's question hanging in the air. The ride home was quiet and bumpy. It was possible Daisy hit the ruts on purpose.

Later, he sat at the kitchen table, steak to his eye, his punching hand soaking in a bowl of ice. Daisy sat opposite him, sipping on her tea, brewed in the sun with berries she'd foraged herself.

I did not move out west to marry a caveman.

Why did you marry me? He was sobering up, feeling sorry for himself and his aching head. He knew they were a mismatched pair, but he'd never cared because from the moment he saw her, he couldn't live without her.

She didn't answer right away, assessing him above the rim of her cup. For a moment he thought she might leave him right then and there. The idea took the floor out from under his feet.

She set her cup down, crossed her arms, and leaned forward, her eyes piercing him like a goddang crossbow.

Because you're the kind of man who will always do the right thing.

Alcohol sticky in his mouth, remnants of his bad night. *But what if I don't?*

Well, that's why you married me. Because I'm very forgiving.

The sweet smell of the meat turned his stomach. *I'll mess up again, in some way or another.*

Well, you're also the kind of man who apologizes. She stood, smiling, and he tossed the meat onto the table, smiled back even though it hurt. She kissed his forehead. *And you're the kind of man who will protect his family at all costs.* She slid onto his lap sideways and slung an arm around his neck, smelling like strawberries and basil, her body soft and strong at the same time and a perfect fit for his own. *But most of all because I love you with my whole goddang heart.* He'd kissed her then, tasting the berries in her tea, running his fingers through her hair, down her spine, and resting them at the rounded top of her backside.

He never drank again.

Her words echoed in the truck cab. *The kind of man who will protect his family at all costs.* They were passing Pike River, getting closer to the pull-off, to Brandi. Mack's body buzzed, his hand on the door handle, ready to jump out of the truck the minute they parked. Fear wrapped around him like a snake, squeezing. He'd promised Sy he'd bring her home.

"Turnoff's about a mile up the road. To the left." He pulled at the fabric of his jeans. "Drive faster, Tom." Tom pressed the gas, lights on but no siren. Mack looked away when they passed the truck he'd stolen from Lander, debated saying something to Tom and decided it'd be better to leave that particular transgression out. "Here, turn here." Tom cut the lights.

The police truck made easy work of the rough road.

"Careful," Mack murmured, worried they'd come upon the trio too quickly and make things worse.

"This is pretty remote." Concern, curiosity, and suspicion in Tom's voice.

Mack leaned forward, an unrealistic hope that he'd see Brandi running toward them. Nothing outside but cracked earth and sagebrush.

The lines that fanned Tom's eyes deepened when he scanned the empty landscape. "You sure she'd take them all the way out here? With nothing to find? They could kill her," Tom said, as if that thought hadn't been on repeat in Mack's head since the moment she was dragged out the door.

His calves tensed; the truck was too slow. Mack wanted to run, to holler her name, to find her alive and bring her home to Sy. But as the minutes ticked by, he felt it all slipping out of his grasp. By his calculations there were forty-five of them behind Brandi. Acid burned up his throat. Could she stall them for that long? "Drive faster, Tom." The SUV shot forward when he pressed the gas.

They drove in a tense silence, and when Mack saw the glint of metal in the distance his heart stopped its beating. He didn't see anybody else. Tom pulled up to a bend in the road, parked where the SUV was mostly hidden. "Stay here," he told Mack, and hopped out of the truck.

Mack followed. Tom shook his head but didn't stop him.

They stayed light on their feet, keeping low behind the same bushes Mack had hidden behind when he saw Sy under the car. A sickening twist in his stomach—where was the girl? A breeze whirled around them, bringing with it a familiar acridness that set Mack's pulse racing.

Gunshot?

He scanned the area, a feeling of hopelessness eating a hole inside him. The doors of the car were open, but there was nobody on the road. Mack got low, temple to the ground, dust tickling his nose when he inhaled. A body, sprawled on the other side of the car. He moaned, eyes burning, and he was out and running, ignoring Tom's hissed command to stay put.

He stumbled, caught himself on the car, pulled up short, hand to his mouth. Nancy, shot dead. A sickening relief that it wasn't Brandi.

He whirled around, frantic, scanning the dirt. There, footprints, over the rise and in the direction of the meadow. He scrambled over the small hill and stopped. His legs buckled on him, and Mack planted his hand to keep from falling. What he saw took him a minute to process. His stump tingled with memory of broken bone, torn muscle, hanging sinew. But it didn't stop him. He pushed to his feet and ran, Jesse's ghost keeping pace and rooting him on.

∽

Her shoe hit a rock that dug painfully into the ball of her foot. Brandi kept running. Behind her she heard Kenny, yelling at her, catching up. No more shooting, but she pictured his reloaded gun or the knife or his bare hands. He'd kill her with all three.

She pumped her arms, pulse beating a stampede in her ears, almost to the base of the hill. Sharp pain in her side—how would she keep going? A growing weakness slid through her legs with her fear that Kenny ran faster. A shot ricocheted off a rock to her right; she veered left, running downslope to a shallow stream.

A few feet down the shore, a bear had one paw on the end of a fish, teeth pulling flesh away from bone.

She cried out and skidded to a stop so fast she sent dirt and rocks flying. The bear looked up, so close she could make out the dirt crusted around her nose. Behind her a cub splashing in the creek stopped its playing, sensing its mother's alarm, and it too stared at Brandi.

Mack's words. *Don't surprise her.* Too late. *Back away slowly.* Toward Kenny? Her throat closed. Her instinct was to run. *Then you might trigger an attack.* She took a step back, hands out in front of her, and stumbled on the uneven ground. She fell to her butt. At the sudden movement the bear stood, sniffing the air. Sweat trickled down Brandi's spine.

Her mind spun. What else had Mack said? Kenny appeared over the rise, running at full speed, gun drawn. When he saw Brandi, his crazed eyes widened with a smile. He ran straight at her so that he didn't notice the bear looming just feet away.

A low growl froze the blood in her veins and sucked it from Kenny's face.

He halted, turned.

"Holy fuck!" he yelled.

The bear fell to all fours, pawed at the ground, and huffed. Kenny turned and sprinted back the way he'd come.

Mack's words through the haze of panic. *Play dead.* Brandi rolled to her side, eyes squeezed shut, knees drawn up to her chest, and hands covering her head and neck. In the dark, her last words to her mother. *You never protected me.* Nancy's body pitifully small and torn apart by the bullet she'd taken to do just that. A scream ping-ponged against her skull. Her skin tingling, waiting for claws to sink into her arm, teeth to tear away her scalp. Heavy thumping reverberated up from the ground. She scrunched into a tighter ball, whimpering. A skunk-like stink in the air, but the sound faded.

Kenny screamed. Brandi's head shot up. The bear had clawed his back, pulled him to the ground. Kenny on the ground, shirt torn, blood pouring from a wound on his face. He fumbled with the gun. It went off, scaring the bear, who bounded backward but didn't run away. Kenny screamed and grabbed his leg. Blood poured through his fingers. He'd shot himself. The bear swayed on her feet, head swinging.

Brandi stayed put. Mack's words ringing in her ears. *Wait for the bear to leave. As long as you're not a threat, she'll leave you alone.*

She tucked her head again, tried to slow down her frantic breathing and shut out Kenny's agonized cries. *Don't be a threat. Don't be a threat.*

And then a shout, a voice that Brandi would know anywhere, and she saw Mack coming down the little hill arm raised high above his head, stump along with it, shouting, "Go, bear! Go!" His voice loud, deep, authoritative.

Air filled her lungs, tears flooded her eyes, but the relief was too profound for Brandi to make a sound. The bear looked up at Mack, and her back puffed. She bounded forward, but Mack kept coming like he was going to take her down with his bare hand. Brandi stiffened, but the bear stopped her charge short, veered to the left, swayed back and forth like she was going to charge again.

Brandi sobbed. "Mack, no."

A figure appeared on the rise, air horn raised and flooding the air with a series of sharp honks. The bear huffed, shaking her head, then suddenly turned and loped away.

Brandi stayed in the fetal position. Kenny moaned; Brandi didn't care. She felt her mother lying on the ground with her, spooning her like she used to when Brandi was little. Pushing the damp strings of hair from her forehead, her palm cool, comforting. Brandi cried. Everything hurt, her heart most of all.

Her mother disappeared and Mack was by her side, hand on her shoulder, searching her from head to toe. "You're okay, Brandi. You're okay." He was breathless, soft-spoken. Scared, she realized. He'd been scared.

After Kenny's violence, Mack's kindness broke her, and she crumpled under the weight of the horror, the fear, and the aching sadness of the last hour. Her body hot and cold. Memories of her mother screaming, falling. The only way Nancy had left to prove her love. She stared past him and to the sky above. A pale blue, wispy clouds dotting its canvas. "She saved my life."

"She loved you in her own way, Brandi."

"Yeah." She tried to swallow, couldn't, overcome. "Is Sy okay?"

"He's probably going to go to a foster home."

Tears leaked from the corners of her eyes, and there was nothing she could do to stop them. She wanted to believe what her mother had said about Heather, but after everything, it felt unreal, a dream. Something Nancy had said out of desperation.

Kenny's screams wiggled inside her ears, and her gut clenched. "Kenny?" *Asshole* didn't flow so easily off the tongue after what just happened to him.

"Got some scratches, nothing too bad. Shot himself in the goddang leg. Tom's already got a tourniquet on him and handcuffs."

"Good." She pulled her knees closer to her chest, too exhausted to get up. "Kenny ran."

"Looks that way." He touched her shoulder, and the contact stilled the shivers that ran up and down her body.

Carefully, she unraveled from the fetal position until she was lying flat on her back. She wiped at her face, her snotty nose, met Mack's level gaze. He took her head and cradled it in his lap. She felt like a baby, but she didn't care. "I did like you said."

"For once," he said. "The way I see it, you saved yourself."

She thought about that and decided she liked the way it sounded. "What will happen to Kenny?"

Mack shrugged. "Hopefully he'll go to prison for murder."

"Where there's worse things than grizzly bears."

Mack barked a laugh, shaking his head like he didn't know what to do with her. "I guess."

A breeze kicked up, brushing cool over her wet face. She inhaled, the leather of Mack's belt melting into the scent of pine, the clean country air. "Thank you, Mack." She could hardly get the words out, because now the tears just wouldn't stop.

Mack patted her head and nodded down at her. No words. But none were needed. Right then, Brandi knew exactly what Daisy had loved about Mack. He was fierce, he was protective, and he was safe.

Twenty-Nine

Five Days Later

In the span of a few days, Mack's life had forever changed.

The Department of Family Services took over Sy's case and ferried him away to figure out a placement for him. Mack didn't even get a chance to say goodbye. His heart hurt so dang bad he thought he'd lost a chunk of it to the boy. At night, he couldn't sleep without hearing Sy's cries, imagining him in a strange house with a strange family.

Brandi's absence had been reported to the courts, and after she was treated for her scrapes and bruises, she was taken away to face whatever consequences were decided for her. Tom said he would keep Mack informed as much as he could. Mack didn't have a phone, so he gave Peggy's number. Another piece of his heart went with Brandi too.

He felt the pull to be by Daisy's side, but he had a feeling he couldn't ignore. So he took the borrowed truck and drove back to Casper and straight to 4425 Delgado Street.

~

A few days later he was back in Pike River, standing outside the Jackelope Saloon. From his pocket he pulled the flyer he'd found nailed to his cabin door that morning. Memorial Service for beloved and longtime Pike River resident Mack Anders. Saturday at 2pm at Jackelope Saloon.

First round on Peggy. Instead of flowers, please donate to the Alzheimer's Association. With a handwritten note from Peggy on the back. *I expect to see you there. You can explain to everyone why you're not dead. I'll be drinking a beer either way.*

He walked into Pike River, nervous to face the folks he'd deceived but determined to set things straight. Daisy would expect that of him, and he couldn't sit by her side until it was done. Jackelope Saloon was around the corner, the oldest bar this side of Wyoming, with the mythical creature in colored lights that lit the night and made visitors think of Vegas. Or so they said. Mack had never been to Vegas.

The door to the saloon was thick and heavy wood, with a long, twisted brass handle. He pulled it open to the smell of stale beer and popcorn. Empty barstools, one bartender—a young girl in a pink flannel shirt. She looked up and smiled, went back to filling a pitcher with beer. Pool tables sat empty; electronic dartboards flashed. Voices came from behind a closed black curtain that led to the back room where they held events and potlucks. He stood by the curtain, listening.

"Mack helped me bag my first antelope. A beauty it was. He was the finest hunter I've ever known."

"Remember the time he had to make an emergency landing with those business boys out of Denver? And one of the men shat his pants. Mack walked into this bar with those fellas, asked for a change of pants and a beer for his friend."

"He and Daisy, now that's a marriage I've always wished for myself. Never could find it."

"You've a wandering eye to blame for that, Derek!"

Laughter, the clink of glasses. Mack's chest tightened.

Someone pushed through the curtains, sending him hopping away. Peggy with an empty pitcher. The curtain swung closed behind her. "I wondered if you'd show up."

Peggy. The kind of woman who would give Daisy the ending she deserved. Even if it cost her a friendship.

Mack had no idea how to start, so he took his hat off, pressed it to his chest. "I'm here to set things straight."

Peggy pursed her lips, then pushed past him to the bar. The bartender handed her the full pitcher. "Thanks, Cora." Wide smile for the bartender fading as soon as she turned to face Mack. "You old coot. Tom phoned me, told me all about your little Grizzly Adams adventure. What is this obsession with bears?" Peggy never held back. Mack had missed her.

He shrugged. "There was this girl who needed saving."

She leaned an elbow on the bar. Cora slid a glass to Peggy, eyebrows raised. "You don't know Mack, Cora, but you're one of the first to hear he's alive after all."

Cora looked amused, raised her own glass to Mack. "Here's to premature memorial services."

Peggy laughed, clinked glasses, and with a long swallow drained the beer. "Whiskey this time, Cora. I could use the fortitude." Cora poured the amber liquid, smirking, quick glance at Mack. "So what now?"

Peggy was a salt-of-the-earth woman. Strong, outspoken, never afraid to say what needed to be said, the kind of friend who wouldn't run from a gunfight. She'd been like a sister to Daisy, and then to Mack. He knew why Daisy had trusted her.

"I'm sorry."

Her eyes went wide. "Well, I'll be damned. Mack Anders apologizing."

Mack leaned heavily against the bar. "I barely survived losing Jesse."

"I know," she said softly. "She knew that too. And she knew it was unfair to ask you to let her die when it was time. That's why she asked me." There were tears in her eyes. "She wanted to spare you the pain."

Mack took a moment to let it sink in before taking a breath, feeling it run down to his feet and fill him up. Something felt stuck in his chest and Mack tapped it, coughed. Goddang heartburn. Letting the love of his life die wasn't something Mack was capable of. Daisy had been right to ask Peggy. He gave his old friend a sad smile. "Well, Peggy, if it's all right, I'd like to move in with you for a while."

She emptied the shot and smiled. "It would be my honor, Mack." There was a pause, long enough for the pair of them to gather themselves.

Peggy grabbed the pitcher and pushed away from the bar. "I don't know how in the world you got mixed up with that girl and her brother, but I do know that Daisy would be proud as hell."

"I suppose she would."

"What's going to happen to them?"

The question pierced him. All he could do was hope that going to Heather had been the right thing to do. "I don't know, Peggy, but I hope I can be there for her when she needs it."

Peggy nodded. "If anyone can, it's you. That girl ever needs a job, you tell her to come my way."

Mack nodded, touched and hoping one day he could do just that. "Will do. And Peggy, thank you."

Peggy let loose with a loud laugh. It shook her body and spilled beer from the pitcher. "It's about goddamn time!" She was already at the black curtain. "Now you get to go in there and explain to a bunch of people why you're not dead."

~

The cemetery was off the dump road on a hill above town. A valley filled with trash on one side, an unparalleled view of town and the mountains on the other.

The sun pushed its weak light through clouds that bruised the sky, and the ever-present wind danced under dead leaves, small tornados of color among the graves. They crunched underfoot. On the other side of the cemetery, a man used a blower to push fallen leaves off a grave. He unfolded a lawn chair and set it facing the leafless plot and from a cooler pulled a beer. Mack watched him hold the bottle up to the headstone before taking a long sip. Music blared from a small radio at his side.

Mack walked farther into the cemetery to a grave on the highest point that got the most sun and had the best view. He knelt, pushed leaves from the plaque, a cold blast around his heart every time he saw his son's name on the cold granite. Hard to swallow. He sat on the ground, huddled against the wind. Time passed. The sun touched the mountains.

"Jesse!" It came out harsher than he meant. "I love you." A dog barked, echoing up from the valley below. The earth was cold; he shivered. "You'll be seeing your mother soon. Take care of her, son." Footsteps on the gravel path got Mack to his feet. The man with the leaf blower. "Hi, Bill."

He nodded. "Mack."

"Elaine's grave looks nice." Mack remembered he'd lost his wife in a car accident years ago. She and Daisy hadn't been close, but they'd been friendly.

"I stop by every Sunday to tidy it up." He wore overalls over a thick plaid shirt, work boots, hands on his hips. "Heard from the guys at your service that you were alive and kicking."

"Yep."

"How's Daisy?"

"She's dying." Hospice came a few times a week. The rest of the time, Mack sat for hours in a chair by her bedside, reading to her, telling her stories of their young days, talking about Jesse. He tried to focus only on the minutes they spent together, not the time she had left.

"I'm sorry to hear that." The man sniffed and was quiet for a while. They both watched the view, shadows shifting with the evening light. "You take care."

"Sure will. Same to you, Bill."

Bill ambled back to his lawn chair.

Truck tires on Dump Road; Peggy coming to pick him up. He was staying with Daisy in the spare bedroom. Taking care of his wife just like he'd promised.

Thirty

Brandi pulled the sheet tight on her bed, tucking the corners military style. It was how Ms. Foster taught her at the group home, where she lived again. Ms. Foster had been some badass helicopter pilot in the army and, in Brandi's opinion, brought all the good parts of basic training to the group home. Like tucked corners and clean bathrooms, strict curfews and lights out. Brandi loved the consistency and the way Ms. Foster seemed like she was all business but was as enthusiastic about motivational sayings as Brandi. Her first night back after the hearing that blew Brandi's mind, Ms. Foster left a note card on her pillow from some author called Jim Butcher.

When everything goes to hell, the people who stand by you without flinching—they are your family.

Brandi didn't read much, but maybe she'd start with one of that guy's books, because he was spot-on. After everything that had happened—car theft, kidnapping, the drugs, violating her probation, Kenny, her mom. Brandi sat on her bed, holding the note card and breathing in and out. Thinking about her mom was hard. Since that day all her hate had vanished, replaced by something that wasn't so destructive. Pity. Her mom had given up everything for drugs so that in the end, all she had left to give to Brandi and Sy was her life. Brandi set the card back on her nightstand, her heart softer than before.

But after everything that had happened, after all the rules Brandi had broken, in the end she was given a second chance she never saw coming by everyone who was left standing after her life blew up. It had all happened so fast. At night Brandi still dreamed about Sy's screams, her mom's battered body, heard the gunshots, woke up drenched in sweat with Carissa leaning over the small space between their beds, scratching circles on her back with her pointy acrylics and complaining that Brandi's nightmares were messing with her circadian rhythms.

Someone knocked on her door, and it opened to Ms. Foster. "You have a visitor."

Brandi stood and smoothed out her butt imprint from her tightly made bed. She didn't ask who it was, figured it was Ms. Hanno, who visited her frequently. That day of the hearing, Ms. Hanno had led the charge, along with Warden Trujillo, a volunteer from juvie who'd taught Brandi and the other girls how to garden, and someone from DFS who Brandi hardly remembered but who apparently knew her. Plus the judge Brandi had stood in front of on more than one occasion, and her public defender. And the best part, the person she never expected to see inside under fluorescents and wearing pants and a nice jacket, was Mack.

Given how many laws she'd broken and being eighteen now, Brandi figured she was going straight to big, bad, scary adult prison. She'd been so nervous beforehand that she'd had to puke in the public restroom toilet. How would she survive prison? She didn't even have a tattoo yet. But inside the courtroom, it was like a Brandi lovefest. Ms. Hanno spoke about her goals and her love for her brother; the warden mentioned her willingness to work hard and her positive attitude that brightened everyone's day; the volunteer and the DFS person included stories about how Brandi helped others. And Mack, Brandi had no idea how he'd made it in there, since he wasn't family, but she figured the cop friend of his had helped. He spoke about her courage and determination and how much she'd sacrificed to protect her brother. Pointed out that she was far from perfect and made plenty of mistakes, but wasn't that the whole point of childhood? *My son died when he was a boy, but I hope that if he'd ever had a chance to grow up, he would have been like Brandi. She's the finest example of a young person I've ever met.*

Brandi, who'd been stunned silent by the whole thing, cried then, big happy tears that just kept rolling down her face.

And *nobody* mentioned her impulsiveness.

They decided to send her back to the group home, where she could finish her probation and get all the support she needed to figure out her next steps. Talk about a fairy tale.

Except for Sy. He wasn't there. He was in foster care, they'd told her, and he was struggling to adjust. She could visit him eventually, but he needed time. Brandi liked to imagine he was with the Heather from her memories, or at least with someone like her. Her mom's words came to her at night. *She wanted full custody of you.* Brandi was desperate for it to be true. But away from Sy, she felt a persistent sadness that saturated all the good stuff and turned those words into what they were: her mother's last-ditch effort to find out where Brandi had hidden the drugs.

She followed Ms. Foster to the room where they met with visitors. Ms. Foster called it the parlor because the home was super old and Ms. Foster loved history. A woman sat in a chair by the fireplace that didn't work and smiled when Brandi came in.

"Oh, sweetheart!" Arms out like she was going to hug her.

Aunt Heather. Memories flooded her: laughter, snuggles, a freedom that came with feeling safe. It hit her square in the chest, and Brandi paused at the door, arms crossed, overcome.

Heather's smile faltered; her arms dropped to her sides. She looked the same but different too, smaller than Brandi remembered her, older. She'd cut her hair so that it was short, boy kind of short, but it looked fresh on her, and it wasn't pink anymore. "Are you . . . is it okay that I'm here?"

It was and it wasn't. A tender spot in her chest, aggravated by the memory of her bitter rejection from that day and everything that happened afterward. Maybe a part of her blamed her aunt for not answering the door.

Heather pulled at the ends of her hair. "I'm sorry. Maybe I should have called."

"Why are you here? Your girlfriend said I was too much for you."

She looked a little like Brandi's mom, same brown eyes, but it was enough for Brandi to see her mom getting shot, dying in front of her. She sniffed and tried to push the image away.

"Susan's a bitch."

That surprised Brandi enough to enter the room all the way and sit down opposite Heather. "What?"

Heather leaned forward on her elbows, calm, with the kindness Brandi remembered. "She didn't speak for me, Brandi. And I didn't even know you'd been there until Mack came to see me."

A thickness in her throat. "He came back to see you?"

Heather's smile was warm. "Quite a character, huh? He told me everything. It's obvious he cares deeply for you and Sy."

Brandi pulled at her fingers, a sticky lump in her throat. Why hadn't Mack told her in one of his letters? "I didn't know he saw you."

"I . . . I think he wasn't so sure about me. He probably didn't want to get your hopes up in case I was, well, like Susan. And he said 'goddang it' a lot."

Brandi sucked in her bottom lip. Sounded like Mack.

"Your mom . . ." Heather blinked several times. "Did you know she started doing photography when she was in high school?"

"I know she took pictures of dead bodies at crime scenes but that she really loved taking pictures of horses and stuff."

"The dead bodies paid the bills. She loved landscapes and animals and Wyoming in particular. She was good, Brandi, really good. She could have been one of the best."

The sweet hay-like smell of wild horses, her mom's elbow brushing Brandi's arm, the click of her camera. It faded into the image of her drug-ravaged body sprawled on the ground. Brandi leaned away from her aunt. "Yeah, and then she shot all her potential up her veins." Her voice trembled.

Heather flinched. "Did you know that when you came to live with me I was trying to get custody of you?"

Her mother's words. *She wanted full custody of you. So I cut her out.* She squeezed her arms across her chest, shook her head no. "Mom told me right before . . ." She couldn't finish, eyes burning. "I thought she was lying to get me to tell her what I'd done with the drugs." It hurt to say it out loud.

Heather reached out, touched Brandi's knee lightly. The contact settled her. "She didn't want to give you up. She loved you."

Brandi nodded, breathless, the truth a painful throb in her chest.

"I wasn't sure your mom had it in her to get sober, but then she did, and you went home on one condition: that she stay sober." Heather's eyes were bright. "You two were in Jackson, but I visited as much as I could. Do you remember . . ." She paused, ran a hand through her hair. "Do you remember our time together, Brandi? We used to paint and go to the zoo, and I wrote to you later too. Did you get any of those letters?"

She said it all with a desperate kind of hope, in the same way Brandi had first talked to Sy. She softened. "I . . . I remember the paint. And I remembered what you said, about feeling safe. It's why I was trying to get Sy to you."

Heather pressed a hand to her mouth, nodded. "Nancy moved from Jackson without telling me. Cut all her ties. I tried to find you."

That truth came in floodwaters, breaching the last of Brandi's defenses. It was all she needed to know. She unwrapped her arms.

Heather's cheeks had gone pink, and to Brandi she looked ashamed. "It's no excuse, Brandi, but I think a part of me wanted to believe she was okay. That you were okay." She was emotional, but Heather was firm too. "Nancy had a drain inside of her that sucked all the good out, told her she was worthless, unimportant. I think the drugs plugged the hole and made life tolerable."

Brandi's chest hurt. "Am I like my mom?"

Heather didn't speak right away, and Brandi figured that was answer enough.

But when she did, it was simple and, Brandi hoped, true. "You look so much like her, sweetheart. The difference is on your insides. From the moment you were born, you always had this light that makes you glow from the inside out. It's what's made you so strong, so loving. So resilient. Look at what you did for Sy. Look at how strong you've been for yourself."

Brandi let it wash over her. It was what everyone said at the hearing. What Brandi was starting to believe herself. It made her feel stronger, braver. "Why are you here, Aunt Heather?"

Heather was quiet for a minute, not reacting, as though giving Brandi the space to feel. "I've met Sy. He's quiet but sweet, and he doesn't trust me. Not yet. I'm working with DFS so that I can foster him."

Brandi gripped the sides of the chair, too afraid to make a sound that might ruin the moment.

"And when he's ready, I plan to adopt him." She pressed her fingers into the table. "I love you, Brandi, and I love your brother."

It was overwhelming. Brandi wanted to feel happy, grateful, relieved. It was all she'd ever wanted. But in that moment she was like that bear by the creek, on her hind legs, claws scratching the air, protective and angry. Sy deserved that kind of love, that type of protection, and she needed to know that Heather was strong enough. "He's been through some shit, you know. You can't just love him and think that will be enough. It won't. This isn't some Disney movie bullshit where everything works out in the end. He needs therapy and consistency, he needs to be heard, and he's going to have a lot of anger, you know? Like maybe break-your-shit kind of anger. Can you handle that? Can you stick by him? Because if you can't, then go away." She sucked air in and out. It needed to be said, but it came with a paralyzing fear that Heather would do just that.

To her credit, Heather didn't flinch, and Brandi's pulse slowed.

"You're right, Brandi, which is why I'd want you involved as much or as little as you want to be. It's going to be a very long road for Sy, and he'll need all the family he can get." Heather held out her hands, flipped so her palms were up. "You'll always have a place in my home."

"Is Susan still living there?"

Heather laughed. "Oh, hell no, not anymore."

She stared at Heather's open palms, hesitated. "I might have some things to work on myself first."

Heather smiled, reached all the way and took Brandi's hands in her own. Still soft and warm like she remembered. Brandi squeezed back.

"Here's the thing," Heather said. "You've been Sy's mom for most of his life. But, sweetheart, you deserve to go for your dreams too. To live for *you*. Do that. And when you come and visit us, be Sy's sister."

Brandi stiffened at the idea. She was Sy's mom in all the ways. But the kindness in Heather's eyes softened her and she relaxed, thought about the waitress she'd met who was going to college. Maybe that was something she could do too. And knowing that Sy would be safe with Heather made it all seem possible.

Heather released her hands and bent to pick up her purse and set it on her lap. "I have something for you." She rummaged inside, pulled out a piece of blue construction paper, and handed it to Brandi. "On my last visit with Sy, he gave me a picture he'd drawn for you." Heather raised her eyebrows. "I'm not entirely sure what to make of it, but he was quite proud."

Brandi flipped over the paper and smiled. It was a drawing of her— she knew by the frizzy head of hair—standing in a meadow and holding Sy's hand, a bloody sword clenched in her other hand, and surrounded on all sides by zombies with their heads cut off. On the top, in someone else's writing, it read *My sister kills zombies.*

Brandi touched the drawing of Sy. A deep ache in her chest. For Sy's nightmares. For her mother's mistakes and sacrifice. For Brandi herself.

"I helped him color in all the blood," Heather said.

"I love it." Brandi gave her a small smile. "Tell Syborg I love him."

"I will."

They sat in a comfortable silence.

"I'm going to get a job and save up some money."

"That's sounds really good," Heather said.

"Maybe save up for college," Brandi added, chest puffing up at how it felt to say out loud.

"Casper has a wonderful community college."

"Yeah, Mom went there."

"And it's close to me." Heather stood, so did Brandi, and she was surprised to find they were the same height. "Can I give you a hug?" Heather said.

Brandi nodded, and when Heather's arms went around her it felt natural. Like coming home. "As soon as I get Sy settled, I'll let you know. I love you so much, Brandi," she said into her hair.

"I love you too." She breathed in Heather's familiar smell and fully relaxed into her embrace. She'd done it. Sy would live with Heather the way she'd hoped. And they'd all be a family.

~

A few days later, Ms. Foster brought in the mail, and in it was a package with her name scrawled in cursive on the front. She opened it and was hit by the smell of old leather. She pulled out the foraging bag Daisy had given to her, inhaled the spicy echoes of herbs and greens, held it to her chest, and smiled. Underneath the bag lay an envelope and a thin roll of fabric. Stitched across the fabric was a quote from someone called Ralph. BUILD, THEREFORE, YOUR OWN WORLD. She shrugged and opened the letter. Spidery writing stretched across the paper. All in cursive. "Damn." Cursive was like another language. She flattened the paper out on the desk.

> *Dear Brandi,*
> *I'm sorry I haven't been out to visit in a while. Daisy's taken a turn and I can't leave her side. Thanks for your letters. I read them to Daisy and we love hearing about all the things you're doing for yourself.*

Daisy made the cross-stitch with her favorite quote.
I think it's fitting for you too. The foraging bag is yours.
Come and visit me when you can and I'll show you where
to find more free food. I might even be able to help you
find a job.
Love,
Mack

She closed her eyes, letting everything sink in. Sy was with Aunt Heather. Her mother had loved her in her own messed-up way. And the old man was waiting for her. She breathed in and smiled. She was ready AF to build her own world.

Thirty-One

Mack woke to the coyotes howling, a full moon shining white through the window. He was hot, sweating, and when he pushed up, the cot he slept on creaked. He rubbed the back of his neck, blinking sleep from his eyes.

"Mack," Daisy called to him from the hospital bed Peggy had rented for her.

He was on his feet and by her side in seconds, heart pounding at the sound of her voice. It was the first time he'd heard it in weeks. The sicker she became, the more her Alzheimer's advanced, and she'd lost the ability to speak.

But now she was awake and sitting up in bed, hair brushed until it shone and hanging down around her shoulders in snow-white waves. Moonlight across her skin, luminescent in the glow.

Mack's mouth had turned dry. "You're so beautiful," he croaked.

Daisy smiled. "You always were a blind fool." She patted the bed. "Come here, love."

He perched on the edge, and she took his hand in her own. "What happened to Jesse was an accident."

Mack squeezed her hand, overcome. "I know."

"You loved him." She smiled. "And he's okay."

"He is?"

A shadow in the corner rose, crossed the room, and sat on the other side of the bed. Jesse as a child, and also Jesse as the man he might have been.

Tears ran freely down Mack's face—deep longing, grief unbound. They held each other, and Mack cried. "I miss you both so much. I hurt all the time."

Daisy wiped the tears from his face. "That's the price of love."

He held her hand, stroking his thumb along her soft skin, and they sat like that until the coyotes quieted and the sun rose. Mack woke up with a strangled cry, back in the cot, having never really left, grabbing the end of his stump. He ran to Daisy's side, but what he knew had already happened. She was gone. He lay beside her and kissed her forehead one last time.

"I love you, Daisy."

$\sim$

Summer

It had been a busy afternoon at the feedstore, and Mack was more tired than usual. He sat on a crate outside the store, kneading the ache from his legs. Since moving into town, and without having to worry about survival quite so much, he'd lost his edge and started acting more his age. Peggy said she liked him better this way. He smiled to himself. She had helped him buy an old cabin not far from her home. One he could fix up and close enough that he could easily walk to town. He picked up the odd job guiding fishing tours but had slowed down quite a bit. He was mostly retired, taking coffee in town, attending a meeting or two of the Kiwanis club, hanging around the feedstore, and helping Peggy here and there. Peggy pointed out he had a lot of people to make up to after convincing everyone he was dead. She wasn't wrong.

An old Volkswagen pulled off the road and parked in front of the feedstore, sending dust flying into the air. Brandi got out, and Mack about fell off the crate. He wasn't expecting her and hadn't been able to make the hour-plus trip to see her in quite some time. He didn't have a truck anymore, and even if he did, gas was expensive. His "borrowing" days were long gone. But she hadn't mentioned anything in her letters about visiting.

It was a sunny day, the sky as blue as blue can get, and Mack was hidden in the shadow of the building. She didn't see him at first. A pang in his chest—she looked older, more like a young woman. Her brown hair was shorter but tamed. She wore a yellow tank top with those ridiculous jeans he'd seen kids wear lately, so wide they could fit two men. But on her, well, Mack thought she looked just right. The old heartburn crept up behind his eyes again.

She walked into the shade and saw him, smiled, and goddang if it wasn't the most dazzling smile he'd ever seen.

"I was tired of only talking to you in letters. You know kids my age don't know how to read cursive, right? I had to have them translated."

He stood up from the crate. "Kids your age should learn cursive. It's a lost art."

"Maybe." She looked up at the sign for the feedstore. "So you work here?"

"I help out when I can. It gives me something to do."

"With the guardian, huh?"

"Peggy, yes."

"Cool, that's cool." She stood holding one arm across her body, shoulders a little rounded. Nervous, Mack realized. "So you said you have a job for me?"

Mack smiled. "I don't, but Peggy does."

She rolled her shoulders, stood a little taller, then pulled a piece of paper from her bag and handed it to him. At the top it read *Brandi's Résumé*.

"Ms. Hanno helped me put that together. There's not much to it, but you know, it's a start. So um, let's see." Her eyes rolled skyward as though she was trying to remember. "I'm a hard worker. I'm reliable and I'm driven. Oh, and I'm timely, which means I'll get to work on time, not like Carissa, who lost her job on the second day because she was getting her nails done."

Mack narrowed his eyes. "Says here you can be a bit impulsive."

A wrinkle in her forehead. "It does not." Then she smiled, and all the tension fell away and she was Brandi. The girl who loved so hard she gave up everything for it. "Yeah, it's true, I can be impulsive. But I'm working on it."

His heart felt full to bursting.

"Oh, and I'm saving up for college." She stood a little taller and Mack liked the look. "I'm going to go to Casper College so I can see Sy too. What do you think?"

"Sounds like a good plan." He crooked his arm, and she took it. "Let's go find Peggy."

Brandi leaned her head briefly against his cheek. "I've missed you, Mack."

Behind them trailed Daisy and Jesse, and Brandi's mom too. And Mack felt all the love and all the heartache at once. But instead of burning him from the inside out, he let his eyes get a little wet. That was the price of love.

Acknowledgments

Some stories take time and many rewrites to get just right. And some develop so naturally it's like the characters have been waiting my whole life for me to bring their adventure to the page. This is exactly what happened with Mack and Brandi. From the very first synopsis, I knew their trials and challenges and how the two of them were meant to save the other. I couldn't write it fast enough. But as with all novels, this one didn't happen just because I wrote it. Book writing is a singular pursuit that requires an entire team of supporters to make happen, and I'm one lucky author to have an amazing team.

Thank you to my editor, Erin Adair-Hodges, for working so closely with me on the first draft and for enjoying Brandi and Mack's story from the very beginning. I loved collaborating with you. And to Tiffany Yates-Martin for your groundbreaking four-page edit letter. I'm so fortunate to have learned from your guidance through all my books, and I'm a most grateful student. To my agent, Jessica Faust, for continuing to champion my work and support my love and pursuit of this career. And a huge thank-you to the team at Lake Union, including Kyra Wojdyla, Jon, Robin, Kellic, and Jill, for skillfully and thoughtfully shepherding this book through the editorial process. Your eyes and knowledge are a critical part of book writing, and I'm so grateful for your work. Finally, thank you to Shuja K. for your Cultural Research Read that ensured that the characters and other elements of this story were represented with accuracy and respect.

No book can be written without research, and this one afforded me a chance to road-trip through Wyoming a few times. Who doesn't love a road trip? Especially one through such a ruggedly breathtaking and wild state. Thank you to my research travel partner and brilliant writer, Sara Miller, for saying yes to many days in the car with me at the very last minute. I still think our best meal was at Nana's Bowling and Bakery and our most exciting sighting was of the grizzly bear filling up on berries. And to my mom, Phyllis, for joining me so I could drive Mack and Brandi's exact route. Thank you for taking all the pictures and notes along our drive. Our adventures in Lander and Casper and the chance to stand under the antlers again in Jackson are some of my most special memories. I felt like Dad came along for the ride whether it was in the stories we told or being together in a state he loved.

Thank you to my longtime friend, Erik Wilt, for your professional advice on life insurance policies. Who knew, when our kids were riding striders down your driveway, we'd be talking life insurance and faking deaths so many years later? And thank you to the book club at the Tri-County Office on Aging in Lansing, Michigan, for staying online after our discussion on *The Night of Many Endings* to answer my questions regarding elder care.

A very special thanks to Jeremy and Dalton with Flies and Lies for teaching my family the joys of fly-fishing. We loved the experience of being in the water, surrounded by the mountains and the thrill of catching fish. It was some of the best family time.

And thanks to all my early readers who take the time to read and sift through the unfinished product to give me feedback that makes stories better. Taryn, for reading on your phone—you have the eyes of a twenty-year-old. And thank you Sara Haynes for the kind of feedback most writers pay for. You're now on my forever list. To Mom, you have literally read everything I have ever written, and you've made me a better writer for it. And to my fellow author and critique partner, Harper McDavid, for reading and for joining me on some great and some not so great book events.

And to Sean: you stand by me every step of the way, you read with enthusiasm and insight, and you never fail to give me your honest feedback. You're my best friend, my most trusted reader, and my husband. How lucky am I? Finally, to Ella, Keira, and Sawyer: you keep growing up, and I keep having to catch my breath at how quickly time passes. I adore being your mom, even if sometimes I cry in the shower at how soon you'll be flying on your own. But other moms do that too. I asked. Thank you for so sweetly supporting me with every book I write. I love seeing what you are creating for your own lives.

Book Club Questions

1. This is a story about sacrifice, even at the risk of losing what we want the most. What did you think of Mack's decision to fake his own death for his wife? Or of Brandi's spur-of-the-moment choice to take her brother? Have you ever made a rash decision for someone you love?

2. Brandi experienced terrible abuse as a child, yet she had dreams and plans for her life despite the trauma of her past. What do you think made her so strong? Have you ever known anyone like Brandi?

3. Mack tried to care for Daisy for as long as he could, but it eventually became more than he could bear alone. Have you experienced caregiving for a loved one? If so, what were the ways in which you coped? Was there a point when you, like Mack, needed help? Were you able to get it, and how?

4. Brandi and Mack form a quick and tight bond. What about each of them makes this possible?

5. Sy immediately identifies Mack as someone safe. Why do you think this happens?

6. Most of the book takes place on the road, where Brandi and Mack cross paths with a host of characters. How did those characters play a role in Mack's and Brandi's personal journeys?

7. Despite being a poor mother and battling her own demons, Nancy made the ultimate sacrifice for Brandi. In fiction, as in life, most people aren't all good or all bad. From Brandi's point of view, what was good about Nancy?

8. Mack ultimately learns that Daisy did not trust him to make the end-of-life decisions she desired. In your opinion, did she make the right choice? Explain.

9. Brandi loves motivational sayings. Share one of your own that inspires you and why.

10. Daisy once told Mack he was the "kind of man who would protect his family at all costs"—something Mack struggled to believe after his son died. How did Brandi and Sy change Mack's view of himself?

11. Was the ending what you hoped for? If you could have written the ending for Mack, Brandi, and Sy, what would you have done differently?

12. Finally, have you ever had an encounter with a bear? If so, please share. I'll start: We have black bears that roam through our property and for the most part want nothing to do with people but sometimes find a way into unlocked cars or peer through our windows. And once, in Wyoming, I saw a grizzly bear eating berries. It was magical.

About the Author

Photo © 2022 Eric Weber

Melissa Payne is the bestselling author of five novels, including *A Light in the Forest*, *The Night of Many Endings*, and *The Wild Road Home*. After an early career raising money for nonprofit organizations, Melissa began dreaming about becoming a published author and wrote her first novel. Her stories feature small mountain towns with characters searching for redemption, love, and second chances. They have been three-time Colorado Book Award finalists and Colorado Authors League 2020 and 2023 winners for mainstream fiction. Melissa lives in the foothills of the Rocky Mountains with her husband and three children, a friendly mutt, a very loud cat, and the occasional bear. For more information, visit www.melissapayneauthor.com or find her on Instagram @melissapayne_writes.